The Shield Maiden's Curse

BOOK 4 in the LEOPARDS OF NORMANDIE SERIES

Peter Richards

Copyright © 2025 by Peter Richards All rights reserved.

No portion of this book may be reproduced in any form without written permission from the publisher or author, except as permitted by U.S. copyright law.

For all those who gave their lives in the D-Day Landings, 1944

1066: Three Leaders, Three Battles

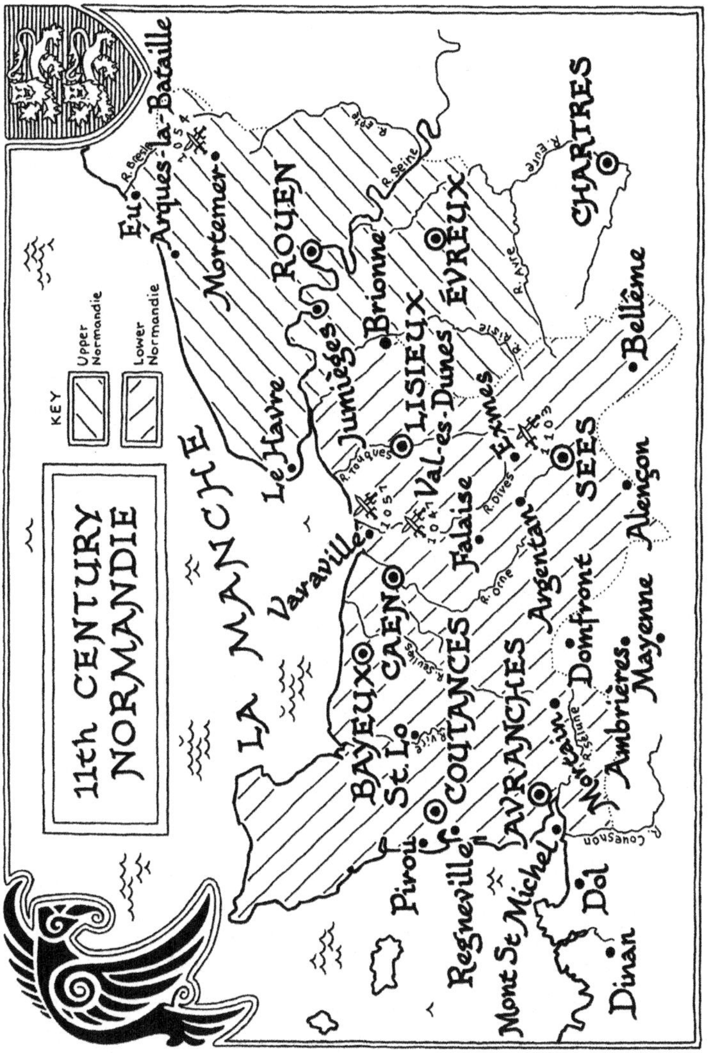

11th CENTURY NORMANDIE
KEY
Upper Normandie
Lower Normandie
LA MANCHE
Eu
Arques-la-Bataille
Mortemer
ROUEN
Le Havre
Jumièges
Brionne
LISIEUX
ÉVREUX
CHARTRES
Varaville
Val-es-Dunes
Falaise
Exmes
SEES
Bellême
Alençon
Argentan
Domfront
Mayenne
BAYEUX
CAEN
St Lo
COUTANCES
AVRANCHES
Mortain
Ambrières
Pirou
Regneville
Mont St Michel
Dol
Dinan
R. Bresle
R. Epte
R. Seine
R. Eure
R. Avre
R. Risle
R. Touques
R. Dives
R. Orne
R. Seulles
R. Vire
R. Sélune
R. Couesnon
1054
1057
1047
1103

Table of Contents

Prologue:	7
Chapter 1: Drowned Gods	9
Chapter 2: Eleanor's News	33
Chapter 3: A Change of Plan	53
Chapter 4: The Return to Maldon	56
Chapter 5: In Search of Welsh Gold	74
Chapter 6: The Shipwright's Promise	94
Chapter 7: Harald's Pledge	118
Chapter 8: The Great Deception	137
Chapter 9: Long Live the King	154
Chapter 10: The Duke's Bitter News	159
Chapter 11: Old Skills Rekindled	165
Chapter 12: The Great Norman Muster	170
Chapter 13: The Warrior Maiden	176
Chapter 14: The Fearful Baronie	189
Chapter 15: The Diplomatic Quest,	199
Chapter 16: Old Friends, New Alliances	203
Chapter 17: The Brotherhood of Norsemen	219
Chapter 18: The Gathering of the Clans	231
Chapter 19: The Duke's Fleet Prepares to Sail	250
Chapter 20: The North in Flames	263
Chapter 21: The Skjaldmaer's Haunting	292
Chapter 22: The Land Ravager Unfurled	299
Chapter 23: Brenier's Stand	309
Chapter 24: The Norman Landfall	327
Chapter 25: The Last of the Sea Kings	335
Chapter 26: The Duke's Great Gamble	349
Chapter 27: Unfinished Business	357
Chapter 28: Battle of the Hoary Apple Tree	367
Chapter 29: Unfinished Business	373
Chapter 30: The Shieldmaiden's Curse	376

Prologue:

When the great Norseman, Jarl Bjorn Halfdanson, led his people to Normandie in 1002 to avoid massacre by the Saxons of England, he created a dynasty. After pledging his allegiance to Duke Robert of Normandie, he fought beneath his liege-lord's banners earning riches, land and reputation. When the old Duke died, his son, the eight-year-old 'William the Bastard' was taken in by the Norseman's family and nurtured to adulthood under their protection. The Jarl's dying wish was for his family to continue this protection and he appointed his grandsons Robert and Harald Fitzroy as companions to the young Duke. They were loyal and diligent fulfilling their duties and fought fiercely for their master whenever their services were required.

By the end of 1064 Normandie was no longer a turbulent cauldron of conflict and it was as peaceful as anyone could remember. This state of grace could largely be attributed to the actions of the Fitzroy brothers. The siblings' support on and off the battlefield provided the Duke with a solid platform for success and expansion. After many years of warring with King Henri of France, William's last major adversary was dead, allowing him to cast his gaze abroad. He set his sights on Saxon England after his uncle King Edward secretly promised him the English throne. William was delighted but knew he needed a Papal endorsement and a mighty army to make good on the offer.

However, all was not well between the Fitzroy brothers; William's jealousy and connivance had caused a schism which festered for many years. The cause of the unrest had come about after the Duke rewarded Robert by giving him Harald's sweetheart in marriage, together with title, wealth and position; the siblings parted on bad terms. After killing a number of men in anger, Harald took flight as a fugitive to southern Italy, the Kingdom in the Sun, where he built a great reputation for himself. In the aftermath of the decisive battle of Civitate in 1057 he captured Pope Leo IX, later saving the man from an assassination attempt and earning the eternal blessing of Rome. Many years later Harald returned to Normandie, after the brothers' reconciliation, and helped defeat a mighty enemy host, bringing peace to the Duchy at last. However, Duke William's simmering jealousy of their fraternal bond re-emerged and he continued to drive a wedge between them. The opportunity presented itself when Harald was reunited with his brother's wife, Eleanor, during Robert's absence from the Duchy. William divulged the news to Robert who swore vengeance for this betrayal. He attempted to kill Harald and imprisoned his own wife. Eleanor later escaped to join Harald and his waiting fleet but, unable to depart with all her children, she was forced to return to her husband. Before Eleanor travelled home, she insisted that Harald take her eldest son into his safe keeping after revealing she was pregnant with his child.

Duke William dreams of the English throne. Harald sails back to Southern Italy to reunite with his old comrades to drive the Moors from Sicily. Robert begins to plan for a greater Normandie. Eleanor returns to an uncertain fate.

Chapter 1: Drowned Gods
The Basque Sea, Autumn 1065

1

Harald was sinking to his death, for the *Norns* had cut the cords that bound him to *Midgard* one final time. As the heavy chainmail shirt and sword of solid Frankish steel that had saved him from death so many times dragged him to a watery grave, the thought that they would now cause his demise somehow amused him.

At first, he had struggled to swim back to the surface where the violent waves were ripping apart the remains of his ship, the *Evas Prayer*, but then he capitulated as the weight of his armour pulled him down inexorably. For a fighting man of his reputation he, the great Harald Fitzroy, was surprised at how little fight there was left in him. He drifted down and knew there would be no return to the Kingdom in the Sun nor a reunion with the Guiscard to rid Sicily of the hated Moors. He was finally at peace, he thought, and although he had no fear of death, his one regret was that he would not die in battle with *Gunnlogi* in his hand, casting doubt over his entrance to Valhalla. He wondered fleetingly what it would be like to drown - an end, to which he had consigned so many men in countless sea-borne battles. Briefly, he recalled the old story of Rán, the sea *Jotun* who caught drowning men in her fishing nets and received them into her halls. He attempted to laugh at the thought but as he opened his mouth, salt water rushed in and forced its way into his lungs. Harald knew he was dying and plummeted into the all-enveloping green-black darkness. He tried to prepare himself for the moment that would soon be upon him and closed his eyes in a final prayer to Odin.

Dragged from this last devotion by a violent tug on his beard, his eyes snapped open. He saw a face in front of him that he recognised immediately as Grandmother Turid. But it was not her, surely, he thought, as the creature, half-woman, half-fish floated in front of him illuminating the darkness with a greenish light, pulsating from her scaly body. Her hair, which waved and caught in the ocean currents was made of seaweed and the skin of her face and upper body were encrusted with barnacles.

"Mormor," he mouthed at her in greeting.

But the *margygr* was angry, shouting at him and he heard her words clearly through the dark water.

"I will have my revenge, Hari. You will not deny me my revenge. You owe me this, boy and I mean to have it," she scolded.

Harald reached out to her, but she swam away from his embrace.

"Do not forsake me, grandson," she called back over a scaly shoulder, "my curse will last for generations, and vengeance is mine."

Then she was gone, leaving Harald alone in the blackness and with his last breath long since spent, he drifted away into his own dark world.

2

Harald tasted salt; in fact, he was covered in it as he lay in the sun drying out. By the time he finally came to, waking from the deep torpor which had consumed him since the previous day, he was almost dry. His hair, beard and clothes were encrusted with salty crystals and sand. The seagulls that had eventually roused him wheeled and turned far above him competing noisily with the waves that crashed onto the deserted beach as high tide approached. He rubbed his eyes and raised his head, looking left and right to get his bearings. He saw nothing but a sandy beach stretching out for several leagues on either side of him. The only other features of note were endless sand dunes that rose into cliffs before descending again further down the coastline. Harald tried to cast his mind back and piece together the events that had led to his arrival in this desolate, windswept place.

The *Evas Prayer* was one of a fleet of five vessels filled with his followers on their way to Italy and the Kingdom in the Sun. She was a beautiful Byzantine *dromon* and named for Harald's long dead wife. With her crisp white sails, black pine hull and decks of oriental pine she was her master's pride and joy - but now she was in trouble.

Their convoy had been at sea for fifteen days since departing the port of Granville in Normandie. Two hundred and thirty-six men, women and children and a hundred horses were sailing south. The journey so far had been unremarkable, and they had hugged the coast of France before setting out across the Basque Sea. At night an oil lamp was lit and hung from the masthead of the *Evas Prayer* so that the rest of the ships could see her and not go astray. On the third night they lost sight of land when a fierce storm blew up, scattering the ships. It grew in strength and venom as it heaved and tossed Harald and his shipmates on the backs of wild, white horses. The storm enveloped them without warning, and he lashed himself to the tiller, steering the craft up mountains of water which having reached the pinnacle, split, at heart-stopping pace into pits of churning foam. As the swell grew bigger so did the noise, and the wind blew the ancient sea-gods' trumpets in a deadly percussion. In this wild cacophony Harald peered into the chaotic gloom seeking a path through the maelstrom of black, white and grey. Water constantly boiled over the gunwales and across the deck, buffeting the oarsmen who laboured in vain while others baled desperately. It was bitterly cold and every person on board was soaked to the skin.

"This cold will kill us," said Harald to himself between prayers, "it will slay us long before the sea does. The ocean might claw and tear at us - but this cold will lull us all to our deaths."

He grimaced again as the ship careered up another mighty swell, but before they reached the top another wave veered across its smaller brother and a mountain of water swamped the stern, shattering the raised deck. Harald, still lashed to the tiller was swept overboard and his helpless crew could only watch as their captain and six of their shipmates were dragged beneath the surface of the angry sea.

3

With a great effort Harald sat up on the beach; his aching muscles and stiff joints protested with each little movement. He brushed some of the sand from his face and clothes and struggled to his feet. He continued to brush sand from his leather tunic and woollen trousers which were heavily marked with dried salt. Then he stretched like a huge dog waking after a deep sleep and got to his feet. Harald looked down to see his stockinged feet and wondered absentmindedly where his boots were. He did not have to look far, for a short distance away he found the answer and breathed a sigh of relief. The boots, *hauberk* and sheathed sword were all together in a neat pile. He turned in a full circle, taking in the new, unfamiliar surroundings. The overhead sun indicated that it was somewhere near noon but there were no other indications of where the sea, which he remembered had so violently taken him and spat him out. There were no signs of the *Evas Prayer* nor the flotsam and jetsam that might be expected had she broken up in last night's storm. He looked out to sea again and the blank canvas of the ocean was devoid of any craft and tried to recall the events that had brought him here. Then he remembered his nephew, Richard and grew frantic. Had not his mother Eleanor's last request to him before they parted been that he guard the boy with his life? He was, she had said, her most precious possession as she handed him over into Harald's safekeeping. The boy was now gone, missing, and Harald's stout heart sank in despair as he desperately scanned the distant, empty horizon.

With limited options he pulled on his boots and the long, heavy chain mail shirt, buckled on his sword and determined to travel west. It was no more than a guess and he resolved to keep walking until someone, or something revealed itself.

He had covered almost six leagues by the time the sun started to sink into the sea and in the half day he had spent walking he found neither hide nor hair of his ship or crew. Harald was hungry and very thirsty, and his aching body cried out for rest. Not that he heeded its call for he could not succumb to hunger or tiredness until he found what he was looking for.

The sun that had burned his face throughout the day, began to depart, quickly leaving the sky to a full moon and glittering firmament. His long hair and beard, sodden with sweat throughout the afternoon's labours were now a gritty dry, and sunset had not come a moment too soon. As he had done at regular intervals throughout the day he looked to the cardinal points for any signs. Imperceptibly, he thought he detected a glint of light much further along his route and close to the sea's edge. He squinted into the distance and gave a desperate prayer that he might discover something - anything that might give him hope.

After another league or so he was close enough to determine that the light could only be from a fire on the beach. Harald's spirits soared and he quickened his pace, oblivious to the parched throat, chaffed skin and tired limbs. He drew to within a few hundred paces of the bonfire which burned fiercely in the lee of a large, beached ship and heard the muffled voices of men and women. He hesitated, putting a chary hand on *Gunnlogi's* hilt and, throwing caution to the wind, raced toward its provenance. Before he knew it he was standing before them; forty-six surprised and seated men and women looked up at the giant, wild-haired warrior standing before them, the firelight reflecting off his unsheathed sword. He span around looking for faces that he recognised.

"Uncle," piped up the eight-year-old Richard from the shadows, "you have come."

Harald, never normally lost for words, was speechless from a large lump in his throat. He thrust his sword in the sand, spread his arms wide and caught the running boy in a fierce embrace that threatened to squeeze the life out of the child.

Others rushed out to meet him but two older boys, Harald's squires Thomas and Gilbert, were close behind Richard. They tried to keep a respectful distance from their master until he grabbed them both, pulling them into his fierce bearhug with Richard, almost crushing all three of them.

"We thought we had lost you, Lord," cried Thomas, the older boy.

His brother, Gilbert, was less successful in controlling his emotions and tears of joy rolled down his face.

"Stop snivelling, Gilbert," ordered Thomas, trying to mask his own feelings. "We have work to do here. Our master is clearly in need of us."

"Gentlemen," countered Harald, "I am delighted to see you too but I shall not need your services tonight. However, I will require something to drink in the very near future before I expire."

By now the entire company were on their feet, smiling and offering Harald their outstretched arms in greeting.

"You are a welcome sight, Lord," said one smiling woman. "One moment you were there at the helm and the next, a huge wave had taken you and the back of the ship with you."

"God be praised, you have been returned to us" said Leif, an old warrior from Puglia.

"Odin protects his own, he would not let the sea *jotuns* have you," said Rolf, a veteran from the Regneville Riders.

"We shall sit together in Valhalla yet, my friend," came his captain's response.

All the people were around him now, clapping him on the back and calling their joyful welcome. He released his hold on the boys and held up his hands, requesting silence.

"Friends, I have been given back to you from the sea and my journey getting here is a little misty. Now, before I try to tell you of that tale, and I confess there is little to tell, I must know what happened to you."

Rolf raised his voice over the others.

"Lord, you were taken by a wave that came from nowhere. It came down on top of us and ploughed the ship into the sea and we all held on for dear life. When she righted herself, you were gone, with some of the crew. The stern was badly damaged, and the tiller and part of the keel were ripped away. The mast had broken and we fought to cut the sheets and get the wreckage overboard. We were shipping water faster than we could bale and I felt we would sink at any moment. Then the winds dropped suddenly, and the swell began to die down. The weather started to clear enough for us to see land, and we rowed and baled with all we had left until we got here. It was all we could do to drive the *Evas Prayer* onto the beach, but she landed us safe and sound. Alas, I feel she will not be taking us much further."

All eyes turned to the battered and broken hull that cast a long, lopsided shadow in the firelight.

"She has been a loyal servant to her crew, but her time is over, and we thank her," said Harald ruefully, raising a skin of wine to the stricken ship. "Now let us be thankful that we are reunited and count our blessings. Come, sit down and we will drink to our fallen comrades."

They took their positions around the bonfire once more and talked energetically. It was not long before Harald fell into an exhausted sleep with one enormous arm around Richard. Thomas and Gilbert, content that their master was comfortable, covered him with his bearskin cloak they had taken from the ship, before curling up at his feet and finally letting sleep take them.

4

Harald woke abruptly. He had been in a deep sleep and dreamt he was fighting with a *kraken* on the ocean floor. The tentacles of the huge beast were contracting around his throat, and he could not breathe. Blinking in the early morning light, he stretched and looked around at the rudimentary camp. On seeing his sleeping comrades lying in a circle around the dead embers of the fire, the deep dread of his nightmare all but faded. He stood up, careful not to wake Richard who snored gently beneath the heavy bear skin cloak. Then he walked over to inspect the *Evas Prayer* and quickly saw that she was damaged beyond repair. The stern of the vessel was completely broken, and the exposed, barnacled hull had several large holes; a small miracle had been performed by the crew in beaching her, he thought. Harald walked around shaking his head and knew that the fate of all of them depended on the survival of the rest of their fleet. It was as if an angry giant had taken his cudgel to the once neatly laid planks of the hull. He also noticed, in consolation, that most of their supplies had not only survived but been unloaded, and barrels of beer, salt pork and mutton lay neatly stacked beneath the ships ragged bow.

"We will not be short of firewood at least," said Rolf from behind him. "How are you faring, Lord?"

Harald turned to greet his old friend, who smiled back revealing a row of broken teeth in a scarred and tattooed old face than resembled tanned leather.

"Well enough, brother. You did well getting her back up here onto dry land," came the reply.

"We were fortunate the storm had all but blown out. Had it not we would have sunk without trace."

"Well, the gods were smiling on us all it seems. Perhaps the sea will return our lost comrades to us as well. Have you seen any sign of local life?" asked Harald.

"A couple of horsemen on top of the cliffs came to take a look yesterday," said Rolf, "but they did not stay long."

"Long enough to count our warriors and assess what we carried aboard, I am sure," said Harald.

They were joined by another warrior, a stout, weather-beaten veteran who had served in Harald's command for more years than any of them could remember.

"A little desperation is good for the Norman soul. Remember Civitate, Lord? When our horses were dropping beneath us from hunger?" said Leif, smiling at the memory. "You were everywhere that day.

There was a moment's reflective silence between the three men.

"There are many more blank pages to write our story on," said Harald. "Now to business. We need to make a wall around us to dissuade any further interest. Take timber from this old girl and build anything you need from that. Then I want sharpened stakes in front, they will need to go deep although the beach seems firm enough here. Set the men to work and then you and I will find our way up to the top of the cliffs. We should build a beacon on high ground. If the other ships have survived, they will be searching for us."

"If our comrades live, they will be here," agreed Leif stoically.

"Indeed, old friend. Now let us eat something and then we shall find a path up those cliffs," said Harald, turning back to his people who were now rousing themselves and getting to their feet to face the day.

There were thirty-six men, nine women and one child in their party. The men, all experienced Norman warriors, were part of a larger contingent that had been chosen to return to southern Italy to join their comrades in a campaign to rid Sicily of the Moors. A few had asked permission to bring their wives with them on the voyage while others left their families behind in Normandie - to be sent for at a later date. They had, to a man, followed Harald slavishly from southern Italy to northern France and now they were on their way back, like their Norse ancestors, in search of land and riches. But unlike their forebears they were now mostly Christian although a few, like Harald Fitzroy, still followed the old gods of Odin, Thor and Freya. It was no secret to his people that their beloved Lord was a pagan and he made little attempt to conceal his faith. With his long, braided yellow hair and plaited beard that reached the top of a flat belly he looked far more like a Norse sea-king from bygone days than he did a general of William the Bastard's victorious cavalry.

By the time the group had breakfasted he had talked to each man and woman. Were a stranger to have observed these little conversations they would have noticed how each person was visibly lifted after they had been spoken to. A familiar word, a casual arm around the shoulder and an encouraging backslap had a palpable effect on each member of the cohort.

Thomas and Gilbert walked respectfully behind Harald and Rolf, young Richard Fitzroy in between them. When they reached the foot of the white, chalky cliffs the little party looked up at the distant summit with trepidation.

"Thomas, you will go first and pick a route for us to the top," said Harald in the full knowledge that the boy was as sure-footed as a goat and had a fearless head for heights.

His brother looked a little crest-fallen before his master added, "And you, Gilbert, will show my nephew how to forage for gulls' eggs. But do not climb too high - I want no broken heads today."

The younger boys looked up as Thomas led the two older men scaling the almost sheer cliff face. The climbers made good progress at first and the young squire was patient with his charges, pointing out foot and hand holes during the difficult ascent. The conversation between the three diminished as they climbed higher, working hard in the rising sun which began to beat hard against the white, crumbling cliff face of chalk. Gulls swooped and dived close to their heads, screeching warnings to them for passing too close to their nests. Harald, relishing the challenge, called to his comrade, labouring beneath him.

"Was it not true that your father was a mountain goat, Rolf? I have no doubt you will beat me to the top yet. Come on old friend, we are nearly there. I will stand you a large cup of ale when we return to the camp."

Rolf muttered something unintelligible as another piece of loose chalk hit him squarely on the top of his balding head. Then he cursed in a mixture of Norwegian and Italian, the sweat dripping copiously into his eyes, and he beseeched the gods to take him off this accursed piece of rock. In another hour they were there, and Thomas called out triumphantly to his master as he reached the final ledge of rock that told him they were home. He put one arm over the lip and felt a springy patch of grass, pulled himself up and over and rolled away from the edge. Then he was on his stomach leaning over to issue final instructions to the other two climbers. Harald arrived soon after and the boy reached for his master's meaty hand placing it where the edge was firm. They soon lay side-by-side calling encouragement to Rolf who was clearly not enjoying the challenge and grabbed the big man, pulling him to safety where he lay breathing heavily and cursing.

Harald and Thomas were on their feet surveying the vista beneath them. They looked down and saw their camp on the beach far below them. Work on fortifying their position had progressed quickly and a large amount of sand and rock had been dug from a deep trench that ran from the bow of their wrecked ship to the broken stern in a circle. The spoil from the digging had been piled high to create 'earthworks' that would reach to the height of a man's shoulders when completed. Another group of men could be seen removing the blades of the ship's oars and whittling the handles to create the sharpened stakes that would be secured around the entrance to their camp.

"What do you think, Thomas? Do you think we might be able to discourage any inquisitive visitors," asked Harald.

Thomas did not answer and was looking away from the sea in the opposite direction.

"Lord, it seems that we are not alone," he finally answered.

In less than a heartbeat, Harald unsheathed *Gunnlogi* from his back and span around to confront whatever enemy awaited him. He relaxed as soon as he saw who it was and smiled in relief. Richard and Gilbert stood about forty paces away next to a raggedly dressed old goatherd in the middle of a flock of about twenty animals. The man stood rigid with fear, and it was only when the Normans lowered their weapons did he appear to breathe again.

"The boys seem to have beaten us here," said Rolf, putting an axe back into his belt.

"At least you won't have to climb back down again," said Harald, walking toward the little group.

Richard ran toward his uncle, his words tumbling out of his mouth in excitement.

"We went to look for gulls' eggs as you instructed, and we found a path further down the beach leading up. We weren't disobeying you, but we could not find any eggs lower down. Then we found Ecto, here, and his goats. He has been kind to us and gave us water."

"Fetch him here. I would like to talk to your new friend," said Harald.

Richard beckoned to the goatherd to advance, and the man shuffled forward, head bowed, with Gilbert just behind him. Ecto, clothed in animal furs and smelling strongly of goats, stood before them waiting to be spoken to.

"Can he speak?" asked Harald.

"He speaks Castilian, Lord," answered Gilbert, "and I know a few words. He lives with his family about two leagues away."

"Have you asked him where we are?"

"We are in the north of the Kingdom of Navarre, Lord," answered Gilbert.

"Ah, the land of King Sancho. That is good, he is well disposed to Normans,"

"But he also said this coastline has constantly been visited by Moorish raiders who are a curse on the land. They killed his brother only last week when they came across his village in search of food."

"Ask him if he will sell us some of his goats. I will give him a good price," said Harald.

While Ecto might have been a little cowed, he was not shy when it came to striking a bargain and he haggled hard with Gilbert. Eventually, a deal was done for five goats, three nannies and two billys, and Harald retrieved a bag of silver from which he paid the man. Ecto thanked him, nodded courteously and bid the visitors farewell, leaving the animals secured by a long piece of twine which he left in Richard's hand.

"Well, it may have been a hard climb, but we have fresh meat and milk at least," said Harald looking about them. "Now let's see if this place suits our purposes. Boys, see what you can find in the woods yonder. We need firewood and lots of it."

Thomas, Gilbert and Richard went off while the two older men turned their attention to the land below them. The deserted beach shimmered for league upon league in the midday heat and the sparkling cyan ocean was equally empty. They knew their camp had plenty of supplies, was well- armed and in a defensible position but they also knew that they needed their comrades at sea to come for them before too long. That is, assuming that they still lived.

They selected a point on the green sward where the land gently rose towards the woods on which to build the watchfire. When the boys returned laden with wood, the pile began to take shape. The nearby copse was full of fallen trees and branches, which meant that it would not be necessary to transport fuel from the wrecked ship. When the stack had reached the height of a man they stopped and Thomas and Gilbert were given the task, for the first night at least, of staying behind to ignite the pyre when it got dark. They were given the bag of dried bread and hard cheese and told to return to the camp at dawn. Harald had no qualms about leaving them here for the night, for they had proven on a number of occasions that they were brave and resourceful young men, but still he sought to reassure them.

"My brother Robert and I went on our first raid into Brittany when we were your ages. I killed my first Breton when I was twelve - unseated him in the first charge and speared him straight through the heart. Now, if there are unwelcome visitors, raise the alarm. Our camp is almost directly below you and we will come to your aid at once. I will see you both in the morning - Richard and I will just have to get by without you for one night."

Then the little party took leave of the boys and the unlit fire and Richard guided them along the cliffs toward the shepherd's path which zigzagged steeply to the beach at the bottom. It was a good deal quicker returning down than climbing up and very soon they were at the foot of the cliff face and walking back to camp. The site had been transformed since he had left it earlier in the day. Sharp wooden stakes now defended an entrance through a thick bank of sand and loose rocks, reinforced with timber and in front of this a deep ditch ran around the circumference. The distinctive kite-shaped shields bearing the insignia of the two ravens of Regneville hung on the earthworks and from the remains of the ship's mast, a flag bearing the two leopards of Normandie flapped lazily in the onshore breeze. They walked through the entrance of their little fortress, where the women had fashioned a trestle table on which they were preparing the evening meal. A man, known as the 'Fighting Priest' stood before them and as was their custom, blessed the food they were about to eat. When it was ready, the people were served and the whole group sat down before the fire as the sun fell into the sea and the heat rushed out of the day. Their mood was good, and spirits were high and the conversation babbled along until everyone had eaten. Then Harald got to his feet and spoke.

"Friends, we have travelled together many times and always reached our destination. This time will be no different and we have been reunited to complete our journey. You will all be wondering how the rest of our brothers and sisters have fared in the storm which nearly killed us all. I have no doubt that they will be looking for us and they will find us soon. Our journey together has been a long one and will continue again, for I know beyond certainty that it will not end here on this barren piece of land. I ask you to charge your drinking cups and toast our comrades lost at sea and thank all the gods for their sacrifice."

Cups were raised high in salute and the priest called out the names of the dead men, asking God to receive their souls. Men and women crossed themselves and stood quiet. The silence was broken by Rolf.

"Lord, perhaps it would be a fitting time to hear the Saga of the Wandering Warriors again," suggested Harald's old friend.

The people called their encouragement to their leader. He smiled and attempted a little modesty before holding one hand up to ask for silence. The only sound that could be heard were the breakers crashing onto the beach as Harald began the famous story of his grandfathers and their epic journey from Haugesund to Regneville.

The words came strong and were spoken loudly with deep resonance. His voice carried on the breeze and there was not a single person that did not crane forward as if to get closer to the storyteller. As always, immersed in the Saga's telling, Harald felt the hands of Bjorn Halfdanson and Torstein Rolloson at his shoulder willing him on. As he spoke, he acted the scenes out in his mind and his powerful voice rose and fell as the rich stanzas rolled mellifluously off his tongue.

> *"Then the burning war-spirit took the warriors*
> *Beyond the great whale-road and on to Wendland*
> *And yielded them up to the Mighty Styrbjorn*
> *Prince of Sweden and Jomsviking King"*

Verse after verse came loud and clear telling the story of the famous Norsemen and their quest for reputation and wealth.

> *"Together they endured the swords and axes*
> *Of foemen sent forth by foreign gods,*
> *They feared neither men's spears nor witches' spells*
> *For Odin's Ravens now walked as men"*

When it was over the audience applauded and cheered, the men and women weeping openly at its conclusion. Richard looked adoringly up at his uncle who reached down and put a hand on the boy's head, ruffling his hair. He noticed it was getting unkempt and the once harshly cropped skin at the back of his head was now a tangle of soft curls.

"I think it is time you learned the story and we shall start tomorrow. Your forebears were great men, and their history is in this story. I shall teach you the Saga, but I warn you I am a harsh task master," said Harald. "Now look behind you, the watch has begun."

Richard looked in the direction of the cliff tops and saw the beacon fire start to catch and burst into life and his heart was filled with hope. He fell asleep to the sound of the storytelling as the people remembered the heroes of past generations.

5

The next day started like the previous ones. The balmy sea breezes stirred the cooking fires beneath an azure sky as the women prepared breakfast. Today would be slightly different, as Lord Harald had ordered that despite their situation, the day should commence with martial training. In the absence of their horses the men trained on foot and the air rang to the clash of steel; swords and axes were hefted and wielded against long wooden kite-shields. After breakfast there was an archery competition in which each man took part, fully testing the bows and, more importantly the bow strings, which had been immersed in salt water only days before. Thomas and Gilbert came down from the cliffs to join their comrades after rebuilding the beacon with firewood from the nearby copse, in readiness for the next watch. They had little to report save for the discovery of a freshwater spring on the cliff top which created a gentle waterfall onto the beach far below.

During the afternoon two parties were sent out along the coast to search for any signs of the missing ships. They returned at dusk with little to report apart from the signs of hoof prints in the sand two leagues away down the coast. This became the pattern of activities in the camp until the end of the fourth day when an event occurred which signalled a change in all their lives.

In the evening Harald and Richard stood on the beach away from the camp looking into the darkening night sky. The older man was explaining the star constellations that were beginning their nocturnal glimmering and the importance to sea farers when he was alerted to a movement less than twenty paces away. He turned to face the sound and instinctively reached for *Gunnlogi,* drawing the blade quickly and raising it in both hands.

"Get behind me, boy," he hissed at Richard who, needing no second invitation, took refuge behind his uncle's huge frame.

"Stay your sword arm, friend," said a soft voice from the darkness. "I mean you no harm. I am a simple traveller walking with my companions.

Harald braced himself as the muffled footsteps drew closer, and in the moonlight, he was able to make out the shape of a man walking toward him with two dogs, one at each side.

"I am sorry if we startled you," said the stranger, "but we were looking for a place to camp for the night and noticed your lights. My name is Grimnir and these are my two travelling companions. They might look fearsome, but I can assure you they will do you no harm."

The man was tall and wore a hooded cloak that almost reached the ground. He carried a large carved, wooden staff and a small leather satchel strapped to his back. He spoke with calm authority and his gentle manner sparked a flicker of recognition in Harald's distant memory. The Norman lowered his weapon and returned it to its sheath.

"My apologies, Grimnir," said Harald "but we are strangers on this foreign shore and are still finding our way."

"It is we who must apologise, Lord, we had no wish to disturb your stargazing," said Grimnir, turning to Richard who was peering curiously at the travellers. "Come out, young man, my companions will not bite a friend."

Richard held out a cautious hand and edged forward, and one of the huge, shaggy beasts who moved forward to meet him sniffed his hand and licked it. Harald stuck out his own hand in greeting.

"My name is Harald Fitzroy, Marchis of Ambrières and the Norman Marches and I am travelling south with my people. Will you join us to sup? I would be keen to hear of these lands. I sense you have a story to tell if you are willing to share."

"It would be my pleasure, Lord. I would welcome some company," replied the stranger smiling back.

"Come then, friend. Richard, run ahead and tell them that we have a few more mouths to feed tonight."

The boy took off at a pace in the direction of the camp and the two men followed the path of his footsteps in the sand. They arrived soon after Richard and walked past the spearman standing guard at the entrance. A woman came over to them with drinking cups full of ale. Grimnir thanked her, raised his cup to his host and to the rest of the camp and drank deeply.

"I am in your debt, Lord, already. This is fine Norman ale I think," said the stranger pulling down his hood and looking around him, taking in the new surroundings. "You have done well. It is no mean feat constructing an impressive fortress in so little time. You are a man who embraces life's considerable challenges, I think."

Harald turned to his guest and regarded him in the light of the blazing fire. Whilst he could not determine his age, he guessed that Grimnir was an old man. The long grey hair was pulled back and braided into a plait that hung down his back. He had a wise and gentle face and a long, white, unruly beard that reached his waist, but this benign visage was offset by a black leather eye patch covering an empty socket. But it was his dogs that commanded the attention of the people for they were huge and appeared more like wolves. They watched them nervously before Richard ran toward the beasts, putting his arms around the neck of one of the powerful animals and embracing her.

"This one is called Geri," Richard shouted to the astonished onlookers, looking up at them in delight. "She can walk a thousand leagues in a single day."

More trestle tables had been built during the day, and one of the women ushered Harald and Grimnir toward one and bid them to sit on some crudely fashioned seats. They sat and talked while food and more drink were bought for them.

"Your people are fortunate to have such a resourceful leader, Lord Harald," said Grimnir "but how is it that you have landed here in the middle of nowhere?"

"That is a long story, my friend, but we have time if you would like to hear it?" came the reply.

The old man smiled broadly and nodded his head.

"It would be my great pleasure to listen," he said. "Leave nothing out."

Harald felt at ease in this man's company and although he had only just met him, he was comfortable telling his story to the stranger. It started with the history of his people and his grandfathers, the Wandering Warriors of Haugesund. He told of growing up in Regneville where he and his brother Robert became companions to the young Duke William. He told of his rise to power as the Duke's 'iron fist' and how he left Normandie for the first time to travel south with the Guiscard. He told of the many battles they had fought and won, and how the Normans had triumphed over the Papal army to secure their future. He told of his return to Normandie and his part in ridding the Duchy of the French King. He spoke of leaving his homeland for the second time and of falling out with his brother again. Grimnir, listened quietly as his host talked into the night until at last he was finished. There was silence between them for a short while. Not the awkward silence of strangers - just a few comfortable moments of contemplation where they thought about what had passed between them. Then it was Grimnir's turn to talk, but before starting his story he took the scraps from his plate and fed them to his dogs, who stirred briefly, ate and then fell back to sleep. He was a Dane from Jelling but unlike the Fitzroy warriors he came from a long line of seers; people who could "read the runes and translate the wishes of the gods." He had left home to escape persecution from the zealous christians who sought only to stamp out the old ways. Now he wandered, travelling the roads and pathways, doing enough small jobs along the way to feed himself and his companions.

"How long have you been travelling?" asked Harald.

"For longer than I can remember, Lord. There are always those who still believe in the old ways and seek the words of one such as me."

"You can tell the future of men?"

"Sometimes, but men do not always want to hear their fate. Particularly when it does not suit them," said the old man wistfully rubbing a finger over his empty eye socket before looking at Harald directly and guessing the next question. "But your fate is one that lies far from here and not where you might think. Your friend in the south can do without you, I believe, at least for the present and there is work to be done in the north."

"The north? Back to Normandie?"

"No, Harald, not there. There is still a debt of blood owed to your people beyond the Duchy. There is a price for the Voyage of Tears still to be paid. No man can fight the Norns when they decide his fate."

Harald stared incredulously at the stranger, not knowing quite what to make of his words for he had made no mention of his grandfather's flight from the old home in Saxon England so many years ago. He had a thousand questions for his guest, but they would not be answered, at least not tonight. Before he could ask them Grimnir, held up his hand,

"My apologies - I do not wish to alarm you; I only speak what I see. Please, I am a little tired and ask that you might excuse this rambling old man before you. You have been most kind and your hospitality does you great credit. Let us continue our conversation another time for the hour is late and a new day will soon be upon us."

Then, he thanked his host, quickly got up and went over to the dying embers of the fire to spread out his cloak and lay down. Harald watched as the dogs got up to join their master.

"The Norns will not be denied," he mumbled to himself with a rueful grin before getting up, stretching and moving to where his own makeshift bed was calling him.

Harald never got to ask the multitude of questions he had for the old seer, for when the people woke in the morning he and his dogs were gone, leaving no trace. Richard was bitterly disappointed when he heard they had departed, and he raced out of the camp and along the shoreline to say goodbye. On discovering his new friends were long gone, he trudged back disconsolately. He stopped and removed his shoes and thick, woollen stockings before paddling through the shallow waters of the incoming tide. The boy was alone in his thoughts contemplating the day ahead of him. He missed his family and wondered what his brother and sister were doing. He missed his mother and their home in Mortain and pondered when he might see them all again. Richard stooped to pick up a handful of pebbles and straightened before throwing the first one as far as he could out to sea. Then he looked to the distant horizon and saw the shapes of four double masted ships and his heart leapt. The lost ships of his uncle's fleet had found them and were coming to take them away to their new home.

Chapter 2: Eleanor's News
Mortain, Normandie 1065

1

Eleanor Fitzroy stood very still as her maid finished dressing her, looking out of the window of the bedchamber. She had spent another restless night worrying over the fate of her son Richard and there were dark rings beneath her eyes. Since parting from the boy and returning to Mortain her life had been, if anything, more miserable than before. But she still had her children, she thought, softly stroking the imperceptible bump of her growing belly that signalled a fourth. The unborn child of her union with Harald Fitzroy was due to come into the world in late autumn and she longed for another daughter. Today was the day, she decided, that she would tell her husband the news. She afforded herself a wicked smile when she considered the pain and embarrassment it would cause Robert Fitzroy, her pious spouse. Eleanor was not a bad person, but the humiliation of her recent incarceration at her husband's hands had been a bitter experience and one for which she was determined to repay him. Were it not for her children she would have fled the marriage bed for her brother-in-law at the soonest opportunity. Today, she knew would be a difficult one but she would handle it with the steely determination for which she was well known.

As soon as the maid finished winding and plaiting Eleanor's hair into an extravagantly long ponytail, she was dressed. Grace stood back, as she did every day, to ensure that she had not missed anything. In truth, thought the girl, there was seldom much to do, for despite her mistress being thirty-five years old she was still a beautiful woman who needed little adornment. However, today's emerald green woollen dress with its abundantly wide sleeves would soon be a little too tight, she decided and in need of letting out, but other than that her mistress was immaculate as usual.

"*Parfait, madame,*" said the maid."Will that be all?"

"Thank you, Grace. I am ready to meet the day," replied Eleanor nervously.

Striding out of the room, Eleanor made for the family's dining room high in the solar of Mortain castle, where she knew her family would be waiting for her. She sighed to herself before entering the room anticipating the sullen atmosphere that normally accompanied each breakfast time. She was pleasantly surprised to find the large high ceilinged dining room bathed in early summer sunlight which streamed through open windows and her spirits lifted a little. Turid and William ran to their mother as soon as they saw her. She delivered a beaming smile and bent down to kiss them both before scooping up her daughter and putting her back on her seat at the long oak table.

"Are you sure you are only three?" she asked the little girl. "You are almost as heavy as your brother."

"Nearly four," said Turid fiercely, "I will soon be able to ride out with him and Papa."

"You'll need to grow a little more first," said her father benignly from the head of the table, while his wife distanced herself at the other end.

"Good morning, Robert," said Eleanor flatly to her husband, without looking at him directly.

Robert Fitzroy nodded silently in his wife's direction. He was now forty-three years old, and his once dark hair was mostly grey. He was still a handsome man and held his athletic frame with a rigid military bearing. The spear wound in his shoulder received in one of the numerous French wars still bothered him, and he constantly flexed it in an attempt to alleviate the stiffness.

The family was served honeyed porridge, bread, fruit and small weak beer. Eleanor picked at her breakfast and did her distracted best to engage in conversation with the children. When the meal was finished, she addressed her husband directly for the first time that morning.

"Robert, there is something I need to discuss with you. I know you are to return to your duties in Caen tomorrow and I would have your attention before then."

"Very well, let us talk later this morning. Come to my rooms later when I return from prayer," came the curt reply.

After breakfast the table was cleared and the children taken away by their servants. Eleanor was left alone to contemplate her meeting with her estranged husband. Since his discovery of the affair with his brother and her attempted escape with the children, a difficult domestic atmosphere had been replaced by bitterness and barely concealed hostility. Husband and wife avoided each other as much as possible and days would pass without the two exchanging as much as as single word. She was watched like a hawk by Robert's odious lieutenant, Gabriel, and she knew that at least for now her life was that of a prisoner - albeit in a gilded cage. She was determined to be as strong and resilient as ever, but she knew that today's news would push Robert's reserve to the limit. A servant came to tell her that he had returned from the chapel. She took a deep breath and walked to his rooms on the other side of the solar.

Before long she stood before the door of his chamber and pounded her fist on it loudly. Robert grunted something inaudible, and she opened the door and went inside. She was no longer taken aback by the austerity of his living quarters, which were sparse to the point of being monastic. A small, solitary window was the only feature in any of the four plain white-washed walls and she had never seen it opened in any of her visits here. There was a wooden cot in one corner of the room and a writing desk in another. His hunting hawk slumbered on its perch in yet another. The only decoration was a large crucifix hanging from one of the walls above a mean fire that gave little heat and even less light. Robert rose to meet her from his desk, and they regarded each other coldly.

"You have something you wish to discuss with me?" he said, preparing himself for another of her incessant complaints. "What is it? You are comfortable enough surely? This is your home, not your gaol. I have made every concession to you since your return."

Eleanor took a step toward him and met his angry look.

"I am with child," she announced defiantly.

Robert's mouth dropped open, and he sucked in his breath, considering the news. His face contorted into a grimace, and he moved toward her, raising a hand to strike her. But it was no weak and cowed woman that stood before him, and she jabbed a finger close to his face. The Lioness of Mortain had returned, and she emoted her angry words through clenched teeth.

"Do not take another step, husband," she warned. "You might be one of the most powerful men in the Duchy, but you do not scare me. If you harm me or this child, you will suffer the consequences. Do not forget that your first-born son is under your brother's protection and if anything happens to us, Hari has promised that you will never see him again."

She let the import of her words sink in and Robert slowly regained his composure.

"So, you carry my brother's bastard," he sneered. "I think it is probably time you joined your mother in the nunnery."

"I think not. I will not be separated from my children and when this child arrives it will be part of the family. Your brother has many loyal and powerful followers in Normandie, despite his absence, and he will know if anything happens to us," she replied truculently.

Robert knew he was bested and fought to control his rage until it began to subside. His shoulders slumped and he shook his head.

"When did you grow so cold, Eleanor?" he asked her calmly.

She was taken aback by the question.

"When you chose duty over your family," she answered.

Eleanor turned and left the room leaving her husband alone with his thoughts.

2

The Lord of Mortain departed for Caen the next day with a squadron of cavalry, and he would not return home for some time. He had business with his liege lord, William, the Duke of Normandie and great changes were afoot. The Duchy had been at peace since his brother had defeated their last enemy, chasing Conan of Brittany all the way back to Dinan to accept the surrender. There would be new enemies trying to wrest Normandie's riches away from the Duke, but for now they had all been vanquished. The bounty of peace was manifold. The Duke's coffers were full, his vassals were wealthy, the church of Rome was supportive, and the people were well fed and content. The desperation that had accompanied the warring years and the fear that came with it had all but gone. Robert knew that this was only a temporary condition, and war would come again soon.

Alone in his thoughts at the head of the squadron he rode the twenty leagues in silence. His men knew better than to disturb him in these quiet moments and did not approach him. Once he arrived in Caen the affairs of the Duchy would consume him and thoughts of his home in Mortain would become a distant memory. But now the last confrontation with Eleanor was still very fresh in his mind and her news had been another bitter pill for him to swallow. When he had first learned of their betrayal he immediately and instinctively exacted revenge against Harald and Eleanor. Whilst he could never forgive them entirely, at least he eventually accepted the situation. He had reasoned that he was not blameless for his part in driving them together and had stoically accepted that things could never be the same again. But yesterday's news that his wife was now carrying Harald's bastard was an almost impossible burden to bear. He thought of Christ on the cross, dying for the sins of mankind, and knew he could persevere with the hopeless domestic situation in which he now found himself. Besides, the thought of never seeing his son Richard was something that could not be contemplated.

They rode hard and fast through the day, it was early summer, and the road was good, providing the party with swift passage. By the time dusk descended, they had reached the long valley approaching Caen where hundreds of smoke trails from cooking fires could be seen on the horizon. The limestone fortress appeared splendid to the travellers, giving off a yellow lustre that could be seen from far away. Soon it was dark, and they stood before the huge gatehouse of the city's castle waiting to be let through the thick oak doors which had been closed for the night. Orders were shouted down from sentries on the battlements and a postern gate in one of the doors swung open to greet the party from Mortain.

"Lord Robert," said the sergeant-at-arms, a large, fleshy man with a pockmarked face, "we have been expecting you, sir. I will send a boy with a torch to light your path."

"No need, Louis. I know my way blindfolded by now," came the reply.

The horsemen walked their animals through the doorway and onto the cobblestones before the keep where an army of grooms were on hand to take the horses off to be rubbed down and fed. Robert stood the men down and made his way to his quarters high up in the keep. As Chancellor of the Duchy he was an important man, but he did not like to be fussed over and insisted on no special treatment.

"Will you be meeting the Duke tonight," said his squire, an earnest young man who struggled along, heavily laden and trying to keep up with Robert's keen pace.

"Not tonight, Henri, it is late. But be assured there will be no rest for me come morning, I think."

He looked up to the top of the *donjon* to Duke William's rooms, noticing lights were still burning.

"Now give me those bags and go to the refectory and get some food before you turn in. We will both be busy tomorrow."

Tired and grateful to be dismissed, the boy bowed and retreated into the night leaving his Lord to his own devices. Robert finally reached his rooms after ascending a host of staircases, each one guarded by a man-at-arms. He sat down exhausted on his bed, but tired as he was, he slipped onto his knees to pray. He asked God to give him the strength to forgive Eleanor and that one day he might be reconciled with his brother. Most of all, he prayed for Duke William's deliverance through the rising storm clouds.

3

As was his normal practice in Caen, Robert rose early and, after making his ablutions, spent the next hour in genuflection in the castle's Lady Chapel. So deep was he in prayer that he did not notice being joined by another in front of the little altar. When he had finished, he got to his feet and turned to find his friend and mentor, Archbishop Lanfranc, sitting in silence on a little wooden pew.

"Father," exclaimed Robert, his eyes wide with delight. "Where did you learn such stealth? You are as silent as an assassin."

"God moves in mysterious ways," replied the Archbishop, smiling broadly.

The two men embraced warmly. They had become close confidantes since their first meeting many years ago and were probably the only two men in the Duchy that Duke William trusted implicitly.

"And how was your visit home?" asked the priest.

"Not easy I am afraid. My brother has left his normal trail of destruction," replied Robert. He sighed deeply, knowing that few events in Normandie escaped Lanfranc of Pavin's attention and his very public falling out with Harald was no exception.

"We cannot choose our kin, and I pray each day for you to find peace," said Lanfranc sympathetically.

"At least our confrontation did not turn out to be deadly. Although at the time I was sure I had killed him," said Robert. "It seems like God is still listening to your prayers."

"And your family?' said the Archbishop, "I have been praying for them, too."

"You are kind father, but it will take a divine intercession to heal the rift between Eleanor and myself."

"Time is a great healer, Robert. There is no doubt that you have been wronged but forgiveness is the greatest gift that a man can bestow on those who have wronged him," continued the Archbishop. "And I have little fear for the well-being of your son. Your brother would sooner die than see the boy harmed."

There was a moment's silence as Robert considered Lanfranc's words, nodding more in hope than agreement.

"I pray that you are right, Father," he replied, remembering his last conversation with Eleanor, before Lanfranc redirected the subject of their discourse.

"Now, there are great changes in the air I feel. I think we should have an interesting council meeting today. Have you seen Duke William?"

"Not yet. I arrived only late last night but he has asked to see me before the council meets today,"

"Then I shall detain you no longer, Robert. He will be pleased to see his Chancellor for, as always you are the voice of calm that has seen him through many stormy times."

"I think you overestimate my influence sometimes, Father," came the reply. "I can only attempt to offer guidance sometimes and I wonder whether he listens to my counsel at all."

Their brief meeting concluded, the two men shook hands and Robert left the chapel and went outside. Dawn was breaking and a chilly breeze blew across the flat concourse within the walls of the castle. As ever, Robert's spirits were always lifted after a meeting with Lanfranc of Pavin, who always seemed to find the right words to say even in the most difficult of times. Now, as he hurried to his meeting with the Duke the thoughts of his domestic problems seemed to dissipate like today's early morning mists in the growing warmth of the rising sun.

After a brisk walk he reached the castle's great hall and was smartly saluted by two spearmen standing guard outside. The building stood alone from the keep and had been a recent edition and it was here that the Duke held all his meetings with important audiences, be it with his liege lords or emissaries from Rome. Like the castle, it was made of robust Norman sandstone and was big enough to seat at least sixty people. Robert had overseen its construction himself during the repairs made to the town after the damage inflicted by the French King's army. He afforded himself a brief smile in appreciation of his work and then crossed himself, thanking God for the Duchy's deliverance and the King's demise. He was not allowed much time to be alone with his thoughts as Duke William's coarse voice boomed out from the other end of a long oak table.

"Robert, my brother. It seems like an age since we saw you last. I am glad to see you safe and sound again."

The Duke was on his feet in a moment, striding toward his guest with arms outstretched in welcome. He cut an imposing figure and although not quite as tall as his Chancellor, was broad and powerfully built, with a thick black head of hair savagely shaven from the nape of his neck almost to the crown of his head.

"It is good to be back in Caen, William," replied the Count of Mortain.

"The Duchy would grind to a halt without you," said the Duke smiling warmly. "Now come and sit by the hearthfire and warm your bones. No doubt you have spent these early hours on your knees in that draughty old chapel."

"You know me too well, I think," came the reply.

"I should think I do. I was but eight years old when your grandfather took me in and made me part of the Fitzroy clan," said the Duke jovially.

"Ah, Grandfather Bjorn," said Robert. "He made men of all of us I think."

"It is the blood of the Norsemen that flows through the veins of Normandie after all - and makes us indomitable - that and the wrath of God. Without it we could not have made peace out of the chaos that was the Duchy. Now to business, we have a busy day ahead of us," the Duke replied, ushering his friend to a seat by the fire.

Robert knew the truth behind his liege-lord's words, for the Duke and his chancellor had known one another for almost thirty years. Bjorn Halfdanson, Count of Regneville, had appointed his grandsons as companions to the young, imperilled Duke on his father's death. The young Fitzroys had sworn fealty to their charge and had discharged their duties faithfully but not without cost.

William and his vassals fought bitterly to preserve the duchy's power, but victory had been hard-won and slowly they prevailed. The fighting had seldom stopped but together they put an end to the internecine struggles that had riven the Duchy. At the age of nineteen, and with the Fitzroy brothers behind him, William had the support and allegiance of all the Norman *baronie* and over the next two decades the Duchy changed slowly from a state of anarchy to prosperity. Peace was enforced by William's own decrees, and he created the law forcibly, proclaiming to any dissenters that it was all done in the name of God. He was ruthless, courageous and cunning in equal measure and, as Robert and Harald came to learn, not above using divisive tactics to achieve his goals.

With the pleasantries over, the Duke turned immediately to the business of the day - the accession to the English throne.

"Harald has left the Duchy for the Kingdom in the Sun," announced Robert without preamble.

"Indeed, he has," said William, "I gave his captain an audience only yesterday. He came with a letter from your brother who 'apologises for his absence from the Duchy but has urgent business in Italy to attend to'. Captain Jeanotte was also at pains to stress that the forces under his command are loyal to a man and that the Duchy's borders to the south are as secure as ever."

Robert rubbed his chin and nodded.

"Well, Jeanotte is a good man, and we should take him at his word. There should be no doubts about his loyalty," replied Robert.

"I agree with you completely. Your brother's exit is regrettable, but we are still in need of his men and support."

"And his eyes and ears in England," continued Robert. "Jeanotte is well regarded in King Edward's court. I will be seeing the captain when our business is concluded here."

"As ever, Chancellor, I have no doubt that you have all eventualities taken care of," said the Duke. "Now, let us get ready to welcome our guests, they must be made completely aware as to their role in our plans."

Robert nodded in agreement, knowing full well that whilst Duke William nearly always heeded his advice, he had made up his mind some time ago the English throne was his by divine right and would crush any resistance that stood in his way. His train of thought was interrupted by a servant announcing the arrival of the other guests and one by one the Duke's advisors made their entrance into the hall. The first to arrive was William's half-brother, Odo, Bishop of Bayeux who despite his title was a fighting man, suitably armed with a cruel looking mace at his waist. After him came Roger of Beaumont, Walter Gifford, William of Warren and finally, Lanfranc of Pavin. When they were all assembled around the table the Duke's *seneschal*, William

Fitzosborne, ordered the doors closed and refreshments were brought to the guests. William greeted each man personally and they sat drinking and eating, waiting for the council meeting to begin.

"Gentlemen," rasped the Duke of Normandie, standing before the influential barons and churchmen of the Duchy. "Thank you all for coming here today. You will know that King Edward of England has promised the throne of England to me on the occasion of his death. This promise has been reinforced by his envoy Harold Godwinson, a loyal knight of the Duchy who has given me his blood oath and fealty. I have news from across *la Manche* that my uncle is ailing and will not make Christmas. As sad as this news is, we must all start to prepare ourselves for taking custodianship of his kingdom."

There was a rumbling of appreciative murmurs from the seated guests, each man calculating the good fortune that was about to fall into his lap if the news was true.

"Now I also hear that my uncle's subjects, whilst they are not in open revolt, are displeased with their monarch and that I will be welcomed to rule a willing people. You, gentlemen, as my own loyal lieutenants, need to prepare yourselves for government of the rich prize of England. There will be grants of land and title for all those who follow me and I can assure you that I have already earmarked substantial rewards for each of you. Gentlemen, this is welcome news, and I am sure that you have questions for me."

William stood there smiling with his arms out, palms upward, inviting discussion. Walter Gifford was the first to respond.

"My Lord, this sounds like a gift from heaven, but my question is this. We have always had to take what we needed by force and then hold on to it with even more force. Are we now to expect that on the death of King Edward you will be asked to rule the Kingdom and we, your *baronie,* be able to take control? Should we not expect some sort of resistance from the Saxons?"

"Walter, my earnest hope and expectation is that this will be a peaceful accession, and I have no reason to doubt it. What God has ordained, men cannot stand against."

Gifford knew far better than to question the Duke in front of his peers but he was only voicing what most of them thought. Could it be possible that the Normans could simply walk into high office? The Saxons were not shy when it came to defending their shores, would they simply lower their defences and let the Normans take their riches? Lanfranc decided to intercede, and the elegant Italian churchman got to his feet.

"I too was a little sceptical when I heard that our Duke would be invited to take the Saxon throne unopposed. All I can add is that we have the unequivocal support of Rome. Not only has the Holy See personally blessed the marriage of our Duke but he fully supports the claim for King Edward's crown. The English church is long overdue for reformation and Rome is actively encouraging us to intercede. I see before us the new Archbishop of Canterbury and know he is the man for the task."

All eyes turned to the Bishop of Bayeux who laughed nervously before speaking.

"I shall do my best to bring the Saxon clergy to heel. I am but a humble servant of Rome," he said.

"The English people shall welcome us with open arms," added Duke William evangelically. "Now, if there are no more questions, my Lords, I have organised a hunt after which I look forward to feasting you all in style."

The meeting was over, and the men got to their feet to leave. It would take a little time to get the coursing horses and hunting dogs ready and Robert went in search of his brother's captain. He left the council chamber quickly and went into the bright morning sunshine.

4

He found Jeanotte with another man of Ambrières, on top of the castle wall near the gate house and hailed him.

"Captain Jeanotte," called Robert to the tall young warrior who span round and visibly stiffened at his approach.

The two had first met in Capulia almost a decade before, when Jeanotte had been a squire to his brother. Since then, the knight had distinguished himself on many foreign fields and returned to Normandie as Harald's trusted captain, assuming leadership of over a thousand men and a string of border fortresses on his Lord's recent departure. He had always liked the young man and secretly admired the manner in which his brother was able to inspire such men in their unfailing loyalty to him. The last time they had met was at the *'holmgang'* when Robert had left the knight's master for dead.

"Count Robert," said Jeanotte, dismissing the man next to him and standing to attention.

"Please, Jeanotte," said Robert. "There is little need for such formality between us. Your Lord, he is in good health?"

"Yes, sir, he was when I saw him last. My Lord Harald is resilient and hard to kill," replied Jeanotte with an almost imperceptible smile beginning at the corners of his mouth. "It is a strange thing, but men still flock to his banner wherever he is - Normandie or Italy. Your brother's reputation seems only to grow - and men will always respond to that."

"Well, I am pleased he is in good health and wish him well on his journey, despite our recent differences. And you, Jeanotte, are something more than a humble captain in my brother's army, I think. A *milites* of some repute if what I understand is correct. You have big boots to fill and the Duke has confidence that you will keep the southern marches secure," said Robert, watching the young man relax a little. "Your meeting with the Duke yesterday was satisfactory?"

"Most definitely, Lord. The Duke rewarded me generously, although there was no need, for he has the fealty of all of us in the Marches," replied the knight with great enthusiasm.

"There was never any doubt in my mind. You know my brother can be a little headstrong sometimes, but like you his loyalty is beyond question," said the Count diplomatically,

Jeanotte bowed his head in silent acceptance of the compliment.

"You have word from England? I understand the town of Maldon is thriving," continued Robert changing the subject.

"Oh, yes, Lord, we have over five hundred souls there now - Saxons and Normans living and working in harmony - the King's patronage has been of great help," replied the knight before moving his head closer in a conspiratorial fashion, "but his health is failing and many at court fear he will not make it into next year. There are constant murmurings of his imminent death - and of course the succession to the English throne,"

"Your sources are reliable?" asked Robert.

"Oh, yes," replied Jeanotte proudly. "The King requested men from Maldon for his bodyguard - we sent our best warriors."

"And the Saxon earls, are there any who the King favours above any other?"

"Earl Godwinson has his confidence of course," replied Jeanotte without hesitation. "He is constantly visiting King Edward's chambers. His visits, I hear, are not without purpose. It is rumoured he seeks power himself."

Robert raised his eyebrows once again.

"Thankyou, Jeanotte. Will you keep me informed of any news that you hear from England?"

"Of course, sir. Lord Harald would wish it."

There was a brief silence between the two as the younger man waited for more questions.

"You have news of my brother, since he left?" asked Robert.

"No, Lord. Nothing new for a while now. His ships were passed going south into the Basque Sea four weeks ago but since then - nothing. He will send word when he arrives," said Jeanotte, "you have a message for him?"

Robert shook his head in reply.

"Just let me know when you have word from the English court, Jeanotte. Much will depend on King Edward's next actions."

"And dying men are not always known for making good decisions," added the young knight knowingly.

The two men shook hands, and Robert thanked him for his time, wishing him a safe journey back to Ambrières. Then he hurried back to his room to prepare himself for the hunt.

5

In truth there was little to do, for Henri had prepared everything for his master with his normal care and attention. Thick woollen hose, a fresh linen shirt and a padded gambeson had been laid on his cot and a highly polished pair of leather hunting boots stood by the fire. Robert nodded his approval as the boy tried to stifle a yawn.

"Ready for some sport?" enquired Robert as the squire finished strapping his master's sword and dagger around his waist."

"Indeed, Lord," came the reply. "Let us hope the boar are not shy today. We have a perfect day for it."

"Come then let us find the rest of our party, and make sure you talk with Lord Giffard's squire. I want to know the state of his fighting force - he tells me he has five hundred *milites* at his disposal and I need to know the truth. Use your discretion."

"Yes, Lord," said Henri knowing full well what was required of him and the details he would need to procure.

They left the room quickly because Robert knew he had spent too long with Captain Jeanotte and did not want to be late joining the rest of the huntsmen. He did not need to worry as the group was still assembling in the courtyard below the keep. Dogs barked excitedly as the coursers were brought out to seat the huntsmen. A groomsmen led a spritely pair of stallions over to the Chancellor and his aide and they mounted smartly before joining their comrades. More servants brought out wine filled drinking horns to the mounted men, and they all toasted the success of the hunt and the health of their benefactor, Duke William. It was noon as the summer sun beamed its warmth down onto the men, dogs and horses. Squires scurried around making final preparations securing boar spears and crossbows to their saddles while kennel masters waited with their noisy charges to leave. The cacophony grew as the last of the stragglers joined the group and a horn blasted out to signify that the hunt was about to begin. With a final shout of encouragement, the Duke led them across the cobble stones of the courtyard and out through the gatehouse in a tumult of clattering hooves and baying hounds.

It was a large hunting party that made its way into the open countryside outside the city of Caen and toward the dense woodland a league away. Forty mounted men led a procession of hounds and their keepers, trackers, cooks and porters. As they approached the forest the *lymers* were brought forward on long leashes in search of the scent of a quarry. It was not long before a cry went up when the scent hounds picked up the trail of a boar and the hunt was on. Half a league further, a large male boar was run to ground within a copse of elm trees and the mastiffs and *alaunts* were released. The enraged animal, now even more aggressive at the height of the mating season, turned to confront his pursuers. It was a massive beast and stood grunting its defiance at the barking hounds, each dog looking for an opportunity to lurch forward and attack. The leader of the mastiffs saw his opportunity and bounded forward to close with the boar, only for its glorious moment to be curtailed by the cornered beast's deadly tusks, ripping its chest and stomach open. It tossed it aside as if the huge dog were no more than a rag doll before turning to face the rest of the hesitant pack. Taking their opportunity two *alaunt* hounds dashed forward and onto the back of the angry boar, trying to sink their fangs into its toughened hide. The air was thick with the noise of the commotion and the pervasive reek of fighting animals. Duke William shouted to Roger de Beaufort,

"Your honour, my Lord."

Beaufort's smile lit up his face at the accolade being bestowed upon him and the burly knight cocked a leg over his saddle pommel and leapt to the ground in a single fluid movement. His squire was behind him in an instant with two short, lugged boar spears, handing one to his master, and they both plunged headlong to engage with the cornered beast. The boar tossed the two *alaunts* off its back effortlessly and pawed the ground before launching itself at the advancing man. The brave charge was met by a spear thrust to its chest which hit bone and glanced off causing little damage. The squire had a little more joy although his spear strike behind the beast's shoulder was wide of the mark and nowhere near its heart. Seeing his baron in danger of being gored to death the Duke ordered crossbows to be discharged, and by the time the fifth quarrel had done its damage the animal relented. With the attack on the prone man over, the boar's legs buckled and fell to its knees in its death throes. Beaufort struggled to his feet and his squire, remarkably untouched from the confrontation, handed his master a hunting sword which was rapidly thrust under the boar's armpit and into the heart.

"Well met, Roger." called Duke William to the perspiring knight, who raised a bloodied sword in salute, first to his master and then to the dead pig.

"Saved by some good Norman mail," rejoined Beaufort panting heavily and looking down at his torn *hauberk.*

"And a few crossbow bolts. At least we should not expect such fight from the Saxons," shouted William to the general amusement of all.

The dead animal's carcass was hung from the branch of a nearby tree from where it was gutted, skinned and butchered. Servants brought the hunters' food and drink and the dogs gorged on the boar's discarded offal. It was approaching dusk when the party packed up and returned to Caen at a far more leisurely pace than they had left earlier in the day.

Robert Fitzroy was thoughtful as they approached the city gates. He drew his cloak around him against the cooling evening, crossed himself and prayed to God the Duke was right and they would not have to fight their way to the English throne.

"There are just not enough of us," he sighed to himself.

Chapter 3: A Change of Plan
Navarre 1065

It took a while to unload a hundred horses from four ships, but soon after noon they were all on dry land - and delighted to be there. The animals had been at sea for many weeks and their joy at being able to exercise stiff legs was clearly visible as they were led along the shoreline by a number of riders. Harald was equally delighted to be reunited with his own destrier and joined the riders in galloping along the empty beach. After a league they turned the herd around and rode back to the camp, where the animals were fed and watered and tied to a hitching line.

"That feels better, boy," said Harald patting Damascus's neck as the horse nickered contentedly in his ear. He loved the powerfully built black stallion who had served him fiercely for more than a decade, and the smell of the perspiring animal took him back to times long gone.

The man standing next to him, attending to his own horse, spoke, breaking his reverie.

"I didn't think we would see you again, Hari," he said to his cousin.

"Nor I you, Brenier, yet here we are, and these fellows are none the wiser," said Harald looking up and nodding in the direction of the long line of war horses, feeding noisily on hay spread out before them. "Tomorrow, we shall graze them on grass, there is plenty of pasture on the cliff tops. We will soon have them back to fighting fitness."

Brenier was a native of Regneville, and they had travelled together to the Kingdom in the Sun over twenty years ago. Five years younger than his commander, the two men looked remarkably similar and were often taken as brothers.

"I expect you will be pleased to see the last of this place?" he said. "It was something of a miracle we found you at all. There is nothing on this shoreline for a hundred leagues or more. The watchman saw your beacon last night and we prayed that it might be you."

"I thought the Norns had cut my cords for good this time," replied Harald. "But our story is not yet complete, I think."

"Will we leave for Italy tomorrow?" asked Brenier, but Harald, lost in his own thoughts, did not answer and continued to stroke his horse's neck.

Since losing contact with the *Evas Prayer*, Brenier had led the little fleet of four ships up and down the Navarrean coastline in search of signs of their lost comrades. The search had been fruitless and despite endless hours of watching, the crews began to lose hope of finding their comrades. All of this changed last night when the beacon fire was spotted. At first light the ships had anchored in the shallows, and their crews waded ashore to be greeted by a delighted eight-year-old boy. He alerted the rest of the camp who streamed out to meet their rescuers. By the time the early morning sun was halfway through its ascent all four ships had unloaded men, women and horses turning the beach into a maelstrom of cheerful commotion. A large fire was built on the beach and many of the remaining pigs and chickens were slaughtered to provide food for an evening feast in celebration of the reunion. It began with the 'Fighting Priest' giving thanks to the gods of different denominations for the deliverance of their fellows. When he was finished, he invited Harald Fitzroy to address the assembly, who stood before the blazing fire, casting long shadows onto the illuminated beach. The Marchis held up his hands for quiet but there was no need as the conversation came to an abrupt halt and the people waited for their Lord to speak.

"My friends, we have travelled far to get here, and my heart is filled with joy at seeing you all again. You have my gratitude for your continuous perseverance in finding us, but I have another request of you. Drink, eat and rejoice here tonight and rest for soon our journey continues. But we will not be sailing to the Kingdom in the Sun, for fate is calling us in the North and we have unfinished business elsewhere. Rest yourselves well for in two days we sail for England."

There was not a single murmur from the audience as they digested the news of the change of plan and Harald continued.

"If any of you wish to continue to Italy, I will provide you with passage and silver? What say you?"

After a moment's silence a single voice answered.

"We will follow you to the gates of hell if you ask us, Lord," shouted Rolf from the darkness.

Harald smiled broadly.

"It is settled then, we shall set sail for Maldon in two days."

Chapter 4: The Return to Maldon
Wessex, England 1065

1

Brisk southerly winds allowed the flotilla to sail in an almost straight line to the tip of France, where they veered into *la Manche*. More favourable winds swept them along the coastline of southern England, before crossing the Tamsye estuary and turning up the River Blackwater toward Maldon.

Harald stood on the forecastle of the *Lady Alberada*, a large byzantine *dromon* leading the ships, packed with people and horses. He pointed out Northey Island to his nephew standing next to him.

"Two battles were fought here, Richard. The first was when your great-grandfathers defeated a mighty Saxon army to win all the land around here, and the second was when they were betrayed and forced to leave it behind them."

"Were they beaten then, Uncle?"

"Alas, they were, but only through the cowardly actions of their Saxon neighbours," replied Harald.

"Do we hate the Saxons then, Uncle?" asked the boy.

"No, not now and neither do we fear them, but it pays to be vigilant at all times. My grandmother Turid also lived here, and she cursed a group of them forever for what they did."

"Was she a witch then?"

"No, but some say she could speak to the gods. She said that a debt of blood always needs to be repaid. Now come, make yourself ready, your new home is waiting over there," replied Harald, pointing in the direction of the town of Maldon less than a league away.

They watched as the town came closer and the *Lady Alberada* drew up to the quay, where men eagerly caught the ropes thrown down to secure the vessel. The other ships did the same, in close succession until all four had been docked and fastened to the wooden pier. Harald, from his vantage point, observed with some satisfaction the development of his town and the changes that had been made since his last visit. The single decaying wharf had been replaced by three wooden piers that stood out at right angles from the stone harbour wall. Behind twelve similarly moored ships some one hundred of the town's houses covered the gentle slope where they had been randomly constructed around a crisscross of tightly packed streets. At the summit of the little hill was the longhall flying the banner of the two ravens of Regneville, built on the site of the original building, burned to the ground so many years ago. Around the town's perimeter stood a large wooden palisade, the height of several men.

Harald's train of thought was interrupted by a shout from the pontoon below.

"Lord Fitzroy, I had no idea you were coming. Jeanotte sent word that you were returning south and would not be back for some time," shouted up Clifford de Courcy, the town's steward.

"A change of plan, Clifford. I hope you have room for our people none the less," replied Harald.

"There is always room for family, Lord," replied the steward. "I will send a servant to get your things and take them to your house."

Harald had by now joined the man on the wharf and they shook hands.

"You have been busy, Clifford," he said to the serious young man.

"Ah yes, you will notice a few changes since your last visit. We rebuilt the palisade last summer as the number of dwellings increased and there is now a regular market every Saturday morning. The new mint has attracted many more new workers,"

"Lots of rents and taxes to oversee then?"

"Indeed, Lord. We have all been busy."

"And what news from Lundenwic? How fares Earl Godwinson since his return to England?"

Clifford drew closer to his master to avoid his words being heard by anyone else.

"I am told the Earl has designs on the English throne," said the steward earnestly. "He visits the King's sick bed daily and is his trusted confidante."

"My friend is an ambitious fellow, is he not? I suppose I had better hurry up and marry his sister then, Aelfgyva will soon be ten years old, and I should not keep a lady waiting," replied Harald.

He looked into his steward's face for a reaction and seeing his confusion, burst out laughing.

"Forgive the levity, but it has been a long and difficult voyage - I have no other desire than to spend some time here and introduce this young fellow to his new home," said Harald beckoning for the boy to come and join him. "This is my nephew, Richard, and he is to be taught how to ride and fight like any good Norman. If you do this for me, I will be in your debt."

"It would be my honour, sir," answered Clifford putting an arm around the boy. "Now come young Lord, let us get you fed and shown to your quarters."

The Lord of Maldon watched them walk up the hill, his mind racing.

"A new king of England and not from Normandie," he thought, "that will surely ruffle Duke William's feathers."

2

Harald and Rolf sat outside the alehouse waiting for the second jug to be brought to their table. The ships were still being unloaded; it was approaching mid-afternoon, and the older man began to feel the effect of the sun on his bald head. They watched the remaining crew of the *Lady Alberada* lead the last of the horses down a ramp onto the pier. The gulls wheeled above them screaming their intent to fight for every last scrap of discarded fish they found. When the animals had all been unloaded, they were taken off to be cared for outside the town's palisade alongside the temporary camp being erected for all of the new arrivals from Normandie. In the short time since they had landed Harald had ordered the provisioning of supplies needed for two hundred men and women. As they sat at their table they were visited by local merchants and tradesman, who were given orders to supply their new charges. Harald's house was readied for his arrival, but he was in no great hurry to go, and there were still people for him to see. The town was already home to over five hundred people and the sudden appearance of almost half that number again would need some planning. His steward was a highly capable young man, and Harald knew that although his unannounced arrival would provide Clifford with a few challenges there was little that would concern him unduly. He was glad to be here, he thought, it was not home yet but the town would provide rest and shelter for his people, who had taken the news of the changes to the plan without demur. The last four weeks had been turbulent and challenging and their arrival in Maldon would provide the respite they needed. Now they were safe he could take stock and secure the best future for all of them.

When Eleanor had informed him that she could no longer join him on the voyage to Italy he had been rocked to his core and subsequent events had convinced him to change his plans. He had not been angry but the bitter disappointment of losing her again was a burden that he would have to bear. The Guiscard could wait a little longer for him in the south, he determined, and if that meant fighting the Moors without him, then so be it.

"Do you think my grandfathers would recognise this place?" he asked Rolf.

"That I cannot say. But since we first came here it has grown so quickly. Why, I remember coming with you on the *Evas Prayer* almost ten years ago when it was a town full of ghosts and now look at it. A harbour packed with ships and plenty of opportunity for a man to do well. The Saxons have it easy do they not?"

"You regret not going back to the Kingdom in the Sun, then?" asked his friend.

"I thought I would be drinking summer wine instead of English ale by now, but I will be happy to make Wessex my home just as easily. How long do you think we will be staying? I should hate to think that our warriors should grow soft from lack of battle?"

"Not long enough to overstay our welcome, just do not get too comfortable," answered Harald vaguely for, in truth, he did not know himself.

3

England, in the year 1065, was not a bad place to be. It was filled with little villages and towns that were self-sufficient, and food and resources were plentiful. The only things that most settlements needed to buy was salt and iron and Maldon had an abundance of the former. Wessex, like Normandie, was a life of endless labour for the common people, but here there was enough to eat and drink and the bounty of fertile land to be worked. Unlike the Duchy there had been relative peace here for many years, and following the depredations of the marauding Norsemen, the Saxons lived comfortably and peacefully enough. Their nearest enemies were the Welsh and the distant Scots who, whilst occasionally appearing to threaten, could be overcome and pacified. Peace had made the country prosperous; the King demanded less taxes and people had the opportunity to become a little richer than those who came before. Without the constant threats of death and destruction from the longships, crops flourished, and farmers grew and reared more than enough to sustain their communities. There were few towns of any note in England and Maldon was now becoming one of the largest. Smaller settlements were dotted around the countryside, where people lived an isolated existence, surrounded by a protective fence. Beyond that there was league upon league of wild forest and heathland that might be negotiated by little tracks wending their way through thickets and marshland. Lundenvic was the exception and home to King Edward and a population of fifteen thousand people. Edward had ruled the country for twenty-four years in peace and prosperity but had never even ventured to the northern part of his kingdom. England was a wealthy country and with its ruler sick and bereft of an heir there was no shortage of strongmen plotting to take it for themselves.

      The arrivals from Normandie fitted into their new home effortlessly and without any friction with the locals. A barracks house was built for the men and the married ones were given permission to repair a number of damaged houses and move in. Harald paid scant attention to running the town and his steward continued to manage things in his normal efficient manner. A monk was appointed from the local monastery to oversea Richard's learning of letters whilst Clifford was charged with the boy's martial training.

4

Harald wanted nothing more than to spend his time hunting and training with the men, but within twenty days of being back in Maldon he felt obligated to travel to Lundenvic to pay his respects to the ailing King of England. The narrow road, he noticed, had not changed since his last visit to the capital but although it made for slow going, it was hard and compact and he and his escort of twelve men made steady progress. Before them they carried the yellow and green papal banner given to Harald almost a decade before. For much of the way they travelled through a dense forest of native oak, beech and chestnut, until they reached the shallow marshland of the Tamsye estuary and headed south-west along the narrowing riverbank. In two days they approached the walls of the city through the Alders Gate, where he dismissed his escort and sent them to a nearby ale-house. He went on alone, led through the narrow streets by members of the King's guard to the royal palace in West Minster.

King Edward had spent the last twenty years constructing a new abbey almost a league away from the main thoroughfares of his city. Thorney Island was a misty, low-lying piece of barren earth, named for the brambles that still grew in profusion despite the huge amount of construction and it was here that he had dedicated his life's work of building his new abbey. The King's Palace was close by, a collection of equally new stone and wooden buildings, including his hall and private apartments. Harald gazed at the awkward-looking site with its muddy bank on the tidal river facing the marshes of Tyburn Brook on the other side and wondered at the wisdom of the construction.

"The King must know something that I do not," he thought, taking in the scale and random nature of the enormous buildings. "And all to the glory of God," he mused.

They drew to a halt on a marble-flagged courtyard where a groom was waiting to take his horse and he dismounted. A brown robed monk came out to meet him.

"Marchis of Ambrières, welcome to the Royal Palace. My name is Osmund and I am the Chancellor here. The King received your message some days ago and has been expecting you," said the man bowing low.

"How is the King's health, Osmund? I have heard he has not been well."

"The malady comes and goes, Lord. Today he is well, not well enough to hold court, but well enough to receive visitors. He has been looking forward to your visit. But first, Lord, if you please you must leave your weapons at the door. It is merely our custom".

Harald nodded in acquiescence and followed the monk through the large oak doors of the palace where he unbuckled his sword and dagger and handed them to a servant. They walked through a cavernous anteroom which echoed with the sounds of their footsteps. Along each wall stood a row of *huscarls* wearing the royal livery, each man cradling a huge double handed axe. They reached the far side of the room and before the doors to the next room, two more *huscarls*, these carrying spears, stood to attention and blocked their way. On a word from the monk they stood aside and Osmund led his visitor into a smaller, well-lit room. They found King Edward sitting on a bench beside a blazing fire, a blanket over his knees and a fur cloak over his shoulders. As they approached Harald noticed the old man was asleep and snoring gently. He was bareheaded and his milk-white hair straggled untidily down to his shoulders. The visitors' footsteps resonated loudly on the flagstones and the King came to his senses with a start, looking up through rheumy old eyes. But despite his great age and obvious infirmities King Edward was quickly alert and aware of everything around him.

"Lord Harald Fitzroy, I am delighted to see you," he said taking the proffered hand in both of his. "It does my old heart good to see you and it is an unexpected pleasure to have you here in my new palace. Now, come in and sit with me and take some wine. It is not every day that I am visited by the famous 'Papal Shield'."

Harald smiled at the reference to the name and bowed low.

"None of that formal stuff, Hari, not while we are alone; we are old friends. Sit down and tell me all your news. I want to hear about Normandie and my nephew William. But first tell me what brings you here to England."

"You are very kind, Lord," came the response. "Normandie prospers and Duke William is well. I have missed my estates in Maldon for some time and the visit is long overdue. I have bought my young nephew with me to show him our English home. And of course, I am at your service for as long as I am here."

Harald spent the next two hours describing events in Normandie to the King who listened intently to every word, occasionally interrupting with questions. Then, seeing his host beginning to tire, the Norman held up his hands and stopped talking.

"I am sorry, my Lord. I am wearing you out with my conversation."

"Nonsense," replied the old man drowsily, "but I must admit to being a little sleepy, if you will excuse me. I insist you visit me again soon and bring that young nephew with you next time." Then he closed his eyes and went to sleep.

Harald looked around for Osmund, who was waiting quietly in the corner of the room and the monk stepped forward.

"I will show you out, Lord Fitzroy," said the monk politely.

They left the King's chambers and walked back into the large anteroom.

"The King is looking better than I had expected," said Harald to the man, who smiled benignly back at him.

"He has good days and bad days, Lord. Today was a good day and he was doubtless cheered by your visit. He is stronger than he looks although tires easily. But he is blessed by God and has strong council to guide him. We pray that he will be with us for many years to come."

They reached the doors at the far end of the building and a servant returned his weapons. He thanked Osmund for his hospitality and stepped out into the summer sunshine, waiting for his horse to be brought out to him. He would rejoin his men and spend the evening in Lundenvic, he thought. Then he looked across the courtyard and saw a familiar figure walking energetically towards him. Striding purposefully in his direction was the unmistakable figure of Harold Godwinson.

The Earl of Wessex approached Harald with a great singularity of purpose. He was bare-headed, and his shoulder length flaxen hair was pulled back from a heavily mustachioed face. An old scar, from the tusk of a dying boar, ran from temple to chin, giving his visage a lopsided appearance. He was dressed in a plain but finely made blue knee-length tunic with the gold wyvern of Wessex on a red background.

"And just how long have you been in Lundenvic?" he bellowed. "What sorcery is this? You should be in Italy by now, if my memory of our last meeting serves me well."

The two men shook hands and exchanged greetings warmly.

"The winds of fate blow us off course on occasion," replied Harald.

"You are here on Duke William's business?" asked Godwinson without further preamble.

"I am released from his service. My time in Normandie came to an end but my oath of fealty is not one I can renounce - not that I would ever wish to do so," answered Harald.

"Nor I, Hari. But the Duke is a wily fox, is he not? He would use us all as pawns in his game. He should know that the world is a bigger place than the Duchy, despite all of his grand designs. Neither of us were born to be the Duke's lapdog were we? Now, I insist that you dine with me tonight. I have a house just outside the city in Southwark and I should be happy to entertain you this evening," said the Earl changing the subject abruptly. "Forgive me but I must hurry. The King frets if I am late."

Their meeting concluded, he watched the Saxon stride off as quickly as he had arrived, the guards on the doors saluting him smartly as he passed. Something about their brief meeting caused Harald to pause and reflect for a moment. The two men had grown to be close comrades during their time together in Normandie, but had something changed between them he pondered? He mounted his horse and rode away from the palace, back toward the city.

5

Harald and Thomas left their men in an alehouse for the evening just outside West Minster. They went west, passing the great wooden cathedral of St. Pauls out of which floated the sound of singing monks at evensong; their chanting echoing through the long-deserted streets. They rode on through the old, abandoned city ruins of Londinium and past the Roman walls that had survived the incursions of so many invading armies. The young squire was full of questions for his master, many of which remained unanswered. Harald was, however, able to point out the building where the old King Aethelred ceded the town of Maldon to his grandfather, Bjorn Halfdanson. The boy reined his horse to a stop and sat in his saddle, bewitched by the decaying palace.

As they got closer to the river bridge the public buildings thinned out to be replaced by single storied houses of mud and wattle in a messy tangle all along the main road. Side-streets careered off randomly along the thoroughfare in untidy confusion, and the air was thick with the smoky tang of a thousand cooking fires preparing evening meals. The warm, dry season had made the ground hard underfoot and dust rose from the continuous traffic of people, carts and animals. The riders reached the south side of the bridge over the River Tamsye and were let through the gates by the evening watch of the guard, out of the city and into Southwark. They asked for directions to Earl Godwinson's house and were told they had not far to travel.

It was getting dark when they arrived at a magnificent villa that had once been the home to a Roman governor and were admitted through a high stone wall into the courtyard. They left the horses with an eager stable boy and a servant appeared to usher Harald into the main building, a single-storied house of marbled stone and granite. Despite its age the house had been well maintained and the obvious patching up to the main walls seemed only to add to its faded glory. Once inside the atrium the servant disappeared, to reappear carrying a tray laden with a wine jug, two drinking cups and morsels of bread and cheese. For the second time in the day Harald was hailed by Earl Godwinson's booming voice.

"Welcome to my humble home, Hari," he called across the tiled floor and waved at the old marble pillars and mosaics. "The Romans knew how to build a house? It can be a little drafty in the winter, but these places were built to last."

"An impressive place to live, none the less," replied Harald looking around and nodding appreciatively. He took a cup of wine from the servant before raising it to his host.

"*Skal*," he said.

"*Waes hail*," replied Godwinson returning the toast and the two men drank deeply before the servant led them through to the dining room, where a table, groaning with food and drink, awaited them.

The Earl was a generous host and had laid on a small feast for his guest. Roasted meats of hare, boar and deer were brought out at regular intervals, with freshly baked bread and a profusion of vegetables, fruits and nuts. He ensured that his guest's cup was never empty, and the servant scurried about bringing fresh wine to replenish the table. The conversation was convivial, and Godwinson was keen to know all the news from Normandie and particularly that of Duke William. He bombarded Harald with a barrage of questions for the first part of the evening, to which he received fulsome answers. Despite the volume of wine he was consuming, his guest remained relatively sober and clear of thought as the Earl probed him for more answers.

"I am not here on the Duke's business, my friend. I am simply in England to tend to the affairs of my estates and to show my nephew the home of his great-grandfathers. I am also at your service," insisted Harald graciously.

"Ah, your brother's eldest boy. His father was happy for you to take him into your care?" asked the Earl curiously. "I have always got room for a new squire in East Anglia if you don't mind him schooled in our Saxon ways."

"An interesting offer, for which I thank you, but his mother would have me flayed if I let the boy out of my care," replied Harald before changing the subject quickly. "Now, I have two hundred fighting men at my command and if you have need of us, just say the word. I would not have them growing fat and indolent in Maldon."

Godwinson remained silent as he considered the Norman's offer, steepling his hands in thought.

"King Edward appears to be improving in health, and I am due to return to my troops on the Welsh Marches soon enough. We have an ongoing quarrel with any number of their princelings. If you would care to join us you would be a welcome addition and the sight of a *conrois* of those black devils of yours in action might be enough to relieve them of their gold," he answered.

"Then we are yours to command, Earl Godwinson. I cannot say I have ever faced a Welshman on the field, but I am willing to try. It would be my pleasure to fight beneath your banners."

"That is settled then, and you will be well-rewarded from the spoils of battle. I know you fight for honour and reputation, but I am sure you will find the booty equally rewarding."

"Oh, yes," said Harald amiably, "a little more gold never goes amiss."

The deal was done, and the two men toasted one another's health again as they continued to talk long into the night, until Harald took his leave and was shown to his rooms. He left Earl Godwinson alone finishing the remains of the wine in his cup.

When he was sure that his guest had been taken to the far side of the villa and out of earshot the Earl got up and walked to the end of the room. A woman stepped out of the shadows, and she smiled benevolently at him.

"You heard all of our conversation, Edith," he asked.

She nodded her head.

"An interesting fellow for a Norman," she said, "but there is deep cunning beneath that burly frame, and it will need a strong plan to force him to stand against his people. Let me think on it. Now it is getting late, come to bed, for the dawn will soon be here and there is much to do."

She turned and the Earl watched his elegant consort walk off, the shadows of her tall frame and long neck accentuated by the light of the hearthfire.

6

The next morning Harald was woken by the crowing of a cockerel. He opened his eyes and took in the surroundings of his bed chamber before remembering exactly where he was. He pushed off the thick woollen blanket and stretched his body awake. Standing up, he walked to the far side of the room and splashed water on his face from a wooden bowl and pulling on his clothes, left the room to go in search of Thomas. The boy was in the stables and his master roused him from sleep, shouting words of encouragement to wake him. His squire was on his feet in moments, rubbing his eyes and brushing straw from his hair. His master told him to prepare the horses, get some breakfast from the kitchens and be ready to leave within the hour. Then he returned to the villa and found the Earl sitting at the table where he had left him the night before. There was a large map of England laid out and Godwinson pointed to St Albans, in the Earldom of Mercia, where Harald's men would meet an escort of Saxon cavalry. They would then be guided to the

English town of Hereford, where a force of Saxons would be waiting for them. Harald needed no more details than this for he had mustered armies far bigger in much less time. He thanked the Earl for his hospitality and left the villa, looking forward to the campaign ahead of him.

Before they travelled home, they had one more task to complete. Thomas was sent off and returned with a struggling piglet, bought from the market on the Southwark side of the bridge. They turned east and left the town, travelling on a narrow dirt road through deserted marshland and followed the course of the river toward the sea. After riding for two leagues the terrain turned from wetland into a dense forest of ancient trees which grew all along the riverbank. The road wound its way through the trees until they came across a crude stone monument, on which was carved the image of the triple moon. Harald motioned for them to halt and dismounted, peering through the trees and listening for the sound of running water. He smiled broadly in satisfaction and took the squealing animal from Thomas, ordering the boy to wait with the horses. Then he set out along an old path and walked up a shallow incline into the interior of the forest. It was not long before he found what he was looking for.

The *Ve* was exactly how Grandmother Turid had described it to him as a young boy. It was at this holy place that his grandparents had rested after their long campaign against the Saxons seventy-five years ago. It was here, she had said, that the gods could be reached, the closest place between *Asgard* and *Midgard*. In a clearing in the trees stood the spring from which bubbled clear water that flowed into the deep pond before it. Harald strode into the clearing, with the wriggling piglet over his shoulder, and its noisy protests disturbed a deer drinking at the water's edge. A rough stone arch had been built over the spring to keep it clear from falling leaves and the detritus of the forest, allowing the water to emerge from the earth to collect nearby, clear and untainted. Butterflies and dragonflies played around the plants and flowers which grew in an untidy profusion, and the place was bathed in summer sunlight diffusing through the branches of the ancient trees.

Harald laid down the animal gently and took his knife to the throat, spilling its blood on the sacred ground but being careful not to spill any in the water. He built a fire and placed the pig's carcass on it, feeding the blaze with more wood until it caught and burned fiercely. Then he turned back to face the spring and gave thanks to Freya for the safe delivery of his people to England and success in their journey to fight the Welsh. After a final message of thanks to his grandparents for their lives, he turned away to rejoin Thomas and the horses.

7

The column arrived back in Maldon around noon the next day and Harald called his captains to a meeting. Before long they were all in the longhouse with their master. Brenier, Leif, Rolf and a German knight named Wolfgang stood expectantly in front of their master.

"Gentlemen," he said, "I hope you and your men have been diligent in your training for in five days' time we shall be leaving to fight the Welsh. Our Saxon neighbours are keen to see your horsemanship. We will be travelling around eighty leagues to the west, where King Edward's enemies have been causing him some difficulty - it will be an opportunity to demonstrate the power of Norman cavalry."

"Will there be much gold?" asked Leif.

"So I am told. The Welsh are reported to hoard the stuff in great quantity beneath their mountains."

"And do we know much about them?" asked Wolfgang.

"We should expect well-trained knights backing up their spearmen and archers, but I am also told they are able to raise many men and prefer fighting on foot in their mountainous country," replied Harald.

"I shall also be curious to see how these Saxon *huscarls* perform," said Leif, "I have heard they can destroy a horse and its rider in one fell swoop."

"Well, whatever we encounter it will be preferable to sitting around here gathering dust," said Rolf,"I am not yet ready for the life of a farmer."

"Then, my captains, we can rejoice in being back on the road together soon. Have your men and their equipment primed and ready. I want our Saxon brothers to see the Norman *conroi* in full pomp," said Lord Fitzroy.

His men nodded their agreement and left to prepare their troops.

Chapter 5: In Search of Welsh Gold
Herefordshire, 1065

1

There were one hundred and sixty cavalrymen and forty mounted archers assembled to travel west. Four squadrons armed with lances, swords and assorted killing weapons formed an impressive looking column, each man dressed in knee length mail and wearing a gleaming conical helmet. On the flank of each horse hung a large kite shield bearing the Fitzroy insignia, two black ravens on a white background. Behind the cavalry came the bowmen, each man armed with a composite Saracen bow that could be fired with great rapidity on foot or horseback. Finally, at the rear of the column came a series of wagons, driven by the squires, carrying a variety of loads including horse fodder, spare weapons and cooking utensils. Harald walked Damascus down the column with a feeling of great pride. He had fought beside these men for nearly twenty years and they had nearly always prevailed, even in the face of the most overwhelming odds. Never once could he recall any man under his command cutting, breaking or running in the face of the enemy. These were his comrades, the elite handpicked veterans who he trusted with his life.

Beside him rode Richard on a little roan mare. When his uncle told the boy he would not be joining them on this campaign his nephew had been inconsolable for several days. It was too dangerous, he had explained, not to mention unpredictable, for an eight-year-old boy to accompany the column into unknown territory. Instead, Richard had been given the honour of inspecting the troop before they left for the west and he diligently executed his duty with great care and attention. Then it was time to leave and the battle horns sounded the advance, leaving a tearful Richard Fitzroy to wave farewell to his comrades.

It was still early summer, and the column wound its way toward St. Albans to meet their escort of twenty horsemen, on the hard, narrow road. The Saxons were initially a little circumspect about their new brothers-in-arms, and regarded them cautiously, but as the journey toward Wales wore on their attitude changed and they became less reserved. In ten days' time they arrived at the Earl's camp and the smoking ruin that was the town of Hereford. Two men rode out to meet the Norman column and Harald drew his men to a halt. He put a hand up to his eyes to combat the glare of the setting sun and recognised Earl Godwinson riding toward them. The two horsemen drew to a halt.

"Welcome to Herefordshire, Lord Fitzroy, I am pleased to have you here. My brother has been eager to meet you," said the Earl formally before turning to his comrade. "And this is the famous Marchis of Ambrières, Leofwine."

Harald shook hands with both men in turn and Leofwine bowed his head courteously in greeting. He looked very similar to his older sibling but lacked his size and bearing.

"It seems like we arrived a little late," said the Earl, "the Welsh got here a day before us and slaughtered everyone and everything, there is no-one left alive in the town. Come, let us ride in and I will show you what these people are capable of."

"And what of the enemy, gentlemen. Will we not be confronting them today?" asked Harald.

"The Welsh are over there skulking in their hills watching us," said Leofwine pointing to the other side of the River Wye. "We will need to lure them down before we can kill them. We'll go after them at first light."

They turned their horses and rode for the nearby town.

Harald did not know quite what to expect from the sacking of Hereford but he soon found out. Bodies were all around, in every street they were prostrated in death where they had been butchered. No one had been spared and even the animals had been slaughtered. Women and children, cats, dogs, pigs and cows lay where they had fallen in their hundreds in the deserted streets. The only sound was the horses' hooves as they walked over the cobblestones of the main street. They found piles of blackened corpses in what had been the cathedral of St. Aethelbert's which now lay in ruins. The once beautiful minster had been fired with many of the townsfolk trapped inside seeking sanctuary and been burned alive. All around, the blackened buildings stood testament to the complete destruction of the town and the stench of the slaughterhouse hung over it in a deadly pall. Bloated crows and ravens hopped from corpse to corpse, struggling to take to the air as the riders approached.

"We must bury the dead before disease sets in. They have lain in this heat for almost two days now," said Leofwine disdainfully, before raising his hand again to cover his mouth and nose.

"Alas, Lord Harald, it is a fine welcome we have given you and your men. Let us repair to my camp and offer you some refreshment. You have come far and we are forgetting our manners. I am sure we can find some decent wine to try and take away some of the taste of these foul deeds."

"And tomorrow we will go and trap the ones who have created this evil," added his brother.

They turned around and trotted their horses smartly away from the utter devastation of Hereford. The riders passed the site of the Norman camp where the erection of tents and a kitchen were already well on their way.

The three generals, seated outside the Earl's own tent waited for food and wine to be brought out to them. Harald was eager to know about the enemy strength for he estimated the Saxons to have no more than a thousand men in camp. Over half of this force were made up the local f*yrd* carrying an assortment of weapons including iron clubs, axes and scythes. He received a vague answer that the enemy could comprise of a force of anything from a thousand to five thousand men, depending on how many of the Welsh princes had the appetite for a fight. The enemy, he was assured, would be weighed down by the vast amount of plunder and slaves taken from Hereford and would probably have little stomach for the fight but they would be pursued in the morning. The combined army would leave at first light to catch the Welsh before they retreated back into their mountains.

A little later, Harald was back with his men, briefing his commanders around the large bonfire in the centre of their camp of hide tents.

"How did you find the Saxons, Lord. Do they look up for the fight?" asked Leif.

In truth Harald had been taken aback by the Saxon's complacency, but he did not let on.

"I think they might be a little war weary after so many years of fighting these people. The Saxons killed the Welsh King last year but it does not seem to have affected his princes' appetite to raid and slaughter. I am promised that if they do give battle we should be ready for a fierce struggle.

"And the Saxon army, are they well organised?" asked Rolf.

"The Earl's *huscarls* seem well disciplined but there is an assortment of local militia who I might not be so confident to stand beside. Anyway, we will find out tomorrow if we catch the enemy. Be sure we are all ready to leave by first light."

2

The next morning as the rising summer sun struggled to penetrate the drizzle of the Welsh Marches, Harald Fitzroy met Leofwine Godwinson at the head of twelve hundred fighting men. The irregulars of the *fyrd* stood at its head in an untidy formation and behind them, ahead of the Normans, the *huscarls* shouldering spears and huge axes stood ready to march out on foot.

"Good morning, Lord Fitzroy, are your men ready for their first visit to Wales," he said jauntily, although Harald could see that the man was a little nervous and did not meet his eye. "My brother sends his apologies, but he received urgent orders from the King to return to Lundenvic and left in the night."

"I am sure your generalship is as fine as your brother's," replied Harald diplomatically, "and yes, my men are itching to fight. If this rain stops we can give of our best. What is the battle plan?

"Our scouts tell us the Welsh are camped on a large hill two leagues away. We shall all cross the river and the men of the *fyrd* will go on ahead and try and draw the enemy down from the heights and onto our axemen. The Welsh can seldom pass up an opportunity for English blood and they see the *fyrd* as easy meat. Your men can then attack their flanks at your pleasure," replied Leofwine.

"And the lie of the land?" asked Harald.

"Firm and flat," declared the Saxon decisively."we don't want too many of these bastards escaping us."

With that the whole column marched forward and soon the Saxon irregulars had advanced over the bridge to gather on the other side. When they were all assembled, they moved off noisily to the sound of trumpets, which echoed up the valleys and into the hills. The rest of the Saxons followed at a distance but stopped after a while and formed up in four well-ordered lines in the middle of a small grassy plain between two steeply rising green hills. Following closely behind, the Norman horsemen trotted off to a nearby wood that shielded them from the sight of any observers from the hills ahead. There was nothing more to do than wait.

3

The first sound of any activity came around midday, when the sound of the battle horns sounded far away, but near enough for Damascus's ears to prick up. The huge black stallion moved around restlessly before receiving some soothing words from his master. When the horns sounded again, this time a little closer, the waiting Normans received the word to mount up and they rapidly moved into line of battle. Eight lines of twenty mounted warriors each formed into tight lines, one behind the other.

"Easy boy," said Harald to his horse, "save your strength for the charge."

He looked around to the men of his command and nodded approvingly at the rows of horsemen, steel-tipped lances pointing skyward while resting the weapon's other end on the stirrup. Each man moved his kite shield onto his left side, transferring its weight onto a leather shoulder strap, protecting that side of his body from neck to foot. Harald looked to the skies and saw them clear of the rain clouds that had threatened earlier in the day. He gave thanks to the gods and touched the amulet of Thor's Hammer at his neck, before feeling for the golden warrior ring on his right arm through his chain-mail *hauberk* as he had done before every battle since boyhood.

Leofwine's *huscarls* stood resolute in their positions and, hearing the enemy trumpets, they too readied themselves for battle. They closed up, standing mid-distance between two hills and prepared themselves for the, as yet, unseen enemy. At first the flotsam and jetsam of the battered remnants of the *fyrd* staggered through the gap in isolated groups. Then the numbers of beaten Saxon freemen increased as they tried to escape the carnage at their backs. Through exhaustion and suffering they attempted to stay ahead of the spears, gisarms and axes that threatened to carve open their backs with every desperate stride. Behind them a throng of red-shirted warriors drove them back toward the Saxon lines in a frenzy of killing. The scarlet horde were marshalled by mailed captains on shaggy horses, urging their men forward beneath banners bearing dragons and wolves.

Harald, a thousand paces away, estimated that between two and three thousand enemy foot soldiers had emerged and were rushing forward to meet the Saxon shield wall. He gave a final order to his mounted archers to move onto some high ground beyond the wood in which they were concealed, and fire a volley of arrows to precede the charge of his *conroi.* They rapidly took up new positions and loosed several volleys of arrows into the advancing Welshmen, who had by now reached the Saxon shield wall. Harald was about to lead the first *conrois* of Normans into the ranks of the enemy who were threatening to outflank Leofwine's men, but paused when he saw the shields separate. The men who held them dispersed to allow themselves space to swing their axes which they unleashed with devastating effect. The first ranks of Welshman were checked by the havoc rained upon their advance by the massive double-handed weapons. Harald saw the English commander unhorsed by several enemy warriors and ordered the first charge.

"Fury," he shouted to his men. "Give me fury, men. There shall be no quarter given or taken."

The horsemen on either side of him bought down their lances and held them in the couched position as the line of Norman chargers launched themselves at the packed lines of Welsh warriors threatening to overwhelm the defiant Saxon axemen. Harald felt an ecstatic ripple of elation as the first *conrois* hit home, shattering the red shirted flanks. His stallion was making himself felt too as the huge beast half-shied as he was trained to, bringing down iron shod hooves onto bare heads. His master speared an enemy foot soldier and expertly tossed the dying man from its lethal point. They drove forward into the mêlée as man and beast worked in unison, their comrades on either side of them within touching distance. Even at the height of his blood lust and killing, Harald felt the next *conrois* of Normans hit home as their enemies were propelled violently sideways like a ship being assailed by an endless waved-filled storm. Just as quickly as they entered the enemy ranks, the men of the first *conrois* wheeled to the left and turned to leave the fight to reform in their original position by the little copse of trees. Harald turned his line back to face the Welsh flank in time to see the next *conrois* strike. Twenty men riding abreast delivered a tidal wave of horse flesh into a surprised enemy who had no counter to the steel-tipped charge. Some of the *huscarls* had been felled by the sheer weight of Welsh numbers but many more remained standing and continued to wield their lethal blades. Harald ordered his men to charge again, and they did so with the same discipline of their first action, riding knee to knee with their comrades on either side with not so much as a glimmer of light between them. His second collision hit home but he did not feel the same resistance as they crashed forward and into the splintering enemy ranks. Discarding his lance in the close quarters he withdrew *Gunnlogi* and set about the red-shirted host which he sensed tire and wither beneath the combined onslaught. Damascus reached for a man who stood in his path, shredding the terrified warrior's face with deadly yellow premolars while his master finished off any resistance with a cut to the neck.

Then like a deadly squall at sea it was over, and the storm died as quickly as it started. The enemy was broken and the last of the Welshman were chased from the field. Most were finished off with a Norman arrow or a lance to the back as they joined their dead comrades in the next life. Harald rode up to Leif and clapped the veteran warrior on the back. It was mid-afternoon and they were all hot and dry in the summer sunshine, and with the killing over, the victorious troops were desperate to slake their intense thirst.

"There my friend, that will have cleared away the cobwebs," he shouted jubilantly to his blood-soaked comrade.

Leif looked up and smiled back.

"Indeed, it has. I was not expecting such a close-run fight," he replied, "at least these barbarians will be a little more careful before deciding to tangle with Norman cavalry."

"Close run?" scoffed Harald, "look about you. I think you must be getting old my friend. Look about you, again."

They both regarded the carnage of the battlefield in the small, contained area where most of the killing had taken place. Whilst over a hundred Saxon *huscarls* lay dead in a small semi-circle, where they had made their shield wall, the majority of the Welsh army had fallen to the devastating combination of repeated Norman charges and volleys of arrows. Nearly all of the Normans were now regrouping near the woods, having their wounds cleaned and bound or taking drinks from a supply wagon bringing them much needed refreshment. Others had dismounted and were searching the corpses of the enemy dead for anything of value.

"And now all we have to do is relieve these fellows of the gold we have been promised," the Commander continued, "but first I think it is only polite to see how our brothers-in-arms have fared. I will rejoin you shortly."

Harald looked over to where the Earl of Hereford was gathering his men beneath his banners a hundred or so paces away. He slipped off the horse's great back and handed the reins over to his captain before walking over to the group of Saxons. Leofwine was being attended by some of his men who were cleaning a wound to his shoulder where, moments before, the shaft of an arrow had protruded. He looked up at the Norman approaching and struggled to his feet.

"Lord Harald, we are in your debt," he said. "I have never seen the course of a battle change so decisively and so quickly. You have my thanks."

"It was no more than one neighbour does for another," said the Norman nonchalantly, "and an interesting exercise for my men who have never fought on these shores before. Linen shirts and drawers are no match for steel. But please come to our camp tonight and we can drink to our victory with our last barrel of good French wine."

Leaving the Saxons to lick their wounds Harald went back to join his men where spirits were high after their resounding victory. Before they made their way to their camp, he dispatched a troop of riders to follow any defeated survivors to the Welsh camp. His cousin Brenier took ten riders with orders to capture any stragglers and bring them back to Hereford. If Leofwine's brother had been telling the truth about the Welsh gold it would surely not be too hard to find, he reasoned, but the very least they needed was solid information on the whereabouts of the booty. The Normans made their way to their tents and supplies of wine and beer were brought up from the wagons that had come from Maldon, the air resonating with the sound of triumphal singing.

"A victory is a victory," Harald said to Damascus softly, as he bent over the stallion's neck, "and we must celebrate it as if it were our last."

Two squires were sent into the town of Hereford to forage for furniture and they returned before sunset with a wagon full of old tables and chairs, retrieved from where it lay discarded in the streets. They also returned with the carcasses of two deer bought from huntsmen they had found on their journey, and five barrels of beer from the Earl of Hereford.

Just after sunset Leofwine Godwinson and three of his captains entered the Norman camp and Harald invited them to sit down with him. The Saxons were carrying a variety of minor wounds and the Earl had his arm in a sling. The 'Fighting Priest' officiated over a brief service of thanks for their deliverance and prayers were offered for the souls of the dead Saxons. Wine was then brought and distributed around the Normans and their guests from large jugs, while the carcasses of deer and boar were turned slowly over the cooking fires. Harald addressed his guests over one of the newly acquired trestle tables.

"Gentlemen, your health. I trust your losses were not too great. Your men fought bravely."

The Earl of Hereford raised his cup to Harald.

"We lost a number of good men today but there are willing replacements to take their place. There always seems to be an endless supply of mercenaries from Scandinavia looking to sell their axes. The men of the *fyrd* are more difficult to replace, of course, and their loss is felt mostly in the fields and on the farms. It is a sad fact but we have to replace their numbers with an army of serfs and captured slaves to work the land," replied Godwinson.

"And the men we defeated today, what shall their fate be?" asked Harald.

"The men we fought earlier will retreat back to the Kingdom of Powys. They took a fierce beating and I do not expect to be bothered by them until next year," came the reply.

"And where do you think we might extract the gold your brother promised me in payment for our services."

"There is little gold in Powys these days, Lord Harald", replied Leofwine with a bitter laugh. "If there was my brother would have insisted we take it ourselves long ago. But Wales is a country of fighting men, and their terrain is wild and mountainous - any campaign against them is not for the faint-hearted."

Harald felt his hackles rise and he fought to keep his anger in check. He had been duped by the Earl of Wessex, he thought, struggling against the sound of his own boiling blood beating in his ears. He took a deep breath and smiled toward his guests.

"Would you advise us against visiting these people, then?"

Leofwinn looked at his captains and they laughed in unison, making Harald feel foolish for his naivety.

"Not without an army. The Norman cavalry are remarkable and a match for anyone but you would need a lot more men to take Caer Gurican," said Leofwine, and realising he may have offended his guest, continued in a conciliatory tone. "I am sorry but I do not know what my brother promised you for your service but I know I am truly glad to have you here. Without you we would have surely perished today."

Harald was impressed with Leofwine's sincerity and resolved to be as hospitable as he could to the younger Godwinson throughout the evening but, he told himself, he would certainly be confronting his brother when next they met. The Earl of Wessex owed him gold and it was not a debt Harald would forget easily.

4

The next day started late as the exhausted Normans emerged from their tents blinking into the new day. They were weary, sore and slightly befuddled having drank most of the wine brought with them. The grateful Saxons had also contributed a great deal of ale to the men of Maldon for their part in turning back the tide of Welshmen on the previous day and the whole lot had been consumed relentlessly throughout the night. Today there would be no work, no training and no fighting; today was a day of rest and they would spend their time playing dice, fishing, grooming their animals or simply sleeping in the English sunshine. Just after noon Brenier returned with his troop dragging a bedraggled line of nine prisoners, shackled by the hands. They were tied in a line behind his horse and led into camp like so many cattle heading for market. Men stopped what they were doing and, curious about the new arrivals, moved toward them for a closer look at the pathetic remnants of Welsh defiance that had so recently sacked the town of Hereford. The prisoners were dragged through the group of gathering warriors, who hurled abuse at them before stopping in front of the table where Harald was sitting with a group of his men.

"Fine work, Brenier," he called to his cousin, ordering his squire to bring out some of the remaining ale to the thirsty troopers. "A successful hunting trip? You seem to have bagged some interesting game. Come, sit down and tell us how you fared."

Brenier dismissed his men, dismounted and sat down at the table. He drank deeply from the cup of ale put in front of him before recounting details of the pursuit.

They had followed in the wake of the retreating enemy who split up and ran in every conceivable direction. Many of the fleeing chose high ground where they could melt back into the hills. They rode down many Welshmen, finishing them off with lance and sword until dusk fell and, fearing getting lost, they stopped for the evening. At daybreak they continued to ride west and came upon a group of exhausted fugitives in some nearby foothills. Most of these wretches did not even have the strength to get up and flee and those that did died soon enough. The living were caught, bound and brought back over the English border. Harald listened intently to his cousin and nodded approvingly.

"Were you able to extract any information that might help us?" he asked.

Brenier shook his head.

"Very little, Lord. We have not been able to understand a single word of what they say. It is a language that is like nothing I have heard before," said the captain.

Harald got up to take a closer look at his prisoners. They were all filthy, tired and suffering. Their clothes hung about them in rags and most of them displayed deep cuts and abrasions. He questioned each of them in turn, but they all remained silent, heads bowed in acceptance of whatever fate awaited them. He stopped at the last captives, looking at them curiously.

"These two, they are not like the others. Have they spoken?" he asked, looking closely at the smaller of them. "And one of them is a woman, if I am not mistaken."

Brenier snorted with laughter at his oversight.

"I thought it was a boy," he exclaimed. "Welshmen all look the same to me."

"These two are not Welshmen either. But there must be someone in the Saxon camp who can understand these devils," said Harald. "Thomas, go to Lord Leofwine and ask for his assistance."

His squire departed and he turned his attention back to the two prisoners and pointed at the woman. She was dressed as a man, and she and her companion looked completely differently from the others. They were both tall and fair in contrast to their dark, swarthy confederates.

"You, what is your name, woman?" he asked her sternly. "Answer me or you will be punished."

She continued to look toward the ground, her dirty yellow hair falling over her face in an untidy mop. Harald repeated his question and shook her by the shoulder. The woman responded, angrily raising her head and glaring at him; he saw no fear in her eyes, only indignation.

"Please, Lord," replied the fair man in the Frankish tongue, "she does not understand you. We are both Icelanders and strangers in this land."

Harald turned to the man, looking him up and down. He noticed the well-made boots and finely tooled *gambeson* but other than that he was ragged and unkempt. The Icelander carried himself with an upright military bearing and looked directly into the eyes of his captor as they talked.

"Then you are a long way from home, friend. Unless you tell me what I need to know you will both be dangling at the end of a rope. First, tell me what two Norse folk are doing fighting in Saxon England."

"Of course, Lord," said the man bowing his head, "I am happy to tell you my story."

5

Halldor Snorrason was a *skald* and a traveller. In the tradition of other Icelandic *skalds* he told the stories of many great Norse kings and warriors, immortalising their deeds and reputations. He was also a veteran of the Varangian guard of Constantinople, a trader, an adventurer and now a reluctant mercenary in the pay of Bleddyn ap Cynddyn, King of Powys. As a boyhood friend and later benefactor of King Harald Sigurdsson, he had recorded the saga of the Norwegian monarch's great deeds and exploits. During his time in the Norwegian court, he had struck a match between Jarl Torbjorn of Rogoland and his daughter, Hedda. The King had provided a ship to take him to Iceland to fetch his daughter and bring her back for the marriage ceremony. Hedda had already been warned of her betrothal to the sixty-year-old Jarl Torbjorn and decided to run away. She boarded the next ship she could take, a wide-bodied *dromon* sailing for Provence, carrying a cargo of walrus tusks, amber and stockfish. Halldor, unable to return to Norway empty-handed, pursued his fugitive daughter to Toulon where he kidnapped her from the fishing boat she was working on and set sail for Norway. When they reached Wales, sailing along the coast, they were beset by a huge storm which drove them ashore, wrecking their ship, and were captured by local tribesmen. They were sold to the King of Powys, who, on learning of Halldor's military pedigree, employed him as a warrior.

When he finished the story Harald questioned him in great detail, to test the veracity of his words, and finding them believable, he ordered the man and his daughter to be set loose.

"A fine tale, Halldor Snorrason. Now my last question is an important one and upon its answer hangs the fate of you and your daughter. Do you understand?" asked Harald, when the story was finished.

Halldor nodded slowly.

"Yes, Lord," he answered.

"Is there gold in Powys?"

"Not enough to risk a single one of your men's lives," came the quick reply.

"Then we are as one mind, and you are free. Besides, my grandfather was also a warrior *skald* and would not possibly countenance me sending you to an early grave. You may return with us to Maldon from where you will be able to get passage north."

Halldor breathed a mighty sigh of relief and Hedda raised her head at this news, tears of relief running down her dirty face. Before her father could respond their attention was taken by one of Earl Leofrith's captains arriving with a group of Saxon warriors. He walked up to Harald's table and saluted him smartly.

"Lord Leofrith sends his compliments," said the large *huscarl,* "but insists that you hand all your prisoners over to him."

Harald looked up and smiled at the man broadly.

"Then he is very welcome to all these prisoners for they deserve nothing more than summary justice," he replied watching Halldor's face change in alarm. "But not these two, they are with us."

"Very well, my Lord," replied the *huscarl* before his men dragged the protesting Welshmen off to their fates.

Before Halldor could sit and take the proffered cup of ale the first Welsh captive had been bludgeoned to death outside the Norman camp.

6

They left the next day and started an unhurried journey home to Maldon. The weather was fine and free of traffic passing west. It may have been an unprofitable trip, thought Harald, but no men had been lost, and injuries had been light. Importantly, it had given him an opportunity for his men to fight beside the Saxons and he wondered, idly, what his grandfathers would have made of the alliance. Halldor Snorrason rode one of the captured Welsh ponies and trotted along in the ranks of the huge Norman horses while his daughter rode in one of the wagons. They both took their share of camp chores in the evening and the girl was not shy when it came to collecting firewood or feeding the animals. On the evening of the second day, she approached Harald as he sat alone eating and stood beside him.

"Come sit down beside me," he said offering her the ground next to him. "It is not a grand place to dine but the forest floor is at least dry."

She sat down next to him, and he offered her some food from his plate.

"Here take this, these Saxon rabbits are more than decent," he said.

She took some meat from his plate and started to eat, giving him the opportunity to look at her for the first time since she had been brought to their camp. She had bathed in the river before they left and had managed to clean her clothes. Hedda was a young woman of twenty years with fine fair hair, the colour of walrus ivory and wide-spaced blue eyes set in a round face. He was reminded of the elven folk his grandmother would describe in childhood stories. A sleeveless leather tunic revealed bare arms displaying a collection of tattooed runes. She ate in silence, unconcerned with him watching her.

"You are glad to have left Wales?" he asked her when she had finished the plate of food.

"I am, Lord, and you have my thanks for getting us out of there. They are strange primitive people.

"It was a close-run thing, nevertheless. The Saxons would have taken their revenge on you had we not captured you first," he said.

She touched the silver amulet at her neck in an involuntary gesture.

"The Helm of Awe?" he asked to which she nodded thoughtfully.

"I am no *seiðun,* my Lord. I can cast no spells," she said anxiously.

"Calm yourself, Hedda. I am sure you are no witch and anyway I am a believer in the old ways," he confided. "There is a great deal of good that the old gods can bring us that will be lost forever beneath the tide of Christianity."

She relaxed a little at his words.

"You are no Christian then, Lord?" she asked.

He laughed and shook his head.

"No, but I have a brother who dreams of being a bishop one day," he said.

She said nothing and reached inside her tunic, pulling out a soft leather pouch and handed it to him. He undid the drawstring and looked inside to see a handful of black pips.

"Magic beans?" he teased.

She shook her head and gave him a stern look.

"These are henbane seeds. If you need to speak to the gods eat one of them - but have a care they can be dangerous if you take more," she said seriously.

He thanked her for the gift and secured it in the belt around his waist.

"Now tell me of the new life that awaits you in Norway?" he said, changing the subject. "My family hails from the west - from Haugesund, you know."

Eva's face changed in an instant and she scowled.

"My new husband is an old boar, but I have been promised to him and the bride-price is a high one. Either way I cannot let my father down again."

"Your days of running away are over, then?"

She looked at him sternly again and then tossed back her head, and Harald heard her laugh for the first time. A beguiling sound, he thought, a reminder of different times, back in Normandie, with Eleanor.

7

In four days' time they were approaching Maldon and dusk was closing in on the long summer evening. The men were dismissed and returned to barracks while Lord Fitzroy went through the town gates with his little cohort and made his way to the house on the far side of the town. The few people who were still on the streets greeted him courteously as he passed by them and he returned their salutations. He had almost reached the longhall when he saw the unmistakable form of his steward running towards him. He drew his horse to a stop as the man reached him, allowing him to catch his breath.

Clifford stood panting, hands on hips, as the words tumbled from his mouth.

"It is Richard, Lord. They have taken him. The Saxons … the Earl of Wessex's men … have stolen him."

Chapter 6: The Shipwright's Promise

Normandie, Summer, 1065

1

The *Mora* pitched forward and plunged into another foamy abyss, waves crashing over her prow. She checked herself and continued up the next steep ascent before plummeting downward again, causing Robert Fitzroy's stomach to void its contents over the ship's side. He wiped his face and turned to the captain at the helm.

"How much longer?" he asked, struggling to keep the desperation out of his voice.

"Not long and we shall turn back, Lord Robert. I want to see what she does in a bit of a squall. This weather has been sent by God to test her," said Stephen Fitzaird, wedged into position at the helm with a bracing leg against one of the bulwarks.

Their conversation was interrupted by yet another wave, crashing over the raised deck and soaking both men to the skin again. Robert was cold, wet and thoroughly miserable and longed to be back on dry land to feel the warmth of the summer sun on his face. He was here at the invitation of Duchess Matilda, who had the vessel built for her husband to sail to England when the time came for his coronation. She had asked Robert to join the ship after the launch for her sea trials, and he had accepted gracefully in the full knowledge of his shortcomings as a seafarer.

The *Mora* was a dragon ship, following the design of a traditional Norse *skeid*, with forty rowing benches and raised decks at prow and stern. Despite her elegant lines and ornate decorations, she was built to meet fierce seaborne challenges, and her captain had been delighted to be thrust into this unexpected summer storm. For three hours the ship had pitched, rolled and yawed in the changeable winds off the coast of Carusburg, much to the joy of

Captain Fitzaird. He laughed out loud as another wave broke over the bow, drenching everyone and everything. To Robert's relief he finally felt the storm's venom begin to weaken until the sea around them took on a flatter disposition and the oarsmen turned her up into the wind and the sail was raised. Her multi-coloured square woollen sheet billowed and filled, and the Mora turned again where the crosswinds caught. She heeled toward her leeward side and left the angry seas behind them, planing smoothly toward calmer water and home.

Although Robert still felt sick, he no longer wished to die, and the feelings of nausea began to lessen. His squire bought him a cloak, trousers and tunic from below decks and Robert, filled with gratitude, changed into some dry clothes. The life started to come back to his limbs, and he climbed the steps to the aft deck to join the skipper.

"You will start to feel better now we have stopped being thrown around. But at least you can tell the Duchess that her gift to her husband will take him safely across the sea to England," said the captain, looking up into the vast expanse of sail propelling the *Mora* at a rate of knots. "You may yet enjoy this part of the journey."

The sun, which had been obscured all morning, emerged, warming the crew who, having shipped their oars, were now resting on their benches.

"The Duchess will be pleased to hear that, she constantly frets over the Duke's wellbeing and the stoutness of this ship will gladden her greatly," said Robert.

"Be in no doubt, Lord, she is a fine ship. And fast and elegant too. We could do with many more like her but I'm afraid the art of building ships like our ancestors did is a thing of the past. This beautiful longboat was built by Norwegian shipwrights in

Barfleur. Can you imagine that - foreigners were bought here to Normandie to build ships for us? What would our grandfathers have said? You are going to need at least two vessels for every hundred men that travel across *La Manche.* Will two hundred ships be enough?" asked the captain.

"Not if we need an army to battle the Saxons," replied Robert flatly.

His seasickness had reduced to a point where he could at least think clearly, and he shook his head mournfully. If they had to fight for England, they would need at least ten thousand men and hundreds of new ships, he thought. Both men looked to the prow of the *Mora* where the figurehead of a golden child with a trumpet in its mouth pointed a finger toward Carusburg.

He left the captain at the helm, walked the length of the ship and stood in the bows, clasping one golden arm of the carved sculpture, and smiled to himself as his sea legs started to return. His brother Harald, a hardened seafarer, would have laughed at him had he seen him only an hour ago, bent over the ship's rail vomiting up his heart and soul. He wondered where his brother and his son were now and prayed for the safety of both of them. In time he knew he would forgive his sibling, and perhaps even Eleanor for her infidelity. He was still angry at both of them but the anger, like the seasickness, would lessen over time and then perhaps Mortain might be a little more welcoming for him. Things would never be the same with his wife for she had committed a grievous sin, but Eleanor was still the mother to his children, and they would soon be joined by a new sibling of their own. All of Mortain knew that his wife would soon have her fourth child but only a handful of Robert's trusted friends knew who the real father was. After all, he mused, it would be the Christian thing to do to accept the things that he could not change. He prayed again but this time asked God to give him the strength to forgive his errant wife and brother. Robert looked down at the bow waves beneath his feet and marvelled at the way the *Mora* glided effortlessly through the flat water. The sun gleamed back off the ocean and, counting his blessings, he felt his spirits soar.

The ship docked in Carusburg by mid-afternoon and Robert was grateful to be back on dry land. He thanked Captain Fitzaird for his service and assured him that he would be seeing the Duchess soon to impart the good news of the *Mora*'s seaworthiness. He walked gingerly down the ship's gangway and onto the stone quay that they shared with merchant ships and fishing boats that had long since unloaded their cargos. The nearby market was still active, and a few women of the town picked among the last remaining fish, hoping to find a bargain to feed their families.

Robert walked past the almost empty stalls to where his escort was waiting for him, the smell of the fish reminding him that his seasickness had not yet quite passed. He had to be back in Caen within the week for a meeting with Duke William and his barons, and he pondered their forthcoming discussions. In truth he had little need of such a heavily armed escort but the Duke always insisted that such an important figure as his Chancellor should never take any risks when it came to personal safety.

The captain of the squadron of twenty men saluted him as he approached, and another trooper came forward with a mount.

"Welcome back, Lord," said the captain, a man of Mortain who had served Robert loyally for over ten years. "I trust the sea trials were successful. Are we to head straight back to Caen?"

"No, we shall go south to Regneville, I need to meet with my father," came the reply. We shall be there for a day or so before we go onto Caen.

There was a ripple of excitement from some of the men, many of whom came from Robert's hometown of Regneville.

"Going home should put a little more spring in your stride," he said to them before mounting his horse and leading his men off to the south.

2

They rode for two days down the west coast of the Duchy, making good time on hard roads that had been largely free of the curse of brigands and cutthroats who made travelling so dangerous in years gone by. The bounty of peace was clearly evidenced in fields full of harvested wheat, rye and barley and they passed any number of high stacked haywains and drovers taking their stock to market. Large herds of pigs and cattle grazed peacefully close by on prosperous looking farms, and the countryside seemed to bask in a golden glow of sufficiency.

The squadron reached Regneville at dusk and Robert was amazed at how much the town had changed. The tall stone towers of the imposing castle keep that had guarded the estuary for three generations of Fitzroys rose majestically above the town, which had outgrown the original palisade. The wooden fortifications that had been so necessary sixty-five years ago, when Jarl Bjorn had settled his people here, had been replaced by high stone walls - although there had been little need of their protection for years. Like the rest of the Duchy the people of Regneville were enjoying the prize of peace, for which so many had given their lives.

The town's feudal Lord, Floki Fitzroy, had seen his brother's squadron riding in from the north and rode out to meet him. He was the youngest of three brothers and had inherited his lands and title from his father. As the commander of the redoubtable Riders of Regneville he was an important cog in the Norman military machine. While his brothers had made their fame and fortune far away from their hometown, he had stayed behind to secure the family fortunes.

Floki rode out at speed to meet his brother, leaving a cloud of dust in his wake. He had only just returned from hunting when he was alerted to his brother's imminent arrival, and he and the hardy little *courser* he rode were still covered in dirt and blood from their days' sport.

"Robert," he shouted, coming to an abrupt stop in front of the squadron, "I cannot believe it is you. Why did you not send word you were coming?"

Without waiting for a reply from his brother, Floki reached out of his saddle and embraced him fiercely.

"It is good to be home again, but I only knew I was coming two days ago," replied Robert when his brother finally released him. "How are our parents?"

"Well enough. They continue to treat me like a small child but I have given them enough grandchildren to keep them occupied …and they are continually asking me if I have news of the Fitzroys of Mortain. And Hari, what news of our famous brother?" came the reply.

Robert held up his hands and laughed.

"Enough little brother. I will reveal all when I have brushed the dust of the road from my clothes, the horses watered and these fellows given ale," he replied, pointing a thumb over his shoulder to his escort.

"Very well, I will be patient until then," replied Floki, but the barrage of questions continued, unrelenting as he turned his horse around and the two made their way back to Regneville.

That evening Robert and Floki sat side by side at the table in the family solar high in the castle keep. Sigrid Fitzroy sat beaming at her two sons before turning her attention to her eldest and launching her questions.

"When are we going to see our grandchildren here. It is many years since I last saw them. And Eleanor, is she well? Are you being a dutiful husband? And what of your brother? We have not seen or heard from Hari, for what is it, Torstein, a year?" she said, turning to her husband who sat patiently beside her.

"Sigi, the boys have been occupied, my dear. You will see your grandchildren in due course. And Hari too. Duke William keeps them all busy."

Torstein and Sigrid Fitzroy were very old and although well past their sixtieth year, they were far from being in their dotage. Floki had taken office from his father ten years previously but when called upon the old man still took an active role in advising the Duchy's ruling council.

"That's all very well but the Duke drives them too hard sometimes. He was never happy as a small boy unless he had his own way," concluded Sigrid. "Now tell me truthfully Robert, what is this latest spat with your brother all about."

Robert sighed, took a deep draft from his cup of wine and told his mother what she needed to hear. He omitted any reference of his fight with Harald or of Eleanor's infidelity.

"And of course you will be a grandmother again soon. Mortain is expecting another Fitzroy before the summer is over," he announced.

"That is joyous news, Robert," cried Sigrid, while her husband regarded Robert sternly.

When the meal was over and all her questions were answered to her satisfaction Sigrid kissed her sons and said goodnight before retiring to her bedchamber, as happy and content as she could be.

Torstein turned back to his eldest son.

"You did well. Many lesser men would have faltered beneath such a withering interrogation. Have you really healed your rift with Hari?"

Robert shook his head with a grimace

"And the child?" asked Torstein.

"The child will be born a Fitzroy that is all anyone needs to know. I will do my best to rebuild bridges with Hari and Eleanor, and the family name will not be tarnished by any of our quarrels."

His father nodded thoughtfully and reached over the table, putting his hand on Robert's.

"I never had the slightest doubt, my son. Tell me, why are you really here?"

Robert, grateful for the opportunity to change the course of their conversation, replied.

"Ah, now that is a far easier subject to address. How does the Duchy build a fleet of ships large enough to carry an army over the sea? I think we might have forgotten how"

3

Olaf Knarresmed was the oldest man in Regneville and had once been a shipwright of great renown. Despite his age he could recall the names of each of the sixty-eight *skeids* he had constructed. Every day he sat on the stone quay of Regneville watching over the estuary, at the ships going to and fro as they plied their trade. Today was no different, and he sat and watched through rheumy eyes as he recounted the names of the great ships he had built.

"Sea Serpent, Orman Lange, Barden," he recanted to himself.

He took another draft of wine and gave a silent toast to their long dead captains, smiling at the memories. His thoughts were interrupted by footsteps approaching and he looked around, shielding his eyes from the mid-morning sun. He squinted for a few moments into the glare until he recognised the men walking toward his table.

"Torstein the Younger," he called in greeting, scrambling to get to his feet, "and if I am not mistaken - your two fine sons."

"Do not get up, Olaf. Is there room at your table for some old friends?" replied Torstein Fitzroy.

"There is always room at my table for the sons and grandsons of the Wandering Warriors," he said before calling for another jug to be brought from the dockside wine shop. "Now, gentlemen I am at your service. I can no longer heft an axe or strike a hammer but if it is good company and a story of the old days you seek, I shall be happy to oblige."

Robert took the man's hand and shook it warmly.

"We need your knowledge, Olaf. We need to build ships again, many, many ships."

Olaf Kanarresmed had been born into a family of shipwrights in Rovde, a small coastal town on the west coast of Norway. He spent the first part of his life learning his craft from his father and together they built many fine ships for the old sea-kings. After joining a rebellion against the King of Norway he was forced to flee his homeland and travelled south in a ship which he and his father had built.

Torstein Fitzroy could not be sure of the shipwright's age, but one of his earliest memories was as a five-year-old boy when Olaf had piloted a ship full of refugees away from England. During the first years of settlement in Normandie the shipwright and his sons still built ships, but as times changed and warriors no longer fought at sea, the demand for his skills dropped away. With no need for a Norman navy, skilled men like Olaf and his sons were not needed.

"Could you teach us how to build new ships?" asked Robert.

Olaf paused for thought, before nodding slowly in consideration at the weighty question.

"To learn how to build the perfect ship takes a lifetime but we could show you how to build a worthy vessel. It could be done, but the men we instruct must be skilled carpenters. We have to work with unseasoned oak, and a lot of it for so many ships. First lay the keel, then build out the ribs as a frame," said the old man gesticulating excitedly as the memories flooded back. "and after that we overlay more planks of wood around the frame and fix them into position. More oak for the mast and oars and you will be ready," he said.

"If I provide the best men and materials, could they build a longship under your tutelage?"

"With the right men, it might be possible. I will speak with my sons who are not yet in their dotage like their father. You shall have your answer by dusk."

The answer came earlier than expected. One of Olaf's sons, a man who Torstein Fitzroy had known since childhood, came to the castle.

"My brothers stand ready with their tools and the old shipyard has been cleared. We can instruct your men as soon as they have been prepared, Lord," announced Kjarten Knarresmedson.

The Fitzroys looked at each other before Robert broke the silence.

"That is good news. Floki, would you mind rounding up as many of the town's carpenters at first light and have them meet in Olaf's yard. I will pay for all the necessary expenses. Now I must return to Caen with all haste. I will be back within the month."

His brother nodded.

"That will be twice in five years that you have returned home. We are blessed," said his father with a mocking grin. "Your mother at least will be delighted. More so if you bring that clutch of grandchildren to visit her. Now go, the Duke is not a man to be kept waiting if memory serves me well."

4

After two days, Robert and his troop rode into Caen. It had been a quiet trip, and they made their twenty-five-league journey in relative silence accompanied only by the creaking of leather saddles and clinking bridle bits. He enjoyed these brief journeys where, despite being with his men, there was little conversation, and he was able to contemplate the many issues that needed his attention. His main concern was the manner by which Duke William would ascend the English throne. It was assumed, at least by the Duke, that the Kingdom of England would be passed onto him without a struggle, and the King's ruling council, the Witan would simply invite him to take the crown. Robert wrestled with the folly of this reasoning and knew that, without doubt, blood would be shed. How much blood he did not know, but what he knew of the Saxons told him that they would not accept a foreigner as their king without a fight. If it came to battle the Normans could muster twenty thousand men, but the Saxons could raise at least three times that number in a heartbeat. Robert had every faith in the Norman fighting machine but how, he wondered, would he get them all to England if they were needed. He was deep in thought as the guards at the gatehouse into Caen saluted him, and his troop passed through the castle walls. But he was also tired and resolved that after prayer, he would turn in early, for tomorrow was a busy day and he would need to be on his metal.

The first hours of the next morning were spent in the lady chapel close to his chambers. These moments of solitude spent in prayer and meditation just after dawn were his favourite part of the day. Robert got up and grimaced at stiff knees creaking in protest. He stood up straight and stretched his body, pulled back his shoulders and calmly went out to meet the day, knowing full well what he had to accomplish.

He walked calmly across the courtyard and into the great hall where his Lord would be waiting for him. It was early and the meeting with Normandie's *baronie* would not start until later that morning, giving the two men time to talk. The Duke was in his normal position at the head of the long meeting table and he got up to greet his Chancellor, scattering the three hunting dogs that had been lying at his feet.

"Robert, it is good to see you. Come, sit and take breakfast with me before our guests arrive. How was your journey?" called the Duke in a loud voice that resonated, deeply throughout the high-ceilinged hall.

"Busy as always but never less than interesting," replied Robert cheerily. "but there is a matter that concerns me that I need to discuss, and it would put my mind at rest to hear your thoughts."

The Duke nodded intently, just as a servant arrived with a tray bearing food and wine. He grabbed at the vittles greedily, motioning Robert to continue as he ate.

"We have no navy," declared Robert.

"I know that. But we have no need of one either, at least not for the last one hundred and fifty years," retorted the Duke brusquely.

"Well, I believe we need one now or very soon will do. If we cannot move our men across the sea our plans in England will be hampered. Apart from a small fleet of merchant ships we have nothing else."

"I will not need to take an army to England. King Edward has promised me the throne and I have taken him at his word," William asserted.

"My spies tell me differently," said Robert, watching the expression on the Duke's face change as he processed the information. "King Edward may well wish you to succeed him, but not every Saxon shares his views and there are those in the Witan who will see his death as an opportunity to seize power for themselves. There are Saxon Earls who will yet oppose us."

Duke William grew angry and hit the table with a fist.

"But I have been promised the throne. It shall not be snatched away from me," he shouted spitting food from his mouth as he did so.

Robert had seen this behaviour many times in the past when the Duke did not hear what he wanted to, and he stood his ground.

"We must be ready for all eventualities. The rumblings from the English court may come to nothing, but if there is opposition, we should have a contingency. We must be in a state of readiness - God is behind you and will not let you fail."

William calmed himself and he sat back in his chair, his inner storm subsiding.

"You know I trust you above all men, Robert? What would you have me do?"

His Chancellor began to explain.

A little later that morning the Duke's senior churchmen and barons gathered around the same table. They were happy men. Not only had their Lord lavished care and attention on them with a sumptuous meal and the finest wines from his cellars, but he had also given each man an early gift of Saxon land. It had been expected but now it had actually been announced and whole English counties been designated, they were delighted. To a man they beamed back at him, estimating the rich yields that these new lands might bring.

"My Lords, it is good to see your happy faces and I hope that my gifts will make you even happier - and not a little richer," Duke William quipped.

They all stood up and applauded him and as the noise of the clapping died down Robert de Beaumont, the new Earl of Leicester spoke.

"My Lord, on behalf of us all I would like to thank you for your most generous gifts," he said to more applause. "May I ask when we can expect to take possession of these new Earldoms?"

"Soon enough. King Edward grows weaker by the day and I expect to succeed him by the mid-point of next year. After this my first duty will be to instal my new Earls to help me rule the Kingdom. But we must start to make our plans now and with that in mind I would like our Chancellor to address a most pressing issue. Or should I say the new Earl of Cornwall?"

There was some polite laughter as Robert got to his feet.

"My Lords and Bishops, within a year we can all expect to be in England enjoying the generosity that our liege-lord has bestowed upon us - but we still need to get there, of course. Now consider this, the defence of our Duchy has always been conducted on land and we have never been threatened from the sea. As such we no longer have the craft needed to build ships. The skills with which our grandfathers built the ships that brought them here have been lost. When we inherit England next year our new subjects will know that Duke William's rule is God-given and beneficial. My men from Mortain and Regneville will not be arriving in cattle transports, but they will land in vessels fit for the new rulers of England, for how else can we command Saxon respect?" said Robert, looking at each bewildered face of the fourteen men in the audience for the answer he knew would never come. "My family have committed to building and supplying one hundred new ships of longboat design as part of a great Norman armada."

Robert let his words sink in, but before he could continue Duke William was on his feet.

"And you, my friends, will need to provide the rest," he said in a voice that did not encourage any comment. The Fitzroy family will lead the way as they have often done before and will show your craftsmen how to build what is required. In three months the first ships will have been finished and within a year all will be ready. My 'Ship List' has been compiled and each of you will be given a quota, and you will start construction as soon as you have been given instructions by our Chancellor here. If my wife can build a ship worthy of taking the new King of England to his coronation, I am sure that my barons and bishops can build a fleet of them. Now we have much to discuss and I would like to move on - the Archbishop of Caen has just returned from Rome with good tidings - and more support for our English venture," said Duke William smiling across at Lanfranc of Pavin.

With the discussion of the forthcoming ship building programme over, the Archbishop rose to his feet to address his peers. The old man was a picture of regal elegance, and his presence seemed to calm the seated men recovering from the surprise of Robert's announcement. He had just visited Rome once again, reaffirming Normandie's willingness to submit to the church, and the Pope reciprocated by giving his blessing to William's impending kingship. The Pope also informed Lanfranc that the Saxons had offended God with their blasphemous preaching of church services in English, and that only the righteousness of a Norman king would save them from eternal damnation. Heads nodded around the table in agreement as Lanfranc continued to pour his balm on any would-be dissenters and concluded the meeting with a blessing. If any of the assembled *baronie* had harboured doubts of whether the Duchy had the backing of God and Rome, by the time the Duke dismissed them - they had none.

5

Although small in stature, Duchess Mathilda of Normandie was a woman to be reckoned with and her husband was proud of his beautiful wife. She had come to him as a nineteen-year-old woman with a large dowry and Duke William had not been disappointed. Mathilda was obedient, fruitful in childbearing and pious in equal measure - attributes that demonstrated the highest qualities of Norman womanhood. While the Duke browbeat and bullied his liege lords into action, his wife achieved her goals more subtly, winning over her opponents by gently coaxing them to perform her wishes. Her kindness and gentleness masked a clever and determined personality that charmed opponents, turning them into supporters before they realised what was happening. She had borne her four sons and four daughters quietly and stoically, never once murmuring a single word of complaint to her husband.

It was with the same quiet determination that the Duchess constructed and completed the magnificent Abbey of Sainte-

Trinité. Today would be its crowning glory, when her 'Abbey of Women' would receive its papal blessing and the adoration of the people of Normandie. She had risen early in preparation for the ceremony and been bathed and dressed by her two maids who continued to fuss around their mistress. Looking resplendent in a silk dress of shimmering gold, the girls covered her head in a plain white wimple and after fastening a simple cross of silver around her neck Mathilda announced that she was ready.

The Duchess of Normandie's piety and good works were renowned way beyond the borders of the Duchy and France. She realised early that the charges of *consanguinity* against her marriage to William would be a serious challenge to his aspirations of kingship. Mathilda had striven to rebalance papal opinion through her good works and the financial support of the church. The lives of many nuns and monks living in penury had been enriched, physically and spiritually by her generosity. The Abbey of Sainte-Trinité was no exception and the lavish masterpiece of Norman romanesque art rose like a beacon over Caen, exemplifying this singular dedication. Her quiet delight at her achievements was barely perceivable, even today, and only those closest to her might detect the merest hint of satisfaction by the occasional upturned corners of her mouth. William, waiting outside the bedchamber, was the first to notice the triumph quietly emanating from his wife's otherwise serene disposition.

"This is your moment, my love, when all of France sees you for what you are - the great matriarch of Normandie's church," he boomed enveloping her in a warm embrace and steadfastly ignoring her protestations.

"William, you know I work only for God's pleasure," she admonished, failing miserably to keep him at arm's length. "Now treat me gently for I am not one of your hunting hounds to be wrestled with."

The Duke bellowed one of his great coarse laughs and released her from his grip, saying,

"You look magnificent and even your great Abbey will pale in your refection. If this does not convince the Pope of our righteousness, nothing else will."

"I am far too simple a woman to be concerned with your politics, husband," she chided gently. "But if the blessing of the Pope today is a sign of his favour, then I shall receive it with all humility."

William wagged his finger playfully at his wife.

"You must take your credit where it is due. Be in no doubt that the Duchy benefits almost as much from your good works as from mine."

Mathilda allowed herself a seldom seen smile that lit up her face.

"I will admit that we are a good match, perhaps. Now come, we have thousands of people waiting for us in the town below. We must not be late."

The Duchess took her husband's arm and they left the antechamber and entered the great hall where her small retinue, including Robert Fitzroy, Archbishop Lanfranc and the Abbess awaited her arrival. Their little cohort were only too aware of the significance of the abbey's forthcoming papal blessing and consecration; it would signify the real birth of the building and more importantly its recognition by the Pope. The procession swept out of the castle and through a vast gathering of townsfolk, lining the street, calling Mathilda's name and throwing flowers at her feet. She waved back to them, nodding her head in acknowledgement of their applause before disappearing into the great church for the service of thanksgiving to begin.

Mathilda and William led them into the huge nave which was packed full of Normandie's dignitaries and the richest merchants, barons, churchmen who sat waiting for their matriarch to arrive. The sound of monks and nuns singing filled the gigantic chamber and their beautiful melodies rose magnificently to the high vaulted ceilings. Finally, the Duke and Duchess took their seats at the front of the church where Phillip, King of France sat with the Papal delegation. The sun streamed through stained-glass windows, bathing Mathilda and those on either side of her in an apparent celestial light. Archbishop Lanfranc, sitting next to her, got to his feet and ascended the steps of the pulpit to address the congregation, and as he turned to face them the singing came to a gentle halt. Robert looked up at his friend and mentor, delivering God's blessing and felt a great wave of emotion sweep over him. The Archbishop led the prayers of thanksgiving for the Abbey and gave thanks to God for his acolyte on earth, the Duchess Mathilda and her diligence in carrying out His wishes. There followed more prayer and liturgies, and psalms were sung by the choir before the formal celebrations were brought to a close and the people filed out into the town where an enormous feast had been organised.

The town square was filled with trestle tables and benches in front of a raised dais where the guests of honour were seated according to rank and importance. Mathilda and her husband were flanked by the King of France and the Chancellor of the Duchy and outside of them were arraigned dukes, counts and bishops from all over the country. At the far end of the square a great kitchen had been built where the carcasses of oxen, boar and deer were roasted over beds of glowing charcoal. Minstrels, jongleurs and mummers entertained the crowd, who grew rowdy in the summer heat on copious supplies of ale and wine from their generous Lord and Lady.

"This feast is a little less boisterous since we sat together in Rouen last year," said Mathilda to her Chancellor. "I shall never forget the excitement when your brother spoke to the crowd."

Robert felt himself blanch at the memory.

"Hari can raise a riot in a nunnery when the feeling takes him," he said, turning his head to meet her smile.

"Well, his people seem to love him none-the-less. You have had word of him since he left the Duchy? I hear your eldest boy is travelling with him?" she asked.

"I have heard nothing of them directly but the Captain of the *Mora* has reported they are in England," replied Robert. "Apparently a storm forced a change of plan."

"Well, your son is in safe hands and I wish Harald well. He has been a loyal servant to the Duchy and without him we would never have stopped warring with the French," she said conspiratorially.

She turned to raise a bejewelled drinking goblet to the King of France who smiled at her before returning to his earnest conversation with Duke William.

"And how is the rest of your family, my Lord? I believe the Lady Eleanor must be close to her time. It is at these moments that we women appreciate the support of our husbands most. Duke William was never one to let his ducal duties get in the way of offering me support when I most needed it. I am sure you are no different," she continued, fixing him with a resolute gaze.

"I believe the child will come soon," mumbled Robert, with the look of a startled deer caught unawares by a hunter.

She smiled beatifically at him and put a tiny, comforting hand on his, leaving it in place for a moment.

"Now, to business Robert. What did you think of my gift to my husband? Is the *Mora* not a fitting way for him to travel to his coronation?" she continued. "The figurehead was my own idea, pointing a golden finger to England where the crown waits for him," she said changing the subject abruptly.

"It is a magnificent vessel, your Grace, but we need many more like the *Mora* if we are to be successful," Robert replied, going on to tell her of the plan to build all the new ships.

The Duchess listened intently, nodding her head as she considered everything.

"Very well, Lord Robert," she said when he had finished. "You must tell me what you need me to do."

6

It was hot in Mortain that summer. Eleanor Fitzroy could not sleep and lay naked on the bed, her arms and legs outstretched in a forlorn effort to cool herself. There was a full moon tonight and beams of pale light shone through the opened windows and bathed her spreadeagled form. Her large swollen belly cast a shadow against the far wall of the chamber and she observed its mass despondently. She knew that the child would not be long in coming into the world and she willed its arrival with every fibre of her being. The child kicked again, causing her to feel a dull pain in her pelvis and she moved onto her side and tried to draw up her knees. The sensation subsided a little and she began to curse the two Fitzroy brothers who had brought her to this point in her life. She cursed Harald, the child's father, for planting his seed in her womb before he sailed away with her beloved first-born son. But she reserved her most venomous profanities for her husband, who had left her alone so often and for such long periods during their marriage. The Lord of Mortain had been absent for the birth of all her babies, and although in the early days he had tried to be a dutiful husband, and she the doting wife, their union was always destined to end in acrimony. She drifted off in a fretful sleep only to wake within the hour. The bed was wet between her legs, and she knew that labour was soon to begin.

"Hurry Grace," she called to her maid who lay sleeping in the cot at the end of her bed. "The baby is coming. Fetch the midwife quickly."

Grace rose to her feet in a heartbeat, rushed out of the chamber to issue a stream of orders and returned to her mistress's side. They had been together in the birthing chamber for almost a month since the Countess had been persuaded to take to her bed, and the girl had faithfully tended to her Lady's needs. She took a linen cloth from a bowl of water at the bedside and dabbed away at the beads of sweat on Eleanor's forehead.

"Not long now, my Lady. Marielle is on her way and all will be well," said Grace.

Eleanor gave another groan and a knock at the door announced the midwife's arrival. Marielle entered the room without waiting for a reply and approached the bed, unceremoniously setting down her large leather satchel carrying the tools of her trade. Another woman followed close behind her carrying the birthing stool.

Marielle smiled down at the Lady of Mortain and took her hand, stating that her fourth child would be delivered shortly in the same uncomplicated manner as she had done with the previous three Fitzroy children. Eleanor nodded silently at the simple words and was calmed. After a brief assessment of the situation and a perfunctory examination, Marille uncorked a vial of rose oil and anointed the swollen belly, hips and thighs. Then she ordered her assistant to arrange a wooden tray with the contents of the satchel on it, and the woman dutifully laid out strips of linen, a knife, bottles of herbal infusions and a scrap of tree bark bearing an inscribed prayer.

"Your time will soon be here, Lady Eleanor. Just as I delivered you safely to your mothers arms all those years ago, so I will deliver this child to you."

Eleanor smiled meekly up at her before being interrupted by the first of many contractions.

"Calm yourself, my daughter," soothed Marielle. "Everything passes and this is nothing we have not done before together."

The old woman began to hum a lullaby that Eleanor had not heard since she was a child and the labour began.

At midday, when the stifling heat of the chamber had long since bathed all four women in sweat, Marielle declared Eleanor was ready. They coaxed her gently to her feet and helped her to walk slowly around the room before lowering her onto the birthing stool. The old midwife got to her knees while her assistant stood behind Eleanor to apply gentle downward pressure.

"Now push," Marielle ordered and Eleanor did as she was told and squeezed her lower abdomen with all her might.

It was getting dark outside when the Lady of Mortain's son emerged kicking and screaming lustily into the world. Despite the summer heat the fire was built up and Eleanor held the infant to her breast where he suckled greedily. The firelight flickered over mother and child, illuminating the scene in a warm glow.

"Take him, Grace. I must sleep," she ordered the maid, detaching her breast from the baby's mouth with a frown.

The girl took the child, covered her mistress with a linen sheet and sat in a nearby nursing chair, watching Marielle and her assistant organise their things and leave.

"The wet-nurse will be here tomorrow. In the meantime the Lady will have to feed the child. He will be hungry again soon, make sure he goes on the tit straight away or he will scream the castle down," commanded the mid-wife on her way out and she and her assistant cackled in unison at the joke. "I will return in the morning to ensure that all is well with your mistress and the child."

Grace looked down at the new born boy whose head nestled in the crook of her arm.

"There is no doubt you are a Fitzroy." she cooed, tracing a gentle finger up the line of the tiny nose and forehead, across the top of his head which already had a tuft of golden hair slicked across the crown. "Wherever your papa is, we will love and protect you until he comes home," she whispered in his ear.

If the child heard her he did not stir, and slept on peacefully in milky dreams with his mother's heartbeat his only memory.

Chapter 7: Harald's Pledge
Wessex, Late Summer 1065

1

Harald Fitzroy stared into the fire morosely. He had not spoken for several hours, and his companions knew better than to interrupt his thoughts. His squires, Thomas and Gilbert, looked at each other and the older boy shook his head, indicating that his sibling should remain quiet and still.

When the news of Richard's abduction had broken, Harald flew into a rage, the like of which few of his company had ever seen before. Those who had witnessed their Lord in full fury knew that it was better to let the storm blow out before approaching him.

Richard had been taken the previous day by armed men bearing the unmistakable colours of the House of Wessex. The sigil of six bears heads had been clearly visible on the shields of the Saxon horsemen who broke down the doors of the monastery where Richard had been studying under the watchful eye of Brother Dominic. The monk had initially stood his ground only to receive a brutal beating at the hands of the intruders who bound and carried the boy off on a spare horse brought for the purpose. They galloped away with their captive on the road west according to Clifford de Courcy who had been the first man to learn the boy had been taken.

Harald had cursed the House of Godwin when the treachery of the act became apparent. He returned to the long hall in high dudgeon, where a fire had been lit and food and drink prepared for his homecoming. He was livid at losing his nephew once again and he seethed at the obvious duplicity to which he had so easily fallen prey. Now the little cohort sat in silence, the only sound breaking the quietude was the crackling of the fire.

"It makes no sense to take the boy to Lundenwic," said Harald eventually, "and I cannot believe that King Edward would conspire in such an action."

"I agree, Lord. The King has been a good friend to us here in Maldon," said Clifford.

"No, my friends I have been well duped - lured away on a fool's errand and leaving the boy unguarded. This is the work of Earl Godwinson who knows exactly the value of his hostage," replied Harald.

"Well, it is a fine way to treat an ally," said Rolf, hawking and spitting into the fire.

"Unless, of course, he feels he needs something to bargain with," said Harald. "I fear that this is no more than a crude tactic to force my hand into lending him our support."

"Why, Lord, when we number so few, and he can muster thousands of warriors? In any case you have already demonstrated your support in Wales," asked Leif.

"Because I suspect our erstwhile comrade may be playing a bigger game than we might imagine. We may number only two hundred warriors in England, but we have a thousand men in Ambrières and even more support in the south. Godwinson has seen what our cavalry can do on the battlefield and covets it. He might even feel that the boy's father could be encouraged to support him if he has Robert's first born under lock and key. Perhaps he believes that even the Normans of Sicily could be persuaded to come to England?" speculated Harald.

"Men will follow you wherever you are, Hari. They will come from the other side of the Byzantine Empire if you ask them. But whatever you do next, I counsel caution - our people have not always had the best of times at the hands of these Saxons," said his cousin.

"You speak the truth, Brenier. We are older men now and have the benefit of wisdom. Tomorrow, we shall travel to Lundenvic. If I find Godwinson has Richard, I may well need a calming influence to stay my sword hand. We will not release the boy with force of arms - guile and cunning must be our only weapons," said Harald with an air of finality. "Be ready to leave at first light and when we return, I want every warrior ready to fight, whatever the outcome."

Harald was left alone, and his comrades retired to their homes, all except Halldor Snorrason who had been invited to stay in the long hall with his daughter.

"Lord, I may well be able to offer some assistance in your search," proffered the Icelander.

Harald looked at him quizzically.

"I am open to anything that will get Richard back, but it will take a little more than Hedda's magic to retrieve him."

Halldor smiled.

"I have friends in the city - men who will know all its comings and goings. If the boy has been taken to Lundenvic they would know of it. There are forces at work there that could well be to our advantage," he said.

Harald looked at him, intrigued.

"But I do not want to complicate matters for you, Lord. Just let me try and provide help where I can. After all, I am in your debt," concluded Halldor.

2

As the first cooking fires of Maldon began to send tendrils of smoke into a clear blue summer sky, Harald's party left the town on the road to Lundenvic. Not wishing to create any interest in their journey, particularly when they reached the city, they travelled lightly armed and without mail. They rode ordinary palfreys, except Halldor, who had taken a liking to his welsh pony and the party of four rode two abreast as quickly as they could, without drawing unnecessary attention to themselves. As evening fell, they passed through the Ald Gate and into the city to find lodgings. Before long they came upon an alehouse near East Cheap and decided to stay for the night. It was a raucous establishment that bustled with off-duty soldiers, whores and merchants; the dingy interior was heavy with the smell of old sweat and stale beer. Brenier found a table outside where they could sit away from the thronging mass of customers in various stages of inebriation.

"To the success of our mission," said Halldor, raising a cup of ale to his three comrades who returned the toast quietly.

Harald looked past the Icelander and pointed to the River Tamsye and the wooden bridge that crossed it not far from where they sat.

"I shall go over there tomorrow with my cousin to visit Godwinson's house. Rolf will stay here to learn of anything worth knowing."

"And I shall be visiting some of the Norse merchants who ply their trade here. There is little that escapes these men," replied Halldor.

They were interrupted by two whores looking for custom.

"Not tonight, ladies," said Brenier politely, "but there is easier custom to be had inside, I am sure."

"Take me up to the loft and I will make you change your mind," said one of the whores, a plump woman of twenty with an ample bosom flowing over the top of a dirty woollen dress.

"Cousin, let us show these women a little Norman hospitality. They look like they have been working hard and could do with a rest," said Harald. "Come join us ladies I will pay you silver for your time, and I would prefer to talk to you first - at least."

"Normans, eh, I was betting you were Danes. But either way I shall be glad to sit with you. I have been on my back most of today and will be happy for the rest," said the older one, a large blonde woman called Mildred, hitching up her skirts to sit down.

Both women joined the table and more jugs of ale were brought out. They drank greedily and by the time the third jug arrived they were chattering away garrulously to their new hosts; they had much to say. There had been a great deal of activity in the past few days with many armed men coming in and out of the city by the main bridge to Southwark where they both lived.

"Then only yesterday, the first thing in the morning, I was woken by the sound of men and horses. They were all in a hurry on their way to the great Lord's house," said Mildred.

"The great Lord?" asked Brenier.

"Yes. He lives in the old Roman palace with a small army to protect him. Hundreds of them, there are. Ask her, she's lain with most of them," answered Mildred, cackling and wiping the sweat off her brow with a grubby sleeve.

The other woman, now in her cups joined in drunkenly.

"Tight bastards as well. Half of them have yet to pay me."

"Well, you will not find me so ungracious," said Harald giving each woman a silver penny.

Mildred snatched hers up.

"For another two pennies you can have both of us, my Lord," she said eagerly.

"Not tonight, I think. But I thank you for your offer and your entertaining company. Now, if you will forgive us we have an early start tomorrow. Good night," he replied.

The women took their cue and staggered off into the night.

3

Harald and Brenier rode over the bridge to Southwark the next morning. They had no way of knowing if Harald Godwinson was at home but hoped he could be found. They were stopped outside the villa, twelve heavily armed *huscarls* barring their way. Harald introduced himself to their captain and said he was here to see the Earl. The man remained impassive, ordering one of his underlings to go inside. Shortly afterwards, they were joined by another man, a well-dressed Saxon who introduced himself as the Earl's steward and asked the purpose of the visit. Harald looked down imperiously from the back of his horse.

"Please tell the Earl of Wessex that Harald Fitzroy, Marchis of Ambrières and his future brother-in-law is here to see him and if he does not wish his little sister to die a spinster he would do well to see me now," he snarled.

The steward was visibly taken back by Harald's fierceness and scuttled away before returning again shortly afterwards.

"The Earl will see you, sir. But you must surrender all your arms and you will come alone," he said.

"Very well, if he fears me that much, surrounded as he is by these fellows, I have no objection," said Harald slipping down from his horse and handing his sword and dagger to one of the soldiers.

He followed the steward through the postern gate, into the palace courtyard and up the steps to the house. Before he reached the top the doors opened and Earl Godwinson stepped out, looking calmly at his uninvited guest. The Earl dismissed the steward and motioned for Harald to follow him into the building. When they were alone Godwinson turned to face him and the two men regarded one another wordlessly. Harald Godwinson was the first to break the silence.

"You should have sent word you were coming, Hari. I could have prepared a decent reception for such an important guest," said the Earl flatly. "I am delighted though that you still see fit to marry my sister. *Aegylfu* - I had almost given up hope."

"Let us not dignify this conversation with any unnecessary politeness. You know why I am here."

"I do and to answer your question - the boy is safe but is not here in Lundenvic."

He watched Harald check himself and pause for thought.

"Then, you must tell me true. Why have you deceived me? I gave you my support, which I have amply demonstrated in the last weeks and yet you conspired to get me out of the way to take an eight-year-old boy, in my care, from his lessons," said Harald, holding his open hands palm upwards to amplify the point.

"Regrettably, it was a necessary deception. I am to be the next King of England," he said unequivocally. "The Saxon people need a Saxon King and they will get one when Edward dies. When Duke William learns that he will not get the English throne, you know and I know he will try and take it by force. I want you and your armies to fight for me for which you will be richly rewarded," said Godwinson.

"I am sure you will make a fine king, but I have no interest in your plans. You know I have sworn fealty to the Duke of Normandie, and I cannot renounce my word," replied Harald as coolly as he could.

"Then your nephew will die and your brother will loose his first born son. How will the Lady Eleanor feel when you tell her that you have fed her beloved son to the wolves?" said the Earl knowingly.

Harald felt his hackles rise and fought to control his temper. He clenched his jaw so tightly that he thought his teeth would shatter and felt the blood throbbing at his temples.

"Just renounce your oath to the Duke and bend the knee to me. Richard shall be returned to you and I shall make you the Earl of Wessex. I know you hate Duke William, and you owe him nothing now. Your debt has been repaid many times over," continued Harold Godwinson casually.

Fitzroy did not, indeed could not, reply immediately and had to breathe deeply before he spoke.

"What would you have me do? Two hundred men of Maldon will not make much of a dent in William's army?"

"Do not take me for a fool, Hari. I know you better than that. You will raise me an army of two thousand Norman cavalry - once you have sworn your allegiance to me, of course. They will come from Normandie and Sicily when you command them. When I am King and all the fighting is over, I will release you from your vows," replied the Earl forcefully. "I do not need to know immediately. Return here tomorrow at this time and give me your answer."

The meeting was over, and the Earl turned and walked off, leaving his guest alone to his thoughts. Harald once again had to breathe deeply several times until he felt the fury that had threatened to erupt, begin to dissipate and gradually leave him. In his younger days his anger had often got the better of him and he would confront his opponents irrespective of the risk and the eventual outcome. But now he no longer had that luxury and was trapped between his sworn duty and what he knew he had to do to get Richard back. He needed guidance but the only man he had ever heeded in his long and dangerous existence had departed to Valhalla many years since. Harald had never felt so conflicted and involuntarily touched the golden warrior ring around his arm. He collected his thoughts and cursed the House of Godwin for the second time in as many days. Then he left the villa, retrieved his weapons and rejoined Brenier outside. The two Normans trotted silently through Southwark and back toward the bridge where they parted and went in separate directions.

Within two hours Harald stood before the sacred Ve he had visited only four weeks before to make the 'blot' sacrifice of the pig. It seemed like a lifetime had passed since then, he thought, and resolved yet again to do whatever was necessary to protect his family. This time the sacrifice needed to be of a similar magnitude to the favour which he was to ask of the gods. He slipped the golden warrior's ring off his arm and looked at it in the palm of his hand, turning it over and watching it catch and reflect in the dappled sunlight. He remembered when Grandfather Bjorn had presented it to him at a great feast in Regneville and made him swear to protect the Duchy. He also recalled giving it to Eva, his wife, before the defining battle of Civitate. He thought of his brother, Robert, giving him back the lost warrior ring, an action which persuaded him to return to Normandie. It provoked many other distant memories, and he spent a moment in quiet reflection before tossing it into the deep water of the pond. The burnished gold sparkled as it flew through the air, then sank quickly beneath the mirrored surface of the water. Harald closed his eyes and incanted his prayer in old Norske.

Yonder, I see the face of my father, my mother, my sisters and my brothers,
I see the long line of my ancestors stretching back to the beginning,
I see the faces of my comrades in the great shield wall,
I see the faces of the slain dead beneath our feet.

They are calling me to join them,
but my time is not yet come.
For I have work to do in Midgard
before the gods of Asgard call me home.
Accept my gift and grant me favour
And return to me what I have lost

He reached for the leather pouch the Icelandic seer had given him and took a single black seed from it. He put it under his tongue as he had been instructed and repeated the prayer again. Harald looked to the sky and saw the silhouettes of two ravens against the sun and felt his legs weaken and buckle beneath him. He was lying on the ground, looking up into a cloudless sky, and turned his head to see the two birds land and hop towards him. He smiled in greeting at them, and they cawed backed in unison. Harald felt his senses swim and he gave himself up to the darkness which enveloped him like a stifling black cloak.

4

He was woken by the sound of seagulls and when he opened his eyes, he found he was back on a deserted beach. Harald got to his feet, brushed the sand from his clothes and stretched himself awake like a bear coming out of hibernation. He lifted his face to the sun and felt its balmy blessing on his skin before looking about him to get his bearings. The sea was in front of him and the cliffs at his back, and to his left and right the featureless sandy coastline wound on forever. It looked almost like the Navarrean coastline where he and his people had been shipwrecked but he knew it was not. A lupine howl to his right took his attention and he turned to see a man walking toward him with the unmistakable forms of two large wolves at his side. Harald stood, transfixed at their unhurried approach and when they were two hundred paces or so away the man raised his staff in greeting.

"Grimnir," he called back as the man and his animals grew closer.

"Lord Harald Fitzroy," came the reply, "it is good to see you once more. You will remember my two companions."

He looked down at the enormous beasts trotting obediently at their master's side. Harald also noticed a change in his friend's appearance. Grimnir was no longer the dishevelled stranger and was dressed in finery fit for a king; his hair and beard had been groomed and cut and he wore a gold band around his head.

"Are these two fine beasts the same dogs that I remember you with last time?" asked Harald.

Grimnir beamed back a dazzling smile, his one remaining eye sparkling with humour.

"When we walk in Midgard it is often necessary to go in disguise," he said "many folk might be alarmed at sitting down to eat with gods and wolves at their table."

Both men laughed and embraced warmly.

"Now Hari come and sit at my table. I have invited some honoured guests to join us. You are hungry and thirsty after your long journey?" he continued, but without waiting for an answer Grimnir turned him around with a hand on the shoulder.

A table had been set on the sand and was piled high with food and drink. Harald gasped in amazement at the two men sitting down.

"My other guests at your feast are the Wandering Warriors of Haugesund. I believe you know of these men."

Harald stood open-mouthed staring at his long-dead grandfathers as they got up to greet him. He looked into their timeless faces with great longing, and they returned his gaze lovingly, their eyes bright and shining with wisdom. Neither man looked like they had aged beyond twenty-five years and their sleeveless tunics revealed heavily muscled arms bearing freshly tattooed runes. Their plaited hair and beards were long and lustrous and displayed not a single grey fleck. Bjorn 'Speararm' and Torstein the Warrior Skald came and wrapped themselves around him in a joyful reunion. Tears rolled down Hari's face as the three stood on the sand clutched in a fierce embrace that he did not want to end. His reverie was interrupted by Grimnir.

"Come my brave warriors, sit down and eat, for this day will not last forever and we have much to discuss.

"And I for one have an appetite that would shame a giant," said Torstein lustily, with one meaty forearm locked playfully around his grandson's neck.

"Why, if I knew no differently, I would swear you two were twins," declared Bjorn.

They all sat and the feasting began. Songs were sung, stories told, and heroes remembered. The drinking cups were always full and the mountain of food never diminished in spite of the ravenous guests.

As the sun began to set Grimnir called for his guests' attention,

"It is good to share the company of old friends and illustrious warriors, but we have pressing matters to discuss, and our friend here is in need of your counsel," he said looking at the grandfathers.

"Indeed," said Torstein putting down his drinking cup, "an oath of fealty cannot be easily broken but I believe our grandson has fulfilled his vow in full and owes his liege lord nothing."

Bjorn nodded sagely and paused before speaking.

"It is true, Hari, your oath belongs only to your people, your *aett*, your family. You have repaid the Duke's loyalty many times over and are free to fight on whatever foreign field and against whoever you choose. Besides, while your grandmother's curse still hangs over the Saxons you cannot be held to account for any promises you make to them," he said with great surety.

"That is settled then, Hari. You are free to make your choice and cannot be bound by the whims of men anywhere outside Normandie," said Grimnir, producing a wrapped silk kerchief which he placed on the table in front of his guest.

Harald looked down and opened it, revealing the golden warrior's ring he had sacrificed to the holy spring.

"The gift was too generous, Hari, even for the gods. Return to your people for you have much to achieve before we see you in Valhalla," continued Grimnir, watching his sleepy guest struggle to stay awake.

"Thankyou, Lord Odin," mouthed Harald before lurching back into unconsciousness.

5

For the second time that day Harald Fitzroy woke up on the ground. He was back in the forest clearing, asleep by the *Ve*. His mouth was dry and he rose on unsteady legs, feeling sick to his stomach. He went to the holy spring, drinking deeply from the stream of bubbling water and felt a little better. It was getting late and the sun which had bathed the little clearing so completely during the day was setting and he knew he should be on his way back to Lundenvic. He walked back to the road and was reassured to find the palfrey tethered to the tree where he had left the animal happily grazing on a nosebag of oats. Horse and rider made their way back to the city and reached the gatehouse on the Southwark side of the river bridge as the watchmen were lighting the torches for the night.

Harald's companions were glad to see their leader as he trotted down the road toward their table outside the ale-house. A stable boy came to take his horse, and he sat down beside them, Brenier filling a cup of ale for him. He raised the cup to them before tossing it back and emptying the vessel.

"The ale has not improved any since last night but it is good to see you all," he said, smiling at the men sitting around the table.

Harald looked about them and satisfied they were out of earshot from the other customers he leaned forward.

"I have a great deal of news to impart but first I am anxious to know what you have learned today," he continued, inviting the others to speak first.

"Then I have some for you, Lord," said Halldor quietly. "Your nephew is alive and well but is on the road to the north of England. He is under the protection of Earl Morcar of Northumbria and will be held at Bamburgh Castle for the time being."

Harald rubbed his chin as he considered the news.

"You can be sure this is true?" he asked, fixing the Icelander with a steely gaze.

"I would stake my life on it, and that of my daughter's. There is much more to tell but let us leave that to when we have a little more privacy," came the cautious reply.

"A troop of horsemen left the city two days ago. About a hundred men of the north according to one of the women working here," confirmed Leif.

"Are we still returning to Southwark in the morning for your meeting with Earl Godwinson," asked Brenier.

"Indeed, but I shall go alone. I do not intend to stay long but I can tell you that I am committing our forces to join the Saxons and fight beneath English banners for the the foreseeable future. There is war coming and I need to confirm our allegiance to safeguard my nephew's life," said Harald looking each man in the face in turn. "Now, let us toast our benefactor, King Edward. We shall drink to his health so that no one here may doubt our loyalty. To King Edward, long may he reign," he shouted.

"King Edward, long may he reign," his men shouted back, and heads turned from the other tables full of drinking men who stood and joined them in the loyal toast.

6

They met at noon by the Ald Gate after Harald's earlier appointment had been concluded with Earl Godwinson. The meeting had been short and perfunctory, and a scribe had been in attendance to record each of the details. In short, Harald Fitzroy agreed to recruit and equip an army of two thousand cavalrymen. The horsemen would be drafted into the service of the King of England for a period of one year in return for one thousand pounds of gold, the Earldom of Wessex and the Lady Aelfgyva Godwin in marriage. The safe return of William Fitzroy was guaranteed on fulfilment of the contract, and the boy would be well cared for until then. Harald promised the army would be ready by the spring and he and Godwinson shook hands. The scribe prepared a carefully minuted document that both men signed, at which point the meeting was over and he returned to Lundenvic to meet his comrades.

He was in good spirits as he led his cohort beyond the city gates and rode hard until they were out of sight of the walls. The weather was warm, and the perspiring horses soon needed watering. They stopped at a deserted point by Walbrook Stream and allowed the animals to drink their fill. Brenier looked at his cousin, anxious to know the details of the meeting in Southwark.

"My friends, I have committed to raise an army of two thousand cavalrymen to support the new King of England when his time comes," said Harald calmly.

"That much we assumed, but when will we need to fight beneath the Saxon banners? Are we expected to fight our own countrymen?" asked Brenier uneasily.

"I said nothing about fighting for them, cousin," he answered with a grin. "The Earl deserves a little deception, after all I am only returning what was done to me. Look, come Christmas Godwinson expects King Edward to be dead and the Witan will declare him successor to the English throne. Duke William will not be pleased and be in no doubt 'the Bastard' will fight for what he believes is his birthright - whatever the odds are. I am sure that none of you want to fight our countrymen but trust me when I tell you that it will not come to that."

"And young Richard, Lord. Will he be returned to us whole?" asked Rolf.

"The Earl has promised to return the boy when I have fulfilled my commitment so we will need to keep the deception going as long as possible. If not, I have no doubt Richard will die once he suspects I have lied about my fealty. I do not trust the man to keep his word, nor do I intend to keep mine. Richard will be rescued before anyone suspects but it is possible we will need to take Bamburgh castle to get him back," replied Harald.

There was a sharp intake of breath at this last comment. None of them knew much about Northumbria but they had all heard of the impregnable castle of Bamburgh which had defeated the best of their Norse fore-fathers. Halldor had remained quiet on their journey home, listening with interest to his comrades, and decided it was his moment to speak.

"Lord Fitzroy," he said seriously, "I should like to provide you with another option which might improve the chances of success in releasing your nephew. As you know, I am taking my daughter to Norway to ensure she marries one of King Harald Sigurdsson's noblemen. The King and I are old comrades, and it might interest you to know that he has told me he too has designs on the English throne. In fact, Earl Godwinson's brother Tostig has persuaded the King of Norway that the Saxons want a strong Norseman to rule their kingdom again."

Harald threw back his head and laughed out loud in disbelief at the thought that the aspirations of the two major antagonists in his life might be thwarted by another.

"Well, I for one would throw my weight behind the King of Norway's bid for power if it meant those two pretenders were cast aside," he guffawed, Brenier and Leif joining him in laughter.

"Would you countenance such a bid, my Lord?" said Halldor seriously once the laughter had died down.

"If it meant my nephew was returned to me unharmed, I would throw my weight behind *Hel* herself," answered Harald returning to a serious demeanour.

"It may well prove a less risky proposition than storming Bamburgh castle," replied Halldor. "Allow me to provide you with all I know of the King of Norway's plans."

"You are a man of many different talents, *skald*," said Harald curiously. "Come tell me everything, you will never have a keener audience."

Halldor's friend and benefactor Harald Sigurdsson was ten years older than his namesake Harald Fitzroy. Although their paths had never crossed, they each had carved indelible impressions on their respective landscapes, forging separate reputations as warriors. Both men were veterans of fighting the Moors in southern Italy and Sicily, and although they often had opposing paymasters, they had never faced one another across the field of battle. When Sigurdsson escaped from the siege of Byzantium with a horde of gold and silver accumulated over many years in the service of the Emperor, he sailed to Kiev to marry Elizabeth, the Rus King's daughter. He took her home to Norway and ascended the throne at the age of twenty-eight to become one of the most famous warriors of his age. Hardrada, as the King was also known, became a ferocious and warlike monarch exemplifying bravery and cruelty in equal measure. He spent much of his early reign keeping his opponents in Scandinavia in check, but when rumour of King Edward's demise filtered through he began to look south to the English throne which he claimed as heir to Cnut, a previous monarch of England. As soon as King Edward dies, said Halldor to his eager listeners, Hardrada will land in the north of England to claim his right.

"And you think he will land in Northumbria? Why there?" asked Harald when Halldor paused to take a drink from his flask.

"It is the most obvious place and he would rather save his strength for the English than the Scots. I am sure that he would appreciate the support of some Norman cavalry when he lands," replied the Icelander. "Perhaps it will be as good an opportunity as any to rescue your nephew?"

"If you are not mistaken it will be the answer to my prayers," beamed Harald, clapping him on the back. "Now let's get back on the road to Maldon while there is still light in the day."

Harald spent the rest of the journey questioning Halldor about Hardrada. He desperately wanted to believe the man but he had not known him for long and there was a great deal at stake. If the *skald* spoke the truth and the Norsemen were coming, it would at least give him a fighting chance to rescue his nephew. But, if his guest was deceiving him, he decided, the consequences were almost too dire to contemplate.

Chapter 8: The Great Deception
Maldon, Autumn 1065

1

The leaves of the great forest around Maldon turned from green to gold, signalling the end of summer. The *haverfest* was a good one for the people of the town, allowing them to fill their grain stores to the brim with an abundance of barley, corn and wheat. Anyone who was not engaged with reaping and preparing the grain was employed in harvesting the plentiful crops of cabbages, carrots and apples, and the workers toiled from dawn to dusk. The town's great autumn fair bustled with traders selling and bartering their excess crops and animals in return for silver, tools and supplies to sustain them through the long winter months.

Lord Harald celebrated the season with a harvest feast in his longhouse, where his loyal lieutenants, their wives and families gathered around a large oak table. When the town had been reclaimed, the longhouse was rebuilt on the site of the old one that had been burned down during the retreat of Bjorn Halfdanson and his people. Now it stood proudly on a hill overlooking the vibrant town, the distinct shape of its hogsback roof dominating the evening skyline. Inside, the wattle and daub walls were hung with round warrior shields and banners decorated with the sigils and runic emblems of ancient heroes and their clans. A large hearthfire, burning with silver birch logs, illuminated the great hall and the smell of roasting meats wafted through the building, tantalising the hungry guests.

The town's priest stood up and the rumbling of conversation died down as he thanked God for the harvest and for the many blessings bestowed on Maldon. When he was finished Harald got to his feet and toasted all of his guests, and when this was finished servants carrying huge trays of food and drink scurried about the table. Brenier sat at Harald's right hand with his new Saxon wife and Halldor Snorrason and his daughter sat on his left. Earlier in the day the Icelander had visited his host asking that he might take his leave of Maldon to travel back to the court of the Norwegian king, who was expecting him. Harald would be sad to see the man go; he had been a fount of valuable information during his short stay but Halldor had to report back to his master on the events in Saxon England.

Furthermore, the Icelander needed to inform his liege lord that he had a new ally in England and that when the great Norse fleet landed in the new year there would be a contingent of Norman cavalry to bolster their ranks. Although Lord Fitzroy had not known Snorasson long enough to fully trust him he judged him to be a man of his word, and they sat drinking to the success of the mission. Harald raised his cup to meet Halldor's and then to Hedda. His daughter looked resplendent beside her father in a light blue woollen dress, gathered at the waist by a simple leather thong.

"I shall miss you both, you have been good companions for these last months," said Harald. "And I wish you luck and joy with your marriage, Hedda."

"Alas, that will have to wait for a while longer," said her father pausing to choose his words carefully. "I would like her to remain with you - at least until our plans have succeeded - it is important that I have your full trust."

"You mean she is my hostage?" came the surprised reply.

"For want of a better word, yes," said Halldor. "I know you will treat her well and she will be happy to work in your service while she remains here."

"And your husband-to-be in Norway? He must wait a little longer for you, Hedda?"

The girl looked up, her pale blue eyes flashing angrily.

"He can wait until Ragnorok and beyond," she said, adding a few Icelandic curses for good measure.

"Daughter, do not forget your manners. We cannot change what has been promised," said her father sternly.

"Hedda, you are very welcome to stay and I need a good housekeeper to make sure this place is run properly. If the work pleases you, of course?" said Harald.

"Thankyou, Lord, you are very gracious. I will not let you down and will be a credit to my father," she answered politely.

"Very well, it is settled. To your journey, Halldor, and to my new housekeeper and the safe return of my nephew," said Harald raising his cup again.

Halldor excused himself for a moment and left the table. The woman leant toward Harald and spoke as quietly as she could, but loud enough so she could be heard above the rest of the voices babbling away in the hall.

"He is safe, my Lord."

Harald gave her a quizzical look.

"Richard - I have seen him in my dreams," she said earnestly. "Your nephew is safe and well cared for. He is many leagues to the north and does not live in fear. He knows that you will not forget him and will come for him when you can."

"How can you be certain?" he asked sceptically.

"Did the gods not talk to you when I asked them?" she said with a certainty that made Harald pause.

He nodded and smiled at her, touching the amulet at his throat for good luck.

2

The next morning Halldor Snorrasson boarded a wide-bodied *dromon*, carrying a cargo of sea-salt bound for Viken. Hedda stood on the stone quay and waved to her father as she watched the ship get smaller and smaller. They had embraced fondly as they parted and agreed to meet in the spring but until then, her father ordered gently, she was to ensure that her service to the Fitzroy household was of the highest order. Determined to comply with her father's wishes she returned to the longhouse to take up her duties and set to work immediately.

Harald Fitzroy had only recently moved back into the building since arriving from Normandie and, although well-constructed, it had never previously been occupied nor benefited from a woman's touch. She loaded the servants up with all the pots, cups and plates that had remained undisturbed from the previous night's feast and ordered them not to return until they were spotless. Then she shooed the hunting dogs outside into the autumnal sunshine and set about cleaning with her normal fierce application. Pulling back the leather curtains from the windows to let in the light, she looked about the room before deciding where to start. She began by clearing the detritus from the feast and then started in the hearthfire, removing the dead embers from the night's blaze, putting the ashes in a wooden bucket and replacing them with new kindling and logs. She took a broom of weeds and began to sweep away at the huge earthen floor, creating a cloud of dust that seemed to follow her as she worked. It took a while, but she eventually swept and cleaned the entire surface of the floor, restoring its original dull lustre. Hedda boiled water and filled a wooden bucket, washing down all the walls and supporting woodwork. The light was starting to go out of the day when she stopped work and retired to her small room behind the longhall to clean herself up and wait for her new master to return.

She was alerted to Harald's arrival by the barking of his dogs and rose from her small wooden cot. Brushing herself down, she drew a comb through her hair and went back into the longhall.

He was coming through the porch at the far end of the building, his dogs jumping up at him in welcome. Behind them came his two squires, Thomas and Gilbert carrying a brace of hares that their hawk had killed earlier. One of the boys went to place the bird on a stand while the other sibling put the carcasses on a table and took out a knife to gut and clean them.

"Good evening, Lord," said Hedda. "Your bird has been busy today."

"As have you, I think," he replied looking around the room, illuminated by the light of a newly lit fire. "your work does you credit. Where are the servants?"

"I dismissed them earlier, Lord. I thought I should set an example of what I expect from them if I am to take charge here."

She moved over to the table and took the hares away from Gilbert who protested meekly.

"I will do this outside," she said to the young squire in a voice that would brook no argument.

The young man began to protest, but he saw from her fierce look that it would do no good and she took the knife and hares and went outside. She returned shortly with the skinned carcasses cleaned, spitted and ready for roasting. Within the hour she presented Harald with a plate of roasted hare and parsnips and set it in front of him with a cup of ale. Gilbert was clearly piqued by his usurpment at the hands of the new woman and sat with his brother at the far end of the hall.

"It will do you no good sulking over there. You had better get used to our new housekeeper, boys. It is time we had someone who can keep a bit of discipline here," he admonished. "Now come, sit down, Hedda, I do not wish to eat alone. Join me, please."

She sat down opposite him and together they ate. It was a long time since Harald had been joined at the table by any woman, much less a young one of such unusual beauty and he suddenly remembered how much he missed female company. They ate in relative silence but when they had finished, he coaxed her into conversation, and she began to tell her story.

Hedda Halldorsdottir came from a long line of *seiðuns* and *skalds.* Over one hundred and fifty years ago her antecedents discovered the land of ice and fire, which they believed was the realm of the gods. It was an easy assumption to make in a country full of stark contrasts. The middle of Iceland was unable to sustain life of any kind while the verdant, coastal pastures supported all manner of existence - except man. At the island's centre volcanoes spewed devastation, killing everything in their path and left geysers, quags and boiling mud in their wake. Here, there were also barren mountain ranges issuing fierce, uncontrollable rivers that tumbled out of the high rocks in a tumult of cascading falls. Conversely, the coastal region where the Norse folk settled were the complete opposite, characterised by long green valleys, broad hills and undulating uplands, providing a comfortable habitation for men and cattle. Trout and salmon filled the lakes and rivers while the seas teamed with whales and seals. Where the pastureland ended, the forest began and stopped only when great barriers of volcanic detritus prevented their progress any further. The settlers, believing they shared their new home with the gods worshipped their neighbours with a zealous fervour, proliferating great legends and sagas.

Hedda's mother, Beata, was a witch, as was her grandmother and great grandmother, and their craft was considered the most powerful magic among the Norsemen and women. Not only could they cast spells and see the future, but, it was rumoured, they could transfer their souls into animals and monsters. In the new land of Iceland such supernatural women became powerful and feared in equal measure. The inexorable growth of Christianity brought an abrupt stop to the practice after the country's pagan law speaker, Thorgeir, renounced the old religion and threw his idols into the great waterfall at Godafoss. Overnight the *seiðuns* became outcasts and the followers of the old gods were pushed to their communities' boundaries.

To escape persecution Hedda's mother joined the expedition of Leif Ericsson with five hundred doughty souls, and sailed west to settle in far off Vinland. They husbanded the new land but hostilities with local tribes were bitter, and farmers were killed one by one as they worked. After two years, when their numbers dwindled below two hundred, they returned to their boats, loaded their families, possessions and animals and braving the ice flows and angry storms, returned home to start over.

Hedda's father was a poet, a warrior and an adventurer and met her mother during a fleeting visit to Iceland. After a brief romance they married. He left to join his friend and brother-in-arms in Norway where he served as the King's advisor, returning home infrequently until the birth of his daughter. Halldor Snorresson was a besotted father, and the King of Norway allowed him to leave his court and return to Iceland to care for his new family. He was getting a growing reputation as a *skald,* earning him fame and a modest fortune. Halldor forbade Beata to practice any more witchcraft, which by now had long been outlawed, but during his time away from home she secretly schooled her daughter in the ancient craft. The young girl became a practised *seiðun* revealing her skills to Halldor only after her mother's death. Angered at first but, knowing his daughter's wilfulness, he agreed to turn a blind eye to her art.

"That is an interesting story that deserves retelling," said Harald.

"Please, Lord, may we keep it between ourselves? My father would be angry if he knew I told you and I have no wish to shame him," said Hedda, fighting to stifle a yawn. "But, may I hear your story?"

"Not tonight, I think. Perhaps when you are not so tired. Feel free to retire, you have doubtless planned another busy day's toil for yourself. Just remember you are also my guest and you are not required to labour like a thrall. You have been far better company than these two anyway," he said, gesturing to the two squires whose snoring could be heard from the far end of the longhall.

"Very good, Lord," she said demurely, got to her feet and left.

He watched her walk to the doors, admiring the lithe form and athletic gait that reminded him so much of Eleanor. He counted the days since they had parted and wondered when and if he would see her again. Harald could only guess at Eleanor's fate and that of their child, resolving to send word home before winter grasped Normandie and England in its icy grip.

3

Harald was woken by the sound of a woman's voice raised outside the longhall. He sat up with a start, trying to fathom its provenance before he realised that it was his new housekeeper berating the servants. He could not hear what she was saying to them, nor did he have to understand that she was angry and in no mood to be placated by any of the wretched women feeling the lash of her tongue.

He smiled to himself at the jolt of lightening that these placid Saxon women were receiving but felt no need to intervene.

He had been too easy on them in the past, he resolved, it would do them no end of good to feel a firm hand.

He sat up and stretched, throwing back the thin, woollen blanket that covered him. The seasons had changed, temperatures had dropped suddenly, and he would ask one of the servants to retrieve his thick bearskin cloak from the sea-chests in the hall. Better still, he thought, he would ask Hedda. He got up and, stumbling naked to the table on the other side of the chamber, poured water from a jug into a wooden bowl, splashing some on his face. He washed and dried himself with a piece of linen fabric that had been neatly folded and placed next to the bowl. Then he dressed himself in the same woollen trousers, shirt and tunic he had been wearing for the last two days and pulling on his boots, he left his bed chamber. The dogs roused themselves at the sight of him, bounding across the hall. They jumped up joyfully and he returned their greeting with some robust petting. His squires slept on undisturbed, on hard wooden benches.

Harald walked the thirty paces of the longhouse and, followed by the hounds, went through the porch, into the bright morning sunshine to greet the day. He sat down at a bench and a cup of weak beer was presented on the table in front of him.

"Good morning, my Lord. I trust you slept well. Do you have any instructions for me today?"

He shook his head before remembering the need to retrieve his bearskin cloak and told her where she might find it.

"I have meetings this morning but please tell the boys to start cleaning my arms and equipment," he continued.

"Certainly, Lord. Will you be back for supper?

"I will," he said, "but I will not eat alone. You will join me?"

She nodded her acceptance, and he was about to call the stableboy to prepare a horse for him to ride into town, but before any order formed on his lips he heard the clip-clop of iron clad hooves on hard-packed ground and looked up. Damascus's coat had been groomed to a high lustre and his mane and tail had been combed through. The stallion stood proudly before his master and neighed softly, his saddle and bridle cleaned and polished.

He thanked Hedda for the ale, mounted the horse and rode down the hill toward the town. As he had done every day since his return to Maldon he trotted outside the perimeter of the palisade fence, ensuring that it was completely secure. It was a discipline that his father had instilled in him from an early age and the daily chore of checking the defences had not been forgotten. Satisfied with his findings he returned through the gatehouse and rode toward his cousin's new house.

He found Brenier sitting outside in the sun preparing for another day's training with the men. He was repairing a piece of kit and looked up at Harald's approach.

"Married life, spending your days sitting in the sun, seems to suit you, cousin," called Harald.

Brenier laughed in response.

"Not a bit of it. When my work with the men is finished, I am given another load of chores as soon as I return home."

His wife appeared at the doorway and called a greeting to the Lord of Maldon before disappearing again. Harald slid off the horse's back and sat down on the bench next to his cousin.

"She is a fine catch that one and I have no doubt she will be filling your new house with babies before long," said Harald.

"Well we are both trying hard enough. It is all I can do to get on my horse most mornings. Anyway, will you be joining me on the training field this morning?" asked Brenier.

"Of course I will, but first we must discuss a trip to Normandie."

"You want me to return home, Hari?"

"I do - but don't worry, you can be back in time for Christmas if things go well. I need you to visit Ambrières to see Jeanotte. He must prepare the men to leave in the new year and be here by early summer. I will send all the ships he needs."

"And may I share our destination with him?" asked Brenier.

"You may, but with no one else, there are spies all over the Duchy. I should know - I put them there myself," came the reply. "I would also like you to travel to Mortain to see Eleanor."

Brenier looked up with start.

"The last time I was there it ended in blood and death. I do not think I will be made welcome," he replied.

"Do not worry, Jeanotte has settled matters with my brother and there will be no hostilities. You will tell her that Richard is well and that we thrive in England after the change in our plans. Tell her she will see her son returned to her safe and well, soon enough. The *Lady Alberada* will be ready to leave in two days. Please give her this."

He slid a delicate bracelet of twisted gold over the table.

"Very well. I am no diplomat, but I will do my best," said his cousin.

The two men shook hands and no more was said on the matter. Brenier understood the importance of his mission and exactly what was required of him. He also knew that Harald craved news of Eleanor and the new baby, and would be ill-at-ease until he discovered their fate.

When they reached the training field they were greeted by the sight of two hundred mounted cavalrymen waiting for them.

Since the return from Normandie each warrior had been given a parcel of land in return for their service. The transition from soldier to farmer was not an easy one and many of them preferred just to take the rents on offer while they waited for the next opportunity to fight for plunder. These were men who had been trained since boyhood to fight from horseback, and although they did not know exactly when, they knew they would be all be marching to battle again soon enough. When they saw Harald riding to meet them, there was great excitement in the ranks, and they cheered and shouted to him as the riders approached.

The men formed up in their designated *conrois,* lines consisting of twenty horsemen and each stood in close formation. They were all dressed in uniform full-length *hauberks*, a long chain-mail tunic reaching the knee, and a conical *spangelhelm* to protect the head. In their right hands the warriors carried a steel-tipped lance while over the left shoulder, a large kite-shaped shield. Ten lines of huge horses stood fretting, with the riders facing an 'enemy' shield wall made up of volunteers from the town, a thousand paces away. Battle cries emitted from the enemy lines as spears were beaten against round wooden shields in a fierce challenge. Anxious Norman stallions pawed at the ground, snorting and whinnying their defiance and fighting against bits and bridles, their riders trying to rein them in. The battle horns sounded and the first *conrois* of twenty men advanced, lowering their lances into a couched position. They started at a trot, each man so close to the next rider that their legs were touching. The same tight formation persisted as the horses accelerated into a gallop, throwing up a shower of earth clods, as the next line of riders began their charge. There were now ten *conrois* in full flight across the field and as they got to within a hundred paces of the shield wall, the first line expertly wheeled away to the left and trotted back to their starting place waiting for the other *conrois* to join them. The exercise was repeated over and over again, stopping only for the heavy beasts to take water from a nearby stream.

"That should blow away the cobwebs. I noticed a few gaps in the *conrois* when we charged the Welsh," said Harald to one of the captains, a crusty old veteran from Rouen.

"Yes, Lord. Too much time at sea makes a warrior a little rusty. When there are no more battles to fight we can all take up the plough," said the captain phlegmatically.

"Does life as a farmer not suit you well?"

Both men laughed knowing that the next new conflict would soon be knocking at their door.

4

Autumn moved in on Maldon and cold winds blew in from the North Sea, denuding the trees of any remaining brown leaves that had not yet fallen. The forest floor was emptied of fallen wood as firewood was collected and piled high and fattened hogs were prepared for slaughter. The traffic of cargo ships making their way up the River Blackwater slowed to a trickle as the town readied itself for the long winter months.

Harald's longhouse remained one of the few areas of activity and visitors came and went with regularity. Men still arrived routinely, delivering messages from London, Normandie and Norway. Halldor Snorrason sent word of Richard Fitzroy who had been seen alive and well in York and the boy now served as a page to Earl Morcar of Northumbria. Brenier also sent word, and a simple message was delivered by the captain of a merchant ship on his way to London.

"All is well in Ambrières and Mortain. The Lady has delivered a fine, healthy son," the man said to Harald, standing before him outside the longhall one morning.

"That is all? Nothing else?" asked Harald.

The man shook his head, and a gold coin was thrust into his hand.

"This is most generous, Lord," said the sea captain, "but your comrade has already paid me well."

"Keep it," came the swift reply. "Good news should always be rewarded. Now come and join me in a drink - this calls for a celebration."

Without being asked Hedda appeared carrying a tray full of food and drink.

In Brenier's absence Harald had taken charge of training the warriors and although the exercise field was now a morass of mud, he worked them hard on a new stone square constructed just outside the town. Twice a week the air rang to the clash of steel weapons as he drilled them relentlessly. On other days he hunted with his hawks or travelled into the forest with his dogs in search of boar or deer. In the evenings when he had no visitors, he would spend time with Hedda, who continued to run his domestic affairs with supreme efficiency. She was a good listener, absorbing his words like an eager scholar and always keen to know more. After much encouragement, he told her his story one evening and she sat with rapt attention until he had finished. She was particularly taken with the tale of the Wandering Warriors and would not stop pressing wine on him until he could be persuaded to retell their saga in full. Beneath a torrent of questions, he agreed to take her into the marshlands to where his grandfathers fought and lost their last stand together.

The following morning, he sent to the stables for horses and took Hedda out along the river and over the causeway to Northey Island. They followed the path of his grandfathers' retreat, and when they stopped at the causeway where Torstein Rolloson fell they stood for a moment in quiet reflection. She asked him to be shown where his grandmother issued her curse to the Saxons on the other side of the river, and they walked their horses to the place where Turid had defied her enemies. As they stood looking over the flat, limpid water of the channel in front of them, the sun emerged from behind the clouds with a great rush of wind causing the water to ripple and shine in a sparkling wave of energy. There was another movement above their heads and a vast murmuration of starlings began swooping, diving and whirling in unison, creating extraordinary black, smoke-like swirls across the sky.

"Black Sun," said Hedda, looking in awe at the many thousands of birds moving as one above them. "Her magic is strong here, Lord. I feel it in my bones."

Harald looked at his companion laughing joyfully at the striations of black against the clear blue sky. She looked back at him and her delicate features seemed to come alive in a face free of all care. As quickly as it had arrived the wind died down, the sun disappeared behind clouds and the birds were gone. The starlings had disappeared, but Hedda's smile remained as she talked animatedly. Delighted at the transformation, from the serious young woman who kept house for him, he responded good-naturedly.

The rest of the day, in contrast, was unremarkable and he took her to the place where the longboats departed over half a century before. Harald looked down the river and out to sea where Bjorn had once led the diaspora of Maldon away from danger on the 'Voyage of Tears'. In his mind's eye he saw the desperate bloodied survivors struggling at their oars to get away on the tide. Beside him, Hedda was lost in her own world, and she prayed, giving thanks to the goddess Freya for the great sacrifice of the people. She looked up at him, still smiling radiantly.

"They shall not win, Lord," she said with great certainty. "Be patient, your grandmother shall have her victory."

The longhouse was empty when they returned that evening. There were no visitors and even Thomas and Gilbert were nowhere to be seen. Hedda prepared supper and they sat and ate before the great hearthfire.

Harald had not previously harboured any desire to make her his mistress but the day on Northey Island had changed all that. For the first time since her capture in Hereford he saw her in her own vibrant colours, as if she had shuffled off some dusty, old cloak to reveal herself to him. He had known a multitude of women in his lifetime and had always been comfortable and assured in their presence but there was something about Hedda that slightly unnerved him. It was clearly not enough to deter his growing fascination with her. He watched her bring a jug of wine, her catlike movements sending long, slow shadows across the room. She poured his wine, and he raised his cup to her without speaking.

"Lord, you need to take a wife," she said without preamble, causing Harald to splutter and spill his wine.

"Aelfgyva Godwin, you know of her?" he asked, recovering his poise.

"No, Lord, a real wife. One of flesh and blood who will warm your bed at night. She will be your sun and your moon. I do not know her name but trust me she will soon be at your door," she said dabbing at his tunic where he had spilt his wine, "but until then I know the person who will suffice until she comes to you."

She lifted her face to meet his gaze and he looked into her fierce blue eyes, knowing that things would never be the same between them again.

Inn matki munr, the great passion, devoured both of them that night and neither of them emerged from his bedchamber until midday. His squires and servants continued with their duties seemingly oblivious to the new mood in the longhouse which had changed so dramatically overnight. The boys no longer had to walk around as if on eggshells, although Thomas earned himself a cuff to the head for sniggering out of turn.

Harald was happy and content for the first time in a while. He knew that retrieving Richard from Northumbria would be difficult but not impossible and the news that Eleanor had delivered their child into the world safely had delighted him. He also knew that, beyond any doubt, the loyal Jeanotte would be here by Easter at the head of at least a thousand men. Hedda's unexpected arrival into his bed was a blessing that would see both of them through the long winter nights in joyful companionship. As the Fitzroy household approached the Yuletide festival with a feeling of cautious optimism, Harald knew better than most that the Norns could cut the cords that bound him to his fate within a single heartbeat.

Chapter 9: Long Live the King
Lundenvic, Christmas, 1065

1

Although Harald doubted the power of the christian God, there was something of a holy miracle witnessed when King Edward recovered from his malady enough to be able to attend the Christmas services in the newly built church of West Minster Abbey. The Lord of Maldon had been invited to the capital by the ailing monarch earlier in the year, and he now sat at the front of the congregation with the Saxon earls and thegns and their families. Harald sat between Earl Godwinson and the *Ætheling* Edgar as the packed church listened to the rich intonations of the Archbishop of Canterbury speaking from the pulpit on Christmas Day. Whilst most eyes were closed in prayer, Harald could not take his off the old king who sat slumped on a wooden throne in front of the altar facing the people. Beneath the thick ermine-trimmed cloak and regalia of his office, the King sat shaking as if from the cold. Below the crown that perched perilously on his nodding head with its sparse remnants of hair, King Edward slipped in and out of consciousness in a state of bewilderment.

Harald had not wished to travel to Lundenvic along the narrow, muddy road at this time of year but he was obligated. His thoughts drifted to Hedda in Maldon where he had left her in a warm bed three days ago. She did not want him to go but he knew he must and in the company of twelve cavalrymen, beneath a gonfalon bearing the papal colours, he led his party of Norman knights to the capital. He now sat with the peers of the realm watching the death throes of King Edward of England, wondering, as did so many others in the church, how events might unfold over the next few days. The banquet that followed was a stiff, regal affair unlike the many Yuletide feasts that Harald had attended in the past, but he did his duty and made polite conversation with the many important guests seated around his table. Despite endless jugs of wine, ale and mead, the occasion was muted as the people watched and waited for their monarch's inevitable demise. Cups were raised to the King and his crowning achievement, the Abbey, which had been consecrated earlier in the day. Harald looked across to Earl Godwinson in deep conversation with his brother Tostig, and wondered how many others at the vast banquet were also scheming. When King Edward was carried out by the members of his household, the occasion became a little more relaxed and drink flowed freely until Harald felt he no longer needed to stay. He excused himself and a servant showed him to his bedchamber in the palace and falling exhausted onto his bed, he was soon sound asleep.

      He had no engagements the following day other than to meet with the Earl of Wessex. The palace and buildings were crammed with people that Christmas, expecting the death of their monarch and it was no private agony which they shared. The Queen and her attendants, the King's Household, the Benedictine monks of the old foundation and the craftsmen who built the great edifice took up every available bit of space. The Witan had also been summoned and forty of the most important churchmen, earls, abbots and thanes, all with their retinues, gathered to deliberate on the future of the kingdom. Their difficult duty would very soon be to choose a new king.

      Harald met his namesake in a small anteroom in the abbey of West Minster, and despite the crowds elsewhere, the room was empty. The two men greeted each other cordially and shook hands.

"It will not be long, Hari. I would be surprised if the king lives another week," said Earl Godwinson, his face drawn and tired from lack of sleep.

"And has he given his blessing to his successor yet?" asked Harald.

"He has," replied Godwinson with the hint of a smile.

"And will the Witan endorse his choice?" continued Harald.

"They will have little choice," said the Earl confidently. "Can I still rely on your support?"

Harald nodded.

"The muster will be complete by Easter. We will be ready to meet whatever stands in our path," he replied.

"Then all will be well," said Godwinson, and the two men shook hands again and departed.

Harald made his way back to the palace to look for some breakfast.

"The cat will soon be amongst the pigeons," he said to himself quietly "and he will wreak havoc."

2

King Edward lasted until the first week in the New Year, attended by his wife, the Archbishop of Canterbury and Harald Godwinson, he died. On the day the old king was buried in his beloved abbey, the new monarch was crowned and King Harold of the Saxons ascended the English throne. He took the triple oath of peace, justice and mercy to his people, and his head was ceremoniously anointed by the Archbishop.

Harald led his party home to Maldon the next day on a grey, foggy morning, to the sound of monks singing in the nearby abbey. They walked their horses across the city and left by the Ald Gate.

"Long live the King," shouted Harald to the guards on the gate, huddled around a brazier as they passed through at a trot.

Brenier looked over at him, chuckling to himself and Harald regarded him sceptically.

"You doubt my sincerity, cousin?" he asked.

"Not I, Lord, but may I suggest you are keener to return home than you are to stay in Lundenvic celebrating the new king," said Brenier good-humouredly. "You seem to have more of a spring in your step on our return journey."

"And you will not be as keen to warm your new wife's bed?" said Harald with a grin. "Now, tell me again of your trip home I have many questions for you."

There was a two day ride ahead of them and their horses stepped ponderously through the quagmire that served as a road, negotiating the large pools of meltwater that gathered frequently along its uneven path.

Brenier had returned to Maldon on the *Lady Alberada* the morning the party was leaving for Lundenvic. No sooner had he landed than Harald had ordered him to mount up and join them. They had had little time to talk on the journey to the city such was their haste but on the return trip home their pace was a good deal more leisurely, allowing the two men to talk at length.

The journey to Normandie had been a fruitful one and Brenier was delighted to report that Harald's fiefdom in Ambrières was in robust good health under Jeanotte's leadership. The borders of Normandie were safe and secure and no report of any hostilities on 'the *Marches*' had occurred since Harald's departure. When the ships arrived in Normandie in the spring, there would be at least twelve hundred men ready and willing to cross the narrow sea for 'the English campaign', as Jeanotte named it. Furthermore, he anticipated there would be no problems leaving the Duchy, and the remaining garrison would be more than adequate to cope with any matters arising from Ambrières.

Brenier travelled to Mortain to deliver news of Robert and Eleanor's son, Richard. When he arrived at the castle, he discovered that Lady Eleanor had been joined by her husband returning from Caen for the christening of the Fitzroy's fourth child. At first Brenier had been a little circumspect when he learned that Robert was at home, but any doubts were soon dispelled after the Count welcomed his cousin warmly.

"They both asked me many more questions about Richard than I could answer but I think they were satisfied that he is safe."

"And how was my brother in his wife's company?" asked Harald. "Was there animosity between them?"

Brenier thought for a moment and shook his head.

"None that was obvious. Robert could always mask his feelings but Eleanor never could. Perhaps they have both accepted what neither of them can change?" ventured his cousin.

"Spoken like a true Byzantine philosopher," mocked Harald, "and you say mother and son are both in good health."

"Indeed, young Thurstan is a happy and contented child and his mother is besotted with him. I slipped the bracelet to her when we were alone and she accepted it with good grace. She said nothing more but before I left she asked me to give you this," said Brenier reaching into his tunic to retrieve a locket that contained a tiny, lock of a baby's hair.

Chapter 10: The Duke's Bitter News
Rouen, Normandie, January 1066

1

At the request of his wife, Duke William had taken his winter court to Rouen to spend the Christmas festival. The old capital of Normandie was Malthilda's favourite city and she had prevailed over her husband to move into the comfortable surrounds of the Episcopal Palace for the cold winter months. It had been a pleasant but uneventful season, and the ducal couple looked forward to the time when they would be King and Queen of England. When the news came from over the narrow sea it was not what they had been expecting.

The day had started with the gathering of the Duke's companions and counsellors on the flag stones in front of his palace. A gap in the foul winter weather enabled the first hunt of the year and twenty-five fur-swaddled hunters stood waiting for the hounds to arrive. It was bitterly cold and Normandie had been covered with snow and ice since November. Jugs of mulled wine were served to the huntsmen, anticipating an exciting day's sport. Blades were whetted and bows were strung as a mid-winter sun struggled into the sky, providing light but little warmth for the first time in the new year. It did not take long for the mood to change.

The news from England reached Normandie very quickly and broke like a bursting dam on a sleeping village. A messenger arrived on an English ship and approached the Duke of Normandie who was in deep conversation with Robert Fitzroy. They looked up together at the man who stood before them.

"Speak," commanded William to the Englishman.

"King Edward is dead, and Harold is raised to the Kingdom," he said in a deep voice that carried around the hushed courtyard.

William looked from the messenger to his Chancellor with a look of bemusement.

"Harold Godwinson is King of England?" asked Robert in disbelief.

"Yes, my Lords. The old King was buried, and the new King crowned only four days ago," said the messenger nervously watching the Duke's face blacken with violent, uncontrollable anger. His rage was beyond anything Robert Fitzroy had ever experienced from his liege-lord in over thirty years of service.

"This cannot be," screamed William, beginning a spit-flecked tirade that threatened vengeance with every word.

The messenger blanched visibly, and Robert put a gentle, restraining arm on the Duke's shoulder as he screamed in the Englishman's face.

"Please, my Lord, he is only the messenger. Let us go inside - we should discuss this in private."

Duke William turned on his heel and, speechless with fury, ascended the steps to the palace three at a time and disappeared from view. The astonished huntsmen looked at Robert, who composing himself, spoke in a clear, untroubled voice.

"Gentlemen, there will be no hunt today. I shall contact you all as soon as we have clarified matters."

He turned and went inside in search of his liege lord and found him seated on a bench in the chapel, his head resting against the cool of a marble pillar.

"William," said Robert, sitting down next to the Duke, "this is no time for grieving. You have been bitterly betrayed; something must be done and God will deliver justice. Speak to me, for we must make a plan to ensure the English throne is yours."

The Duke looked at him, and speaking in voice that exuded both clarity and singularity of purpose he said,

"The Saxons shall suffer for this, Robert, upon my dear mother's grave and on the heads of my wife and children I swear vengeance on this usurper Harald Godwinson. Do we still have his sons?"

"Indeed. Wolfnoth and Hakon Godwinson are hostage in Caen."

"Well, they shall be the first to suffer for the sins of their father. Do not spare them," said the Duke menacingly. "Now please leave me, I need God's guidance in this matter. Call a council meeting for this afternoon and we shall sit together and make our plan."

Robert bowed his head and went without a further word. He left the chapel and wandered out through the numerous anterooms back onto the courtyard where the hunters had been gathering only an hour before. The promising early morning sun, presaging so much, had been replaced by a thick freezing fog that descended without warning. Guards huddling around a brazier saluted the Chancellor as he drew his cloak about him. Robert had not been the slightest bit surprised by the news from England and had always harboured a suspicion that Earl Godwinson would renege on his promised fealty to the Duke. It seemed like everyone in the Duchy, from his highest baron to the humblest ploughboy, had expected the Saxons to name William their King, but the messenger's earlier announcement had only confirmed Robert's suspicions that the Duke had been duped. There would now be a considerable price to pay, and William would demand justice for this public betrayal. Robert knew his liege lord was a primitive and barbarous man who had pacified the rebellious warlords of Normandie by bending them to his iron will without mercy. However, in his heart of hearts, he had always doubted that his master was what England needed or wanted. A voice from behind him interrupted his thoughts.

"We should not be completely surprised," said Archbishop Pavin. "England is a jewel that many covert, after all. Harold Godwinson was just quicker than the other pretenders to the throne."

Robert span around and recognising the hooded figure of his friend, smiled and held his hand out in greeting.

"Whatever the reason, for fifteen years the Duke has believed the English throne was his by right. He cannot and will not accept this without a fight, for to do anything else will make him look weak and foolish," replied Robert quietly, ensuring they were out of earshot.

"Indeed, it is pride that drives our leader, an eminence that will ensure a dangerous enterprise which none of us want - much less the Duke himself," replied Lanfranc. "What next, Robert? You are closest of any of us to the man. What shall be your counsel?"

"You flatter me, my Lord. Our Duke listens only to his own heart now and very soon we will be back at war," replied Robert flatly. "All I can do is make sure we are in a condition that allows us to prevail."

"Then with God's will, we shall, my friend," replied the Archbishop. "God favours the brave - and the just."

Robert ordered the counsel to meet in the early afternoon and it was well into the evening before the barons and churchmen were allowed to return to their quarters. William was clearly in a truculent mood and the men sitting around the table of the great hall listened intently at the Duke's tirade. Harald Godwinson was a perjurer and a usurper, they were told, and it was the moral duty of the Duchy of Normandie to do God's will and kill him. Not only this but he had also reneged on his promise to wed the Duke's daughter, Agatha, adding further to his list of felonies. There would be holy war against the English, he promised, and the Church of Rome would not stand idly by while the Saxon King spouts his blasphemy. It was at this point that he looked to the Archbishop of Caen, inviting him to give his thoughts.

"My Lord, you have the unequivocal support of the Holy See and with the news of this betrayal I cannot see Pope Alexander changing his mind."

"Well, you will travel to Rome to make sure he does not, Lanfranc. Our crusade might depend on his repeated blessing," ordered the Duke and looked around at the rest of the assembled Lords. "Now, gentlemen, it seems we will be fighting a war across the narrow sea before long and I will need every man and horse you can supply. As always, I rely heavily on our Chancellor for his support, and who will doubtless have considered all our options. Lord Robert, please give us your counsel."

For the first time since the meeting started William smiled, putting a hand on his friend's shoulder. Robert took a deep breath and spoke.

"I am sure we all share in the Duke's righteous anger and our response must be swift and clear. We must provide at least ten thousand men and a thousand ships by the end of the summer - probably more - if we are to go to war in England," said Robert to a sharp intake of breath around the table.

Duke William interrupted and banged his fist on the heavy oak surface.

"Do not sound so surprised, my lords, the Lord of Mortain tells us only what we already know, surely?" he asked, looking around malevolently at the other barons.

"But first, may I suggest that we send a message to the English court and allow 'King' Harold to fulfil his promises and step aside for the rightful heir to the throne. The Duke is a man of wisdom and honour, after all, and it might not be too late for the 'pretender' to recant," said Robert in a conciliatory tone to which many heads nodded.

"And if he does not?" asked the Duke.

"Then England will be consumed in the fire of our crusade and we shall take what is rightfully ours," said Robert.

"I concur," said the Duke after a moment of thoughtful deliberation. "We will meet here in four weeks and each of you will commit your holy word to the number of men and ships that you will provide. If Godwinson does not reconsider, we will be sailing for England by the summer. If anyone here harbours any doubts - say now?"

The Duke looked each man in the face, searching for any sign of doubt or dissent and seeing none, he called the meeting to an end, dismissing his silent barons.

Chapter 11: Old Skills Rekindled
Regneville, January, 1066

The journey to Regneville from Rouen was cold and bleak, fierce winds sending angry clouds, black with rain, scudding across the sky. It was only when Robert looked down from the hill overlooking the town that he realised how much he missed the place. He envied his brother Floki who lived a simple existence here, far removed from the bitter politics of Caen and Rouen. His younger sibling had not been made to swear to protect the young Duke as had he and Harald, so many years ago, and Floki was probably all the happier for that. The ride had been long and uncomfortable but above all necessary, and he was desperate to get some news of the progress of the ship building he had commissioned. He strained his eyes through the gloom to see the winking lights from the houses guiding the company home.

He was challenged when he approached the castle gates before the captain of the guard recognised him and called a welcome from up high on the walls. By the time Robert reached the keep his brother was there to welcome him and, dismissing his men, he hurried through thick oak doors and out of the bitter cold. The two men embraced fondly.

"We had given you up for lost, brother," said Floki, "we expected you a couple of days ago. Perhaps you are getting a little old for these long rides."

Robert snorted with derision.

"You are lucky to see me at all, little brother - the roads around here could swallow a horse and rider whole."

"Nonsense! However a man of your age cannot be too careful on these rough tracks," jested his brother. "Now come let's get you some warm wine and a seat by the hearthfire and then I have something to show you - that is if your old bones will allow another trip this evening."

A little later the two brothers sat next to each other in the hall of the shipyard on the stone quay by the sea. A great fire burned in the centre of the floor throwing out heat and light to the men gathered around the table. Olaf Knarresmed and this three sons sat opposite as an old woman brought bread, cheese and beer to the table. When she finally shuffled off, Olaf got to his feet and cleared his throat.

"My Lords," he announced formally as if addressing a gathering of the kings and queens of Europe. "It is with great honour and joy that I can reveal the fruits of our labour."

"Father, please let us not delay" declared Kjartan Knarresmed in kindly tone, "Lord Robert has travelled far to see what we have built. Let us not keep him waiting."

"Very well, light the way and let us not be shy. Gentlemen, forgive my prevarication," said Olaf with a theatrical bow.

His three sons disappeared into the gloom and reappeared with large lanterns, casting light on the rest of the hall. The hulls of five longships, supported on wooden spales were revealed. As the party drew closer the air was filled with the smells of newly milled wood; the mossy aroma of sawn oak mingled with the resinous tang of pine.

"Behold," said Olaf waving dramatically to the five identical *skieds*. "These craft will make you proud. Each one is fifty paces long from prow to stern, double ended and will take a big sail. They will accommodate forty seated oarsmen and there is room for another fifty to sixty men at a push."

He touched the hull of one of the ships, running a gnarled old hand over the clinkered planks of oak.

"We'll finish caulking them in the next couple of days and they'll be ready to go to sea. The masts and keels are already built, and the sails were delivered yesterday. What do you think, my young Lords?" said Olaf with a toothless grin.

Robert looked at his brother and for the first time in a long while, he burst into long and joyful laughter. He turned back to the new ships and walked the length of the nearest one, running a hand over the long planking from bow to stern.

"You have worked wonders," shouted Robert to the Knarresmed men who watched him in anticipation. His approval set off an eruption of exited chatter as each of them spoke at once. Olaf held up his old hands calling for quiet.

"We are only glad to have been of service, Lord. Now let us return to the table and drink to the health of these fine ladies. We have plenty of good wine to chase away the winter sprites and much to discuss," said Olaf.

The shipwright of Regneville had been busy, tirelessly working away with his sons, building and initiating the local carpenters in their craft. After a trepidatious start, the framework of the first hull was laid down and the work gathered pace, their combined output becoming highly productive. Skilled hands could work quickly, Olaf told them, provided the raw materials were there to be worked.

"A hundred and fifty ships by summer?" Robert asked cautiously.

Olaf rubbed his chin, pulling at his unkempt, grey beard. He fired off a barrage of questions to his sons in the old Norske language they used together.

"It can be done, but I shall need a lot more men, wood and silver," he said finally.

"And you shall have it, Olaf," declared Robert raising his cup. "To your skill and fortitude. May the craft of our ancestors never be forgotten."

It was late when the Fitzroys returned to the solar in the castle's keep. The tallow candles burned low as they made their way to their bedchambers. As he always did Robert prayed before he lay down to sleep and losing himself in his devotions, he asked God for many things, guidance, humility and above all forgiveness for him and his family. Sleep did not come to him easily that night and he tossed and turned on his cot, calculating the numbers of men and *materiel* needed for the forthcoming campaign in England. It was in the small hours of morning before he finally fell into a deep and impenetrable sleep.

He met his mother and father for breakfast shortly after sunrise and Floki joined them. As ever, Sigrid Fitzroy greeted her eldest son with warmth and affection before admonishing him for not visiting home more often. Then she bombarded him with questions about her grandchildren which he answered patiently until his father interceded with questions of his own.

"The news from England is not good, then?" asked Torstein. "I am still advisor to the Duke. Tell me all I need to know. If there is war coming you will need every hour that God gives you to plan for success. We will share the burden as we have always done, as a family"

Robert told him all the news from Rouen and his father, having listened intently throughout, spoke again.

"Ten thousand fighting men might be enough but you will need luck and fair weather to prevail over the Saxons. If Duke William is as hell-bent on this venture as I suspect he is, there is little point in persuading him otherwise. Your main challenge will be to convince all the *baronie* that their fealty extends to fighting battles over the sea. Are the council members firm in their support?

Robert nodded slowly as he considered each of the barons.

"I believe so, Father. De Beaumont, Gifford, de Montford, Roger Montgomery, Warren, Fitzosborn. None have wavered yet."

"Not enough. You will need many more and foreign venture can be a costly affair. I can almost hear the dissenting voices," said Torstein cynically. "You can of course count on the Riders of Regneville."

"We will provide at least five hundred men and horses," rejoined Floki, "and one hundred and fifty ships."

"You approve of Olaf's work, Robert?" asked their father.

"Who could not admire the craftsmanship, but we must harvest trees from all the great forests around the Duchy to build more," he replied.

"Indeed. If I can live with a smaller forest to hunt in, so can all the great lords of the Duchy. Regneville will provide what we must. Now, what of Hari? He has always answered Normandie's call to arms, in spite of what the Duke thinks of him," asked his father.

"I have not had news of him directly, but he sent word to Mortain that he has settled in Maldon and that your grandson is safe and well," replied Robert.

"Ah, yes, I heard Brenier brought word from England but perhaps it is now time for a more direct intervention with your brother?"

Robert did not reply, his thoughts returning to the bloody memories of his last encounter with Harald Fitzroy.

Chapter 12: The Great Norman Muster
Mortain, January 1066

1

The company's horses made the last of their journey from Regneville to Mortain on tired legs. The mud that had sapped their energy throughout the fifteen leagues journey had taken its toll, and the dirt-spattered animals walked slowly up the final hill to the castle overlooking the town. Their riders were equally tired and there was not a man amongst them who was not looking forward to warming himself by the refectory's hearthfire with a cup of wine in his hand.

"We have made good time, comrades," shouted Robert as they reached the cobbled courtyard in front of the keep. "Now go and refresh yourselves. We will be staying put for a few days."

A small army of stable boys took the weary horses off to be rubbed down, fed and stabled for the evening. Robert looked up to his family's solar and wondered what sort of reception he might receive from his estranged wife on this visit. In truth, he reflected, the atmosphere between them on his last return had not been quite so strained and whilst the ice between them remained, at least there had been less hostility. They had been civil to one another and at the christening ceremony of her son they had stood together in the church for the first time in many years without so much as an angry word or an embittered glance. After Brenier's visit they had both delighted in the news of their eldest son's wellbeing and the promise of his return home before too long. Tonight he was hopeful of joining his family for supper and was pleased to find them all sitting at table, about to start to eat.

The children welcomed him energetically and he returned their fond embraces. His wife cordially invited him to sit with them and he sat at the far end of the table opposite her. She asked Robert to say 'grace' before a substantial meal of pottage, veal and duck was put in front of them. He chatted to Richard and Turid throughout and the children responded enthusiastically to their father's questions. Robert stole the odd glance at his wife as he listened and noticed the return of her healthy pallor following the problematic childbirth.

"It is good to see you looking well once more, Eleanor," he said.

He registered the look of surprise at the compliment, and she forced a smile. No more was said between them, but after the final fruit and jellies were consumed with gusto by the children he called the maid and asked her to take them off. When his wife got up to leave, he stopped her.

"Please, Eleanor. May I have a moment of your time?"

She nodded demurely and when there were only the two of them left alone, he cleared his throat to speak.

"Things between us have not been easy," he began, "and my duty to the Duke and the long periods away from home have caused you great anguish. For that I apologise and ask for your forgiveness. I cannot condone or forgive you for lying with my brother, but what is done cannot be undone. I am not a proud man but this has caused me great pain."

She interrupted him but he held up his hand.

"Please, let me finish," he asked softly. "I have treated you harshly in my anger and have been little more than your gaoler. For this cruelty I also ask your forgiveness. You are a good mother and deserve better. I know you sent our son away with Hari because you feared for your own safety, but let me reassure you that you no longer have any cause for alarm. I pray for Richard's safe return home to his family."

He looked over at her and saw tears rolling down her cheeks.

"I promise you that I will treat your new son, Thurstan as my own and he will have no less privileges than his siblings. You are no longer under the scrutiny of my servants and any restrictions I have placed on you are lifted. I will treat you with respect and consideration as a decent husband should and you may come and go as you wish," he said, pausing to finish the statement.

"But…?" asked Eleanor.

"But, if you decide to leave me and join my brother our children must remain here, and you shall never see them again."

There was silence as she digested his words before nodding slowly.

"Thankyou for your candour, Robert," Eleanor replied as calmly as she could and looking him directly in the eyes continued. "I, too, long for the return of my first born and will do whatever is necessary to keep my family together."

Then, she excused herself, left the room and went in search of her children. When she closed the door on her way out Robert expelled a huge sigh. It was partly in despair at what he had lost and partly relief at the prospect that his domestic turmoil might, in some small way, be coming to an end. He spent the remainder of the evening alone in quiet reflection, and when the last logs of the fire had burnt down, he realised how tired he was and made his way to his bed.

2

Rolande of Coutances was one of the Count of Mortain's most trusted friends. From an early age Robert had served as his squire and the two had ridden to war many times together. Rolande had taught the young Fitzroy how to fight and win on the battlefield, lessons that had served him well in dozens of conflicts. For his part, Robert had been generous with his rewards and the loyal Marshal of Mortain could always be relied upon.

Robert found his friend and mentor in the castle yard. The sun had only recently started its ascent into the sky but the old knight had already been hard at work instructing swordplay to a dozen young pages. His face was coated in sweat which, in spite of the freezing temperature, ran in rivulets into his thick grey beard. The object of his sword play was a cloth dummy stuffed with straw and set on a rotating pole at the height of a man. After demonstrating a variety of cuts to the 'enemy' soldier's body the first six boys were ordered to 'attack' the dummy directly in front of them. They stepped forward unleashing a flurry of blows on their hapless victims, one of which swung round and knocked the assailant flying, encouraging a stream of invective from their instructor. The boy was saved from any more of the tirade by Robert's approach and Rolande looked up and raised his sword in salute to his liege lord.

"Boys, you will do battle in pairs with wooden swords until breakfast - but not before you are fully padded - I want no broken bones or faces requiring stitches," barked Rolande to his charges, before turning back to the Lord of Mortain. "I heard you come in last night, Robert - I thought you might be joining me and your old comrades for a cup of wine."

"Sadly not - but tonight is different and I am duly refreshed and will be ready to take my place in the great hall with you all," came the reply.

"What do you think of your new warriors," asked Rolande, waving his sword at the mêlée of seven- and eight-year-old boys hacking away at each other.

"I am sure that under your tutelage they will be ready to fight before too long. It is good to see the 'Marshal' still taking such a personal interest in their development," said Robert.

"I seemed to remember that both you and Hari benefitted from the experience - that is whenever your brother could be persuaded to listen to me."

The two men laughed and shook hands.

"Do you think I might drag you away from your pupils for a while."

"Of course. Let's go into the refectory and get breakfast before these young pups get there and eat everything," replied Rolande, before issuing a final set of instructions to the battling pages.

They were some of the first men to arrive and sat down at a bench and table in the corner of the empty room where they would be out of earshot. A servant arrived with bread and ale and curtsied clumsily when she saw that it was the Lord of Mortain at the table.

"This year will be an interesting one. There will be war and we shall have to travel to England to find it," said Robert perfunctorily. Mortain will be sending five hundred mounted men on ships that we will also be providing."

The older man spluttered into his cup of ale.

"We will send men of course - but ships? What do we know of shipbuilding here? We are at least twenty-five leagues from the sea and most people here have never set foot on board let alone sailed to sea. As for building them we know nothing of the shipwrights craft which died out with our fathers and grandfathers," blustered Rolande.

"Calm yourself, my friend. I would like you to gather up the best carpenters in Mortain and send them to Regneville with the tools of their trade. They will be well rewarded, and they will build ships under the guidance of shipwrights in that town. The lost skills are being rekindled, and we must all play our part," answered Robert calmly. "We also need oak - lots of it - and trees from the forest will need to be culled in great number and sent on wagons on to the sea. We will ride out today and decide where our wood cutters will begin."

The older man shook his head in disbelief.

"You are still full of surprises, Robert and it is no wonder the Duke relies on you so heavily. How long do we have to accomplish the task?" asked Rolande.

"Early summer at the latest. Do not worry, the same exercise will be going on the length and breadth of the Duchy and we shall prevail as we always have done," answered his friend.

They left shortly after breakfast and rode along the River Cance, travelling deep into the nearby forest to an area where ancient oak trees were plentiful. The following day men from the town arrived with saws and axes and began the great harvest. A large area of woodland was cleared and the huge trunks sawn into shape, loaded onto wagons and taken seaward, where the shipwrights and carpenters awaited their arrival.

Chapter 13: The Warrior Maiden
Maldon, England February 1066

1

It had not taken long for Hedda Halldorsdottir to establish herself as the head of Harald's household. It had taken a little longer for her to become his mistress, something that she had neither planned nor foreseen despite her prowess as a *seiðun,* which he had sworn to keep secret. The serving women feared her presence and their jealousy fuelled a great deal of hearthside gossip throughout the long winter months. However, whatever they thought of her did not matter, for their master found himself spending more and more time with Hedda during the cold, dark mid-winter months. The Christmas festivals had come and gone, the Lord of Maldon spending his days hunting with his hawks or his hounds. He made a point of rising early to train at arms with his men, before disappearing into the forest or marshlands in search of deer, boar or the hares to which his falcons were so partial. Come the evening, he would spend the first hours drinking in the company of his comrades before returning home to Hedda and her welcoming bed. It was not as if he had forgotten Eleanor and he thought of her often, longing for the day when he could return Richard to his mother. As time passed, he knew in his heart that she would never be free of Mortain or Normandie, and it would take an intervention by the gods to reunite them. In the meantime, his new mistress occupied much of his time, and what had begun as a beguiling diversion was turning into something quite different. Their affection for one another was strong, and when the great passion of their love making had passed, they would talk of their families, their people and their history.

Then, one dank February morning as a sea-mist hung over the town, the first ship of the new year arrived into the harbour. A longboat, expertly rowed by forty oarsmen emerged from the fog and tied up on the stone quay. It carried no cargo but a man wearing an expensive wolf skin coat, who stepped nimbly down onto to the quay, enquired where he might find the house of Harald Fitzroy. The tall, well-dressed Norwegian, made his way through the town as another day began, the smoke from hundreds of cooking fires mingling with the fog. He knocked at the door of the longhouse and was taken to a seat by the hearthfire, where he was given food and drink. Harald emerged from his chambers and walked toward the visitor, taking in his well-groomed appearance and confident manner.

"Lord Fitzroy, I am Jarl Oystein of Bergen. I hope I am not disturbing you too early in the day. I come from the court of King Harald of Norway who sends you his greetings," he said as he rose and bowed low from the waist?

"*Góð dagr, Jarl Oystein, þú eru mjök welcome*," replied Harald.

Oystein smiled at the response.

"Ah, you still speak the mother tongue," said Oystein. "So many of our people forget it when they leave Norway and settle elsewhere ."

"It is the language of my grandparents now, but I do not have much opportunity to practice it," said Harald. "You have come a long distance when the seas are at their least friendly and I am honoured and intrigued by your visit."

"I shall get straight to the point, Lord. My King has a trusted friend in his court who is known to both of us. Halldor Snorrasson?" said the Jarl choosing his words carefully. "He says you are friendly to the King's intentions and might be disposed to offering him support in his forthcoming venture?"

"Halldor has been a friend, but not for so long. We must all be careful in these uncertain times so I would be happy to speak freely if there was some way of verifying that you are who you say are."

Oystein smiled and pulled out a ring from his tunic.

"This is Halldor's ring, my Lord. He said you would recognise it as his."

Harald took the gold ring with its black garnet stone in the shape of a raven's head and inspected it.

"It looks familiar," said Harald. "But come, I am forgetting my manners. Please return to the fireside to warm yourself. The old whale road is bitter at this time of year and you are welcome to such comforts as my house can provide. When you are warm, I must take my leave of you briefly, and you should return here for supper to be properly fed and quartered. What do you say?"

"I should be delighted," replied Oystein with a smile, and they both sat down at the bench and felt the comfort of the roaring fire.

When the Norwegian left, Harald called to the far end of the longhouse and Hedda stepped out of the shadows and walked towards him.

"You heard most of that?" he asked, putting the ring into the palm of her hand.

She nodded and inspected it.

"It is my father's and that man is who he says he is. He is Harald Hardrada's man and speaks for him," she said confidently. "He is also known as Silvertongue and will report back to his master every word that is spoken."

"Then I shall be on my guard, Hedda. It is a complicated game we are playing."

Oystein returned as the light was leaving the day and he came with a gift for his host, an elegant carving of two ravens made from the ivory of a walrus tusk. Harald thanked him and inspected the sculpture, running his fingers over the delicate object and turning it in his hands .

"It is a fine piece of work. A gift to grace the gods of Asgard," said Harald delightedly.

"Your grandfather's legacy will be long remembered in Norway, and the 'Saga of the Wandering Warriors' is often told around the hearthfire. Were they truly Odin's Ravens walking as men?" asked Oystein earnestly.

Harald chuckled at the notion.

"Nothing more than skaldic legend, I think, but a fine story nonetheless."

They were interrupted by Hedda, carrying two cups of wine. She wore a simple blue woollen dress, and had braided her fine fair hair into long plaits, reaching down her back.

"And this is Hedda Halldorsottir," said Harald, noticing Oystein's admiring look at his mistress.

"Your father sends his greetings and looks forward to being reunited with you soon,"said the Norwegian politely.

Hedda nodded back courteously to the Jarl, who continued to smile radiantly at her. She thanked him for the message and left them.

"A rare beauty," said Oystein when she left the room, "the Jarl of Rogoland is a lucky man."

"She has been a welcome addition to my household. I shall be sad to see her go. Now come I am keen to hear your news from Norway - your King is a man of great reputation is he not?"

Harald led his guest to the table and the two men sat and talked as the servant women, under the strict guidance of their new mistress, provided a constant supply of food and drink. It was not long before Oystein drew their conversation around to the new King of England, and in the diplomatic manner in which he had conducted himself, asked Harald for his thoughts on the new monarch.

"An opportunist, I feel, but no less than the rest of us," he said plainly, fixing the Jarl with a steely gaze, "Now come, Jarl Oystein, we have some real business to discuss, I think. Your master has a claim on the English crown, and I can help him to seize it. I can put an army of Norman cavalry at his disposal if he so desires. This you know, otherwise you would not be here, but I must know his intentions before I can make this pledge to him."

"And the cost of your fealty, Lord?" asked the visitor.

"The safe return of my nephew," answered Harald, "Oh, and a share of the plunder."

"The King welcomes your support. You are a man after his own heart," replied Oystein after a moment's thought, producing a vellum map from the leather bag he had brought with him.

He cleared a space on the table and spread it out, pointing to where the Norwegians would land come summer. Harald Hardrada planned to land his host at a rallying point on the Northumbrian coast, where he would make camp. From here his army would begin to raze the countryside along the coast, steadily moving southward, forcing the Saxons to try and stop his progress. The King's first major target was to retake the old Norse capital of Yorvic and when this was done, he would shatter each of the Saxon armies that were sent to deny him. Oystein spoke with an almost evangelical fervour as he described Hardrada's plans, using his hands and arms to accentuate the inexorable progress of the Norwegian army as it swept south toward Lundenvic.

"A bold plan," said Harald looking down at the map in consideration, "but one that relies on speed and rapid troop deployment. The fleet will need to move quickly down the Northumbrian coastline to be effective. Are you sure that the Saxon commanders can be drawn out so quickly."

"Oh, yes," said the Norwegian confidently, "my Lord has the Saxon King's brother in his thrall. There is little that this man has not revealed."

Harald laughed at the revelation.

"Ah, Tostig Godwinson. A man of little honour and a great lust for power. Let us drink to favourable winds and greedy turncoats," he said, raising a cup of wine to his guest.

"And to the next King of England," replied Oystein, his eyes shining like a zealot.

2

Harald's guest stayed for two days. Oystein of Bergen proved entertaining company and was full of good stories. He was keen to know about the size of the Saxon army and its fighting capabilities and Harald told him everything he knew. He took the Jarl hunting and along with Brenier, Rolf, Leif and the two squires they spent a fruitful day in the forest returning at dusk with the carcass of a large boar on their wagon. A feast had been organised and that evening the longhouse was filled with Harald's comrades. There were still several barrels of wine and ale that had survived the Christmas festival intact and the cohort from Normandie made short work of them. As the evening wore on songs were sung and stories told, and the Lord of Maldon was inevitably called upon to recite the Saga of the Wandering Warriors. He received a thunderous applause at its conclusion and then called for Hedda to come and sing for his guests. She protested at first, but her master would not take 'no' for an answer, and he called for quiet before picking her up as if she weighed no more than a small child and putting her on the table. With a little encouragement she began to sing the first tremulous lines of 'Emla's Journey' but as she continued her voice got stronger until the room resonated with the melodious sound of her voice.

> *Once again she sees the earth rise up*
> *from the ocean, lush and green.*
> *Waterfalls cascade, an eagle soars above,*
> *one who hunts fish upon the mountain*
> *She sees a hall stand more radiant than the sun,*
> *adorned with gold and silver.*
> *And there her lover waits patiently*
> *To wrap her in his ardent embrace*

She finished her song and the guests shouted their appreciation and clapped loudly, even louder than they had done for the previous performance.

"I cannot compete with entertainment like that," shouted Harald and swept her off the table and into an ardent embrace, drawing even more applause.

The rest of the evening heard more songs sung and tales told, and Oystein needed little persuasion to recite 'The Death of Baldr' to a drunken audience. Finally, when the guests had supped their fill and the words to songs and sagas could no longer be remembered, the fire had burned low and the evening petered out. Those who could make it staggered off to their homes and quarters while others simply slept where they fell, sharing the floor with the hunting hounds. The Lord of Maldon, however, was not one of the drunkards, and taking Hedda's proffered hand he was happily led to his chambers.

He rose early the next morning and walked with his guest to the waiting longship. The Norwegians left as soon as the Jarl was aboard, and Harald watched it as the oarsmen pulled out into the channel and on past Northey Island toward the open sea. Then he pulled his cloak around him tightly against the winter chill that seemed to be coming directly from the North Sea, and walked back to the longhouse deep in thought. He arrived as the last of the evening's revellers had roused themselves and were on their way home and they called their thanks for his hospitality. He was gratified to find the servants had rekindled the hearthfire and took a seat close by, holding out his hands to feel its warmth. Hedda came to sit by his side.

"I had no idea you had such a fine voice," he complimented her.

"There is much about me that you do not know," she said and returned his smile.

"And I am delighted to discover all your secrets," he answered. "The land of ice and fire clearly produces women with hidden virtues."

"Some women have secrets that are worth discovering, some women do not ," she said coolly before changing the subject. "You have agreed to join forces with the King of Norway."

"You know I have. We shall meet at the muster point in the summer," he replied.

"Take me with you when you go. I do not wish to stay here without you."

Harald shook his head.

"No, Hedda. The battlefield is no place for a woman," he said sternly. "I do not want to return a corpse to your father."

"I can fight well enough - even for a woman," she said defiantly, "and anyway, I do not want to return to Norway to marry a fat old man. Besides when you retrieve your nephew, I can take care of him while you have your revenge on the Saxons," she insisted.

He shook his head again but knowing how obdurate she could be, he relented.

"Very well, I will give it some thought," he declared.

She made herself scarce for the rest of the day and they did not see one another until later that evening. When she bought his supper, she put the food and drink in front of him and sat opposite watching. He ate in silence and when he had eaten his fill, he pushed his plate away and looked at her. She returned his gaze with large, beseeching eyes.

"I will take you with me on one condition - that you learn how to fight. Your training will begin tomorrow," he said sternly.

Hedda proved to be a willing pupil and the next day at first light her instruction began. Gilbert was given the job of working with her and the first hours of his day, from then on, were spent teaching the housekeeper how to fight with a sword. Harald picked out a light blade and watched her and his squire work diligently as she grappled with the rudiments of swordplay.

Every day Hedda was the first to rise in the house and would be waiting for her tutor to join her and the air would ring with the sound of blade on blade.

As the days grew longer Harald focused on the serious business of preparing Maldon for the influx of at least a thousand fighting men. A new blacksmith's forge was built, and many more smiths were recruited to cope with the demands of shoeing horses and repairing weapons that the arriving army would bring with them. The garrison's barracks were extended, new latrines dug, and temporary stables erected. When Jeanotte arrived the size of the town would double, and food and grain would be needed in great quantities; Clifford the Steward was kept busy from dawn to dusk.

At least twenty new ships were required and Harald travelled to Lundenvic with a bag full of gold. He found what he needed on the quayside of the old city and procured a small fleet of sturdy-looking cogs from a Hanseatic trader who was looking for a quick sale. While he was in the capital, he visited the royal court in West Minster to update his new liege lord on the progress of the muster and request news on his nephew. They met in private and King Harold told him that word had been received from Normandie; Duke William had asked him to reconsider his decision to take the throne. The two men had laughed at the arrogance of the suggestion. They both knew the likely outcome and that when the weather calmed the narrow sea there would be war. When he enquired about his nephew, King Harold reassured him that the boy was safe and well in the service of Earl Morcar and reiterated that Richard would be released back to him as soon as the Kingdom was safe. It was a brief meeting, no longer than it should have been, and safe in the knowledge that he knew everything he needed Harald made his way quickly to the banks of the river, where Brenier and his men were waiting.

"All will soon be ready," he said to himself, standing at the helm of the first of the ships that would bring his men from Normandie to Maldon. He led the little fleet along the Tamsye River and across its estuary toward the open sea. Where the river currents met the incoming tide, the wind blew harder, and he felt the exhilaration of sea spray hitting his face. It had been a while since he sailed across the narrow sea to Maldon, and he realised how much he had missed the freedom of this life. It would not be long before he would be sailing to war with his comrades and, despite his years, the thought of the new campaign filled him with excitement. He knew, as he had always known, that he was destined to live and die the life of a warrior. He also knew that a new chapter of his life was about to begin and he was completely unsure of how it would conclude.

3

The hauberk, helm and sword sat in a neat pile on the table in front of them. Hedda had just finished two hours of swordplay with Gilbert and despite the freezing weather she was covered in sweat beneath her padded leather *gambeson* and woollen trousers. Her efforts to learn how to fight had not gone unnoticed and although Harald had said little about her progress, he had been impressed by the way she continued at her lessons. Her body had slowly changed shape and her soft, willowy limbs became harder and more defined with the constant repetition of working with sword and shield. Today she was sporting a black eye from colliding with the rim of Gilbert's shield.

"I have something for you, Hedda. If you are to become a Norman warrior we cannot have you dressed like a Saxon peasant when we go to war. Now let's see what you look like dressed in your new finery. Try it for size to begin with," Harald said, pushing the small, scabbarded sword toward her.

Her eyes lit up with delight, taking the weapon and unsheathing it in a single fluid movement. She smiled broadly at the finely crafted blade, testing its balance in either hand and nodded her satisfaction.

"It was made for a Frankish princess, but the merchant did not say what happened to her," he added with a laugh. "Now for the *hauberk*. I told the smith to make it as light as possible without losing any strength."

He helped her on with the long chain mail shirt which reached her knees and she winced at the weight of the garment.

"Heavy?" he asked.

"I will get used to it," she said stoically.

"Good because it might save your life one day. You like your new uniform?"

"They are fine gifts, Hari," she said grinning broadly and buckling on her new sword.

"I have one more surprise," he added. "Today you will be joining Brenier's *conroi*. From now on you must learn how to ride and fight from the saddle like a Norman cavalryman."

Winter was passing into spring and the need for battle-ready troops was an imminent requirement. The frequency of their training increased and they gathered daily at first light to practice an endless round of training drills. Hedda took the news of her promotion to the ranks of the cavalry in her stride, and an hour later found herself on the training field alongside two hundred horseman. She had been given a lively colt to ride and the young stallion curled and flapped his lips as he accustomed himself to the weight and smell of his new rider. Hedda knew that all eyes would be on her and resolved, as she always did, to give a good account of herself as she took her place in one of the *conrois*. She had seen them train many times before but now she was sailing in completely uncharted waters. Wedged between two huge black stallions on either side of her, she realised her determination would be tested to the limit. The first charge was uneventful but as the troop wheeled and turned, her colt lost his footing and threw her off. She landed unceremoniously on the soft, muddy ground and struggled to her feet to the derisive jeers of her comrades. Hedda felt her face redden and, with her jaw set defiantly she gritted her teeth and went to retrieve her horse.

The day was a long one for the new recruit and there followed two more falls from the saddle but after each one she hauled herself unaided onto the animal's back and rejoined her *conrois,* each time earning a little more grudging respect. By mid-afternoon the light began to leave the day and the men were stood down. Hedda returned the colt to the stables and prepared to groom him but found she could not reach the animal's back. She cursed in frustration and felt a gentle hand on her shoulder.

"Here, stand on this," said Brenier, putting a large piece of wood at her feet. "You have earned a little help today."

Chapter 14: The Fearful Baronie
Normandie, February 1066

1

"Calm yourself, my love," said the Duchess soothingly to her husband, who seethed visibly in front of her. "Your rage will do you no good. I know your pride is wounded but it will not help you win the support of your barons and magnates."

"They will feel my wrath soon enough - as God is my witness. All of them have sworn oaths of fealty to me and now half of them are fearful of crossing the narrow sea to fulfil those very vows," retorted Duke William angrily. "They are ingrates and cowards."

"Not all of them, husband. Your loyal companions have never let you down yet," she chided.

Mathilda was diverted momentarily, giving instructions to her two maids as they finished dressing her, and then she turned back to her husband who was pacing her bedchamber like an angry bear.

"A little gentle coaxing might serve you better than inciting fear. You must use all your powers of persuasion to convince them - after all, an invasion of England is the road to riches. Normandie has a moral duty to punish Harold Godwinson for his wickedness. Why even the Pope has said as much. Let Robert of Mortain speak your mind for you, he has worked wonders getting them to build your ships - I am sure he can reassure the timidest of doubters," she said.

William stopped pacing and considered her words before nodding in agreement. Duchess Mathilda always seemed to have an innate capacity for calming her husband at the very moment when it seemed he might explode. He had recently been informed that over half the counts and viscounts in the Duchy were murmuring their discontent over the invasion. Nearly all the required ships had been either built or acquired as the Duke had ordered, but now the commitment for men and arms was called for, many were baulking. At yesterday's council meeting his most loyal companions agreed unanimously to support their liege lord in the invasion and all had pledged their troth. Between them they could muster four thousand men, but the Duke would need at least double that number to ensure a successful venture. A second, larger counsel meeting had been convened in the ancient town of Lillebonne in a week's time for all the barons of the duchy, where their loyalty would be put to the test.

"Your wisdom is infallible, and I am blessed to have you as my wife," said the Duke, in response to the calming words.

"Not to mention a substantial dowry and the ability to bear you many sons and daughters," she replied brightly. "Come now let us have breakfast in peace and you can reserve your anger for those who deserve it most."

2

Robert had chosen Lillebonne for the great gathering and as with everything he managed for the Duchy there was little of his plan that was left to chance. He had prevailed upon the Duke to give each attendee the chance to have their say, and once their objections were overcome and consensus reached, an unwavering commitment could be demanded. The dangled carrot of Saxon land and wealth was his obvious ploy and those who still dissented would incur the Duke's displeasure and all that it entailed.

The town had once been the military and commercial centre of Roman Gaul and sat at the meeting point of the main roads through Normandie. Over five hundred men from all over the Duchy braved the late winter weather at the invitation of the Duke. All of William's relatives and allies would attend, as well as his loyal companions. There were also many others, local rulers and men of authority whose loyalties were less certain, and all would be given the chance to speak and voice their feelings on the invasion plan. Their support was vital, for Duke William needed all their knights and men-at-arms to conquer England.

The roads on which they travelled with their various entourages were barely passable having suffered the winter depredations of snow and rain. There were counts and viscounts, archbishops and bishops as well as their attendant squires, pages and bodyguards who all needed a place to sleep and stables for their horses. The town's great hall had been fitted out with tables and benches for the assembly, and such was its significance that there were few absentees.

The meeting was opened by Duke William, who welcomed everyone from a raised dais at the front of the hall which he shared with his inner council. His convivial and amicable address was in stark contrast to the brutal reputation he had built during the two decades of his ducal reign and each man listened in respectful silence.

"I have invited you here to share my plan with you," he rasped in a booming voice that carried to the rear of the great hall. "God has given Normandie a purpose and in doing his holy duty we will be rewarded both in heaven and on earth."

The Duke nodded to Archbishop Lanfranc who got to his feet and, smiling beatifically, blessed the assembly before commencing his address.

"My friends, I have just returned from Rome. As God's defender of the faith, Pope Alexander has asked for Normandie's aid to rid the world of the pretender to the English throne. Harald Godwinson is a blasphemer, a murderer and a breaker of holy oaths who must be held to account. We will lead the crusade against the Saxon enemy and return this errant church to Rome. All those who take part in the crusade will earn eternal salvation," said the influential Italian to a rapt audience.

Lanfranc continued in a similar vein for some time and Robert watched the expressions on the faces of those assembled. There were nods and mumbled approvals, but he sensed that there were many here who would need a great deal of more convincing to undertake the bloody enterprise of conquest. When the Archbishop concluded his address, it was the Chancellor's turn to speak and taking his cue, Robert stood up.

"Gentlemen, you are all men of honour. You are also men of wealth, made so by the grace and favour of our Duke, and each and every one of us has sworn fealty to him. That duty now compels us to fill our ships with men and arms and take what has been promised to him by King Edward and ordained by God. We have travelled far together and defeated all those who have tried to take the Duchy away from us. It is now time to go beyond our borders to make a greater Normandie," said Robert, pausing for a sign of approval from the assembly. Apart from a little applause from the dais there was no other sound and he ploughed on.

"There are many of you here who have built ships to take us to England and I thank you for your contribution and efforts," he continued, signalling to a herald sitting beneath the platform to read from a parchment unfurled in front of him.

"Lord Robert of Mortain commits one hundred and fifty ships and a thousand men," called the man in a loud, resonant voice which was met by loud applause from those seated on the dais. "Oddo, Bishop of Bayeux, commits one hundred ships and two hundred men, William of Evreux commits sixty ships and three hundred men," continued the herald to more applause.

He worked his way to the end of the list until it was completed and the clapping died down.

Robert turned back to the audience who had so far shown little in the way of reaction to the reading of the 'Ship's List'.

"We need more men - your men," he implored the seated assembly sitting impassively before him.

There was still little movement until one man rose to his feet. Raul de Tosney, a nobleman with a small fiefdom near Chartres, stood up and called for attention. All heads swivelled around to hear what the old knight had to say and in a loud voice he introduced himself.

"Those of you who know me know that I am plain spoken and do not mince my words. I have been moved by the words of the noble Lord Robert and the Archbishop, they have stirred my blood in no small measure. My fealty has been promised and given to the Duke and I will not renege on it, but this is a risky business, and I am no-seafarer like the Norse ancestors of my line. My feudal duty does not include fighting on a foreign field, and I fear the sea. I have no desire to be the richest corpse in Christendom. We will be wiped out by the Saxon navy before we set foot on their land. I will not go - I say no," said the old man.

There was a deathly hush in the room until more men stood, in turn, and voiced their disapproval of the invasion plans. The volume of noise grew as more men shouted their opposition and very soon no-one could hear himself speak. As the din of the hubbub grew, Jeanotte of Ambrières slipped out of the hall unnoticed.

"At last," said Robert to himself, holding out his hands for quiet, "the dissenters are revealing themselves."

He knew there would be objectors to the plan and now he knew who they were, they could be dealt with. One look at the

Duke told him that William was shocked at the manner in which he was being treated by the very men he had enriched. Eventually, calm was restored to proceedings and Robert spoke again to the assembly.

"Gentlemen, it is important that we hear all your concerns. The Duke will meet each and every one of you," he said and looked across at William, glowering angrily at the assembly.

As he had promised, the Duke sat down with all the magnates and churchmen and listened. Some of them picked a spokesman or came alone, but it was late in the evening by the time the last man visited his liege-lord. Count Conan of Brittany sat across the small table from Robert and Duke William. He had been waiting patiently for an audience with them all day and wine had got the better of him.

"Will you be joining us in our venture, cousin?" asked the Duke as brightly as he was able.

"No, I will not - the risk is too great, but I wish you good fortune in your venture. Take care, my Lord, for your absence will provide me with an ample opportunity to take the Duchy for myself," slurred the Count belligerently, and before either could answer he staggered from the room.

Neither of the two men could believe the audacity of the Count's rashness and looked at one another incredulously. Duke William gave his Chancellor a tired smile; he was clearly perturbed at the reception he had been given by men who had sworn their allegiances to him, and they would suffer his vengeance.

"You were right to give them a voice, William," said Robert knowing full well that his liege lord would soon respond to the ingratitude of his *baronie*.

"At least we have separated the sheep from the goats. There is nothing more dangerous than having half-hearted men under your command and it is well we know now. Doubtless you have a plan to raise the extra men we need," came the reply.

"Indeed, I have but tomorrow is another day. Let us drink to those loyal companions you **can** rely on," said Robert raising his cup.

They were interrupted by a knock at the door and the guards admitted an elderly knight into the room. Count Eustace of Boulogne stood before them and bowed his head respectfully to the Duke.

"It is not too late for one more deputation?" asked the tired-looking man, still mud-spattered from the road. "My apologies for the late arrival but the road from the north was impossible."

"Not in the slightest. Loyal kinsmen are always welcome whatever the hour. Take some wine and warm yourself by the fire," replied the Duke.

"With pleasure, but first let me have my say," said Eustace proffering the hilt of his sword and bending an arthritic knee to the floor. "I do not approve of these turncoats who wriggle from their duty at the first sign of danger. I pledge twenty-five ships and one hundred men."

Duke William reached down and helped the old man to his feet, embracing him warmly.

"Hope is never lost when there are men like you at my service," replied the Duke, his face wreathed in smiles. "God, bless you, Eustace."

3

Duke William, Robert and their escort left Lillebonne early the next morning and arrived back in Rouen by nightfall. A gap in the inclement weather ensured the trip was at least bearable and the two men talked at length during the journey. Despite the disappointing reaction from at least two thirds of his barons the Duke was not downcast in the slightest. Robert had, for many years, learned to anticipate a mood of high dudgeon, following every bitter disappointment but today he was surprised. From the ashes of Lillebonne, the Duke emerged with a far more pragmatic realisation of the forthcoming invasion than Robert had ever thought possible. Until Eustace's entry late in the evening Robert had begun to harbour fears that the campaign would not be able to take place at all. By the time they had reached the welcoming gates of Rouen, Robert had unwrapped his recruitment plan for five thousand extra men and the Duke was delighted. He had started with a statement of the obvious, in that if they could not raise the men from the Duchy they would get the requisite mounted knights, men-at-arms, archers and foot-soldiers from elsewhere. This would require a lot more money than they had anticipated but since the Duchy's coffers were full it could be achieved with a degree of comfort. When Robert suggested that the '*knight's fee*' for all participants should be doubled, the Duke did not prevaricate in the slightest. Robert reassured William that with a ring containing a relic of St. Peter on his finger, the papal banner to rally his troops, and land to reward them all, there was little to fear.

When they parted that night and left for their separate quarters, the Duke embraced his Chancellor fiercely.

"Rest well, my friend for tomorrow our journey begins in earnest," said Duke William fervently.

4

In the morning, prayers in the chapel were followed by the staple of breakfast, and Robert strolled through the palace grounds trying to stretch the rigours of the previous day's ride from his weary bones. He had a meeting with the Duke later and needed to consider the finer details of his plan; before then, fresh air and a little exercise were called for.

He found the Duke in his quarters in the same robust good humour in which he had left him the night before. Robert politely turned down the offer of breakfast and the two men sat down at the table.

"Before we start I have a little news for you," said the Duke brightly. "Count Conan of Brittany is dead. He dropped out of his saddle on his way home yesterday. Apparently he had been poisoned. The toxin was smeared all over his bridle and gloves."

Robert's mouth fell open in surprise at the swiftness of this retribution.

"Not by my hand. Poison is a coward's weapon, is it not? But the world shall not mourn him too much I think," added the Duke with a little twinkle in his eye. "Now, of more importance I think is who shall lead our deputations to the Danish and German courts? You and I shall be busy with our near neighbours I think."

" Fitzosborne to Denmark and Warrene to Germany," said Robert without prevarication. "And might I suggest also going to Brittany, Conan will be succeeded by his sister Hawise who is a little more sympathetic to our cause?"

"I agree. And after that we will visit my father-in-law in Flanders and then the French court. King Phillip is still only a boy and is easily swayed by a little flattery," said William.

"I will also despatch a ship to Italy. My brother Floki will go, we were successful raising men from the Kingdom in the Sun before when we needed them. But ...." said Robert pausing.

"But Harald Fitzroy was at the head of that army," completed the Duke. "Let us hope we do not have to call on his aid again."

"He still has the men of Ambrières in his thrall," suggested Robert.

"Nonsense, I believe the new Lord there can be trusted well enough," spat the Duke, "Captain Jeanotte has been amply rewarded for his continued loyalty to me."

Robert did not take issue and moved their conversation onto other matters, of which there were many. They would take the *Mora* on her first official voyage and sail her first to Nantes to meet the new Duchess of Brittany. They would travel on to Flanders and then to Paris to petition for support for the invasion. If men and arms were not offered by the respective heads of state, they would seek permission to recruit directly from the companies of avaricious knights looking for their next opportunity for plunder. It might not be the invasion army that William would have chosen but, as he knew only too well, a greedy warrior was better than a timid one and greater France was full of them.

Chapter 15: The Diplomatic Quest,
Brittany, 1066

The *Mora* was readied for her inaugural diplomatic voyage under the eyes of Duchess Mathilda, who wanted the world to see her gift to her husband in its very best light. The ship stood proudly on the quayside having been fitted with new sails which flew the papal banner of green and gold, newly consecrated from Rome, at her masthead. She would carry Robert Fitzroy and the Duke of Normandie to all the destinations around northern France where they hoped to gain support. The trip could have been made far quicker by land, but William wanted to make a great show of their journey; the sea and river route in the glittering *Mora* provided the perfect means for an impressive arrival. On the day of her departure she sat, fully laden with her cargo of forty oarsman, ten knights, the Duke and his Chancellor. They were accompanied by two other vessels carrying men-at-arms, horses, hunting dogs and supplies for the trip. A crowd gathered to see the flotilla off, and once the enterprise had received God's blessing from the Archbishop, Captain Fitzaird gave the order to cast off. The *Mora* pulled out elegantly into the main channel of the River Seine and headed seaward, waved off with great theatre by the Duchess and her gaily clad ladies.

Robert was thankful for the calm weather *en route* to Nantes as they rounded the tip of the Cotentin, and a favourable northerly wind filled their sails and blew them comfortably down to Britanny. They reached the estuary where the River Loire meets the Atlantic Ocean and rowed inland to Nantes where the new Duchess awaited them. They arrived at the riverside capital to be met by a small crowd, alerted to their arrival by the sound of a trumpet from a Norman herald standing in the bows. Duchess Hawise sent an escort of Breton guards to meet the party, and they all rode together through the town to the grand castle. The local people came out onto the streets and cheered the magnificent sight of the Duke, his Chancellor and ten Norman knights, resplendent in shining hauberks and dazzling surcoats, riding in pairs behind impressively attired Breton horsemen. They swept through the town toward the gleaming walls of the grand castle of Nantes and clattered past the gatehouse in the ancient Roman walls and onto the flagstones before the ducal palace.

The Duchess stood on the white granite stairs of her residence to greet her guests, wrapped in a blue, ermine trimmed cloak to ward off the early spring chills. Duke William leapt from his horse even before an attendant groom had a chance to take the reins and strode purposely toward her. He took her proffered hand and kissed it, beaming up at her.

"It is wonderful to see you once more, Lady Hawise," he said before dropping his smile for a moment, "but first let me offer my condolences on the sad passing of your brother."

She returned an enigmatic smile.

"You are most welcome," she said courteously. "Alas my brother had many enemies and was not a man to keep his friends. Now come cousin, we have prepared a little dinner for you. I hope we can improve on the vittles you have onboard."

"You are very gracious, Duchess. But first let me introduce you to my Chancellor, the Lord of Mortain," responded William as she turned her gaze on Robert.

He was instantly struck by her piercing green eyes set in a stern, rubicund face that contrasted starkly with the girlish cascade of red curls falling to her shoulders. She nodded courteously toward him.

"Welcome to Nantes. The name of Fitzroy is well known to us in these parts. Please, gentlemen, follow me," she said.

She took William's arm and led the little party up the remaining steps and into the palace, through a huge anteroom, towards the great hall. A long table had been elegantly laid out for her guests, and it was quite obvious that in the short time she had been Duchess she had made her mark on the place, for a woman's touch was much in evidence. There were no lounging dogs or hawks asleep on their roosts, and the hall was perfumed with burning beeswax candles and spring flowers. Clearly glad to be out of the cold, the Duchess gave her cloak to a servant and served her guests wine by the hearthfire. There was a good deal of polite conversation and news of Brittany and Normandie was swapped. She was attended by her husband, a grey-haired, sallow-looking man of about forty who stood at her shoulder, and although he said little, he listened intently to every word Robert and William said.

They were served a fine meal of oysters, scallops, venison and roasted fowl and gradually the atmosphere between guests and hosts became less formal. At the end of dinner Hawise fixed William with another intense look,

"Cousin, we both know that relations between Brittany and Normandie have not always been convivial. You are our sworn liege-lord, and I remain loyal to that oath. I am aware that you intend to invade England, and you well know that our last Duke was bitterly opposed to sending men overseas and was quite vocal in his sentiments. Is there a finessed proposition that you would like to discuss perhaps?"

"Indeed, there is, Lady Hawise, and I would like my Chancellor to explain some of the finer details," said the Duke, nodding to Robert.

"The proposition is a simple one, my Lady. We will be embarking on a pilgrimage - a crusade blessed and consecrated by the Pope of Rome to rid England of the blasphemer, Harald Godwinson. We have a fleet of ships ready and waiting to take our army across l*a Manche* to depose him. We have gold and land in abundance for those that support us," said Robert unrolling a parchment map on the table in front of them. "The Earldom of Wessex is rich and fertile and for your support we will cede a large part of it to you. We will pay your men handsomely and will give you enough gold to make a decent profit on the enterprise."

"Gold I believe your brother Harald relieved us of on his last visit here," retorted Lady Hawise.

"Normandie was at war with Brittany and Harald was only doing his duty," said Robert. "We will return that gold and give you the opportunity of being richer than you have ever been. For that we need at least five hundred men."

Lady Hawise considered his words carefully.

"No, I will not provide you with five hundred men," she said forthrightly, and Robert felt his spirits plummet. "But I will provide you with a thousand - if the price is right."

The Duchess of Brittany proved to be a hard negotiator and paid meticulous attention to every detail of the proposed plan, which she scrutinised assiduously as Robert unwrapped it; in the end both sides got what they wanted. Lady Hawise called in a scribe and the man recorded every detail of their discussion, and hours later the deal was signed and sealed. William raised a cup of wine to her in salute.

"You drive a hard bargain, my Lady," he said, watching her face as it finally cracked into a smile.

"To the success of our mission," she said triumphantly. "It is our holy duty, is it not?"

Chapter 16: Old Friends, New Alliances
Flanders, March 1066

1

Two days later the Norman party were back aboard their ships and heading down the river to the sea, where they would travel back up around the Normandie coast to Flanders. Robert was a relieved man. To have secured the support of Brittany and the promise of a thousand mounted warriors and archers was a welcome addition to the growing invasion force - but they would need many more. Twenty thousand men would be more than enough, and even ten thousand might prevail, but any less than that he knew would be a risky business. Still, he reasoned, it was a good start to their recruitment campaign. He afforded himself a brief smile at the thought of William's extravagant pledges of Saxon land that they had not even won yet, wondering how much there would be left before they sailed. His thoughts were short-lived as the *Mora* headed into choppy waters and his seasickness returned with a vengeance. By the time they rounded the top of the Normandie peninsula he had stopped being sick, but it would be a full three days later, when they docked in the county of Flanders, that he began to feel normal once more.

A bitter wind from the north greeted the Norman flotilla and their crews dropped the sheets as they came to rest by the stone dock. A huddle of horsemen, illuminated by flaming torches, could be seen waiting patiently in the dying light on the quayside of Damme, the outport of the Flemish capital of Bruges. It was approaching dusk and the three ships threw down mooring ropes to cold hands on the quayside to secure the vessels. Robert was one of the first to disembark, and thanked God for the feel of solid ground beneath his feet. Duke William jumped down from the ship after him and the two men made their way toward the group of waiting horsemen less than a hundred paces away.

"William, we had almost given up on you," called a booming voice from the gathering darkness.

"Father-in-law, I am honoured you should have come all this way to greet me," shouted back William in an equally loud voice.

A muffled clip-clop of iron shod hooves sounded from the mist, and Count Baldwin of Flanders emerged from the gloom on an enormous black stallion. The man was huge and in a single fluid movement he cocked his leg over the saddle pommel and leapt to the ground, embracing his son-in-law in a massive bear hug, pounding his back in greeting.

"It is good to see you again, my boy. I trust all is well at home and my daughter is a dutiful wife," he bellowed before releasing Duke William from his grasp and turning his attentions on Robert. "And the Lord of Mortain is also very welcome here. Now, come let us make haste - we have two leagues to ride before we can show you and your men some proper Flemish hospitality."

"All is well at home and Mathilda sends you her fondest regards, Baldwin," said William looking round to check on the progress of his men in the second ship, unloading the horses.

Two Flemish squires hurried forward with skins of wine for the Norman guests and both drank deeply as the Count of Flanders continued his noisy welcome. Despite Baldwin's advanced years he did not have a single grey strand in a full head of flaming red hair and luxuriant beard. He was sixty years old and had the energy of a man half that age. The Count was a man of enormous appetites for wine, food and women, but despite these excesses he was as lean as he was broad, putting Robert in mind of his own father. For all his rambunctiousness and good humour the

Count had a reputation both as a shrewd diplomat and ruthless general and was without doubt a man to be reckoned with. Seven years previously, Baldwin had been appointed the regent of France for his nephew, the Dauphin and the boy lent heavily on his uncle's guidance. If young Phillip could be persuaded to support the Norman cause, France might provide men for the campaign. Count Baldwin had interests far beyond Flanders including close ties with Saxon England through his sister's marriage into the Godwin clan. Despite the obvious bonds with the Duchy of Normandie, Robert knew that hard bargaining and clear logic would be needed to gain Flemish support for the invasion of England.

Within the hour all the horses, hounds and knights had disembarked from the ships and were ready to leave. More torches were lit and the Count roared the order to depart. The whole party left the dockside and hurtled down the road to Bruges in a cacophony of sound that fractured the early evening darkness.

The capital of Flanders was illuminated by the lights from thousands of homes by the time the party clattered through the gatehouse, and the doors were slammed shut behind them. They made their way to *Het Steene*, the Count's palatial castle in the centre of an energetic city whose streets still bustled with the activity of traders selling their wares in the great square. An army of grooms came out to meet the party, and the horses were led off to the stables while the hounds were taken to the kennels. The seneschal of the castle, a large middle-aged man dressed in merchant's finery stood waiting for his lord. His expensive beaver skin hat, elegant silk coat and finely buckled shoes were in stark contrast to the chainmail and armoured helms of his guests.

"Are they ready for us in the great hall?" bellowed Baldwin without breaking step and his seneschal nodded. "Come my friends, you will be thirsty and hungry."

With one arm around Duke William, the Count marched up the steps to the hall, leading his entourage of Flemish and Norman knights. He was interrupted by half a dozen hart hounds, bounding energetically toward their master who bent down to greet them.

"I hope your own hounds are in good fettle, William, for tomorrow we shall see what Norman dogs are made of," he shouted above the din, and without waiting for an answer marched on, men and animals trailing in his wake.

An enormous hearthfire roared its welcome at the far end, bathing the whole room in heat and light. At the centre of the hall sat a gigantic wooden table festooned with spring flowers, silver drinking vessels and baskets of bread, and the knights were shown to their places and seated. Count Baldwin stood before his guests offering words of welcome to the Norman visitors. At his signal a multitude of servants appeared bearing all manner of roasted meats, sea-fish and vegetables and the banquet began in earnest. Duke William sat at the Count's right hand while Robert sat at the other and the great hall, bedecked with sigils and battle standards, resounded with the sound of feasting. Baldwin was a consummate host and quickly learned the names of all the Norman knights, engaging each one in conversation across the noisy table. Every man was called upon to deliver a story or a song, and even the Duke got to his feet to deliver a soliloquy about the feats of his great-grand father Rollo, Normandie's founder. When Robert's turn arrived his choice was made for him, and the men called upon him to narrate the Saga of the Wandering Warriors which he did with great gusto and not a little feeling. At the end of the story

Count Baldwin stood and, with tears running down his face, applauded louder than any man in the room. After each man had contributed his part, the noise died and the atmosphere became less raucous until Duke William excused himself and retired to his quarters. He was followed by many others until only a handful were left.

"For a man of great religious conviction you have an enviable capacity for wine and good company," said the Count toasting the Norman Chancellor. "I know you have come to talk and what you need but have patience and let us enjoy the company of fellow warriors."

"And you are no mean host, my Lord," said Robert returning the toast. "Your reputation for great hospitality is vastly underrated."

"And long may I live up to it. Now rest well my Lord of Mortain for tomorrow we must do battle with one of the great stags of Flanders. There is a giant hart who has reigned imperiously in my forest for many years and let us hope he gives us some sport," said Baldwin before draining his cup one last time, saluting those who remained and taking his leave. "Good night, comrades. Until tomorrow."

2

The courtyard in front of Bruges castle was alive with frenetic activity as the Norman horsemen milled around, getting used to their new mounts, the hardy, little coursers that Count Baldwin had provided them with for the hunt. They were joined by their Flemish companions from the previous evening, and the conversation, still fuelled by the residue of wine from the recent bout of drinking, filled the early morning air. Dawn had only recently broken and the songs of blackbird, thrush and linnet poured out a far more harmonious melody. The cacophony was completed when the kennel pages brought out their charges and the hounds joined the huntsmen in a maelstrom of snarling and barking. A multi-coloured riot of tan *lymers*, brindle mastiffs and milk-white *talbots* moved about anxiously waiting for the hunt to begin, while aquiline, greyhounds jittered and trembled at the end of long leashes. Each dog, horse and man had responsibilities in the hunt and each participant had been trained from a young age to play their part.

"Not long now, Duke William, we are nearly all here. The Saxons are always late," shouted the Count to his guest. "Ah, here they are now."

The party was joined by three English noblemen who strode over to take their horses. They were all long-haired, bare-headed and extravagantly moustachioed and carried hunting bows across their backs. The men announced their arrival with morning greetings and bowed courteously to the Count who introduced them to the Normans.

"I have pleasure in introducing you to my other honoured guests. This is Earl Tostig Godwinson, brother to the King of England, and his companions," declared Baldwin. "Our company is complete. Let us make the most of this fine morning and the devil take the hindmost."

With no more ado, he dug his spurs into the flanks of his robust hunting horse and led the company clattering out over the flagstones through the waking town and into the open countryside.

In just over two hours the party was in the middle of the forest and one of the scent-hounds picked up the spoor of a deer and pulled against his leash in complete silence, as he had been trained to do. His companions felt the frisson in the air and soon they were all pulling at their traces, before a magnificently antlered stag stepped out nimbly into the grassy clearing where hunters and quarry observed one another in a moment of quiet. In less than a heartbeat the hart realised the danger he was in, turned and vaulted away with an impressive turn of speed. The hunting horn was sounded, the greyhounds were released, and the hunt was on.

It took three hours of hard chasing before the quarry was run to ground. The stag, its throat parched dry from exertion, stood facing its pursuers turning its back to the forest stream that it had sought in vain. Too exhausted and wary to drink, it raised its head in defiance at its pursuers and waited, panting and winded from the long chase. Three huge *alaunt* hounds were unleashed and send careering toward the trapped beast to bring it down. Despite being desperately tired the animal met their charge, impaling one of the dogs on its antlers while battering away the abortive efforts of the other two, who scurried back to their masters in whimpering defeat. Streaked with sweat and snorting blood from streaming nostrils, the stag faced the hunting party again.

"It falls to my son-in-law, to put our magnificent friend out of its suffering," shouted Count Baldwin to his comrades. "Duke William has the honour of sending him on his way."

William nodded his gratitude and withdrew a short, single-edged hunting sword in preparation to deliver the *coup de grace.* He spurred his courser toward the dying hart who spied him warily from the corner of his eye. In a final charge the stag accelerated headlong into the horse, causing it to shy and throw his rider unceremoniously to the ground, knocking the wind out of him. It turned on the prone figure, lowering its antlers to deliver retribution to his tormentor and Robert spurred his own horse forward in an effort to save his liege lord. Before he had the chance to close in on the stag who was intent only on goring William to death, the hart dropped to its knees with the fletchings of three hunting arrows protruding from its broad chest. Robert leapt from his horse's back and pulled the blood-spattered Duke away from the dying stag which threatened to collapse on top of him.

"You are hurt, my Lord," he shouted fearing the worst.

"It is his blood not mine," retorted William. "Now finish him, Robert. The beast has earned a noble end."

Robert turned toward the stag who had collapsed onto its side and finding the top of its sternum he thrust his sword deep into the chest, piercing the still beating heart. He withdrew the heavy blade from a wound that continued to pump blood from the dead animal for several minutes after it had expired. Willing hands came forward and helped Duke William to his feet, who fought to compose himself after looking death so closely in the face. Count Baldwin was at his side thrusting a skin of wine into his hands.

"That was a close-run thing, William," he said heartily. "It would have been shear carelessness to lose a son-in-law on my hunt and after all, how could I have explained that to my daughter. If it was not for the quick thinking of these fellows, I might well have been sending a corpse back to Normandie."

He waved his hand to where Tostig Godwinson and his two comrades stood together holding their recently discharged hunting bows.

"My thanks, gentlemen," called Duke William to them.

"It was our pleasure," replied Tostig, smiling broadly. "But please, Lord, do not let my brother Harold know that I saved the life of his most bitter rival."

With the tension of the final kill released, the hunters settled down to wine brought forward by eager servants. Fleming, Norman and Saxon stood around the forest glade sharing convivial conversation and laughing together as the deer was unmade, its warm offal tossed to the ravenous hounds. Before long the skinned and gutted carcass was loaded onto the wagon, and a jubilant

Count Baldwin led his weary hunting companions back to Bruges for another evening of his famous hospitality.

3

The second night of the Norman stay was marked by a grand affair to which many influential noblemen, merchants and churchmen had been invited. Together with their wives and paramours the most important men of Bruges, Ghent and Ypres attended the feast at the behest of their Count. As Robert was introduced to the gathered lords and ladies, he was immediately struck by the wealth on display and the richly adorned women who lit up the room in their expensive dresses of multi-coloured Flemish cloth. Jongleurs, minstrels and mummers performed for their guests and the sound of music and conversation filled the huge hall. He found himself in front of an exquisitely dressed woman, her dark hair coifed and garlanded with spring flowers, and around her neck hung a bejewelled crucifix. The Count's much younger sister, Judith, nodded her elegant head courteously in acknowledgement.

"An interesting day's hunting, Lord Robert?" she enquired formally, although the two of them had known each other for over a decade.

"It was not without incident," he quipped with a smile. "It is well that your husband is such a fine archer, or I might well have been looking for a new master,"

"You know these Saxons, they are seldom without a bow in their hands," she returned with a dazzling smile of her own.

When Judith of Flanders married Tostig Godwinson she also became the Countess of Northumbria and produced three children during the decade of her tenure in Saxon England. Her great beauty and generosity earned her wide renown in her new home, and she was beloved by the church and the people within her husband's fiefdom. Earl Tostig was a far less successful diplomat, and his antipathy for his people ended up in open revolt which he dealt with his customary brutality. It was even rumoured in many quarters that one noble Northumbrian family had ended up in pies and served to the local people at one of Tostig's feasts. A lengthy rebellion soon became inevitable, and the rebels cast out their liege-lord, forcing the Earl to go cap in hand to his powerful brother for support. Harold Godwinson was many things, but he was no fool and refused his support in favour of Morcar of Mercia who became the new earl. Tostig swore eternal damnation on his brother and fled in ignominy to his wife's former home in Flanders, where the Count provided them and their entourage with a comfortable refuge.

"And how does being back in Bruges suit you and your family?" asked Robert.

"Oh, well enough. I am actually quite delighted to be home with my books and libraries. Baldwin has been very generous, but Tostig still dreams of the day when he can regain his fiefdom," she said before being interrupted by her husband.

"May I commend you on your marksmanship, Lord Tostig," said Robert offering his hand in greeting. "On behalf of the Duchy of Normandie, you have all our thanks."

"It was nothing, sir. No more than one great Lord would do for another, I think," said the Earl bombastically, emptying his cup of wine while looking around for a servant to refill it. "I look forward to hearing of his invasion plans, if he cares to part with them. We appear to have a shared ambition."

Robert observed the man briefly. He was clearly a Godwinson and had the strong Germanic features of his brother, the King of England. However, he was now half-drunk, and his garrulousness and swaggering manner was not endearing him to anyone, least of all the Chancellor of Normandie.

"Let us drink to the defeat of our common enemies then, Earl Tostig. God shall reward the righteous," said Robert offering a toast to the new arrival.

"As long as my treacherous brother gets what he is due, I would enlist the help of the Devil himself. Take care though, Lord Fitzroy, the Saxon throne will not be relinquished easily and my brother has a powerful army of *thegns* and *huscarls*. Why, there is even a rumour that your own brother, the fabled 'Papal Shield', has bent the knee to him," said Tostig watching closely for a reaction.

"My brother has no duty to the Duchy, my Lord. His vows of allegiance have long been paid and he is free to choose his home and his master. It is of no concern to Normandie," said Robert coolly.

He excused himself to the Godwinsons politely and continued on his round of introductions. On the surface Robert exuded his normal diplomatic conviviality, but below that he seethed with anger at the possibility of his brother's treachery. Surely, he reasoned, Hari would never betray the Duchy, whatever had passed between them as brothers. His attention was suddenly taken by the sound of Count Baldwin's bellowing voice clearly audible above the rest of the noise in the great hall. He walked over to find his host with one arm around Duke William in a fraternal embrace.

"Robert Fitzroy, your skills as a huntsman surpass that of your reputation as the great diplomat you have become, and I salute you. But let us put our statesmanship aside for tonight and we will drink and dine as brothers for tomorrow I have some interesting news to give you both," said the Count winking at Duke William and tapping the side of his nose with his index finger.

The Duke beamed broadly at Robert.

4

As always, Robert rose early, and with a local cock crowing the world awake he made his way to the castle's chapel and spent his first hour of the day in prayer. He prayed for the Duke, he prayed for his family, but he prayed hardest and longest for his brother, asking God to guide Hari's way in Saxon England. The sun's early morning rays illuminated the exquisite stain glass windows of the chapel, but by the time Robert got to his feet, his belief that Harald Fitzroy was no traitor was reinforced.

He and Duke William were due to attend a meeting in Baldwin's private chambers and he made his way purposefully through the labyrinth of hallways. Two smartly liveried guards allowed him entry into the opulently decorated rooms where he found the Count and his bother-in-law with Eustace of Boulogne waiting around a table set for breakfast.

"Ah, we have a quorum," announced Baldwin as Robert took his place. "Now gentlemen, we have much to discuss but I will be as brief as I can."

Robert shook hands with the Count and sat down. He looked up at his host who continued to speak, noticing the change in the man's persona as the details of the proposal began to take shape. Gone were Baldwin's genial and bluff mannerisms to be replaced by those of a man looking to drive a shrewd bargain.

"Normandie calls and I intend to answer even if I will be the second Flemish nobleman to do so, but I will say from the outset that I need to be careful with how I offer you support. You will know that I am related, however tenuously to both the Kings of England and France and my actions should not disadvantage Flanders. Now, I also intend to give my backing to my brother-in-law Tostig to regain his former fiefdom. He is an impulsive fellow and talks before he thinks, but I have decided to furnish him with a small fleet to harry the English coastline that will divert his brother's attention from the Norman invasion. This will also give me ample opportunity to spread a little false information into the Saxon court about your plans, where no one can keep a secret. I will also advise the young French King that it is in his best interests to allow you to recruit troops in France to fight under your colours. There are many idle free companies that will jump at the chance of booty, particularly at the expense of the English," he said, pausing while the audience took in the import of his words.

"And what of Flanders, will you come with us on this pilgrimage?" asked Duke William.

"Not directly, for my neutrality will be questioned but I will be there in spirit. My *castellan* Marshal Brio will lead his free company of cavalry and crossbowmen on your campaign with ships of our own, and they shall fight beside their brothers from Boulogne," continued the Count, nodding to Eustace.

"And your price, brother-in-law?" asked William.

"I will accept the county of Northampton as the price for my service," answered Baldwin looking at William who nodded his acceptance immediately. "And there will be a tax of ten points on everything you pay to each Flemish soldier, be he high or low-born, to be paid when you take control of the English coffers, of course."

The Duke did not even look at his Chancellor before he consented.

"A generous offer, my Lord and one to which I am happy to agree," said William. "Do we need a scribe to record our dealings?" he asked.

"There is little need, we are family after all," said the Count, offering out his hand to seal the deal.

5

Within the week, the *Mora* was on her way up the River Seine, where King Phillip of France expected the Norman party. At the Isle de la Cite they attended a brief and formal meeting, at which the young monarch followed Count Baldwin's advice given to him in a letter that arrived two days before. They were given permission to recruit an army from the Kingdom of the Franks, during a courteous reception in the royal palace. A nervous young monarch presided over the conference, with every reason to fear and despise Duke William, the man who had beaten his father so many times on the battlefield. Their meeting concluded and with no reason to stay, they thanked their host and returned to their ship which was rowed back down-river toward Rouen and home.

Two days after their ships left Paris, they returned to the busy quayside, where Duchess Mathilda had organised a welcoming party and the noise of the excited crowd could be heard from a league away.

"A successful trip, I think, and in no small thanks to you," said Duke William as he stood with his Chancellor on the raised deck in the bows. "But it is a shame your brother will not be joining us on this campaign. Let us hope the rumours have no founding."

Robert continued to look ahead, waving to the distant crowd, with an expressionless look on his face.

"You are right, they are just rumours but be assured I would stake my life on my brother's loyalty," he replied flatly before turning to face the Duke. "He is no traitor, my Lord. There is no way he would raise his sword against you."

Duke William put a comforting hand on Robert's arm.

"Alas, Harald would not be the first warrior whose head was turned by land and gold. He served us well in the past, but where is he now when we most need him? I hope you are right, my friend and that all this talk of defection is nothing more than Saxon deceit. Come now, let us make ready for our homecoming, we have much to be thankful for," continued the Duke, indicating that the matter was closed.

The *Mora's* oarsmen pulled the ship expertly out of the river's main channel and soon had her nestling up against the side of the stone quay, where she was joined by her sister ships. It was mid-afternoon when the Duke leapt down on to the dockside to meet a delegation of noblemen and women led by Duchess Mathilda. Soon after, the rest of his party of knights, men-at-arms, servants, horses and hounds disembarked. After a brief speech welcoming the company home, the crowd dispersed leaving Robert and his squire alone on the harbour.

"Shall we go to your rooms, sir?" asked the boy interrupting his master's train of thought.

"Take the bags to my quarters, Henri. I shall remain here a while," ordered Robert.

When the boy was gone he went to a riverside wine shop and sat at his table watching the river flow languidly toward the sea, sipping slowly in contemplation of his recent efforts. He was satisfied with the outcome of their mission and confident they could now raise the men and arms they needed for the invasion. Robert was content that he could do no more to fulfil his duty, but he was deeply troubled by the news of his brother's actions in England. As convinced as he was of Hari's loyalties to his family and to Normandie there was something about the news that he could not quite fathom. His thoughts turned to his son, Richard, and he wondered how the boy was faring under his uncle's care and guidance. He knew that all he could do was trust in his brother's integrity and sighed at the notion. Robert raised his cup to his lips and, once again, vowed to himself to accept the things that he could not change.

"I hope you know what you are doing, little brother," he said to himself under his breath.

Chapter 17: The Brotherhood of Norsemen
Maldon, Summer 1066

1

The clash of steel blades resounded outside the town's longhall as Harald Fitzroy watched, with some satisfaction, his mistress train at arms. Hedda and Gilbert circled one another looking for an opening to attack, and after almost an hour of intense practice both protagonists were beginning to tire. Yet again, the girl hefted her shield above her head to absorb the blows of her heavier opponent, and with the back of the hand that clutched her sword she wiped her eyes of salty sweat threatening to obscure her vision. Despite being almost twice her weight, Gilbert did not hold himself back and attacked his obstinate rival with unrestrained fury, but to her credit she did not buckle. Hedda dropped her shield in front of her, anticipating the boy's next move as he committed to a full-blooded thrust to the body. He met nothing but air as she stepped nimbly away from the danger, leaving a trailing leg over which he tripped and fell. Gilbert's surprise gave way to anger as he saw the ground rise up to meet him, and moments later felt the tip of Hedda's blade needling the back of his neck.

"*Rendement,*" she called to him, and he duly offered his surrender.

Panting heavily, she looked over to Harald, who acknowledged her small victory with a cursory nod.

"Well met, but you might find those Saxon *thegns* better prepared for your box of tricks."

She allowed herself a smile knowing that this was as much praise as she could expect from the Lord of Maldon, at least in public. In six months of intense military training Harald had been a harsh task master and subjected her to the same rigours that the rest of his warriors went through. To her credit she had gone about her work with a quiet, uncomplaining stoicism that dispelled any murmuring of favouritism within the ranks of his veteran fighters. She was now a competent horsewoman, capable of holding her own in the disciplined ranks of her troop and more than capable of wielding a lance from horseback. Hedda still resembled a boy on her horse when she took her place in the *conrois* of grizzled cavalrymen. When battle came, which it surely would, she knew she would fight as hard as any man, and they would respect her for that.

Before she could respond to his faint praise they were interrupted by excited shouting.

"They are here, Lord. Captain Jeanotte's fleet has been sighted - they will be here in two hours," shouted Thomas from a galloping horse.

By the time Harald had ridden down to the quayside a sizeable crowd had gathered. He dismounted and made his way to the front of a throng of several hundred people waiting patiently for the ships. It had been an anxious wait since Brenier had first delivered Harald's orders to Ambrières. He knew that a departing army of a thousand men would have aroused suspicion in Normandie and had sent his fleet of twenty ships to St. Malo in Brittany for the rendezvous. It would be good to be back in the company of his army, and the thought of a new campaign with his comrades excited him. He found himself standing next to Brenier and the two cousins shared a skin of wine as they waited in the balmy sunshine on the dock.

"When Duke William discovers that he has lost the support of the men of Ambrières there will be hell to pay," said Harald.

"And Robert will be none too pleased either," added Brenier." You think they will have left undetected?"

"I doubt it. That number of men travelling to the sea will not have gone unnoticed, but St. Malo is a den of pirates where no-one cares about the comings and goings of an army. I would still like to have seen the Duke's face when he discovered Jeanotte's deception," replied Harald wryly and put a hand on his cousin's shoulder. "But do not trouble yourself, we have not betrayed our countrymen and will not be raising arms against them. It is Harald Godwinson who will reap the whirlwind."

Brenier nodded thoughtfully before raising an arm and pointing toward the ships.

"Look, here they come," he said, raising a hand to shield his eyes against the mid-afternoon sun, "the *Lady Alberada* is leading them in."

A great cheer went up from the crowd as the first of the ships appeared around the headland of Northey Island, until all twenty vessels of the fleet rowed toward Maldon. Banners bearing the two ravens of Regneville flew from each masthead in the gentle breeze as the oarsmen expertly manouvered their craft over the flat water. There were ships of all sizes carrying men, horses and equipment, and Jeanotte stood in the prow of the Lady Alberada like a sea king of old as she glided majestically toward the harbour. Harald felt a frisson of excitement, looking on proudly, as the convoy approached and docked. Jeanotte jumped down onto the stone quay even before the shipped was tied up and sought out his master. The two men embraced warmly.

"Late as always, Jeanotte," shouted Harald joyfully enveloping the young man in a powerful bear hug.

"The winds were against us, Lord, but we are here now, over a thousand men and ready for the fight," he replied.

"Well, it will not be long in coming, I think. You had no problems leaving Normandie?" asked Harald.

"None to speak of, the Duke will know of our departure by now. The castles along the Marches are all fully garrisoned by trusted men as you ordered."

"You are a man to be relied upon," beamed Harald. "But first things first; let's get the men and horses into camp before we talk of business."

Clifford de Courcy stepped forward and held out his hand in welcome.

"Jeanotte, it is good to see you again. We have prepared quarters and stables only a short walk away. Everything is ready for you," he said pumping his friend's hand.

"I will come and find you later, we have much to catch-up on," added Harald before leaving the two younger men. "And you will be staying with me in the longhouse," he concluded, pointing a long finger at Jeanotte.

Five of the larger ships had now tied up alongside the stone dock and men started to disembark, while further down the shoreline other boats had been driven into the shallows and were disgorging their cargos. The air resonated with not only Norman voices but with Italian and Greek tongues, shouting orders and calling to their comrades. Nervous horses were led cautiously down wooden steps into the shallows, coaxed by patient grooms. Byzantine knights waded ashore with Neapolitan infantry, and Sicilian archers carried their composite bows in the air to protect the strings from the salt water. Slowly they gathered on the beach beneath their company standards before local men arrived to guide them to the nearby camp. Harald moved amongst them, reuniting with old comrades and veterans of distant battles. It took him an age, as he stopped frequently to greet friends and comrades. There was a great deal of handshaking and back-slapping as the men of Ambrières were reunited with their liege-lord, who spoke animatedly to each and every man who waylaid him, reminding him of past glories.

"Will we be fighting the likes of those Swabian knights again, commander? I will be ready for their swords this time," cried one veteran from the Kingdom in the Sun.

"Who will be brave enough to fight us, Lord? Will there be plunder?" cried another. "My wife has developed expensive tastes since Italy,"

"Remember how the French cut and ran at Val-es-dunes, my Lord? You were everywhere that day"

"Patience my friends, do I still have your trust?" shouted Harald. "I promise there will be plunder for all. Enough for each man to buy women and drink for many years to come."

They cheered him wholeheartedly as he walked through the ranks. When men, horses and materiel had finally been unloaded the order was given to march to the camp, where groups of long wooden barrack rooms and tents of hide were neatly laid outside the town's palisade. By the time dusk settled and the warmth began to leave the day, lines of tethered horses nickered happily as they fed from oat filled troughs. Large cooking fires had been prepared to cook the food sent from the town and by the time night fell each man was replete. A huge bonfire had been lit in the centre of the camp and the men settled down in its glow to drink the night away, renewing old bonds of friendship with their old comrades who had sailed to Maldon the previous year.The fighting force of Harald's army now exceeded twelve hundred men and their commander stood before them.

"My friends, this is the day that I have long prayed for, when we should be reunited once again to stand together. Your captains have told you little of the enemy that we will shortly be confronting, and you have demonstrated your loyalty by answering my call. May I crave your indulgence a little longer before I reveal our plans to you?"

The seated warriors roared out their approval and Harald continued.

"We have fought many foes together and defeated them all in their time. The Moors in Sicily, the Greeks and Germans at Civitate, the French at Laraville - none stood a chance against us. Soon we will be facing a new adversary - one who will line our pockets with gold and silver. When you have rested, we will be sailing again to fight. Tonight, I drink to your health and to the death of all those who take the field against us," he called to them raising his drinking cup in salute.

His comrades answered again but this time louder and longer and the night air resounded to the sound of their raised voices.

"Har-ald, Har-ald," they chanted in unison.

Their commander drained his cup and raised his hands in acknowledgement, with the light of the fire at his back, casting his huge shadow over the ranks of his newly reunited army.

It was late when Harald returned to the longhouse with his guest, and Hedda was waiting for them. She had hectored the servants throughout the day to ensure that the hall and quarters were spotlessly prepared and there was food and drink in plenty laid out on the long wooden table.

"And this is the lady of my house," announced Harald as he entered the hall. "But beware, she is as fierce as she is beautiful so have a care."

Hedda got up from her seat by the hearthfire and moved toward them. She nodded demurely to Jeanotte.

"You are very welcome here," she said, "the servants have your quarters prepared if you are tired."

"Thankyou, Lady Hedda, but I am not tired and we have much to discuss before I am allowed to reach my bed," he replied looking admiringly around the longhouse. "This place has changed a good deal for the better. A woman's touch here is obvious."

She felt herself blush at being addressed as 'Lady' and hoped it would not be noticed in the dim light of the hall.

"And you will be travelling north with us? I for one am glad to hear it - the company of so many fighting men gets a little dull after a time," Jeanotte continued.

"You might not be so polite if you saw her coming at you with a lance tucked under her arm," interjected Harald. "Let us sit - there is much I still need to know."

Hedda said goodnight and left the two men alone.

"The rumours are true, she is a rare beauty," said Jeanotte.

"Now, news from Normandie," said Harald changing the subject. "I hear the Duchy is a cauldron of activity. I swear that sometimes I can hear the Duke's war drums from England."

Jeanotte raised his cup to his lips, drained the contents and paused for a moment.

"Now, where to begin. Your brother, Robert, has been as active as ever and seems to have worked a miracle. He has replaced the Duke's timid barons and men are now flocking to join the invasion force. The promise of Saxon land is tempting enough to bring in free companies from all over Europe. The Duke's host should well exceed ten thousand men by the time he sails - that's even without the men from Ambrières," said Jeanotte.

"Ah, Robert has surpassed himself again, that is good to hear. Alas, your departure from the Duchy will not have gone unnoticed by now. There will be some consternation, of course, but the fog of war creates a good deal of confusion and our friends in the Normandie will have more than enough to concern themselves with," said Harald thoughtfully. "Duke William will doubtless have assumed that I have taken Harold Godwinson's gold and that I am raising men to fight beneath his banners. We will leave Duke William and King Harold to fight each other. While two mad dogs are fighting nobody else gets bitten."

Jeanotte chuckled.

"I think this will end the promise of my becoming a Norman Lord," he said ruefully.

"Do not be so sure about that, my boy. War has a habit of changing the fate of all men and the conflict that is coming will have far reaching effects. If the King of Norway has his way, he will be sitting on the English throne by Christmas and you might yet have a new master," replied Harald.

"I am happy with this one, thank you, Lord," replied Jeanotte raising his cup in toast. "And what of our plans?"

"We wait for word of the Norwegian landing in the north and will join them there. Earl Morcar of Northumbria holds my nephew at Banburgh castle and we must find a way to retrieve him - as well as helping ourselves to any riches that might fall into our path. But our little deception must be maintained. When we leave Maldon it must look as if we are sailing in support of the Saxons," said Harald.

"And after that, Lord?" asked Jeanotte.

"You know better than to question the Norns. After that we will see what the gods have in store for us, but until then let us enjoy the company of reunited comrades and the promise of the road ahead.

They talked long into the night until Harald finally took heed of his captain's exhaustion and let him go to his bed.

2

It was not long before Harald received the visitors which he was expecting. Five days after the arrival of his army, a group of Saxon horsemen led by Earl Leofwine and an escort of twenty riders were spotted from a watchtower on the town's palisade fence. The Lord of Maldon, flanked by Brenier and Jeanotte, and at the head of his own fully armed escort, met their visitors on the incoming road. It had been a dry summer, and there were clouds of dust as the companies of horsemen rode toward one another. Despite the summer heat Harald had insisted that his horsemen were dressed for battle wearing long, heavy *hauberks* and carrying lances. The Saxons on the other hand were lightly armed on swift moving horses and the two companies drew to a halt less than half a league out of the town. Harald called a hearty welcome to the Earl of Kent and trotted forward to greet him. They exchanged pleasantries before he turned and led his guests back into town and past the garrison, where twelve hundred men could be observed preparing for war.

The air was thick with a cacophony of noise from the camp. Blacksmiths' hammers beat out discordant rhythms mending weaponry and preparing horseshoes. Captains shouted orders from the training grounds as horsemen wheeled and charged at invisible enemies. Swords pounded away at heavy wooden shields as men-at-arms toiled in the heat. The company entered the town gates and into a maelstrom of activity, with traders noisily vending their wares from both sides of the main thoroughfare. They passed wagons full of supplies, wending their way toward the garrison and clogging up the busy road with traffic. Smoke from furnaces and cook-fires hung over the town and mingled with the bitter tang of tanneries, human and animal waste. Harald led the party up the hill, away from the town centre toward his longhouse where an awning had been constructed over a long wooden table. He dismissed his men and invited the Saxon noblemen to sit out of the heat of the sun and take some ale.

"You have been busy, Lord Fitzroy. Is this your full company?" asked Leofwine Godwinson, brushing the residue of beer from his bushy moustaches.

"Not quite – we are still expecting a cohort from Italy before the muster is complete. Warriors spend half their lives readying themselves for battle and this is no different. I find that good preparation nearly always delivers the best results," declared Harald confidently. "Your brother's army is ready for the invasion I am sure."

"Indeed, the men of Kent and Wessex stand ready on the south coast. King Harald sends his greetings and requests that you and your men join him as soon as you are able," declared the Earl.

"And we shall do just that. One more week and my men will be ready to join yours. We are just awaiting the last of our ships," replied Harald. "Now how is that arm of yours? The last time I saw you it had a couple of Welsh arrows sticking out of it."

"It has healed well enough, and I am happy to report that the Welsh Marches have been pacified now - thanks in no small measure to the efforts of your cavalry," replied the Saxon.

"Ah, undisciplined infantry are no match for armoured horsemen. Let us hope the Welsh have learned their lesson," said Harald.

Leofwine was about to respond when his attention was taken by Hedda who appeared from inside the longhouse. He gave her a long look as he struggled to recognise her from their last meeting, but his host interrupted his thoughts.

"When do you think we might expect the invasion to begin?" asked Harald.

"A good question, my Lord, and one to which we have no answer. We know that the Bastard's fleet has been assembled, but not what is holding him up. Suffice to say that when he does move our navy will be ready for him, and if he survives that he will die on our southern beaches," said the Earl haughtily and fixed his host with a steely gaze. "And you will have no qualms about doing battle with your countrymen?"

Harald, no stranger to using his powerful physical presence to impose his will, leant over the table and spoke calmly in a tone that each man seated understood well.

"I have given my word, Earl Leofwine and that is good enough for the King of England," emoted the Lord of Maldon.

The Saxon did not meet his gaze and looked away nervously.

"Now come, where are my manners, you must be famished after riding all day in this heat. Drink up and we shall eat - an army marches on its stomach and ours is no different," said Harald, reverting to his former convivial tone and motioning to the serving women to bring food.

It was past dark when they had finished eating and drinking. The evening drew to its natural conclusion and the Earl excused himself. Harald's invitation to join him and his household in the longhouse was politely declined in preference to spending the night in camp with the rest of his Saxon noblemen. They left in the morning at first light, Harald and his captain watching them leave from a vantage point on the palisade fence.

"They suspect nothing?" asked Jeanotte.

"I think not but they have spies everywhere and we should not let our guard drop," came the reply.

3

Two days later more visitors arrived in Maldon but very few of the locals noticed them arrive or depart. In the early hours of the morning a longboat beached on the muddy shoreline at low tide. There was a full moon, and the forty rowers shipped their oars in the silvery light. A cloaked figure slipped over the side and waded through the shallow water toward a bonfire that had been set at the high-water mark, where Harald's two squires waited warming their hands. The brothers squinted through the darkness toward the vague silhouette of the longship, listening intently. Gilbert thought he could discern the sound of wet leather boots squelching through mud, ordered his younger sibling to stop talking and drew his sword. For a few anxious moments they stood stock still until a hooded form emerged from the gloom.

"Stay your sword arms gentlemen. A friend is approaching," said Oystein of Bergen, letting the hood drop to his shoulders.

"Welcome, my Lord," said Gilbert sheathing his weapon. "Please follow me, they are waiting for you in the longhouse."

The Norwegian did as he was bidden, and the three men left the beach and walked silently toward the town. Oystein came bearing important news; a fleet of three hundred ships had landed an army of Norsemen in Northumbria. It was time for Harald Fitzroy to join them.

Chapter 18: The Gathering of the Clans
August 1066, Northumbria

1

Hedda Halldorsdottir was cold, and she leant into the folds of Harald's bearskin cloak. She was no sailor but felt completely safe with his meaty arm wrapped around her, as the ship pitched and yawed in the colliding currents of river and sea. He gripped the tiller of the *Lady Alberada* which led the fleet across the wide estuary of the River Tamsey and out into the open sea. The crew raised the sail, and the great ship turned to starboard. With the convoy following the light of an oil lamp at their masthead, they swept north, aided by favourable southerly winds.

Like the rest of her comrades-in-arms, when the order came to leave, Hedda had been ready, and with her belongings packed into a small wooden sea chest she joined the well-oiled machine that was Harald Fitzroy's army. Following Oystein's visit, he had called his captains to a meeting and the plan for embarkation was put into motion. Warriors and horses assembled rapidly, together with cooks, farriers, armourers and sailors. Supplies for the voyage had already been collected and stockpiled and within two days the expedition was ready to depart in a variety of longships, cogs, galleys and *dromons*. They left quietly just before first light and by the time the summer sun had started its ascent, the town of Maldon and Northey Island had disappeared behind them, they were five leagues down the Blackwater River.

Harald laughed as the spray from another wave broke over the bows of the *Lady Alberada* and soaked the ranks of resting oarsman. He was in his element and standing at the helm of his beloved warship beneath the banners of the two Ravens of Regneville, he was leading his warriors to war again. It filled him with an excitement that he had almost forgotten, and despite his forty years or more he felt renewed by the daunting challenges that awaited him, which seemed only to heighten his excitement. It had been a long winter and spring of waiting and whilst Hedda, had brightened his existence, he knew that his real destiny was on the field of battle. He was back on the great whale road of his grandfathers and the spirit of the Wandering Warriors of Haugesund coursed through his veins once again. Harald Fitzroy's reputation, forged by numerous bloody encounters the length and breadth of Europe and Asia Minor, was to be tested by a new challenge and he embraced it wholeheartedly.

Their summons to war had been brought by the Norwegian longship, *Sea Viper* which waited for them further up the East Anglian coast in Gernemwa to pilot them to the muster point in Northumbria. In four days they reached their destination and the thirty ships under Harald's command rowed along a huge sandy beach festooned with longships to where they would camp in a place of honour beside the King of Norway. As dawn was breaking, they followed the *Sea Viper* along the coastline. Harald stood in the prow of his ship observing the frenetic movement on the beach as newly built camps of disparate war bands seethed with activity. He recognised many of the fighting standards of northern bondesmen that fluttered onshore. Banners from Viken, Oppland and Frostaping fluttered next to those of the Orkney Islands and the Faroes and their encampments spread for almost a league along the sandy shore. As his grandfathers had done so many times before him Harald experienced the same frisson of excitement in anticipation of joining his fellow warriors marching to the drums of war. He reflected that he was now more than twice the age of either Bjorn Halfdanson or Torstein Rolloson when they first joined the great war fleet of Norsemen sailing to the killing fields of Fyrisvellir. Harald wondered for a moment what fate had in store for him. Hedda came and stood next to him, interrupting his thoughts.

"It is a long time since a Fitzroy fought as a Norseman," she said knowingly.

He smiled at her uncanny ability to read his thoughts and looked at her. She had caught the sun during the voyage, and her tanned arms and face enhanced an already an healthy visage.

"You are looking forward to seeing your father again?" he asked her absent-mindedly.

"My father -yes. Some of his friends - no," she said obstinately.

"I have told you, Hedda, you will not be given to a man who is not of your choosing. I will speak to Halldor in due course and will match any bride-price that has been promised," he said firmly.

"You know who I have chosen," she replied.

"I do - the matter of your betrothal will be settled and you are going no-where - besides you are one of my warriors now and I have no wish to let all that training go to waste," he said trying to lighten her mood. "Now look lively, the *Sea Viper* is turning for shore. I don't want our entrance to look sloppy. I want no slovenly Norman seamanship here."

Ahead of them the *Sea Viper* turned sharply towards an area of empty beach and the oarsmen drove her onto dry land. Several smaller ships of Harald's fleet did the same whilst the larger ones anchored in the shallows and prepared to disembark their cargo. An area of approximately one thousand paces of shoreline came alive as men and horses were expertly marshalled up the beach to make camp. Neighing beasts were led down from wide-bodied cargo ships on rapidly affixed wooden ramps, through the shallows and up the sand where their grooms tethered them in long lines. Warriors from the deeper-drafted *dromons* waded ashore carrying their arms and equipment above their heads and out of the salt water. Servants and squires ran hither and yon unloading a variety of different cargos needed to build and sustain the camp.

Harald watched the operation with satisfaction from a vantage point on the beach and smiled with quiet relief to see his huge black stallion, Damascus. The stallion was led down a ramp into the shallows, through the small waves that lapped at his fetlocks and onto the sand to join his comrades.

Just before noon the whole operation was complete, and a rudimentary camp had been made. The horses were fed and watered, tents erected in the dunes away from the beach and the standard of the two ravens of Regneville flew above them at the rallying point. Harald and Brenier stood together in conversation.

"A neat and precise operation, as always," said the Commander to his cousin.

The feverish activity that had boiled all around them slowed down dramatically.

"It is no small wonder, after all we must have done this a hundred times before. I hope we have at least impressed these Norsemen with a display of efficiency," replied his cousin.

They looked to the left and right of their camp, along the crescent of the shoreline that was filled with ships and warriors of the King of Norway's host.

"How many men do you estimate?" asked Harald.

"Three hundred ships? Eight thousand men? And they are still coming," ventured Brenier.

"More than enough to give the Saxons a kick up the arse then?" said Harald nodding in agreement. "If I were Harald

Godwinson, I would be roundly aggrieved to discover that I had another deadly foe waiting for me where I least expected. But after all, oath-breakers deserve nothing less. Perhaps the Norns have something in store for him?"

"And for the rest of his Kingdom too," said Brenier. "Let us hope there is enough plunder for all of us here."

"There will be more than enough to satisfy the greediest of raiders but let us not forget the purpose of our journey. We are here to retrieve my nephew, and after that we can all fill our pockets," reiterated Harald.

Their conversation was interrupted by a horseman trotting toward them and they squinted into the afternoon sun trying to recognise him. Halldor Snorrason shouted a greeting and dismounted.

"You have made fine time, my Lord," called the Icelander, "we were not expecting you for another few days."

"Halldor, it is good to see you," shouted Harald, delighted to see his friend. "This is quite a reception party that you have organised for me."

"We are all delighted to see you, Lord Fitzroy," said Halldor with a wide smile across his face.

"And none more so than one of our number," returned Harald calling behind him to the line of horses where Hedda had been tending her colt.

She looked up from the pail of oats from which she had been feeding her horse and exclaimed her joy at seeing her father for the first time in six months. She rushed over and flung her arms around him delightedly. He returned her embrace fondly and stepped back to look at her.

"You have changed," he said laughing as he took in her short hair and muscular physique, clearly discernible beneath a sleeveless cotton shift and leather breeches.

"I am a warrior, now Father," she said seriously, before joining in the laughter.

"And a fierce one, too," said Harald. "You left me a housekeeper and I got a bodyguard."

"Well, I am sure she will honour her family either way," retorted her father unlocking himself from Hedda's powerful embrace. "I look forward to hearing all your news, daughter. But before that I am on official business. Lord Fitzroy - King Harald invites you to dine with him later today in his camp."

Halldor bowed low from the waist.

"Please tell the King I should be delighted to accept his invitation," said Harald politely. "But first let us get out of the sun and take some wine - there is much that I would know of you."

"And I you, my Lord," he said, glancing at his daughter one more time. "We have much to discuss."

Harald led Halldor to a small wooden table and chairs that had been placed outside his tent, and they sat down to share a skin of wine brought by one of his squires. The two men drank and talked until it was time for the Icelander to return to his master. Halldor reported that his network of spies had been busy and reported that Richard Fitzroy had been seen in York only as recently as a few days ago in the retinue of Earl Morcar of Northumbria. News of the approaching Norwegian fleet had reached the city, accompanied by scenes of great panic, as fearful local residents made frantic plans to defend themselves. In the south, the massed Saxon armies of Harold Godwinson which had waited in vain for the Norman invasion began to disband; harvest time was approaching and the men of the *fyrd* were needed in the fields. As English eyes turned North, the sibling Earls of Mercia and Northumbria began to rally their *thegns* and *huscarls* and another great muster began. When their inevitable clash with the Norsemen took place the opportunity to rescue Richard Fitzroy would reveal itself.

"There is another matter which we need to discuss. You will know that my daughter has been promised to the Jarl of Rogoland," said Halldor, shifting uncomfortably in his chair and, taking his time to speak, he chose his words carefully. "She was never happy with the match and now that she has a home in your household, I expect her to remain with you for as long as she pleases you - but it does complicate matters."

Harald stroked his beard, contemplating a response.

"I cannot deny that I have grown fond of Hedda and have given the matter much consideration. She is strong and willful, and I was in two minds to bring her here at all. But here she is and I must confront the problem with her suitor. Will Jarl Torbjorn accept the bride price in gold in lieu of a wife? I would be very generous," he asked.

"It is unlikely - he is an old man but an honourable one. If he thinks his reputation has been slighted it will take more than gold," replied Halldor.

"Then I shall do what I must to avoid conflict in this matter, but I will not jeopardise my plans to retrieve my nephew at any cost,"

"A wise decision, my Lord. Now I must go, the King is not a man to be kept waiting," said the Icelander as he downed his wine and got up to leave. "It is good to see you, Lord Fitzroy and my daughter has a smile on her face that I have not seen for some time."

No sooner had his guest left than Harald was joined by Hedda who stepped out of the shadows from beside the tent.

"You were listening?" asked Harald.

Hedda nodded stoically before launching into a different matter.

"It is time I prepared you to meet the King of Norway. The Papal Shield cannot appear before his peers looking like a sea gypsy," she said and went into his tent.

She opened one of the sea chests which she had prepared for him before they left Maldon and emerged with combs and clippers. Then she set to work on him combing and trimming his hair and beard. Neither had been cut since Christmas, growing wild and unkempt but by the time she was finished with him his luxuriant growth of silver flecked hair had been groomed and plaited, hanging neatly down his back. She also cropped the unruly tangle of his beard before standing back to admire her work and smiled with satisfaction. Then she led him into the tent, where a clean set of clothes and boots had been laid out for him on a cot.

"There, I have made a good start, but I will trust you to do the rest yourself. Your squires have been working hard on your attire," she said with a grin.

Beside his clothes lay *Gunnlogi*, gleaming dully in the half-light of the tent. "They have also done their best with this," she continued, handing him a thick band of solid gold.

"Ah, the warrior's ring from my grandfather," he turned it over delightedly before sliding it on to his forearm, remembering the day he had received it as a ten-year old boy.

"He would be proud, I am sure. Let us make haste - your audience awaits. I will wait for you outside - I know how you hate to be fussed over," she said leaving the tent.

Harald emerged shortly afterward looking resplendent in a white shirt beneath a black leather *gambesson*. The jewelled hilt of his *ulfberht* sword caught the last of the sun's rays, reflecting small shards of refracted ruby-red light. Thomas stood holding the halter of Damascus who had, like his master, been groomed to perfection. The horse's coat shone with a deep black lustre and the silverware on the saddle and bridle had been polished to a brilliant sheen. Hedda and the two brothers stood and looked on, gratified by the result of their labour.

"Am I fit for an audience with the King?" asked Harald.

"You need no great horse or fine clothes to announce your arrival, my Lord," said Thomas, handing him the reins. "Your reputation goes before you."

"I thank you, my friends," said Harald before putting a foot in one stirrup and hauling himself into the saddle.

The great horse needed only a deft squeeze of his master's knee to know which way they were to travel, and he turned and walked obediently across the beach to where the King of Norway's camp lay less than half a league away. Before long horse and rider had left their own camp and passed through the perimeter of the Norwegians towards the King's pavilion at its centre. They were scrutinised by many pairs of eyes as they rode past the great lines of tents bearing the battle standards of the Norse clans. It was approaching dusk when they arrived at their destination, and the sun was descending rapidly in the west as Harald dismounted and gave the reins of the horse to a waiting servant. As he approached the entrance to the enormous tent, his way was blocked by two guards, each man bearing an enormous dane-axe.

"Your weapons, my Lord," said the first guard, in old Norse. "We cannot allow you any further until you give them to us."

Harald said nothing and was about to unbuckle the belt that held his sword and seax when a loud voice erupted from within.

"Let him pass with his arms intact," boomed the voice. "If a king has to fear his allies we will never get anywhere."

The guards stood aside allowing Harald to pass between them and he entered a large, sparsely furnished tent illuminated by numerous torches. At the far end stood three men, Oystein of Bergen, Halldor Snorrason and the King of Norway. They looked up from the table at which they had been poring over a map and watched their guest approach. He walked toward them and stopped in front of the table, looking only at the King who regarded him without a word. Both men held each other's gaze until Harald lowered his head in a brief bow to the Norwegian monarch.

"My Lord, may I introduce you to ….," began Oystein breaking the silence.

"Yes, I am well aware of who he is," snapped the King stepping toward Harald until they were within an arm's length of each other.

Harald Hardrada, the King of Norway was as tall as his namesake, if not quite as broad and was ten years older. His sandy shoulder-length hair was tied back from a heavily bearded face that revealed a fierce disposition. Deep set green eyes beneath a furrowed forehead gave him an angry look, and he regarded the man in front of him in complete silence. Harald continued to return the gaze and the moments of this first encounter seemed to last for an age. It was the Norwegian who broke the silence, and he extended his hand in greeting, a hint of a smile formed on his thin lips.

"Welcome to my camp, Lord Fitzroy - I trust our alliance will be long and fruitful. You are everything that I was told to expect," said the King, gesturing to a servant to bring beer for his guest.

"Thankyou, my Lord. Our paths may not have crossed but I am more than familiar with your reputation," returned Harald.

"And I yours. But I am intrigued that you still speak the language of your grandfathers with such fluency." replied the King.

"*Dǫnsk Tunga* was the language of our house," said the Norman. "And my late wife made sure I never forgot it."

"Then let our first toast be to our families and ancestors and that we should honour them with our deeds," said Hardrada raising his cup. "Now you are familiar with both of these fellows, I am sure," he continued, waiving an arm to Oystein and Halldor, who had retained a deferential silence.

Harald nodded, raising his own cup to his host and then to the two other men.

"*Skål*. To Norway, the birthplace of heroes; let us empty our cups and break the chains that seek to bind us," he said loudly.

For the next two hours the King bombarded his guest with an intense barrage of questions which Harald patiently answered. He wanted to know about everything from Norman battle tactics to details of the English King's court, to the balance of military power in the Kingdom in the Sun. Hardrada contemplated each response carefully before moving on to the next question, as if testing for signs of weakness or falsehood. Finding none, the King relented in his questioning and his disposition seemed to change in moments.

"You are a man after my own heart, Harald Fitzroy," he said as his face cracked into a broad smile. "Now, you have indulged me for too long with my incessant quizzing but humour me a little longer, if you will. Is it true that you have come all this way to fight for plunder alone? Is there no other reason for your quest?"

"I seek the return of my nephew who is a hostage of the Earl of Mercia, and I have unfinished business with the Saxons," replied Harald without a moment's hesitation. "Besides, you are known to be a generous Lord who rewards his warriors once the battle is done."

The King steepled his hands in thought.

"Ah, a blood-feud will out-last many generations. Come my friend, it is time to meet your comrades. You will know only too well how we Norsemen like to feast. It might be poor fayre but will be better than the hard bread and dried fish we have all endured during the voyage to get here," said Hardrada standing up from his chair and stretching.

Harald stole a look at Halldor, who smiled back and nodded his silent support. They all made their way out of the tent into a refreshing onshore breeze and, led by a group of torch bearing servants, they walked to the top of the sand dunes where a long table had been laid out beneath a large silken awning. It was now dark, and the clear night sky provided a backdrop for countless twinkling stars. After the stultifying heat and gloom of the King's quarters, the smell of kelp and sage brush provided a welcome change, and Harald breathed in the salty tang deeply as they walked in silence. It did not last long for already seated were over fifty men, the Jarls of the territories and allies of Norway awaited their leader and loudly applauded his arrival. They stood, clapping and banging drinking cups on the table until the King raised his hands for quiet.

"Welcome my friends, you have travelled far, and it is my pleasure to see you all again. Tonight, we shall eat and drink our fill, but as soon as our host has gathered, we shall be moving down the coast to take what is rightfully ours," called Hardrada in a voice that carried on the wind. "But before we sup together, I have the honour of presenting my ally Harald Fitzroy, the great war leader of the Normans whose bloodline is shared by many of you here."

There was some polite applause, and the King put his hand on Harald's shoulder inviting him to sit down on his right. At this signal, servants began to appear, pouring beer for thirsty guests from huge, seemingly bottomless jugs. More servants came with trays of roasted meats from the adjacent mobile kitchens, and the air was filled with the sounds of men's voices in lively conversation.

"You did well, my Lord. I have seen lesser men wilt beneath such an intense interrogation," said Halldor leaning across the table to Harald.

"A man must be as certain as he can of those who stand beside him in the shield-wall," he replied. "Now tell me which of these fellows is the Jarl of Rogoland?"

"He is the old man in a blue cloak with silver hair, halfway down the table on your left," said Halldor.

Harald followed the directions and looked into the face of Jarl Torbjorn. He nodded politely to the old man, who did not acknowledge the gesture but simply glared back at him with undisguised fury.

The evening passed without incident, despite the amount of beer that was consumed, and the company was good-natured and entertaining. The gathering lost its formality as more drink was consumed; tales were told, and songs were sung. Harald was introduced to many of the Jarls, who were keen to meet him, and he received compliments about the impressive appearance of his cavalry earlier in the day. The Jarl of Haugesund approached, announcing himself as a distant relative and invited him to visit their camp before they left on campaign. The feasting continued long into the small hours until the King departed for his bed and one by one his captains returned to their camps. Harald went to find his horse and wearily rode Damascus back to his tent where he crawled, exhausted, into bed. He found Hedda fast asleep and wrapping an enormous arm around her, he drew her close and collapsed into a deep dreamless slumber.

2

The following day started in a lively manner and Harald woke abruptly as Hedda shook him out of a deep sleep. There were raised voices coming from the camp and he dressed quickly and went outside to investigate. He looked toward the source of the commotion at the perimeter, to see that a number of armed men had been stopped from entering further and were surrounded by a group of his own warriors. He strapped on his sword and strode swiftly toward the knot of men with Thomas and Gilbert falling in behind him. They arrived to find the Jarl of Rogoland and six Norsemen in a heated conversation with Leif and a cohort of guards who had prevented them from progressing toward the centre of the camp. On seeing their commander approach, Harald's men parted, allowing him to walk through their ranks towards the Jarl, who was still remonstrating with Leif.

"Good day, my Lord. You are welcome to our camp, but we are just finding our bearings here and you must pardon us if we appear a little defensive," he said to Jarl Torbjorn convivially. "May I offer you and your men some breakfast"

It was still early in the day and despite a nip in the air the old man was red-faced and sweating. As Harald approached him, he saw that the Jarl was older than he had originally thought, perhaps sixty or seventy years old and clearly agitated.

"You have something that is mine and I want it back," the Jarl answered unequivocally.

"We are both men of good reputation, my Lord. Please stand your men down and let us talk without rancour," offered Harald.

The Jarl, surrounded by fifty or so armed Normans, muttered something to his men and Harald came closer and led him away from the throng with an arm around the shoulder.

"You will have to forgive my men, my Lord, we are veterans of a thousand campaigns together and when one of us is threatened - we all are," said Harald soothingly as they walked together past a line of tethered horses. "Now, my Lord, you speak of Hedda Halldorsdottir?"

"I do," blustered the old man who had managed to calm himself a little. "She has been betrothed to me and is to be my wife. It is a matter of honour that needs a resolution, and I cannot let it drop."

"This I understand," said Harald, "but the woman has no wish to be your wife, whatever you have agreed with her father. I have no desire to fall out with you when there are far more important matters at hand. But you are right, this does need to be settled. Are you proposing settling this in the old way? By *holmgang* perhaps?"

The old man turned and faced him, knowing there was no way he could physically enforce his claim.

"The King has forbidden such competition. Not that I would oppose such a resolution, of course and honour must be satisfied," said the Jarl in a slightly more conciliatory tone.

"I would not insult you by offering gold in settlement, but perhaps you would accept a more suitable exchange? My warrior's rings that have been bestowed upon me by great men? Perhaps my sword which has won me and my kin many battle honours?" proposed Harald.

"That is too great a sacrifice, Lord Fitzroy. I could not presume on such a resolution," came the immediate response.

Harald thought for a moment and turned toward the sea, where *Lady Alberada* lay anchored in the shallows and pointed toward the beautiful black hulled *dromon* with an outstretched hand.

"You are a seafaring man, Jarl Torbjorn. That ship is as dear to my heart as anything. Two rows of double-banked oars for forty rowers, decks of oriental plane, strong and fast as anything you will find at home," said Harald. "It will carry you back to Rogoland in triumph with as much plunder from the coming campaign as you can carry."

Jarl Torbjorn looked at the ship with interest and then back to Harald.

"That is a fine offer, my Lord and one which deserves consideration," he said before adding "And when might I take her?"

"Then allow me to sail her to battle, if you will," replied Harald, knowing that the deal was as good as done. "I should like her to terrify the enemy one last time."

The two men shook hands and the matter was settled.

3

For the next three days they waited. More men joined Hardrada's army until the last expected ships arrived. Tostig Godwinson's warriors were the final war band to join the great host of Northumbria. The Earl's longboats drove up onto the furthest part of the beach and three hundred loyal *thegns* and men-at-arms came ashore. In a ceremony the following day, the brother of the English monarch bent the knee to the King of Norway pledging an oath of fealty. The significance of the event was not lost on the Norwegian Jarls, who took this as a sign that many other Saxon nobles would also swap their allegiances, helping them take the English throne. It was certainly not lost on Harald Fitzroy, who stood watching the brother of the King of England pledge his loyal oath to his brother's enemy.

"When brothers fallout, no-one can be sure of the outcome," said Harald quietly to Jeanotte as they observed the swearing-in. "Betrayal is not easily forgiven."

"We can be sure of that, my Lord," agreed his young captain, recalling the rift between the Fitzroy brothers.

"And perhaps to answer your unasked question, I would dearly love to make things right with my brother, but I think that would be stretching his abilities for forgiveness a little too far," said Harald.

"Have you had any word from the Lady Eleanor?" asked Jeanotte.

Harald shook his head and gave a rueful smile.

"Brenier reported that she and the child appeared well, when he visited Mortain, but beyond that - nothing. Perhaps it is for the best - little good will come of rekindling the ghosts of the past. Anyway, we appear to have our hands full here for the moment," he answered.

"As does the rest of Normandie, Lord, but I am happy to confirm that I have never seen the men in a better state of readiness. I almost pity the Saxons who will be reaping our whirlwind soon enough," said Jeanotte as they watched Earl Tostig get to his feet and accept a fraternal embrace from his new liege-lord. "And what do you make of this particular Saxon?"

"I have heard nothing good. He is a desperate man clutching at straws - and one not to be trusted by all accounts. I should not like to rely on him in the heat of battle."

Their conversation came to an end as Harald Hardrada walked amongst his Jarls with Tostig at his heels.

"Ah, Lord Fitzroy," he called, seeing the pair of Normans in front of him. "You have met our new comrade-in-arms."

"I have not, my Lord, but his reputation precedes him," answered Harald with a benign smile, inclining his head diplomatically to the Saxon Earl.

Tostig Godwinson displayed a surprised look, and he returned the greeting. Harald observed that the Saxon had none of his older brother's assuredness and looked distracted and agitated.

"Then I will be fortunate enough to share the battlefield with two great warriors," he said a little too obsequiously. "But surely, Lord Fitzroy you are a long way from home?"

"Fate takes the warrior where the opportunity is greatest," retorted Harald, before Hardrada broke in.

"And fate brings us all together finally, gentlemen. Tomorrow we shall be leaving on the high tide and heading south. In ten days' time the city of York shall be ours," said the King with undisguised enthusiasm.

4

The *Land Ravager* sat broadside to the beach about five hundred paces from the shore. It was a beautiful ship and every part of her had been finished with exquisite care by her builders. At the bows there was a large carved dragonhead, while the tail of the mythical creature featured at her stern. The clinkered planks at the top of her hull were of gilded pine, and below this line were seventy *tholes* at which her oarsmen toiled to keep her steady in the freshening sea breeze. The sails, anchors, rigging and cables were all of the highest quality, and she glistened and sparkled in the autumn sun. At the King's order a man stood at the prow and blew the great war horn, summoning his forces to war. Moored vessels pulled up the anchors and those on shore were manhandled through the breaking waves and manoeuvred into position to join the great fleet. The huge red and white sail of the *Land Ravager* was hoisted, and she turned to sail off a northerly wind, leading the great armada of three hundred ships to war. Standing at the helm of *Lady Alberada,* Harald looked up at the grey clouds scuttling across the northern welkin and mouthed a few silent prayers. He leaned all his weight into the long wooden lever of the tiller and as the craft turned, the mainsail snapped into life. The vast sheets caught the wind and the *dromon* led her sisters out to join the biggest naval force that had ever assailed the English coastline.

Chapter 19: The Duke's Fleet Prepares to Sail
Normandie, August 1066

1

"We all saw the sign, my friends. What else could it have meant but His divine blessing on our pilgrimage to England?" asked Duke William of the assembled council, the last one before he left Rouen to join the army on the coast.

"I would question the shooting star as a sign of God's will no more than the three kings did when a similar celestial event led them to Christ's birth in Bethlehem," rejoined Robert of Mortain, to which the Duke's own wise men around the table nodded in agreement.

All eyes turned to Lanfranc of Pavin, as if he were able to divine the thoughts of God.

"What say you, my Lord Archbishop?" asked the Duke.

"There is no doubt in my mind that the Lord has given his blessing to our endeavours. We here believe it, Rome believes it and the thousands of men who have rallied to our colours are all similarly disposed," said the Archbishop of Caen.

There was another general murmur of approval from around the table and many of the council members crossed themselves.

The Duke was in good humour and the feeling of bonhomie ran through the room. Events following his diplomatic efforts earlier in the year had proved fruitful. After the disappointing decision by many of his barons not to join the invasion force, the tide of opinion had turned dramatically and warriors from all over Europe responded to the promise of plundering the Saxon Kingdom. They came from far and wide. Men from Brittany, Anjou, Burgundy and Flanders started to arrive in May, and by the summer the trickle became a flood. The muster point of Dives had grown into a large town almost overnight as soldiers of fortune including substantial numbers of the Norman diaspora from the Kingdom in the Sun arrived by land and sea. The news from England had been equally encouraging and the landing in the north of the country by the King of Norway had been received as a further blessing to the Duchy.

"Gentlemen," continued the Duke, "the campaign will not be an easy one and God intends to test our resolve. We could well be in England for many years. In my absence I am appointing my wife, the Duchess Mathilda as regent and she will rule the Duchy in my stead. Do we all concur with this decision?"

There were more rumblings of agreement from around the table.

"Your assent is duly noted," he said, waving at the attendant scribe, furiously scribbling away. "Now the Chancellor will deliver his report."

Robert Fitzroy took a deep breath and began to speak.

"Eleven hundred ships, ten thousand men and three thousand horses will be ready to depart from Dives in the next few weeks. You are to be congratulated, and I applaud your efforts," he said clapping his hands slowly.

Before long all twenty council members joined in the applause and the sound resonated out from the chambers, ringing through the halls and rooms of the ducal Palace of Rouen. Robert held out his hands calling for quiet, which came eventually.

"The Saxon army that have been waiting for us all summer is about to be stood down and the *fyrd* sent home to gather the harvest - we shall continue to keep them guessing about our own arrival. To add to their problems a great army of Norwegians have arrived in Northumbria to challenge for the English throne, and we expect the Saxons to meet this threat with all the forces they can muster. It would seem a perfect time for us to strike at English hearts," continued Robert.

"Might the Norsemen threaten our own plans?" ventured William Fitzosborne.

"It is possible but unlikely. They are currently over a hundred leagues away from where we intend to land and Harald Godwinson cannot fight on two fronts. We are hoping that they will destroy one another - after all when two mad dogs are fighting no-one else gets bitten."

More discussion followed but Duke William drew the meeting to a close, announcing that they would all meet on the road to Dives at first light the next morning.

"My Lords, destiny awaits us. What God has ordained neither Saxon nor Norwegian pretenders can deny. Let us take the rest of this day to say goodbye to our loved ones, for we will not be seeing them for some time," he said before sweeping out of the room.

One by one the council members got up and left until only Robert and Archbishop Lanfranc remained.

"The Duke has much to thank you for," said Pavin when they were alone.

"I am happy to do my duty," replied Robert.

"But at no small cost to your personal life, I believe," said his mentor. "How are things in Mortain?

"My family are well and relations between my wife and I are cordial enough. The new child occupies much of her time, but she frets over the fate of our eldest. Whilst our marriage will never be harmonious again, we share a common purpose which has brought us back together in some small way," replied Robert before changing the subject. "You have heard the rumours about my brother?"

"I have and I do not believe a word of it. Harald Fitzroy is many things but is no traitor. Despite your personal differences, he would die before he betrays us. Have faith he will not let you down and your son will come home soon," said Lanfranc, reaching over the table and putting a hand on his friend's arm.

They sat in silence for a while and then as they had done so often before, they left together for the chapel to pray for guidance.

Robert had a great deal on his mind and if God was listening to him that day, the requests for heavenly assistance would be numerous. The Norman fleet needed steady southerly winds to take them to England and the summer had been stultifyingly hot on the coast, without as much as a breath of the required sea breezes. Whilst the ships had been swiftly procured, he was concerned that the Duke's enormous fleet did not have enough competent mariners to negotiate the tricky conditions of *La Manche*. Fickle weather conditions could potentially sound their death knell without God's blessing. Robert was further concerned by rumours that the Saxon war fleet lay in wait for them and might even be encouraged to launch a preemptive strike at the Duchy. He had a lot on his mind aside the perils of the forthcoming invasion; his beloved son was in enemy territory, his brother was a suspected traitor, and he could not be sure of where his wife's loyalties lay any more. As he had done so often before, he put his faith in the Almighty and prayed with all his heart for the safe deliverance of all of them.

2

In contrast to his Chancellor's concerns, Duke William appeared carefree and joyous as his cohort of companions approached the great city of fifteen thousand tents housing the men of numerous different regions and nationalities that made up his army. His continued high spirits were available for all to see as he chatted to each of them during the forty-league march to the west, where his host awaited their commander in the small seaport of Dives. The Duke's strict instructions to his commanders that the local population should be treated with respect during the army's buildup had been observed to the letter, and locals appeared at regular intervals along the way. Men cheered him and women presented him with summer flowers as he passed along the route to the sea, and in contrast to his normal gruff persona he returned their greetings with great gusto.

Robert was no stranger to the road from Rouen, having travelled it many times this year as soon as it was decided that Dives would be the place where the Norman host would assemble and disembark. He had persuaded Duke William to gather his army here after a lengthy deliberation. The port had been chosen for its ability to safely harbour the large, improvised fleet and there was a plentiful supply of grain to feed both men and horses. Robert had toiled with his customary diligence to plan and provision the enormous camp. As the group crested the rise leading down the coast, he looked out with satisfaction at the fruits of his labour as it stretched out beneath his gaze. He turned in the saddle to look at his squire Henri, who crossed himself before smiling back at his lord. The long line of carts carrying supplies into the camp moved to the roadside allowing the troop of sixty horsemen to ride along swiftly. They paused briefly at an abbey outside the perimeter of the camp, where a group of Benedictine monks joined the procession beneath a golden cross held high on long wooden pole. To the homophonic chants of plainsong, the party made the remainder of their journey on foot, where the whole garrison waited for them in the stillness of another warm summer's day. When the group reached his pavilion, Duke William stepped up on a makeshift dais and raised his hands to acknowledge the cheers of his army. They were happy and well-fed, having received additional rations for the previous week, and the promise of Saxon plunder ensured the whole camp was in good spirits.

"My friends," the Duke called in a loud, coarse voice that carried to the furthest ranks of soldiers, "you have journeyed far to get here and I thank you for your efforts. Remember you are doing God's will on this most holiest of pilgrimages and I guarantee that each man will receive great rewards for his endeavours both here and in the next life. When our work is done you will return home rich in body and soul. *Dex aie.*"

The men cheered and answered the rallying call by chanting his name and soon the whole camp resounded to cries of "William, William." He raised his hands to quieten the crowd before inviting Oddo, the Bishop of Bayeux to join him on the platform. The warrior priest stepped up, resplendent in a gleaming *hauberk* and blessed the now silent assembly, leading them in enthusiastic prayer. The brief service concluded, the monks struck up with a loud chanting of psalms and along with the Duke's companions, the whole throng was dismissed. Robert stood beside the platform watching the men return to their quarters until only he and Duke William were left. Then both men turned and walked the short distance to where the Duke's pavilion had been erected at the top of a hill in the centre of the camp. A servant came out to meet them and guided them to a table upon which food and drink had been laid out. They sat for a few moments taking in the sight of the vast array of sigils and banners that hung limp and loose all around them, barely stirring in the early evening stillness.

"We need wind from the south, William," said Robert, breaking the silence as he looked beyond the camp and past the harbour where the Norman fleet waited listlessly across the expanse of the river estuary.

"There are some things that are beyond even the 'Genius of Dives'," replied the Duke good-naturedly. "The wind shall come in due course. Mark my words, God is with us and he will provide what you cannot."

Robert managed a weak smile through his tiredness. At the same time a faint breeze wafted the smell of equine waste from the column of dozens of carts that snaked slowly out of the camp. The gust was short-lived and the pervading reek from latrines, tanneries and smoke of a thousand cooking fires resumed their prominence.

"The wind cannot come soon enough," replied Robert. "I am not sure how long I can live with the stench."

"Nonsense, but you have worked wonders. The camp is a small miracle and here we sit looking over our well-fed, well-equipped army with a fleet of ships at our disposal, safe from any of the predations of the Saxon navy. I drink to your health, Robert. The success of our mission will be laid at your door," said the Duke with uncharacteristic praise.

He raised his cup to his Chancellor and the two sat in silence watching the red orb of the setting sun descend into the sea, knowing that this was probably the calm before the storm. Their reverie was interrupted by the approach of the camp marshal; Floki Fitzroy strode purposefully toward them.

"Permission to join you, my Lord?" he enquired, standing before the table.

"You need no invitation, we are family here," said the Duke to Robert's brother. "It is good to see you. Now pray sit and join us. Tell us the news from the camp."

Robert stood up and embraced his younger brother who then sat beside them and helped himself from the large earthenware jug of summer wine.

"I am pleased to say the muster is complete, my Lord. We have a few stragglers still awaited from the south but with no wind it is a fearfully long row from Italy," said Floki jauntily. "I can report the camp is in good health and there has been no sign of disease. The warhorses are in fine condition and they are all under the care and attention of the stable boys of Regneville. What is more, I can report that your army is in harmony - the old quarrels have been forgotten - at least for the moment anyway."

"Any sign of Saxon ships?" asked his brother.

"Three warships were spotted offshore a few days ago but we caught them cold and took them without much of a struggle. Two dozen good oarsmen are an ill-match for any size sail in this weather. Anyway, we let one of the ships escape once they had seen the size of our fleet," said Floki.

"Excellent, let's keep the English pretender guessing about our next move. Did you learn anything from the prisoners about the Saxon force that will oppose us?" asked Robert.

"Little we did not already know, although the Norwegians are creating havoc in the North of England and diverting the English king's attention from our own invasion. The Saxon fleet lies becalmed on the coast and a good wind from the south will enable us to slip past them unopposed," replied Floki.

Duke William nodded contentedly.

"You are the bearer of good news, Floki Fitzroy," he said getting up. "Now gentlemen, please excuse me. I must go and pray for those winds and ask for God's continued blessings before I can allow myself to retire. Please stay here and eat - I am sure you have much to catch up on."

The Fitzroy brothers waited for their liege-lord to retire into his tent before continuing in low whispers.

"What news of the men of Ambrières?" asked Robert anxiously.

His sibling leaned into their conspiratorial conference.

"Well, they are not here, brother. Jeanotte took most of Hari's army and sailed to join him in Maldon. And there the trail grows cold - our brother simply vanished. He was due to join the English King in the defence of the south coast, but his ships were rumoured to be heading in the opposite direction."

"To where?" asked Robert.

"Toward the Norwegian fleet of course, brother. Surely, you did not think he would be joining the Saxons to fight against his own kin?" said Floki softly.

Robert threw his head back and almost emitted a joyous laugh before he checked himself.

"My prayers have been answered," he said dragging his brother toward him and embracing him fiercely.

"Have faith, Robert. Do not waste your prayers asking for Hari's continued loyalty. It was never in doubt - as well you know. Whatever our brother is up to it will not be to our detriment on the field. It is a stiff southerly we need now - one that will blow us across *La Manche* and will render the Saxon fleet impotent. Come now let us finish off these fine vittles before we retire - I have had enough of camp food to last a lifetime," said Floki with a grin. "Do you think that the Duke might spare us another jug of this very fine wine?"

"You grow more like our brother every time I see you," replied Robert before summoning a servant to replenish the jug.

3

Despite the prayers offered to God from William, his companions and a small army of priests and holy men, the weather did not change, and the sultry heat of August carried forward into September. Far from being downbeat the Duke seemed to revel in the suspense, asserting to his confederates that the wait would gull the Saxons into believing that any invasion might be called off at least until the following year. While Robert busied himself administrating the demands of keeping the camp healthy, nourished and motivated, Duke William took an active part in martial training and proved to be a rumbustious combatant whether on foot or horseback. He showed his delight at being reunited with the Riders of Regneville, with whom he first learned his skills as a warrior and joined their *conroi* whenever they took to the drill field. It was after one such training day, when the Duke was returning to his pavilion, that the winds began to blow hard from the south, thirty days after he had first arrived at the camp. He and Robert were deep in conversation when the first gust of wind blew so hard that the sound of the pennons above the ducal pavilion snapped hard and caused them both to look up. Then they looked seaward to see the mouth of the Dives estuary awash with white horses, causing the anchored Norman ships to buffet and pull against their chains.

"It is here at last, Robert," shouted the Duke exuberantly, clapping his Chancellor heartily on the back, "the breath of God that will sweep the Saxons into the sea."

As dusk approached the wind was still blowing strongly from the south and the decision to sail imminently was made. The following day the army with all their accoutrements of war had been loaded and the ships were ready. As dawn broke the early morning sun shone over the estuary, and the first ships, led by the

Mora, set out on the high tide heading for the narrows. Behind the deserted camp the brown, grazed-out land was engulfed in a dust cloud as the warhorses were herded together by Floki's horsemen, to be shepherded down the coast for a shorter sea passage to England. Robert, aboard a robust longship, the *Sea Winds,* together with fifty men of Mortain, almost forgot his seasickness the moment they reached the open sea, and he looked back to see their fleet in full sail. He marvelled at the magnificent spectacle of the wind billowing the colourful flags, banners, pennants, streamers and painted sails of the armada and crossed himself as he muttered a prayer of thanks. In that moment he knew beyond doubt that they were moving inexorably toward victory across the narrow sea of *La Manche.*

What had not entered the Chancellor's meticulous calculations was the capricious nature of the sea. After a morning of sailing, free of incident, he looked over the port-side gunwale toward the west and noticed a squall of black clouds scudding across the blue skies toward them, and the words of his long dead grandfather echoed back at him from the past.

"The sea is a cruel mistress," Bjorn Halfdanson would often tell his grandsons, "you can love and revere her but be wary of her soft embrace for she will break your heart and take your soul."

Around midday the storm announced itself with heavy gusts that rocked and pounded away at the fleet as it made its presence felt. Shortly afterward the skies darkened, blocking out the sun and the temperatures dropped alarmingly, forcing men to pull their sodden cloaks about them in an effort to keep warm. Then the full force of the tempest struck and howling winds assailed the rapidly de-rigged vessels, hitting them hard amidships and scattering everything in its path. It was as if an angry giant were lobbing rocks into a pond full of toy ships and Robert lost sight of the other craft of the invasion convoy as they careered off in all directions. As the *Sea Winds* pitched and yawed, other lost and uncontrolled vessels reared up in front of her before disappearing again in the roiling spume as fast as they had appeared. They ascended great mountainous swells, descending into huge foam-filled troughs before reappearing at the peak of another wind-blown summit. He lost sight of the *Mora* which vanished as another tumultuous gust of wind launched itself across the gale-ripped sea. Robert felt another wave of nausea threatening to overcome his senses and dug deep in an effort to control the rising gorge. It seemed to erupt from the soles of his boots, and he vomited onto the heaving wooden deck which took away the last vestiges of strength from his pain-wracked body. When things seemed like they could not get any worse the wind changed, veering from south to west, setting up cross seas which drove the *Sea Winds* east and back toward the rugged shoreline of Normandie. Her oarsmen struggled in vain to control her progress until they collapsed, exhausted over their looms. The froth-flecked winds howled through the ship's shrouds making her timbers shudder with terror and Robert sank to his knees in submission. He mouthed prayers asking for God's deliverance for it seemed like nothing man-made could withstand the bared fangs of the storm.

In the hours that followed, the storm kept up its vicious assault but miraculously the *Sea Winds* refused to buckle and break, which owed more to the shipwrighting skills of Olaf Knarresmed than to any divine intervention. Robert stood on unsure legs at the ship's aft gripping the sternpost next to the battered helmsman and together they peered through the gloom to discern a stretch of sandy shoreline racing toward them at great speed.

"Brace yourself, my Lord. We are coming in fast but with God's grace we may yet avoid the rocks and land safe. Please, lend me your weight - we need to hit the land straight and true, " shouted the helmsman.

"As long as you don't ask me to pray - I'm not sure there is another prayer left in me," shouted Robert back with grim humour, clutching the rudder shaft desperately in both hands.

Both men leant into it, aiming the bows of the craft directly at the beach which seemed to rush up to meet them. There was a sharp, grinding sound as the shallow keel made contact with the shore and the ship juddered with the impact, galvanising the exhausted crew into life. The momentum propelled her at speed, hurling her through the shallows until she came to an abrupt stop and every man who had not braced himself against something solid was thrown forward. The crew reacted immediately, and each member, bar Robert and the helmsman, launched themselves overboard to grapple the *Sea Winds* out of the clutches of the pounding surf and up the beach. They pulled her as far away as they could, past the high-water mark with the remainder of their strength until, exhausted by the effort, staggered up onto dryer land and collapsed onto the shale. The helmsman turned to Robert and shouted,

"Thankyou, my Lord. We have been delivered. Rest now and gather your strength - you have earned it."

Robert put out a weary arm and clasped the man's shoulder before succumbing to exhaustion, falling into a deep, dream-filled sleep on the deck of the ruined craft.

Chapter 20: The North in Flames
Northumbria, September 1066

1

Skardaburg was an unimportant town on the east coast of England and of scant strategic importance to any invading army. The King of Norway considered this fact to be of little significance when the fickle winds blowing his fleet south died and progress came to a temporary halt. As he had done on so many previous campaigns in Europe and North Africa, he beached his ships and laid waste to the land, stripping it of every last piece of food and anything of value. His first act was to send out teams of foragers to gather and burn, and the Norsemen set about their task with practised brutality. Full grain stores were emptied and cattle and sheep were slaughtered where they grazed, to feed the rapacious appetite of the invading army. The local population suffered from the wanton depredations of the raiders who roamed at will beneath the sigil of the 'Land Ravager'.

There was more to Hardrada's actions than merely provisioning his army and terrorising the Northumbrians. Earl Edwin and his brother Morca were mustering an army of defenders in the city of York, fifteen leagues away, and the King of Norway knew he must draw them out and defeat them before advancing any further into England. As his longboats wrought carnage along the coastline of the north-east, Harald Fitzroy took a party of mounted warriors on the road to York. He tasked Jeanotte with selecting a hundred and fifty men to ride inland on fast, mobile coursers and announce the arrival of the invading army to any Saxon warriors they might encounter.

As dawn was breaking on another mizzling Northumbrian day, Harald's men rode out of their temporary camp and headed west. They were an assortment of mounted infantry, archers and skirmishers, adept at travelling quickly overland to engage in lightening strikes on the enemy. Each man was a veteran of numerous campaigns under Harald Fitzroy, and after the tedium of months of travelling and training they were all keen for the opportunity to be fighting again. Earl Tostig had provided two local scouts from his meagre army and the company set out at pace to cover as much of the fifteen leagues to York as they could before they needed to turn back. When Hedda had learned of Harald's mission she had begged him to take her, until he had finally relented. Lightly armed astride a sleak Norman courser she proudly took her place in the flying column.

It was not long before they passed the first deserted farmhouse and its smoking remains announced the presence of Norsemen in the area. Blackened corpses of unlucky Saxons who had failed to outrun the pillagers were in great evidence as Harald's party progressed, and by midday the road ahead of them was full of the detritus of a local population on the run. There were broken and abandoned carts, discarded belongings and the carcasses of dead horses strewn over the road as people fled to the sanctuary of the city.

"It seems that we do not need to announce our presence," called Harald to Jeanotte.

"It is small wonder," said his captain, turning to the skyline behind them which was dark with the smoke of the fires engulfing Skardaburg. "The Land Ravager has begun his work in earnest."

"It seems like we have company," he answered as a group of warriors appeared on the rise of a nearby hill.

He ordered the column to halt and waited for the scouts riding back toward them at speed.

"A company of Mercian infantry, Lord," said the first scout as he approached. "About two hundred men-at-arms. They will want to test our resolve."

"And they will find out very quickly. Let them come if they are willing and we shall see how inquisitive they are. Make ready the archers, Jeanotte," said Harald decisively.

As the Saxons moved down the small hill and onto the meadowland between the two groups of warriors, fifty Norman archers rode up and halted a thousand paces away from them. They dismounted and formed into a line and the other half of Harald's mounted company drew up behind their comrades, watching the advance of the Mercians who marched steadily towards them. The archers waited patiently for the enemy to close on them, nocked arrows and drew their bows. Jeanotte gave the order and a shower of arrows were loosed simultaneously, raining down on Saxon heads. Multiple volleys followed, bringing down warriors who were too slow to raise their round wooden shields and men howled in pain as the treacherous steel bodkins penetrated boiled leather tunics and mail vests. The Saxon advance was checked momentarily but encouraged by the shouts and threats of their *thegn* riding behind them they tentatively moved forward until a Norman arrow pierced their leader's helmet dropping him stone-dead from his horse. The Saxons moved closer together and with thirty of their number dead or dying, they formed a shield wall a hundred paces away from their enemy. The Norman archers answered by mounting, moving position and peppering their flanks with more arrows. When their work was done, Harald ordered his skirmishers into action and they raced behind the line of their foemen, into the rear, causing mayhem with a volley of hurled javelins. The battle horn sounded, and he called his men back, allowing the bewildered enemy to run from the field in a disorganised rabble.

"A successful first venture?" suggested Jeanotte wiping his face clean of the blood from a fallen Saxon warrior.

"Small victories don't often win wars," replied Harald, "but this little sortie will at least have announced our arrival."

"Are we to pursue?"

"No, let them go back to their masters and report our presence. We must get as close to the city as we can before our work is done and leave them guessing and confused," replied the Commander.

A brief check on the column revealed a few light injuries but none that would halt progress and they followed the path of their defeated enemy. They crested the small hill to see the city of York on the horizon, eight leagues to the west. Below them the narrow road, snaking through recently harvested fields, was full of movement. The old Roman thoroughfare that had recently been so empty was now busy with Saxon peasants joining the exodus from the countryside. In the distance ox-drawn wagons, flocks of sheep, families on foot and armed men could be seen joining the retreat west as news of the Norwegian invasion spread like wildfire among a desperate population. The stragglers at the back soon caught sight of enemy horsemen on the hilltop and their cries of alarm alerted the rest to the imminent danger and panic ensued. What had been a slow retreat began to gather momentum as the crush of humanity tried to escape the danger that threatened to envelope them, and many in front succumbed to those pushing from behind.

Harald turned his attention to a village below, comprising several farmsteads and a larger manor house. It nestled in the lee of the hill by a flat-meadowed plain, and he ordered his company to advance down the slope. According to his scouts, it was the hamlet of Ryeton, a community of over one hundred souls who, in peacetime, had farmed the land. Now, it was deserted save for the abandoned cattle in the fields and pigs and chickens who roamed through its main streets unchecked. It was well into the afternoon when they entered unopposed, and orders were given that the company would be stopping for the night. After the horses were unsaddled and fed, and perimeter guards posted, they settled down for the evening. Harald took the manor house for his quarters and found the large, rectangular stone building to be well-stocked with food and ale. Hedda came to join him and, swapping her combat duties for domestic ones, she slaughtered a roaming chicken and roasted it, inviting Jeanotte to join them for the meal. She also found several barrels of the departed *thegn's* ale which she gave to her delighted comrades, and when all had eaten and drunk their fill, they settled down for the night.

"The boy is safe and in the service of the great lord of Northumbria," said Hedda, looking into the flames of the hearth fire she had prepared earlier in the evening.

"That is just what your father told me, yes," said Harald.

"No, I have met him since - in my dreams," she said, "he is a fine young boy and will grow to be tall and handsome like his uncle. I told him to make himself ready for escape," she said.

Jeanotte stole a wary look at the Commander before getting to his feet and bidding them both 'good night'.

"You must defeat his gaoler on the field of battle first if you are to free him," she continued oblivious to the captain's departure. "The Lord Morcar is a fierce warrior with thousands of *huscarls* at his back. It will not be easy for you."

"Where and when will this be? Did you really see that?" asked Harald.

"I saw a great battle with many slain. I saw Richard through the fog and getting on a horse. I saw you reunited with him," replied Hedda flatly. "No more than that."

Harald nodded at her words.

"Then we must wait to see what fate delivers. As long as he comes back to me safe, I do not care how," he said, watching her suddenly shudder uncontrollably.

He moved closer to her, put an arm around her thin shoulders and taking one of her hands was surprised to feel it cold to his touch.

"Rest now, my love," he whispered gently. "I shall need the strength of all my warriors come tomorrow."

2

The column left in the stillness of a bright early morning. Their last act was to set fire to the buildings which had given them refuge the previous night. The thatched roofs caught easily and soon the whole village was ablaze and the flames consumed everything they touched, sending black smoke into the clear blue sky. They avoided the road which would now be impassable with the press of people trying to escape and rode through fields and meadows stopping at more deserted hamlets to burn the houses. Harald was alone with his thoughts as he watched his men go about their tasks. This was not work for seasoned warriors, but it was a necessary tactic to show the enemy how close they were, spreading alarm among the locals.

He made sure that Hedda rode beside him. He had watched her in the action against the Saxon shield wall and was more than satisfied that the hours of training on horseback had served her well. She had been impulsive, even reckless, as she rode behind the enemy to discharge her throwing spears and she would need to take more care in future. For now all was well, she was safe and so was his nephew it would seem. It was almost a year since he took her to his bed and he had come to believe in the prophecy of her dreams, which were nearly always correct. Whilst he developed no more than a vague plan to free his nephew, he was gratified to hear that the rescue, when the opportunity arose, would occur soon and probably during the forthcoming battle. Harald was brought back to the present by the sound of galloping hooves, and he looked up to see his scouts approaching at speed.

"Lord, we are but a league away from York. There are many troops camped outside the city walls and the flags and sigils of Northumbria and Mercia are everywhere."

"Numbers?" asked the Commander.

"Perhaps two thousand in camp and many more marching toward the city from the west. There are many *huscarls* amoung them and the *fyrd* has been summoned. Perhaps another two days and there will be a mighty host," replied the man.

"Any sign of the King of England's standards?" asked Harald.

"None," said the scout.

"That is a pity but unsurprising. Unless he has sprouted wings he will still be in the south," said Harald with a rueful smile before turning to Jeanotte. "We shall not be charging the enemy today I think."

The scouts led them to a nearby hill where they could observe the city, but safely enough away from it to see any sign of hostility towards them. Harald looked down at the flurry of activity within the old Roman walls that had long since been replaced with brick and stone. Although there was no castle, as was customary in any major Norman town, there was a stout stone fortress built on a huge mound in the centre of the city, that appeared well fortified. He looked at it with interest musing on how he might breach its defences should it become necessary. There was little need for concealment, and they watched in plain sight of the inhabitants of York. The gonfalon bearing the emblem of the two Ravens of Regneville was unfurled and raised so that everyone in the ancient walled city could see them high on the promontory of their vantage point. There would be no one in the frantic citadel below who did not know that the enemy was almost at their gates.

It was not until midday that the defenders of York responded and the huge city gates opened allowing a large troop of mounted warriors out. They moved swiftly in a beeline toward the hill and by the time they had all left the city Harald counted eight hundred heavily armed men.

"Time for us to take our leave," he said calmly to Jeanotte, before leading his troop back over the other side of the hill the way they had come earlier.

3

Skardaburg was a smoking ruin by the time they returned to meet up with the invasion fleet. They had ridden hard on their return and the ships were preparing to get underway once more, having stripped the town and all the surrounding area of every last morsel of food. The people of Skardaburg had made the mistake of resisting the King of Norway and he had rewarded their valour by setting fire to their homes with them inside.

On his return Harald visited the King's pavilion to report on his mission, and the two men pored over a parchment map of Northumbria, discussing troop numbers and tactics. They would be heading south once more but on reaching the Humber estuary they would row inland and make their camp. The journey proved a little more testing than expected as the fleet of longships crossed the mouth of the Humber and into the tributary of the River Ouse, where a spring tide carried them along at breakneck pace. Three hundred ships packed the fast-flowing river and the master mariners piloting the fleet were sorely tested as they rushed past steep mud banks searching for a point of ingress. As mid-afternoon approached, the horns from the lead ships signalled that a gateway through the muddy banks had been found and they turned to make their approach into the large ox-bow lake that would provide a safe harbour. Every ship's oarsman now fought against the treacherous current as the vessels were manoeuvred through the gap, where the slightest miscalculation from the tillerman could spell disaster. More than a few ships missed their mark and were carried on down the river into hostile territory. Harald watched helplessly as a ship full of Faroan warriors capsized as their longship turned and became swamped by the racing water. The Norman fleet suffered no such misfortune, and their commander was secretly elated when the last of his ships anchored safely on the far side of the lake.

They disembarked close to the deserted Saxon village of Riccard and made camp once again alongside the King of Norway. Tents were erected hurriedly, for tomorrow the army would be on the move toward York to meet their foemen. As soon as the whole fleet had anchored and the warriors landed, the King called his banner-men to him and the battle plans were revealed.

"Gentlemen, we are here together at last on the eve of battle and tomorrow we shall strike our first blow against the usurper Godwinson, who has stolen my kingdom," shouted Hardrada to the commanders gathered outside his tent as thralls scurried amongst them dispensing ale. "Ten thousand of us is surely enough to defeat him but victory will be hard won. Tomorrow we shall march and see what the best of our foemen can do. I will leave a strong force here to guard the ships and we shall meet the enemy somewhere between Riccall and York. My scouts have informed me that a large force of Saxons have left the city, and we shall meet them, head-on, come tomorrow. The Norwegian host will take the left flank, and I want Jarl Siward and the men of Orkney in the vanguard. Earl Tostig is to lead the rest of our allies on the far left."

He turned to look at Harald and fixed him with an intent look.

"Lord Fitzroy and his army shall remain in reserve ready to deliver the killing blow," continued the King.

"Where will the enemy be met, my Lord?" asked Harald

"They are camped no more than three leagues away on the road to York, six thousand Mercians and Northumbrians.

"And ready to die beneath our axes," shouted Jarl Siward of Orkney, a large, bearded warrior.

"And die they shall," shouted back Hardrada holding his drinking cup high, "for they are about to reap the wind from the North."

His commanders, already excited by the prospect of battle returned their leader's toast with great gusto and the sound of their cheering echoed around the shoreline of the huge lake. When it had died down the King moved amongst them speaking to each man in turn before dismissing them for the evening with orders to be ready to march at first light.

4

It was mid-morning when the King of Norway's great host approached the massed Saxon army. The Earl's of Northumbria and Mercia stood in opposition behind their respective shield walls, on the far side of a brook that was slowly getting shallower as the river tide ebbed out. A long phalanx of men lined up, three deep, in battle formation waiting for the arrival of the Norsemen, whose trumpets could be heard getting closer beyond the small hill that stood opposite them. The *huscarls* and local men of the *fyrd* stood perspiring in the late summer heat, flicking flies from reddening faces, their weapons seemingly getting heavier as the day wore on. Many had arrived the previous day and slept beneath their shields in readiness to meet a spiteful enemy, who had razed their homes and laid waste to their lands for generations. When their Saxon ancestors had first met the Norsemen they had fallen prey to vicious raiding and had been forced to bribe the invaders with dane-gelt to keep them at bay. That was many years ago, and victorious encounters had given successive Saxon rulers confidence. Today that confidence was strong, and the men trusted their commanders, the siblings Morcar and Edwin, to deliver victory. The Saxons stood rigidly in lines that stretched for half a league in each direction, daring Hardrada's main force to show themselves over the brow of the hill.

    The King of Norway had decided to split his army in two and was converging on Fulford Gate from separate directions. Norwegian warriors led the march on foot with Harald Fitzroy's heavy cavalry walking behind them. When they reached the hill in front of the brook their allies had already arrived, and the fighting commenced. The Norsemen of Orkney were advancing beside Earl Tostig's men, and had engaged the Saxon shield wall. Harald and his captains crested the rise and looked down at the developing situation below them; a Mercian army stood on the left and a similar-sized Northumbrian force to the right. Although Hardrada and the Norwegian contingent had not yet entered the fray and were still mustering on the hidden left flank getting ready to face the Mercians, the battlefield was already alive with activity on the right. Jarl Siward with his wild and undisciplined band of warriors from the Orkneys and Faroes had charged pell-mell into the Saxon shield wall of the Northumbrians and, despite ferocious axe work were unable to make a dent in the enemy's ranks. Earl Tostig and his cohort of loyal *huscarls* and European mercenaries fared with even less success. His vain attempt to jam in and roll up the enemies left flank had failed spectacularly and his men were in danger of being enveloped by Morcar's Saxons. The Normans looked down from their vantage point as Hardrada's standing army moved into position and began to march down the hillside toward the Mercian shield wall in front of them.

"These Saxons are showing promise," said Jeanotte.

"Too early to wager, I say," replied Harald.

"And too boggy for our cavalry," rejoined Brenier grimly.

"That, I agree with at least. I am sure none of us has forgotten how to fight on foot," said Harald assessing the battlefield as it unfolded below him. "Now quickly, I have little time to explain and no time to discuss. We shall be called upon sooner rather than later to join battle and I fancy, from what I see before us, that our heavy horses will founder on the soft ground. We shall fight on foot except for your *conroi,* Brenier. You will charge the causeway across the brook on the firm ground and will not stop until you have cut a bloody swathe through to the other side of the Saxon ranks. And then …."

"And then I shall proceed to the Northumbrian baggage train, yonder and retrieve young Richard. Do not fret, we shall not leave without him. We will find him and bring him home as we discussed," interrupted his cousin patiently, for they had spent much of the previous night finessing the plan.

"Good. When you find him, see he is mounted behind Hedda - her horse is strong and quick enough to carry the two of them away from danger," continued Harald. "Now, back to your men. The King's trumpets will be inviting us to join him soon enough."

His two companions wished him luck and left him alone. Harald continued to observe the plot unfolding below as a group of Norwegian berserkers, stripped to the waist and wielding huge, double-handed Dane axes charged ahead of the main group and into the enemy shield wall waiting across the beck. The Mercians seemed stunned by the ferocity of the wild charge and a gap appeared in their lines through which the crazed Norsemen entered before disappearing from view. Their bloody corpses reemerged shortly afterward; prone, lifeless forms kicked unceremoniously down the bank and into the shallow muddy water. Harald shook his head at the reckless sacrifice of life and turned to watch the disciplined lines of thousands of Norwegian warriors march down toward the brook and wade through the water toward the enemy lines. He squinted into the sunlight, trying to discern the figure of King Hardrada and found him within a tight knot of heavily armoured men beneath the the banner of the Land Ravager, a single black raven on a white background. Looking ahead of the advance he saw that the water filled ditch was a little wider than a man could throw a spear and, to reach the enemy lines the attackers would have to emerge from the water and climb a further twenty paces up a muddy bank. The King marched forward, exhorting his veterans on the left and right to deliver the hammer blow. When the first ranks reached mid-point in the stream the Saxons unleashed a torrent of javelins, bringing down many Norwegians in the water. Their volleys pierced the shields of others, rendering them impotent and opening up their lines to a Saxon counterattack. Hardrada's attack stuttered but did not falter. When the two lines of advancing Norsemen hit the English shield wall, the Saxons took a single backward step before advancing into the fractured enemy lines, pushing the enemy back into the water from which they had only just emerged. The Mercians did not pursue the Norwegians who were now reforming on the far side of the brook which was filling up with the dead bodies of the fallen. Further up the Saxon lines, the Northumbrian shield wall was not quite so disciplined, unravelling as they first beat back and then pursued Tostig and Siward's men.

The King's war trumpets sounded, calling for reinforcements and Harald raced back to join his men who had already dismounted and were awaiting the Commander.

"*Svinfylking,*" he called and without a further word each man of his command knew exactly what was expected of them.

The horses, now under the charge of many of the squires who had ridden to battle with their masters, were led away. Three cohorts, each comprising three hundred warriors and archers rapidly grouped into triangular 'boar snout' formations and when they were ready, marched to the top of the hill and down the other side to join their Norwegian comrades by the side of the brook. The King, now bareheaded and shield-less, waved a double-handed axe toward the Norman cohorts and Harald waved *Gunnlogi* back in response to signify his mens' readiness as they took their positions on the far-left flank.

The war horns sounded once more and as Hardrada's men re-entered the brook, three Norman formations did the same, marching forward relentlessly. As the first Norman battle cry of "*Diex Aix*" went up, the archers within the three triangles of massed ranks released volleys of arrows dropping numerous Mercians in the shield wall in front of them. Harald, the first man at the apex of his *Svinfylking* felt the hairs on the back of his neck rise with the primal intensity of battle; the spirit of the Wandering Warriors coursed through his veins again. He touched the amulet of Thors Hammer for luck once more, before drawing *Gunnlogi* from her sheath and preparing the longsword to strike as the first targets drew closer. Propelled up the far bank by the weight of men in the formation, he was in amongst his enemies before he knew it, driving the point of the wedge through a gap in the Saxon shield wall. He dispatched his first foeman, a tall *huscarl* armed with a giant axe, with a vindictive thrust of his sword over the top of his shield and the man dropped to the ground and perished beneath hundreds of stamping feet. The air was putrid with the stench of spilled blood and feaces as men voided their bowels in terror, and the three formations each gained a foothold on the far bank before pressing their advantage home. Harald felt the shield wall in front of him buckle, give ground and appear to snap beneath the crush of the relentless s*vinfylkings,* which hewed and slashed at the bewildered enemy. He looked up to take stock of the situation before him and saw that the Saxon flanks, that had defiantly given so much opposition to the King of Norway's army, fold in on itself. He shouted an order to wheel to the right and his contingent swung round, as one. As they did so the other 'boar-snout' formations repeated the movement until they were all driving at right angles into the enemy lines. The Norwegians, having benefitted from the press of the Norman effort, were gaining ground. Harald's men hacked through the melting Mercian flanks enabling the Norsemen to cleave channels into the enemy's shield wall and before long the Saxons were forced to turn and flee. The confrontation with the Mercians was over and the Norwegians pursued the vanquished with venom. Fleeing men threw away their weapons and shields in an effort to escape but few were lucky to make it from the field alive.

    For Harald Fitzroy there was no respite, and he urged his cohort forward leaving the Norwegians behind to loot the dead. They carved through the lines of running Saxons toward the causeway and beyond in search of the man who had been holding his nephew hostage for almost a year. When they reached the causeway, a road made of rock and stones that traversed the brook, he raised a hand and called for his men to stop and take a drink. He looked around and took an offered flask of wine, which he raised to the surrounding press of his bloodied comrades. He knew that Brenier would need time to search the baggage train for Richard and his efforts might yet be thwarted by too many returning soldiers.

"Brothers, I salute you all," he shouted, taking a huge draft of wine. "Our day is nearly done but I invite you for one last foray today. Will you join me?"

A huge answering cry went up just as Brenier led his *conrois* of fifty riders thundering over the causeway toward the Northumbrian camp. When the Norman cavalry had galloped away, he led his men, still in their wedge-shaped formation forward along the side of the brook which was now clogged by the press of dead warriors.

Earl Morcar, unlike his brother Edwin, was returning from his victorious rout of Tostig and Siward to the far right of the battleground. Whilst his victory had been complete, it had been hard won, and he was returning from a lengthy pursuit of the men of Orkney and the renegade Saxons. On seeing the red and yellow stripes of the Northumbrian banners flying a thousand paces away, Harald marched his men toward the force of two thousand Saxons. However, in his enthusiasm to advance he had lost sight of the King of Norway's banners and now the Norsemen were behind him, following his advance. Hardrada's bloodlust had not yet been fully slaked, and anxious to make the victory complete he ordered his men up to where his Norman allies were preparing to confront the Northumbrians. They now outnumbered the remaining Saxons in the field by four to one. The King stepped out in front of his own troops and hailed Harald.

"I believe I am in your debt, Lord Fitzroy. Your intervention was telling back there, but please, my Lord. Do not deprive me of the pleasure of rubbing the Saxon noses in it," said Hardrada who was covered in dried blood from head to foot, and his eyes glinted malevolently through the rust-coloured mask.

Harald nodded graciously.

"You are my general, Lord. What is your pleasure? I would be happy enough just to take the head of Earl Morcar."

The King looked at his weary troops in contemplation.

"I would be willing just to accept his surrender, and we can go and loot York at our leisure. We will need to be at our best to defy Godwinson's host before the English throne is mine, after all. But if you can tempt them into battle, I would gladly fight beside you, once more," said the King grinning widely, making his face look even more demonic.

Harald bowed his head and turned back to the Northumbrians, who were forming a long shield wall in front of them.

"Looks like they intend to make a fight of it, my Lord," said the King.

"Let us see what they have left before we commit ourselves," replied Harald. "Might I have the use of your herald?"

The King shouted to where a group of his captains stood in a huddle and a smart young warrior bearing his standard stepped forward. Harald beckoned the man to follow him and, with Jeanotte on his shoulder he stepped out and walked toward the Saxon lines. When they had covered half the distance they stopped and Jeanotte called out in a loud voice,

"My Lord Morcar of Northumbria. Lord Fitzroy of Ambrières wishes to parlay with you so that we can keep further bloodshed to a minimum," he shouted in a voice that carried on the wind and could be heard some distance away.

The Saxon line parted and a group of six warriors strode out toward them, stopping within twenty paces of Harald. The leader of the group, a tall, powerfully built man wearing a bejewelled helmet with a full-face mask, observed them in silence. A coat of mail reached down to his knees and around his waist hung a long sword in an expensive-looking scabbard inlaid with gold and silver. He pulled off the heavy helmet with some effort before speaking. Morcar was thirty years old, and his long fair hair was wet with perspiration, clinging damply to his head. He looked directly at Harald and spoke in a voice that did not betray any sign of fear.

"A Norman some way from home, I think? What brings you here to trespass on my land," he asked in a commanding voice.

"I fight for the King of Norway and I am here to honour my oath to him," returned Harald confidently. "You are heavily outnumbered, my Lord, and as one nobleman to another I ask you to yield before you suffer the same fate as your brother, who lies in a marshy grave with his comrades."

Morcar looked at the long line of his enemies, beyond Harald's shoulder, which was growing in length, the longer he looked at it.

"Surrender the field and we will let you return home with your lives. Fight us and you will die in this forlorn marshland. If you are expecting help from the south, I can tell you that your King is a hundred leagues away. Come, Lord, your men look weary enough to drop - we will let you return to York with your honour intact and maybe we can face one another on the field another day," said Harald.

The Earl of Northumbria stroked his thick moustaches as he thought and inhaled deeply, considering his answer.

"The King of Norway does not have a reputation for dealing leniently with his enemies," stated the Earl.

"He wishes to take York without further resistance. Let him have his victory and you can go in peace," said Harald, watching the Earl consider the odds that he knew were stacked so heavily against him.

There was silence as the Saxon lord considered the offer, but he shook his head saying,

"I cannot surrender to Lord Hardrada without a fight, my Lord but if you defeat my champion I will leave the field, and you shall have your victory. And if my man triumphs?" asked Morcar.

"That will not happen but if it does so we shall gladly leave the field to you. Send your man forward and we can settle the matter," replied Harald Fitzroy with a broad smile.

The Saxon leader turned away and headed back to his lines.

Jeanotte stepped forward to speak to his leader.

"Who will you designate to fight for us. Rolf lost an eye earlier today and will be of little use to us in single combat," he said of the Norman champion, "Leif took a spear to the gut and will be similarly indisposed, I fear. There are many in the ranks who can fulfil this role, but none so deadly as either of those two."

"Do not fret, my friend. Have you no faith in your old Commander? Now hand me your spear and pray that I can still remember how to use it. I do not wish to burden any man with a task I can do myself. Step back and give me some room."

They did not have long to wait, for the Saxon champion came roaring out from the lines like a wild beast shouting to the heavens and cursing. The Northumbrians began to beat their weapons on their shields until the valley resonated with the sound. The gigantic Saxon hefted a huge single bladed Dane axe over one shoulder and marched purposefully toward Harald to the rhythmic tattoo. The man threw off his bearskin cloak revealing a semi-naked and heavily muscled, oiled frame, glinting in the late afternoon sun. He wore only leather breeches which seemed to struggle to contain the huge legs, bearing him remorselessly toward Harald Fitzroy with murderous intent. When the Saxon was within fifty paces of his target he broke into a loping run to the cries of encouragement from the Northumbrian lines. It was only at this point that his fellow combatant made any move, and Harald took five rapid paces forward. For a man of his age and size he moved like quicksilver, breaking into a short run and releasing the javelin with a deft movement of his arm and wrist. The spear went into a swift, shallow arc and hit its target squarely in the chest, dropping the Saxon champion to the ground like a felled tree. The warrior did not have time to utter a single cry of pain as he tumbled backwards. Harald walked slowly toward his fallen foe, stopped only to retrieve the fallen giant's axe and in two blows removed the man's head from his shoulders.

It was now the men of Ambrières's turn to cheer, and they hooted cries of derision at the Saxons who stood in silence at the demise of their great champion. The Norwegians soon joined them, and seven thousand men cursed and insulted their enemy, who ignominiously left the field on the road back to York. As much as they were abused by their enemies as they slunk away, more than a few Saxons gave thanks that they had faced the army of Hardrada of Norway and yet still lived. The Normans crowded around their leader, feting their own champion but Harald Fitzroy's thoughts were elsewhere, and he prayed hard that Brenier had enough time to retrieve his lost nephew.

5

Brenier's *conroi* scattered any Saxon warriors they confronted on the causeway like dust in the wind. There was a fury to the gallopers' charge as they pressed on over the brook and along the stone road wide enough to accommodate ten horsemen riding abreast. The couched lances of the Norman cavalry spared no one foolish enough to stand before them, and any Saxon warrior who managed to evade the steel spear tips met their end beneath iron-clad hooves. In truth, with the battle ended and the Saxons on the run there was scant resistance to the charging *destriers* and the sound of their pounding hoofbeats cleared the road some distance ahead. Very soon they were clear of the marshy hinterland that would have bogged down the heavy cavalry had they been deployed in the battle. The ground became firmer and the tightly packed *conroi* spread out as they approached the camp on the rise of the next hill. A few sentries, old soldiers who were better suited to guard duty than combat, sounded the alarm at the sight of the charging horsemen. They shouted in vain, for the camp of over a thousand tents was largely empty save for the small army of blacksmiths, grooms and armourers who plied their trade to the Saxon host. A group of thirty or so young squires who had been left behind made a desperate muster beneath their Lords' banners and faced the *conroi* with axes and swords. Their bravery was short-lived, and they dispersed, dropping their weapons and running for cover as the Normans drew to within a hundred paces. They raced to the questionable sanctuary of hundreds of heavy wagons filled with camp supplies of hay, food and wine. With any sign of resistance at an end the search for the Norman boy began in earnest and the horsemen rode up and down the camp calling his name. They were looking for a nine-year-old boy, but it had been almost a year since Brenier had seen him last, and the captain harboured the fear that unless Richard was able to reveal himself their search might prove fruitless.

Hedda discovered a group of ten page boys hiding in one of the tents and she ushered them outside with curses and threats. She unleashed her sword urging them to tell her what she needed to know. Several of them dropped to their knees fearing they were about to be killed. Some called for their mothers and began to cry.

"Where is the Norman boy? Richard, his name is Richard," she shouted in their native tongue but they just looked back at her blankly or continued to wail.

Just as she was about to abandon them one brave soul walked toward her. He was about seven or eight years old and pointed to the train of wagons that stood at the side of the camp. Taking her hand, he led her to a large merchant's cart. The glowing embers of a fire still smouldered beneath an awning attached to the wagon and she held out her sword in one hand whilst keeping hold of the little Saxon boy with the other.

"He is in there?" she asked the boy who simply nodded. "Very well, go and join the others again. Tell them they will not be harmed."

Hedda looked around for her comrades but all she heard was their cries far off as they continued to search. Time was short and she decided to go into the wagon and investigate and sheathed her sword transferring her dagger to her right hand.

"Richard," she called, "my name is Hedda. I have been sent by your uncle to take you back to him. Come out if you are in there, you will be safe."

There was still heat in the day and rivulets of perspiration ran down her face and neck and inside her padded tunic. She became intensely aware of the noise that the linked chains of her *hauberk* made as she moved nervously toward the door of the wagon. She climbed the creaking wooden steps to the door and pushed it open carefully with her foot, tentatively edging forward. The inside of the wagon was dank and gloomy, and she looked around as her eyes adjusted to the dark. She sensed a blur of movement out of the corner of her eye and turned to see a dark figure swinging a cudgel at her head. Ducking at the last minute to avoid the blow, she sprang up and caught her assailant with the point of her blade in the side of his neck. Even in the half-light she saw the spurt of blood from the wound and felt its warmth trickle down her face. Her attacker collapsed to the floor of the wagon, his life's blood draining from him and she heard the sound of a child whimpering in the darkness.

"Richard," she hissed, "come to me. You are safe."

She felt a small hand touching hers and grabbed it with a powerful grip, feeling the child wince as she did so. Hedda moved toward the door, stepping over the prone figure and into the light. She was holding the hand of a young boy, covered in blood, and he trembled with fear.

"Richard, is your name Richard?" she asked him urgently and the obvious tension in her voice only seemed to add to his distress. Salty tears ran down his face and he sobbed uncontrollably. She wiped away any visible sign of blood but could not find any trace of an injury, constantly repeating her questioning but he did not answer and kept nodding his head. A shout went up from another part of the camp sounding the alarm that the Saxons were returning, and she grabbed the boy's hand, dragging him back to where her horse had been tethered. Brenier saw them coming and rushed toward them. He bent down to look into the face which was caked with blood and dirt.

"Richard?" he asked the boy who continued to nod at the sound of the name before turning to Hedda. "Now mount your horse and let us leave - the Saxons are returning in great numbers and are not far away. They will soon discover our presence, and we must be gone."

Hedda leapt up onto her horse's back and Brenier lifted the boy up behind her.

"Put your arms around my waist, Richard. We shall have you back to your uncle in no time," she said as gently as she could and felt the boy slip his arms around her middle and press his face into her back. She turned the colt and joined her comrades, and the *conroi* galloped away from the camp with their precious cargo safely behind her.

6

In truth, the returning Saxons had little interest in Brenier's *conrois* and even less interest in trying to stop them from fleeing back to the rest of the Norman warriors, less than a league away. The battle of Fulford Bridge was over, and in its aftermath, King Hardrada's men began to celebrate. Harald Fitzroy breathed a sigh of relief and turned to face the men who had followed him across the entire length of the battlefield with unquestioning loyalty. Jeanotte called to him from the wedge-shaped *svinfylking* which was only now beginning to lose its shape as the men lowered their weapons and looked around at each other as if seeking confirmation that they had made it, alive, through the hell of battle. It had been a hard-fought fight, but the losses of Harald's men had been mercifully light, considering the bitterness of the engagement.

"Well met, my Lord," shouted the captain from beneath the battle standard of the two ravens.

"I salute you all, my friends," returned the Commander raising a skin of wine to his comrades. "I could not have asked anymore. Tonight, I shall drink with each and every one of you - the warriors of Ambrières have only added to their illustrious reputation. Then we shall fill our pockets with Saxon gold and silver - that is if our Norse brothers have left any for us."

A great cheer went up from his warriors and Harald turned his gaze to the battlefield, which was littered with the dead of both sides. In the distance he saw that both banks of the beck were festooned with the bodies of dead and dying men and the water of the brook itself could no longer be seen. The water was clogged with huge numbers of fallen warriors who had met their end in the ebb and flow of the fighting. Harald's pride at the disciplined display by his men was only tempered by his consternation for the whereabouts of Brenier's horsemen, and he began to steal anxious glances to the causeway for signs of their return. His attention was taken by the presence of Halldor Snorrason, appearing at his shoulder, who despite looking battered and bloodied gave him a wide grin.

"Lord Fitzroy, it is good to see you looking so well after such a day?" said the old Icelander.

"And you too, my friend," rejoined Harald pressing the skin of wine into his hand. "Let us wait here together for the return of your daughter. She has been on a very important mission."

Halldor nodded knowingly and they were interrupted by the sound of galloping hooves as Brenier led his troop back over the causeway. Hedda's father let out a sigh of relief as Harald slapped him heartily on the back.

"It was never in any doubt," said Halldor, mightily relieved. "but alas our liege lord requests your presence before darkness comes."

"Then I must answer his call. Let us hope he has called an end to the fighting for a little while, at least," said Harald good naturedly as the two walked away to the King's enclave without waiting for the riders to arrive.

They found the King of Norway in a jubilant mood. Dusk was falling as Hardrada greeted Harald with a massive bearhug. Whilst his army had suffered many losses, the opposing forces of Earl Edwin's Mercians had been destroyed and once the Earl's brother Morcar's men had left the field, victory was complete.

"Your reputation does not do you justice, Lord Fitzroy," he boomed in Harald's ear. "The Saga of the Wandering Warriors of Haugesund will soon have a few new verses I believe. The actions of you and your men have carried the day. I am in your debt, my Lord."

The King released Harald from his grip and stood back, his face wreathed in smiles and motioned to one of his servants to come forward. The man presented Harald with an exquisitely designed helm of shining steel inlaid with gold and silver across its full-face mask. The Norman looked down at the beautiful piece of armour, turning it over in his hands, admiring its splendour. The King began to applaud loudly and soon the attendant jarls all joined their leader in the hand-clapping. Harald took the accolade modestly and nodded his thanks.

"It belonged to a Byzantine king," explained Hardrada, "no more than a trinket but a small token of my appreciation for your valour."

"It was my honour to join you on the field, Lord. I serve at your pleasure," replied Harald, above the noise.

"At the very least we have sent a message that the English King cannot ignore," shouted Hardrada. "But tonight, we will celebrate our first victory of the campaign - I have sent wagons of ale and food to your men. Tomorrow we shall take our rewards in York."

The reverie was interrupted by the disheveled figure of Tostig Godwinson entering the camp. He limped in, his long hair matted with blood and dirt, the remains of his expensive chain mail coat hung in pieces from his tall frame. The King spotted the Saxon lord and greeted him heartily.

"Earl Tostig, it is good to see you again. I hear your former bannermen gave you a difficult day," he shouted to the amusement of many of the Norwegian Jarls.

Tostig Godwinson grimaced at the remark.

"Yes, my Lord, it has been a hard-fought day, but we have prevailed as you see,"

"Indeed, but do not be too hard on yourself, Lord Fitzroy saw your foemen off the field without much more blood being spilled," said the King. "Now tell me Lord Tostig - are you ready to sack the city or shall we ransom it?"

Harald, realising that the King was toying with his Saxon ally, looked from one man to the other. King Hardrada beamed a brilliant smile at Tostig as he waited for an answer.

"My Lord King," spluttered Tostig, "I believe we have already agreed that we shall accept the city's ransom and hostages from all the noble families. I cannot rule Northumbria if my capital is burnt to the ground."

"Quite so, but your comrades in arms here have paid a heavy price for victory today and many of them would prefer more immediate gratification," said Hardrada warming to the task of baiting the Saxon.

Despite his weariness, Tostig did his level best to contain his anger and continued to bluster but the King put up a hand to quieten any more argument.

"Then let us do this as ancient Norse custom once dictated. Every man here shall have a vote, and we will all abide by that decision," said the King slyly.

There followed a good deal of discussion and drinking after which the commanders cast their vote in a show of hands. Sixteen men voted to sack the city, and sixteen men wanted to take the *Dane gelt*. They all looked toward the King to make his casting vote and with a great deal of showmanship he put an arm around Harald's shoulder and announced,

"I give my casting vote to the noble Lord Fitzroy, no man of us has shown greater valour today and it is his honour to decide the fate of the city," said the King.

Harald, entering into the spirit of the spectacle, stroked his beard in deliberation and made a decision for which he would thank the gods for many years to come.

"Gentlemen, I must admit to being somewhat undecided but having weighed up every consideration I have decided we shall hold the Saxon feet to the fire and command a great ransom from the city of York. Each noble family shall provide at least one valuable hostage."

The assembly erupted into raucous laughter and servants scuttled amongst them carrying huge pitchers of ale. Harald looked over to Earl Godwinson, catching his eye, who returned the look with a weak smile. With the business of the next stage of the campaign settled, the evening continued in good humour and it was not long before the King dismissed his commanders, with orders that they be ready to take the road to York in the morning and the wounded sent back to the boats in Riccall.

Harald, anxious to rejoin his warriors and be reunited with his nephew, took his leave of the King and retraced his steps by torchlight. He found the men of his command gathered around a huge bonfire where they stood eating and drinking. Hardrada had been as good as his word and three large wagons filled with ale, bread and meat had been dispatched. His men greeted him warmly as he passed through them and despite the pressing need to find Hedda, he stopped to exchange words with any man who wanted to talk to him. He felt a strong hand on his shoulder and turned to see Brenier smiling at him.

"All is well, Hari," he said, "The boy is over there with Hedda."

"They are both unharmed?" asked Harald.

"They are well - which is more than I can say for the fool who tried to cross her. Come now, they are by the fire."

Harald followed the direction of Brenier's pointed finger and saw a woman and a child huddled together, with a blanket wrapped around their shoulders. It was not cold, but the boy leant into her comforting embrace, resting his head against her breast and snored gently. Harald looked down at her tenderly and was about to speak but she put a finger against her lips. Then he knelt down in front of her and examined the face of the boy without waking him before getting to his feet silently. He turned and took a few paces to look despairingly at his cousin.

"Whoever that boy is - he is not my nephew, Richard," he said quietly before walking disconsolately into the night.

Chapter 21: The Skjaldmaer's Haunting
September, St. Valery, Normandie

1

Robert Fitzroy was back in Jerusalem on the pilgrimage that changed his life, or at least he dreamt he was. After his visions at the Church of the Holy Sepulchre he was taken outside to be met by a group of scourge-wielding monks who whipped his naked back as he carried the heavy wooden cross. The road to Golgatha, the place of Christ's crucifixion, was a bitter one but he had refused to cry out despite the agonising pain. After one particularly brutal flaying he bit his tongue in an attempt to stifle the cry of anguish rising from his throat, before turning to look at his assailant who had somehow beaten him more painfully than anyone else. But it was not a man who had struck the blow, and he looked directly into the face of his grandmother. Turid Halfdanson, the Skjaldmaer of Laeso looked back at him, her cold blue eyes seemingly boring into his soul.

"Grandmother, I did not forsake you - I turned my back on the old gods and found a new path," he whimpered, huge salty tears running down his cheeks.

"The old gods do not care that you found a new totem. There is enough room in the firmament for an army of gods. Now put down your burden for we have important matters to discuss," she said in a kindly tone that resonated with something he could not quite make out.

He dropped the heavy, wooden cross and looked up at her to find that they were no longer in the dusty streets of Jerusalem but sitting beside the holy *Ve,* where she used to take her grandsons to pray to the old Norse gods when they were small boys. He looked into the still waters of the spring and saw the face of a young boy looking back at him. Then he looked at his grandmother and saw the beautiful woman he remembered, and she reached over and put his small hand in hers.

"You are going on a difficult journey and there will be war with the treacherous Saxons. You know how I feel about them, do you not?" she asked, fixing the small boy with a benevolent eye.

Robert looked up at her and nodded.

"You also know that I have cursed them, and that curse will last for generations until my children's children have wrought bloody vengeance on them," she continued.

He nodded again and looked up at her, her golden head of hair wreathed in sunlight.

"Good. Now come here and give your Mormor a kiss," she commanded, and he got to his feet and ran into her embrace.

He inhaled her old familiar scent of crushed lavender and put his child's face up against the soft flesh of her cheek. As he did so he felt its texture change, and instead of gentle skin he felt only feathers. Her voice had changed, and he no longer heard his grandmother talking to him in her soft, sweet voice but the harsh caw-cawing of a raven. He pushed away and looked directly into the bird's jet-black eye.

"Do not forsake me, Robert," said the bird. "We have a pact, do we not?"

Before he could answer the giant bird reached over and pulled at his earlobe, drawing blood.

It gave another squawk and took to the air and Robert felt the wind from its enormous wings. He covered his head with his hands and when he took them down, he was looking up at an empty sky where white clouds were racing across an expanse of blue.

2

"I am looking for the Lord of Mortain," shouted a familiar voice, reaching into Robert's unconsciousness and dragging him out of its murky depths.

He struggled to open salt-encrusted eyes and blinked at the brightness of the day. Looking about him, he saw the prone body of the *Sea Winds* captain, with a huge shard from the splintered mast protruding from his neck. Two more bodies could be seen amongst the shattered oars on the lower deck, and a large seagull pecked at the face of one of the corpses in search of easy pickings. Grabbing the remains of the gunwale, Robert pulled himself to his feet stiffly and quickly checked himself for injuries. Finding none, he looked over the side of the beached longship to see the remnants of the crew sitting or standing on the shale and talking to a group of horsemen. Floki looked up to see the groggy figure of his brother peering down at him.

"Saints be praised, Robert - there you are. We have been searching this beach for days looking for you," he called jubilantly, jumping down from his horse and walking swiftly toward the wreck of the ship.

Robert rubbed his head to discover an egg-sized lump where he had struck it during the great storm.

"Have you anything to drink?" he croaked between parched lips before draining a proffered skin of water.

"Come brother, take my arm. You have been missing for some time, but now we have found you all is well," said Floki.

"And the Duke - he lives?" asked Robert, trying to piece together the events that brought him here to this deserted length of beach

"He is well enough and will delight in the news that you have been found. Now let us get you out of here and onto a horse and I will tell you all you need to know," said Floki, helping his brother down from the stricken craft.

Robert gratefully accepted the assistance of two men-at-arms as they hoisted him into the saddle of one of the many spare horses that had been brought to carry any survivors back to St. Valery. It took them until nightfall to reach their camp and during the journey Floki told his brother all had happened in the past few days.

The Norman armada of a thousand ships had been hit by an enormous storm from the west, scattering the great fleet. While Floki had marshalled a herd of three thousand war horses from Dives to St. Valery, he had watched the storm gather in its ferocity. The plan to follow the fleet on a shorter crossing with the animals had been abandoned until they learned the fate of the Duke and his company of eight thousand warriors. By some miracle the storm had not resulted in disaster and by the time it had died down only forty ships were still unaccounted for. However, the bodies of the misfortunate mariners were still washing up along the coast and the Duke had ordered that they be buried immediately without ceremony to avoid spreading panic among the troops. Fear of the impending journey to England was spreading among the more skeptical elements of the army and desertions were expected.

By the time the column had made it back to St. Valery, Robert had almost recovered from his ordeal. He felt alive and well and more than ready to resume his duties. Despite his brother's protestations, he insisted on being taken to the Duke's quarters in the fortified chateau in the centre of St. Valery. When he got there, news of his safe arrival had preceded him, and Duke William was waiting in the courtyard of the building to greet him. No sooner had Robert dismounted than William rushed to him and embraced his Chancellor in outstretched arms.

"Robert, my brother," emoted the Duke, "you are safe, and our great work can continue. Come in, my physician is here if you are in any pain."

"I am fit and well, my Lord, and there is nothing else I need save a good night's sleep and sometime in prayer thanking God for my deliverance," replied Robert.

"And you shall have both, my friend, for tomorrow our whole camp will be rejoicing in your safe arrival and the escape of our company from the elements. Now, I command you to come inside to receive some sustenance before you retire," said the Duke jubilantly.

He thanked Floki for his diligence in finding his brother and putting an arm around Robert's shoulders, led him into the chateau and out of the rapidly cooling evening.

3

Robert woke late the next day and prayed for the next few hours in a nearby church. After the service of thanksgiving, he spent the rest of the day moving about the camp which was, after all, only two days old and began to assess what needed to be done. Many of the ships had sustained damage and were in need of repair and the Chancellor gave orders for teams of shipwrights to be brought in to start work. Men and horses required shelter and nourishment, and the surrounding countryside was scoured for enough food for an indefinite period. Morale in the camp was not as low as Robert had feared and although there were no more than five hundred desertions, the Duke still felt he needed to incentivise each warrior with increased rations and further inducements for the trip to England. More land was promised, and any seeds of doubt seemed to disappear. After a week regrouping in St. Valery the effects of the storm damage on the invasion force did not appear as serious as he had feared and once again all eyes turned toward the Saxon Kingdom.

News from England had been scant, but a Flemish merchantman carrying a cargo of leather had arrived a week after the storm to report the waiting Saxon fleet on the south coast had not been so lucky. Much of the vaunted English navy was badly damaged and the rest blown to the four winds. Duke William had been jubilant at this news and insisted that whilst God had merely been testing the resolve of the Normans, He had savagely punished the Saxons for their blasphemy which was only a portent of things to come. Besides, William would often add, the wait for the Norman invasion force would keep the Saxons guessing. It only remained for the wind to change direction and for the Duke to countenance restarting the campaign once again. Robert spent any spare time in counsel with his liege lord and they watched and waited for the wind direction to move.

A month later, as Robert sat in the saddle beside Floki, watching the Riders of Regneville going through their regular manoeuvres - the wind finally altered direction. He had been looking at the lance pennants blowing in the westerly wind, that had been so constant, and they suddenly changed, snapping into their new position and pointing out to sea. He looked at his brother and laughed.

"The time has come. God favours us with a second chance," he said with relief.

"Then let us make haste, before He changes his mind" replied his brother.

It did not take long for the Duke to give the order to sail. After four weeks of alternating moods between elation and despair his prayers were answered, and the southerly winds arrived. Within two days, men, supplies, arms and the precious war-horses and been loaded aboard their respective vessels and the fleet put to sea. To avoid collisions every ship was equipped with lanterns at each masthead and on an evening high tide the *Mora* led the procession of ships over the mouth of the river's estuary and north across l*a Manche* toward their destiny.

Chapter 22: The Land Ravager Unfurled
Northumbria, September 1066

1

The King of Norway's army stood in front of the main gate of the city of York in a long line of warriors several deep, beating swords and axes against their shields. They had no need to cow the local population into submission, for the destruction of the Mercians and the retreat of the Northumbrian armies had already consigned the city to defeat. King Hardrada, the 'Hard Ruler', had always insisted that vanquished foes should never forget to fear him, and today was no exception. However, he had been persuaded to treat the people of York mildly, belying his ferocious reputation, and their citizens would be grateful. As the battle standards fluttered in the wind he stood before them waiting for the English Earls to present themselves. Beside him were Harald Fitzroy and the former Earl of Northumbria, Tostig Godwinson. All that remained was for the terms of the surrender, which had been delivered earlier, to be agreed and the victory would be complete. The city gates swung open, and the Saxon leaders trudged toward them with a small contingent of spearmen. As they approached it became obvious that one of the Earls was suffering from a number of injuries; Edwin of Mercia was limping badly, and his bare head was bandaged over one eye. Feared dead and given up by his men during the battle, the remnants of his bodyguard had returned to the field and retrieved him from a pile of corpses.

They stopped within ten paces of Hardrada, and the King spoke.

"You have considered our terms," he said without preamble. "You may walk away with your men and arms intact if you agree."

"We have and we accept them," said Morcar, "but five hundred pounds of gold and a thousand pounds of silver will take two days to collect.

"Very well," replied the King, "you have until the day after tomorrow to deliver your dues and you shall accept Earl Tostig as the new Lord of Northumbria. My commanders will return with you to the city today to take the hostages. They are our guarantee of good conduct but be in no doubt if you raise arms against us, they will all perish."

Harald studied the face of the English Earls, listening in resignation and considered the events of the last day. It had started brightly enough and fighting beside his men had been a sweet reminder of his calling, but he had ended the day in high dudgeon. He had been in despair when he realised the boy with Hedda was not his nephew and had walked away from her in quiet rage. As always, she read his mood easily and let his anger relent before going to him. When they sat beside the bonfire, she explained that all was not lost and the boy from the Saxon camp told her that Richard had been taken back to York earlier in the day.

"Trust me, Hari, she had insisted, "I have seen him and he is safe. Be patient - he will be back soon."

He had desperately wanted to believe her and submitted to the hope that his nephew could be returned when they took control of the city.

Now, with the formalities of surrender completed, he rode behind the defeated Saxons into York and through silent streets lined with frightened local people. They bowed their heads as his victorious cohort passed, reminding him of so many other cities that he had conquered in the past. Benevento, Civitate, Rennes, Dol and countless others were just fleeting memories now, but the lost faces of the local people never seemed to change. Harald was brought back to the present as they approached the cathedral of York, and he noticed the behaviour of the crowd change. They began to cheer as Tostig Godwinson passed by and he returned their greeting by waving back. The Earl noticed Harald looking at him and called.

"They are only welcoming home their true lord," he shouted jubilantly. "Rejoice, my brother's yoke is not wanted here."

"Enjoy your return, my Lord. Every man needs to come home sometime," Harald shouted back.

As they drew near, a line of folk emerged. They were mostly women and children; the wives and offspring of the prominent families of Northumbria - all to be taken back to the Norwegian fleet at Riccall as hostages. There was one name on the list who was not a Northumbrian - a young Norman boy named Richard Fitzroy.

He spotted the boy coming out of the cathedral and tried hard to conceal the relief that flooded through his body. Richard was a small figure in the line of people making their way toward the wagons provided as transport back to Riccall. At first, he did not hear his name being called and Harald raised his voice and shouted again, waving enthusiastically from the saddle. The boy lifted his head in recognition and saw his uncle for the first time in a year. He cried out and dropped his small collection of possessions, running to the group of horsemen. Harald could contain his excitement no longer and leapt off the back of Damascus and ran toward his nephew. They met somewhere in the middle of the courtyard and Harald swept the boy up in a fierce embrace before tossing him up into the air as if he weighed no more than a bundle of rags. Richard, unable to contain his emotions, began to cry and his tears ran down his face and into his uncle's beard.

"I have missed you, my boy," he cried, kissing Richard on the cheek. "Now, pull your shoulders back and follow me, let us show these Saxons how a Norman warrior conducts himself. Dry your tears, you are back amongst your own people, and I will never let you out of my safe-keeping again - at least until you have grown a little taller."

Richard composed himself and brushed his wet face with a sleeve and the two Fitzroys walked back to the horses. Harald moved to bend down and lift the boy onto the palfrey mare that he had brought with him, but Richard stopped him.

"It is alright, Uncle. I am a man now - I can mount alone," he said.

Harald stood back and nodded approvingly, watching his nephew confidently put one foot in the stirrup and pull himself up into the saddle. Tostig Godwinson moved to Harald's shoulder and spoke quietly.

"It is good to get a reminder of home, is it not? No matter how far away you are," he said.

Harald turned and saw that the Earl was smiling - perhaps for the first time since he had met him.

"Thankyou for your efforts in finding him, my Lord. I doubted if I would ever see him again," he replied.

"It was nothing. No more than one comrade-in-arms would do for another," said Tostig, taking Harald's proffered hand to shake it.

2

The gold and silver demanded by the Norwegian King was delivered in less than two days and his army returned in triumph to the fleet in Riccall where a victory celebration would take place. Harald decided that as his cavalry horses were in good condition, having not been involved in the battle, he would remain in Fulford with his army. King Hardrada would be returning the following day to take delivery of supplies for his army and the rest of the hostages before marching south, and Harald saw little point in riding the heavy horses when they could be rested and cared for. The citizens of York had accommodated Tostig Godwinson's request for hay and oats, and the horses were now tethered in long lines where an army of grooms attended them. The King had been happy enough for Harald to remain behind and had left a considerable amount of looted food and ale for the Normans to have their own victory celebration. In addition to the supplies, Hardrada also insisted on giving Harald his share of the ransom immediately, which was delivered in a sturdy wagon drawn by a pair of oxen.

So it was that, two days after the victory, Harald's army were camped within sight of York, where almost a thousand men took their respite. His army had acquitted themselves well on the field of battle and had taken a great deal of plunder from the land and the purses of their vanquished foeman. This last fact was greatly appreciated by several wagonloads of whores from York who worked through the night to relieve their customers of any newfound wealth.

Harald and his comrades sat in the firelight around a large makeshift table. Between him and Hedda sat the small figure of Richard Fitzroy, eagerly observing the sights and sounds of the merry-making all around them. Brenier, Jeanotte, Rolf, Leif and Wolfgang and all their squires were there, having made it through the battle alive, despite carrying a variety of wounds. Their commander got to his feet, no worse the wear for drinking copious amounts of English ale.

"My friends, we are still alive and still together and long may that remain so. We are far from home and yet none of you have ever questioned me, and I thank you for that. I do not expect the fighting is over yet and our fealty to the King of Norway has been rewarded with much gold and silver. I raise my drinking cup to you. I could not wish to fight beside so loyal a band of brothers," he said, raising his cup to all of them.

The table resounded to the sound of fists pounding the rough, wooden surface.

"To the men of Ambrierres," rejoined Brenier, who got to his feet.

"And the Kingdom in the Sun," added Jeanotte who now stood next to his friend, an arm slung around his shoulder.

Harald raised his arms, calling for quiet,

"I have one more toast to make," he called as the shouting died down. "I should like to make a toast to one of our number. Please raise your cups to Hedda Halldorsdottir, the Lady of Maldon and soon to be my wife."

Hedda looked up at Harald as if she had just been struck by lightning, tears rolling down her face. He looked down at her, grasping her hand and it was now her turn to get to her feet and receive the toasts and applause of her comrades-in-arms.

As the evening wore on tales were told and songs were sung. Inevitably Harald was called upon to recite the Saga of the Wandering Warriors and he was about to get to his feet when Brenier stopped him with an arm on his shoulder.

"Surely, it is my turn after all these years, cousin," he said, "and besides you will want to lavish all your attention on the Lady Hedda."

"Then I am sure that you will do the story great justice," bellowed the Commander.

Brenier stood in front of the large bonfire and took a breath before launching himself into the great saga of their ancestors from Haugesund. His cousin's expert rendition of the story took Harald's breath away and he marvelled at the detail and precision of the delivery.

> *Five ships and five times valiant men*
> *the Wandering Warriors sailed West*
> *Two shields, an axe and sword they shared*
> *And bid farewell to their Jomsvikings*
> *In search of gold and reputation in Saxon lands*
> *Odin's Ravens now ranged as men*
> *To plant their seed deep in conquered lands*

The audience hushed as Brenier recited the stanzas with great drama, and as he did so warriors from other parts of the camp drew close to hear him. By the end of the recital many more men stood in rapt attention listening to his words, which carried on the warm, evening breeze to the outer perimeter of the camp. When he finally took his bow, almost one thousand warriors cheered his efforts and no-one applauded louder and longer than Harald Fitzroy, his face glistening with tears in the bonfire's glow. As the fires burned low and warriors succumbed to drink and exhaustion, they began to drift off into the night. Harald sent his loyal companions to their beds and dismissed his squires, Thomas and Gilbert, with a final instruction. They were to take his young nephew and not let him out of their sight. Dutifully, they carried the young boy who had fallen asleep many hours before and covered him with a blanket before lying down, one on each side of him. Seeing they were finally alone, Hedda took Harald's hand and led him to a small makeshift bed she had prepared for them both. They laid down on a bearskin cloak that she had taken from the Saxon camp, and beneath a clear Northumbrian sky that glittered with a million stars they let the *manakti manir* - the great passion - consume them until dawn's early light.

3

The morning came too soon, and Harald raised his shaggy head and looked down at the sleeping form of his bride-to-be. Her short boyish hair and elfin features reminded him of a character from one of his grandmother's stories. His heart skipped a beat as he could not remember where Richard was, and he jumped to his feet and breathed a sigh of relief to see the boy wedged between Thomas and Gilbert, the swords of each of his guardians lying resolutely by their sides. The early morning sun was starting its ascent, and he resumed his position next to Hedda who had yet to stir. He drew her in close and inhaled the scent of crushed lavender in her hair before resolving to send her back to the ships with his wounded comrades, Richard and the wagon load of gold and silver. Then he pulled her in closer still and fell asleep again only to be woken for the second time by the sound of the camp kitchen coming to life.

The army began to get to its feet and the activity all around the Commander's central position intensified. Warriors suffering from a surfeit of last night's ale made their way to the kitchen and horses nickered softly by the supply wagons, waiting patiently for their oats. Exhausted whores began to leave the camp in droves as they counted their wages from the night's unbridled coupling while squires and pages ran round doing their masters bidding. The smoke from the cook fires pulled still-drunk warriors from their dreams, threatening, at least temporarily, to overpower the stench from the newly built latrines and dung-piles.

One of the Norman scouts came thundering into camp and Harald was interrupted at his breakfast. They reported seeing a large body of Saxon warriors camped five leagues away on the road to York. The King of England and an army of fifteen thousand men was but half a day's march away and would be on them by noon. After ordering Hedda and her contingent of wounded warriors back to Riccall he gathered his captains together. As he suspected, Harold Godwinson had finally marched to the aid of his northern kingdom, gathering men and arms as he did so. He had been joined by the defeated forces of Morcar and Edwin and they were ready to join battle against the Norwegian invaders and their allies. Brenier spat at the mention of the English Earls' names.

"We should have gelded them when we had the chance," he said angrily. "These Saxons have little sense of honour when keeping their word to stay out of the fight."

"Fifteen thousand warriors are going to keep us busy, treacherous or not," said Brenier.

"But hold them we must," said Harald, "at least until King Hardrada arrives with reinforcements."

"What then, my Lord?" asked Jeanotte. "Do we stand and fight? Perhaps a fighting withdrawal to the ships?"

"Let us not be too hasty until we look the enemy in the eyes, it may well give us the opportunity to finish our foemen for good. Anyway, it is far too early to concede our position although I must admit the odds are not stacked in our favour," said Harald stoically. "Provided King Hardrada's army is here in half a day we have a fighting chance."

They were interrupted by the arrival of Tostig Godwinson who had ridden the short distance from York with his men.

"Good morning, my Lord," called Harald cheerily, "your brother seems to have sprouted wings to get here so quickly."

"He is not a man to be easily denied but I must admit a sneaking admiration for his fortitude. Let us hope the march from the other end of his kingdom has tired him a little," said the Saxon with grim humour.

"I doubt it - a driven commander such as he can overcome many obstacles, but we should be wary all the same. We have little to lose and everything to gain and I have long prayed for the opportunity to face your brother on the field. Now come my friends, let us make ready and see what the Norns will throw at us next," replied Harald.

Chapter 23: Brenier's Stand
Stamford Bridge, September 1066

1

It was an unseasonably warm day that saw Harald Fitzroy's army deployed in front of the Stamford Bridge, an ancient structure of wood and stone that spanned the River Derwent. In its long lifetime it had seen a great deal of traffic, from passing Roman legions marching beneath the imperial eagle to itinerant cattle drovers moving their animals. Today would be another chapter in its history as Norman cavalry spread out in front of it waiting for the enemy. Earlier in the day, the bridge, broad enough for ten dismounted men to march across, had bustled with activity and now the army of Ambrières patiently stood in battle formation. Three *conroi* of heavy cavalry were ready and waiting, the horses fidgeting in the mid-afternoon sun beating mercilessly down on the warriors as it had for most of the day. Behind them sat the mounted archers in an equal state of alertness. They did not have to wait much longer, and soon Saxon battle standards could be seen on the summit of a nearby hill, announcing the arrival of Godwinson's army. Harald looked back across the bridge and was relieved to see the first elements of a large force of his Norse allies marching toward him. He ordered the bridge cleared so that the Norwegians could march through their lines to form the vanguard in front of them. They were led by the doughty Jarl of Rogoland and the old man saluted Lord Fitzroy as he drew near. Harald returned the salute and called out a greeting.

"Welcome to the field, Jarl Torbjorn. I think we shall have our work cut out today," he shouted.

"The King sends his compliments and is not far behind us. We have been sent forward to engage the enemy so he might have time to organise on the other side of the river," said the Norwegian.

"Did he not receive my message that the enemy were approaching?" asked Harald.

"Not until we were well on the road, I am afraid. We have had to run most of the way just to get here in time," replied the old Jarl, breathing deeply to catch his breath.

Harald watched the rest of the Norsemen cross the bridge to move out in front of his own troops and was dismayed to see that they were lightly armed with only shields, swords, axes and bows. Most of them had little or no armour or helms and all of them were bathed in sweat. Torbjorn saw Harald's look of concern at the dangerously under-equipped warriors and spoke again.

"Alas we had no time to prepare, the King was not expecting a fight today," said the Jarl ruefully.

"No matter. You shall doubtless give a good account of yourselves, as ever," replied Harald, dismissing the oversight as if it were of no importance.

He turned his head to watch the inexorable advance of the Saxons come streaming down the nearby rise in their thousands, until they stopped at the bottom and formed up in five divisions. Harald looked on as rank upon rank spread out and took their formation before him and he wondered if there was an end to the stream of enemy troops. A familiar voice broke into his thoughts and he looked up to find the King of Norway and Earl Tostig at his shoulder.

"Today shall be testing, Lord Fitzroy," said the King. "But, for all their great numbers, I sense the Saxons still have a soft underbelly that we might exploit."

Harald turned Damascus' head toward his allies but before he could say anything six horsemen broke clear of the Saxon lines and rode steadily toward them.

"Ah, the heralds are calling us to parlay, no doubt offering us ridiculous terms to head back to Norway," added the King jovially. "Let us hear what they have to say before we send them packing."

Despite the warmth of the day Harald had donned his new helm which seemed to make him appear even bigger astride his enormous charger. Like the rest of his Norwegian warriors the King was bareheaded and lightly armed with only a sword and axe at his belt.

"Do not fret, Lord Harald, I have sent for reinforcements, and they shall be arriving, fully armed, in short order," continued the King who seemed completely unconcerned that he and his men would soon be in a pitched battle with a foe that heavily outnumbered them.

The three protagonists walked their horses out in front of the Norwegian vanguard and as they stood waiting for the arrival of the Saxon heralds, the Norman commander recognised one of their number; Harold Godwinson, the King of England was riding in the rear of the group. He said nothing but watched as Earl Tostig also recognised his brother and readied himself for whatever might unfold. On reaching the King of Norway, the heralds stopped and one of their number began to address the King in *Anglisc* but not understanding a single word of it he motioned for Tostig to speak for him. Harald, anonymous behind his mask of steel watched as the English monarch remained silent. Unsure of what to expect from this subterfuge he put a hand on the hilt of *Gunnlogi* and moved closer to King Hardrada to protect his flank. His caution proved unwarranted as Harold Godwinson spoke for the first time, speaking to his brother directly as if there were no-one else present.

"Come back to your kinfolk, brother. All is forgiven and you shall receive one third of my kingdom for your loyalty," he said in his native tongue.

"I have sworn fealty to a different king," said Tostig calmly, "and what would you give him?"

"He is a tall man so I would give him no more than seven feet of English earth to bury him," replied his brother coolly looking Hardrada in the face.

The Norwegian King, still unaware of what was being discussed but reading the petulant 'herald's' body language, brought the parlay to an abrupt halt.

"This nonsense is getting us nowhere - in any case I have no desire to accept any more Saxon surrenders. We shall return to our lines immediately and let battle commence," he announced and turned to leave.

Harald Fitzroy waited for a moment and removed his helm to reveal his face, moving closer to the English king. He saw the Saxon visibly blanche as he recognised his former friend and ally.

"You shall reap what you have sown, my Lord. The only payment for betrayal can be death," spat Harald, unmoving, and waited for the Englishmen to turn their horses and leave.

The Norman commander rode back to join his troops, passing the massed ranks of Rogoland who were now in their battle lines. He stopped to speak to Jarl Torbjorn, standing defiantly in front of his men, bareheaded and with a dane-axe hefted over one shoulder.

"The gods favour brave men, my Lord. We shall be watching for your advance and guarding your flanks," he said to the old warrior.

"Then it is a good job you and your men are mounted, Lord Fitzroy. With no armour to impede our progress you might have trouble keeping up with us," said the Jarl, tossing his head back and laughing.

Harald cast a look along the long line of Norsemen, many of whom were standing bare-chested carrying only a spear or an axe as they waited. He pondered how they would fare against the heavily armoured *huscarls* that had slowly advanced toward them and had stopped less than a thousand paces away. Then he dug his spurs into Damascus's flanks and raced back to join his cavalry and was met with great cheering from the men. Their commander unsheathed *Gunnlogi* and lifting her high in the air, returned their greeting, knowing that it would not be long before battle commenced.

By the time King Hardrada's war trumpets signalled their readiness, from the rear, on the far side of the river, Jeanotte had taken his *conrois* of two hundred horsemen to the right side of the Norwegian vanguard with orders to attack the Saxon flank. Brenier's men formed up on the left and Harald's horsemen were held in reserve. The experienced Norman warriors were in no doubt that they faced impossible odds and their actions might hold the vast numbers of Saxon foot soldiers for a short time only.

There was movement in the English ranks and a large force of men from the *fyrd* began to move toward the enemy lines. As they did so several volleys of arrows sailed over their heads toward the ranks of the Norwegians and Normans only to fall woefully short of the target. In response Harald sent in his mounted archers from the rear who rode within a hundred paces of the charging foemen, dismounted and unleashed a withering hail of arrows of their own. They mounted and fell back to repeat the manoeuvre several times and their commander nodded with grim satisfaction as his bowmen wrought destruction from the air. The Saxon irregulars armed with an assortment of seaxs, spears and cudgels continued to charge on, trampling the bodies of their fallen comrades beneath their feet as they ran, heavily laden, through the afternoon heat. When they were four hundred yards from their target, both forward sections of the Norman cavalry began their charge toward the enemy's flanks. The galloping *conroi*, comprising rows of twenty horses each, were at full pace as the first steel-tipped spears hit home, killing and maiming scores of foemen. Behind the first lines of cavalrymen, riding so close that the legs of each man touched the next, came more disciplined lines. Wave after inexorable wave of heavily armed, mounted troops drove at the 'shoulders' of the body of Saxons, who, in an effort to evade their charge, changed direction, running across their comrades in the centre. The carnage inflicted on the English flanks narrowed the torrent of charging men and the Norwegian vanguard, unencumbered by the weight of armour raced out to meet them. As the last lines of Norman horsemen hit home and retired to the ranks of their waiting comrades, the Norsemen unleashed uncontrolled fury on the broken formations of the *fyrd*, scything through an exhausted enemy.

    Harald gave the order for his *conroi* to retire and lance pennants signalled his instructions across the battle front. As they retired, they were met by a small army of grooms and pages who raced out to water the long lines of panting horses. He watched impassively as the jubilant men of Rogoland checked and turned the Saxon charge and knew that as impressive as this early confrontation was, there were greater challenges yet to come. The

Norman commander did not have to wait long for a response as the Saxon war-horns sounded across the field calling the English King's household troops into action. He patted Damascus on the neck,

"Not long, now my friend. Let us see what these *huscarls* are really made of," he said as the 'tramp, tramp' of advancing feet reverberated over a fluid battlefield. Three thousand armoured warriors marched forward, preventing the Norwegian vanguard from pursuing the *fyrd* any further. Jarl Torbjorn's men having taken a brief respite after enjoying their initial victory, regrouped and turned to face the enemy once more. Their adversaries this time were cut from a different cloth and marched purposefully forward in two uniform and unwavering lines, seemingly untroubled by the storm of raining arrows caught on thick wooden shields. Heavily armoured spearmen in the front rank and axemen to the rear, the lines of *huscarls* pushed forward to engage. Norman cavalry advanced to hit the enemy flanks once more, only to be met by stiffer resistance as the disciplined ranks presented banks of spear tips behind a moving wall of shields. The *conrois* made their presence felt again, but the sheer weight of Saxon numbers was proving to be a harder nut to crack and every enemy felled by a lance thrust was replaced with a fresh warrior.

In the centre of the field Jarl Torbjorn gave the order for his Norsemen to charge and they obliged, hurling themselves at the Saxon lines that were now no more than fifty paces away. As they did so gaps in the first line of *huscarls* appeared allowing those behind them to wield their fearsome Dane-axes. The first Norwegians to reach them were winnowed like summer wheat and their lack of helmets and armour began to tell immediately. Heads and limbs were separated from bodies with ease as huge swathes of onrushing warriors fell in great numbers in a one-sided encounter.

On the right side of the battleground Jennotte's cavalry was in a fierce struggle and he signalled for reinforcements. Harald responded immediately and led his reserve *conroi* supported by mounted archers across the battlefront toward his comrades. In his eagerness to race to their aid he did not see Jarl Torbjorn fall beneath a merciless storm of axes and the old warrior's head was removed from his body and mounted on a spear. Watching their leader fall the fighting spirit of the Norsemen deserted them and despite the bravery of their charge they were pushed back relentlessly and slaughtered.

Harald's entry into the battle could not have come a moment too soon for Jeanotte's hard-pressed men and he found his captain engulfed in a sea of Saxon warriors. The cavalrymen had discarded their lances and were now hacking their way through the enemy ranks in a cauldron of clashing blades. The wounded and dying of both sides screamed their agonies and the ground was thick with corpses. The Commander, unable to use his archers in the close-quarter fighting deployed them quickly, loosing their arrows into the horde of Saxon warriors behind the main mêlée. Riding front and centre in the first *conrois* of gallopers he led his riders into the action, skewering enemy warriors in a slew of killing. He and Damascus were of singular purpose and focussed only on the destruction of their enemy. The stallion's iron-clad hooves cleaved their way through any resistance and as one enemy axeman drew back his weapon to strike, the horse lunged forward tearing the man's face to ribbons with a deadly bite. His master had already broken his lance driving it through the helm of another Saxon head and *Gunnlogi* was unsheathed and brought to bear on other foemen. Behind him, more *conrois* charged in and the Saxon advance, at least on that side of the field was checked to a stunned halt. Whilst the intervention of Harald's reserve was telling it only gave enough of a respite for Jeanotte to extract himself from the very real threat of being overwhelmed. Realising that this particular battle was lost Harald ordered a withdrawal and the two groups of horsemen regrouped and left the fight to rejoin Brenier on the far side of the field.

They found their comrade equally hard-pressed a thousand paces away, having just withdrawn from some bitter action on the left flank where he had been beaten back by an overwhelming force of Saxons. By now, the remnants of the Norwegian vanguard had rallied, and their small knot of resistance drew themselves together for a final charge. Five hundred bloodied and desperate men turned and faced the enemy one more time and knowing that a retreat to the far side of the bridge to rejoin the main army was not viable, they pitched forward. The enemy front line seemed to waver as they closed with them, but this was no sign that the battle's fortunes had changed. A gap in the Saxon lines appeared, into which the Norsemen rushed pell-mell, seemingly swallowing them whole.

Harald looked at both of his captains who, like their horses, were breathing hard. Both Brenier and Jeanotte were bloodied and bore minor wounds but were otherwise intact. Harald raised the mask of his helm and looked toward the furious sounds of battle.

"I believe it is time to leave the field. There is no more we can do here. We shall retire back over the bridge and pray that the King of Norway is ready," shouted the Commander over the noise of the tumolt from nearby as the last of the Norwegian vanguard disappeared from view. "Come, let us leave while we still have time to get our men and horses back over the river," he continued.

Both men nodded their ascent before shouting orders for the troops to form into a single column and hasten from the field.

Stamford Bridge was empty when the first hooves resounded on its wooden planks. The Norman retreat was disciplined and unhurried as the column made its way back over the river. They had put some distance between themselves and the main body of Saxons who were still murderously intent on finishing off the Norwegians. However, a small group of enemy soldiers followed them at a distance and had stopped on the slope leading down to the bridge and were shouting derision, cursing the departing combatants. A few of the Saxons had unslung their bows and were now loosing arrows on the remaining horsemen who were still on their side of the river. Brenier was watching the last of his column withdraw to the other side when three arrows caught his horse in the neck. The great beast dropped to the ground trapping his master's leg beneath it. Harald heard his cousin's curses and turned to see him struggling on the ground. He dismounted, ran back down the line and with the aid of four other men dragged the dead horse off him.

"You are hurt?" Harald enquired.

"It is nought but a scratch, Hari," said Brenier as he coughed and a bright, red flow of blood escaped his mouth and ran into his beard, "but I would be grateful if you would remove this arrow from my back. Alas, I cannot reach it."

He turned around to reveal the broken shaft protruding from his *hauberk* which was embedded in the middle of his back. It had gone straight through his mail shirt and snapped when the horse fell on him.

"Well, what do you see?" continued Brenier,

"Nothing good, my friend. "The arrow is lodged deep, and I cannot remove it," said Harald on closer inspection. "There is nothing for it but to ride out of here - come take the horse of one of these squires. They are light enough to share one between them."

Brenier turned back to face him bleeding heavily from the mouth and shook his head.

"My Lord, it grieves me deeply, but I must deny my commander's orders. Come Hari, you must flee while there is time - the Saxons will soon be upon us," he said pointing up to the top of the rise where, having disposed of the Norseman, the Saxon army were mustering to sweep down on the warriors that had been the cause of so much tribulation earlier in the day.

Harald looked into Brenier's eyes and saw the haunted look of a dying man. He wrapped his arms around him in a tender embrace and kissed his cheek.

"Until Valhalla, then," he whispered.

"I will see you in the great hall, but a long time from today. You have yet to fulfil our grandmother's curse," said Brenier.

"You have seen her?" he asked incredulously.

"She visits me in my dreams - as I'm sure she does you. Now, I shall need an axe - a large one - and I must play my part. I will hold the bridge for as long as I am able - it is my last gift to you all."

"Then my last gift to you is this fine helmet. It once belonged to a king of Byzantium, I want to make sure the gods looking down today see you as you slay our foeman," said Harald.

A warrior at his shoulder thrust a dane-axe into his captain's hands, and Brenier hefted it to feel its weight before turning to face the Saxon horde gathering on the brow of the hill, daring them to come and meet him. No more words were spoken, and the column remounted and left their comrade to his fate, the warm afternoon air resonating to the sound of his voice, heaping scorn and derision on the enemy.

2

Brenier Fitzroy stood with his back to the sun, casting a long shadow. With his full-length *hauberk* and *coif* covering most of his body and the dane-axe over one shoulder he represented a fearsome challenger for any man brave enough to fight him. His cousin's magnificent, crested helm made him seem even taller to the watching Saxons to whom he called to battle with a variety of insults and curses. He cursed their mothers and fathers and homes and families, inviting them to send their best men down to fight him. They did not know he was mortally wounded and there was no visible sign of any injury as he spat his rage at the onlooking host at the mouth of the bridge.

The first man to accept his challenge was a Saxon thegn who had marched all the way from London with his band of local men. He left the cheering ranks and approached his challenger. The *thegn* carried a large round shield and spear and walked purposefully toward Brenier, who mocked his opponent as he drew closer.

"Are you sure you are ready to play with grown-ups yet, Downy-Cheeks?" scoffed the Norman.

The Saxon did not reply but came on with an increased pace and lunged wildly at Brenier. Despite the weight of his arms, the Norman stepped nimbly aside, inviting the man to try again. After receiving several wild spear thrusts, Brenier grew tired of baiting his opponent and aimed a double-handed strike at his opponent's shield, splitting it with a single blow. The Saxon reeled backwards and fell, raising his head belatedly, only to see his opponent's second blow about to remove it from his shoulders.

Brenier kicked the dead man's head away and called up the quietened ranks of Saxons,

"Come down and meet me, Harald Godwinson. You should be a leader of your men, instead of just using them as your shield," he shouted.

The second man to accept the challenge was a *huscarl,* a captain from the King's personal bodyguard and the huge Dane loped down the slope to attack. He charged in to meet the challenge, swinging his own dane-axe, determined to repay the Norman for his insults. Again, Brenier moved quickly to evade the first blow and parried the second with his own axe. As the *huscarl* moved in again he fell to his knee, dropping his axe and withdrawing his razor sharp *seax* in a single fluid movement. He drove the blade into the unprotected area of the man's inner thigh, severing flesh and arteries. The Dane dropped to the ground and watched his life blood drain from the wound, but Brenier hastened the man's journey and cut his throat. Although he was mortally wounded, not a single man in the enemy ranks might have guessed, as he called up to them once again and this time directly addressed the Saxon king.

"Godwinson - turn up to this duel if you have a man's heart, rather than a mare's. And if you fail to come, then a scorn-pole will be raised against him, and you shall be cursed. You will be a coward in the eyes of all men and will never again share the fellowship of warriors. You will endure the wrath of the gods, and bear the name of truce-breaker," he shouted, hands-on-hips throwing his head back and laughing.

Another man came down and was similarly dispatched before two spearmen charged down the slope and were scornfully sent into the next life. After the ninth man fell beneath Brenier's axe blade there was a pause in the activity, and he took refreshment from a skin of wine that one of his men had left him. He was now very hot and close to exhaustion, but the exhilaration of the fighting coursed through his veins, and he called upon the old gods to fuel his inner fire. He felt his spirit rise from his body and watched himself fighting and downing more Saxon warriors as they came and died.

Up on the top of the hill Harald Godwinson sat astride his horse beneath fluttering royal banners, curiously observing the defiant warrior below, denying his army's progress. He reflected that it had been a successful day for his army despite the surprise of meeting Hari Fitzroy at the earlier parlay, but the annihilation of the Norwegian vanguard had soon put it to the back of his mind. Now, for whatever reason, his former friend and ally stood across the bridge blocking his way and defeating the best of his warriors. The English king rejected the entreaties of his captains to have the troublesome Lord Fitzroy finished off by archers, deciding that he would allow him a warrior's death. After all, he reasoned both men had once been brothers-in-arms before the betrayal.

As the day wore on, the Norman showed no sign of weakening and with bodies of the fallen festooning the mouth of the bridge, the King grew impatient. He was persuaded to put an end to the embarrassing resistance by changing his point of attack. He ordered some of his men to take a small boat upriver and float downstream on the current until they were beneath the bridge. One of these men would take a spear and dispatch the troublesome warrior from below while he was otherwise engaged in the fighting.

Brenier felt a sharp pain as a spear entered his body from somewhere beneath his *hauberk.* He took a sharp intake of breath as the steel tip of the spear was rammed up into his body between a gap in the planking. He thought briefly that this was what it would be like for a whale to be caught on a harpoon and reached down between his legs to feel the spear shaft and knew his race was run.

The last assailant to face him had been game but no match, and had it not been for the spearman beneath the bridge, yet another Saxon would have fallen to his axe. The pain began to disappear, and he started to feel tired for the first time and even when the spear was pulled free, he felt nothing. He lay on the ground breathing his last, at peace with himself, knowing that he had given his comrades every chance of escape. The advancing Saxon warriors, under strict orders of their King not to pillage or desecrate the body, picked it up carefully, laying it to one side and cleared the way for the rest of their comrades to follow on.

Brenier opened his eyes and looked out of the face mask of his helm to see two ravens sitting on the fence that ran along the side of the bridge.

"Well met, my boy," said the first, crooking his head to one side, "you fought valiantly and could have done no more. Does he remind you of anyone, Bjorn Speararm?"

"Why he reminds me of you, Torstein Rolloson," said the other.

"Then we have the right man," chuckled the first raven.

"Who are you?" croaked Brenier through cracked lips.

"We are the Wandering Warriors of Haugesund and we are here to take you to the great hall of Valhalla."

"Ah, that is good news then, for today has been thirsty work," replied the dying Norman.

"Just get to your feet, grandson and we will carry you there," said the second bird.

Brenier jumped lightly to his feet and the two ravens picked him up in their beaks as if he weighed no more than a feather. As they flew into the sky he looked down to see the prone, unmoving body of a warrior, still clutching his great axe in both hands and the sun glinting off the inlaid gold and silver of a magnificent helm. The figures on the ground grew smaller and smaller as he gained height and soon he could barely make them out.

"Hurry, grandfathers, make haste for I am keen to meet the rest of my ancestors," he shouted into the wind and the great winged birds carried him away.

3

It was well over an hour before Harald could no longer hear his cousin's threats and curses, by which time his *conroi* had rejoined the main body of King Hardrada's army. There was little to tell the King that he did not already know, for the earlier battle and Jarl Torbjorn's demise had been witnessed by his confederates from the rise on the river's far side. The Norsemen and their allies spread out in a crescent-shaped formation on a large flat plain that sloped down toward the river. Despite the morning's losses Hardrada still managed to field an army of five thousand men, and the arrival of another three thousand reinforcements from Riccall was expected at any moment. Harald led his tired cavalrymen past the massed ranks of Norsemen, who cheered them heartily as they moved to take their positions in the reserve. He stopped briefly to speak with the Norwegian King who stepped out of the lines to greet him.

"A brave action, Lord Fitzroy. The Norman horsemen are every bit as fearsome as their reputation. I commend you for your efforts and your sacrifice. Your brothers have not died in vain," he called.

"We are yours to command, Lord King," answered Harald, "let us give this Saxon pretender what he deserves."

"Indeed, we shall; when the time comes for you to enter the fray look for the banner of the Land Ravager - I shall be where the fighting is thickest. If I meet the English King before you do, I shall give him your regards," said Hardrada and laughed madly before giving a polite, little bow. "Now, take your men to the rear, I need you to hold them in reserve when the hammer blow is called for."

"We shall be ready for your order, Lord," replied the Norman commander, leading his men away.

He passed Tostig Godwinson and his small band of rebels and called out a greeting, wishing him good fortune in the coming storm. The Earl saluted him stoically and Harald was dismayed to see that his men were the only warriors, aside from the Normans, properly attired for the fight. When they were out of earshot of their allies, Jeanotte spoke for the first time since their retreat over Stamford Bridge. He spoke quietly as they watched and waited.

"It is madness, Lord, these Norsemen are dressed as if they are out for a day's hunting. They will need more than a few bows and spears to hold the Saxons back. Surely a fighting withdrawal would have suited our purpose better? Why fight with one arm tied behind your back?" said the Norman captain, apprehensively.

Harald shrugged and sighed.

"Spoken like the veteran warrior you are, my friend. But sometimes even a King has to choose reputation over wisdom. But let us see how this day ends, it is not the first time our backs have been to the wall and yet still triumphed," said the Commander, with as much reassurance as he could muster. They both watched in silence as the King of Norway strutted before the lines of his warriors, axe in one hand and sword in the other, extolling the gods, old and new, to give them victory.

In truth Harald knew that Jeanotte was right, and the disciplined savagery of their enemy's actions this morning only confirmed that he had every reason to be cautious. He touched the amulet at his throat as he watched the Saxon hordes come streaming over the river and spread out in front of them. As the two sides swapped the inevitable insults that precursored the battle's beginning, Harald found himself thinking of Hedda and whether he would ever see her again.

Chapter 24: The Norman Landfall
The South Coast of England, September 1066

Robert Fitzroy was also deep in thought as he stood at the gunwales of the *Mora,* gray waves lapping softly against her hull. Dawn was breaking and he called up to the sailor at the mast head to ask if the man could sight either land or ships. The man replied that he could see nothing and shinned back down, Robert shaking his head in frustration. The night voyage had been surprisingly calm and their sleek vessel with the best of crews had sailed far ahead of the rest of the fleet across the calm surface of l*a Manche*. Duke William had insisted that Robert, against his better judgement, should sail with him rather than with the men of Mortain. The Chancellor argued against the decision, saying that it would be folly to have both of them aboard a single vessel, but the Duke had been adamant. Now they were lost at sea and there was no sign of any of the following four hundred ships, fore or aft. The ship bobbed around in the gentle swell with the sail dropped as they waited for their comrades to catch up. The Chancellor cut a frustrated figure and cursed beneath his breath, eager to get to England to feel *terra firma* beneath his feet. He turned to the sound of the Duke's voice, calling him to join him for breakfast.

"My friend do not fret so. What God has ordained no man can change. Come and join me in these vittles - a little food might settle your stomach," shouted the Duke.

Robert left his station looking out to sea and sat with William at a little table in the stern where a servant bought him a cup of spiced wine.

"Captain Fitzaird, are we still headed toward the English coastline?" continued the Duke to the man at the wheel.

"To the best of my knowledge," shouted the ship's captain above the screeching of the herring gulls. "We sailed with such speed we have simply left the rest behind."

"There you are, Robert - Stephen Fitzaird is never wrong when it comes to navigation. Let us concern ourselves with the sort of reception we shall receive when we arrive. You will be glad of a stout breakfast if we have to fight our way ashore," said the Duke.

"If my spies are correct the main strength of the Saxon army has gone north to fight the Norsemen," answered Robert. "Godwinson cannot be in two places at once."

"And you too are seldom wrong. But let us not take anything for granted, although making an easy beachhead would be an agreeable way to start our campaign," said the Duke.

Their conversation was interrupted by a shout from the lookout who spotted four sails on the horizon. Within an hour the same voice reported that a forest of masts was in sight and the *Mora* hoisted her sail again and led the fleet onward. After another hour, the heights of Beachy Head, on the English coast, hove into view and a great cheer went up from the tightly packed fleet. As they grew closer the *terce* bells of the local monastery pealed the hour of nine o'clock and the first Norman ships drove into the shallows. The shock troops of the advance party urged their horses overboard and up the stony beach to secure the landing point.

The speed with which the Riders of Regneville assembled was impressive but ultimately unnecessary, and they failed to encounter resistance of any kind. Five hundred cavalrymen stood ready and waiting on the beach but with no-one to fight Floki Fitzroy stood his men down and they used the opportunity to stretch the legs of their mounts, running them up and down the beach. The rest of the ships moved to nearby Pevensey Harbour and began to disgorge their cargo at a more leisurely pace. By noon the invasion force had landed, camping beneath the massive stone walls of the ancient Roman fortress.

The crossing had been slow and, but for the loss of two ships, had been completely successful and the pilots who plotted the course, which for most constituted an inaugural crossing, were jubilant. The calm weather had also proved miraculous and in thanks for this divine intervention, Duke William ordered a service on the beach moments after the last man had landed.

As soon as Bishop Odo intoned the last blessing the very serious business of finding food and shelter began. With the ships packed to the gunwales with men, arms and horses there had been little room for vittles, and the rich towns and burgs on the English south coast were expected to be full of food after a bountiful harvest. A company of a hundred Breton horseman were dispatched to commandeer as much food as they could around Pevensey Bay. Duke William had given strict instructions while his army was camped at Dives that the local people were to be respected and not to be molested or stolen from, but in England there were no such orders. On the contrary, foragers galloped away with a rapacious intent and a license to instil terror in an unprotected population.

Robert joined his brother and, with a detachment from the Riders, they rode into the nearby town of Pevensey in search of accommodation for themselves and the Duke. When they arrived in the almost deserted town they were spoilt for choice, for the rich burghers had all but deserted the place, leaving their homes and property behind them. They selected a number of comfortable houses that would suffice and after posting men at the doors to discourage the foragers they went in search of refreshment. They found an alehouse a short distance away from the homes of the rich merchant's houses where they would be quartered, and after threatening the landlord with burning his property to the ground the terrified man was persuaded to open up. Floki pressed silver into his trembling hand and ordered food and drink for his men with the promise of protection from the depredations of any freebooters. Jugs of ale appeared in copious quantities, soon followed by trays of bread, meat and cheese and the company sat down in the warmth of the midday sun to take refreshment. Many of the men had not eaten since leaving St. Valéry and were clearly famished, wolfing down food and drink with gusto. As they did so, shuttered windows and locked doors opened all along the street of close-packed houses, and timid locals began to emerge. Before long a small group of children congregated in front of the seated troops, observing the company of armoured warriors in repose.

"These folk are the lucky ones," said Floki, taking a bite from a chicken leg, "when our foragers are through with this part of the coast there will not be much left from the flames. The Duke is a master at inducing fear, is he not?"

"Be in no doubt, there will be enough destruction to lure the Saxons onto the field of battle. The Duke will stop at nothing to confront the pretender," said Robert, pushing back his mailed *coif* from his head to feel the warmth of the sun.

"He must at least be delighted with the ease of our landing? I have not seen a single enemy warrior yet," said his brother.

Robert nodded and smiled.

"Indeed he is which is why we must enjoy this tiny moment of respite for there will soon be no rest for you or your men. The Saxon army have left and gone to fight the Norseman and whoever is left standing will come for us next," he said.

"Any word of Hari?" asked Floki.

Robert shook his head.

"None, not since he left Maldon. But you can be sure that whoever stands against him will be feeling some pain," came the quiet reply. "Let us pray it is the Saxons feeling his wrath for I could not bear the thought of him standing against us."

"He will be true to his family. Be in no doubt," said Floki putting a hand on Robert's arm.

The two men looked at each other for a moment, each one wondering the same thing but neither contemplating the remotest possibility of their brother's treachery. They raised their drinking cups in a silent toast to him - wherever he might be.

Their thoughts were interrupted by the sound of wagons rolling along the mud-baked street toward the inn. Six large carts filled with grain sacks were being drawn along by yoked oxen. A platoon of Breton horsemen were lazily overseeing the convoy as it ponderously made its way up the street and back to the camp. The seventh cart in the group carried a different burden and it was loaded to the brim with all manner of household items including cooking utensils, pots and chairs, while on the top sat four children, all below the age of ten. This cart was pulled by four disheveled looking women, their faces bruised and bloodied and their clothes torn and dirty. Robert looked up from his conversation and put his cup down calling out to the Breton serjeant leading the group.

"What have you got there?" he shouted to the man who took a moment to recognise the Duchy's Chancellor before drawing himself to attention in the saddle.

"It has been a busy morning, Lord, and we have been collecting food for the Duke's army. The land is full of bounty and the grain and oxen will feed many men," said the Breton.

"And these people?" asked Robert pointing to the cart at the rear.

"Saxons, my Lord. Nothing creates fear among the enemy like taking their women and children. Besides we can find a use for them back at the camp," said the man leerily.

"We do not take captives for slaves," said Robert, "it is a sin against God. Release the women and children immediately - we have no use for them."

The serjeant began to bluster, arguing that he had been ordered to terrorise the local population and abduction was only another tactic of war. At this, the men of Regneville stopped drinking and rose as one, hands on weapons.

"Cut them loose, I say," ordered Robert firmly.

The Breton, realising there was no point in arguing ordered one of his men to free the prisoners and they ran to the cart to retrieve their children. As soon as the women scooped them up from the wagon, they ran off back down the street and the convoy resumed its progress, the disconsolate Breton horsemen to the rear.

"Alas, some of our ranks do not share our Norman sensibilities," said Robert to his brother before calling for more jugs of beer to be sent from the kitchen.

"Do not fret, the Saxon axemen will be none too picky when it comes to cleaving heads. We shall need them all - good and bad." said Floki cheerfully.

"Unless we have to hang them for their crimes first," said Robert a little too piously for his brother's liking.

"Come Robert, you of all men know that war is a brutal business where only the strong can survive," said Floki in an attempt to assuage his brother's anger.

"True enough but it is always the weakest that suffer most," replied Robert. "Now where is this ale, I am beginning to think the landlord does not want our business at all."

They settled down once more, enjoying this brief moment of calm, which they both knew would soon be a distant memory. The brothers travelled back to the harbour riding side by side and the great food collection was in full swing. It seemed that every man with a horse had acquired a piece of rope with which he had lassoed the townspeople's cattle. Soldiers captured every single sheep, pig and chicken and stolen cauldrons hung over cookfires everywhere.

Robert had one more task to oversee, which was to ensure that the building of the fort within the town's Roman defences was underway. Pevensey had powerful fortifications, built by the Romans, and was enclosed by a stout stone wall with a perimeter of seven hundred paces. There was also a network of docks that had been used by the Saxon navy and merchant vessels of all sizes. Robert's builders were some way along with their task of completing a garrison that could house a thousand men and had already erected the walls with wood brought from Normandie for the purpose. The mound on which it was to stand was the first task to be completed and by the end of the day a deep ditch had been dug around it. Duke William came to join the inspection and both men, satisfied that it would be completed in the next two days and ready to house a thousand warriors, made their way back into town toward their new lodgings.

"A good day's work, my friends. Gentlemen, you have both my respect and gratitude," said the Duke as he dined with his companions.

They sat in the courtyard of his new temporary headquarters in the last of the day's warmth.

"Indeed Lord, we have certainly been favoured by God. But what does tomorrow hold for us?" asked William Fitzosborne.

"What I have seen today tells me that we need a decent road off this peninsula, should we need it. Tomorrow we shall take Hastings," said the Duke, sure in the knowledge that his destiny was secure.

Hastings was a smaller town than Pevensey but being on the road to London Duke William decided he would have it. Splitting his army in two, he sent his foot soldiers for part of the trip by sea, while his cavalry made their way along the coast road and a double trail of destruction was set in motion. Those villages lucky enough to be out of the line of march were spared while other communities were caught in a storm of steel. Their stock was seized, the people killed or chased away, and their villages laid waste. Leaving a path of death and destruction behind him the Duke simply walked into Hastings and occupied it without a struggle. Robert ordered his builders to commence work on a new fortress and within a week that too had been completed.

The Norman army was now fed and quartered and with no opposition the Duke could only wait for news from the north. He prayed that the violent destruction of the Saxon homeland was enough to tempt their King into meeting him on the battlefield or whoever had won the battle in the north.

Chapter 25: The Last of the Sea Kings
Stamford Bridge, September 1066

1

Autumnal sunshine beat down on the bare head of Harald Fitzroy as he watched, fascinated by the unfolding drama in front of him. Damascus shifted beneath him in the heat, effortlessly bearing the massive armoured weight on his back as if it were no more than a child. The stallion nickered with impatience and his brothers, behind him, called back as if to encourage their masters to enter the fray.

The lines of opposing warriors locked shields no more than two hundred paces from each other, perspiring in the heat. The Saxons were still extending their line into battle formation, and it was already three times the length of the Norsemen's shield-wall. In response King Hardrada ordered the ends of his line to fold back on itself and form a defensive circle. Now dressed in a full-length coat of mail, he stood in front of his men calling for great deeds of valour and they responded by cheering their leader energetically. The first sign of any significant movement came from the Saxons and ten axemen ran forward to be met by a dozen semi-naked berserkers and fighting began with several frenzied confrontations. The Norwegians held the sway in the early skirmishing and each personal victory delivered by their heavily tattooed warriors was met with more cheering. The Saxons responded with a charge by a complete division of *huscarls* who advanced and then spread out as they engaged, enabling them to swing their axes in wide, deadly circles. The Norsemen absorbed the impact of the attack, and it was their turn to advance, cutting down many axemen, pushing the rest back. The Norwegian King in feverish excitement burst out of the defensive circle and charged forward leading a cohort of his bodyguards into the enemy ranks.

At the head of a press of five hundred warriors, Hardrada was irresistible, and he and his men breached the Saxon shield-wall and surged through the gap, splintering all opposition.

Harald, still sitting impassively in the reserve on the high ground behind the packed circle of Norwegians, struggled to keep sight of the King. The banner of the 'Land Ravager' bobbed and weaved as the men beneath it forged a path through the enemy's lines. It headed toward the English King's own banner, but its progress slowed abruptly as it approached. After a bloody and prolonged clash, the banner bearing the single raven fell and disappeared from sight. Hardrada had been struck by an arrow to the throat and lay dying within the protective knot of his bodyguard. Their charge checked, the Norsemen that still lived were hurled back from whence they came but the Norwegian King was not to be seen. A huge cry went up from the Saxon ranks as the news of Hardrada's fall spread like wildfire. His army was stunned into shocked silence and the defensive ring buckled at several points as ten thousand Saxon warriors moved to encircle it. The English army soon surrounded their foemen and poured volley after volley of spears and arrows into the ragged ranks of trapped men. Tostig Godwinson was the next leader to fall, and he disappeared beneath a hailstorm of spears as did the last hopes of his loyal Northumbrians.

Harald ordered his *conroi* to retreat further back up the rise and put another five hundred paces between his men and the encircling army. They stopped to turn back but his attention was taken by a large body of men running toward them on the road from Riccall. Fearing being trapped between two armies he readied his troops to charge at the men running to the rear of his *conroi*. Recognising the banners of Oystein Orri approaching at speed, he stood his men at ease. Although Harald had known the Jarl for less than a year, the two men were good friends and quickly recognising each other, they hailed one another.

"How goes the battle?" asked Oystein, breathing heavily beneath a thick mail coat liberally coated with his own sweat.

"Not well, my friend. I lost sight of the King on the field and fear he is fallen," replied Harald, handing him down a water-skin.

Oystein swore and dropped his head in anguish.

"Then if we are too late to save him, we must save our comrades," said the Jarl looking down the slope at the seething mass of men caught in the throes of death.

"We shall go with you," said Harald.

"No, my Lord, if the King is dead then you are released from your oath. This is no longer your fight - take your men and return to the ships," said Oystein firmly.

Harald started to protest but the Jarl raised a hand to stop him.

"If the King is dead - I command here. Leave us Hari, you have done your duty and can do no more," continued Oystein.

His friend nodded his consent and bowed his head in resignation but before he could say more the Norwegian shouted to his captains to ready their men. Two thousand Norsemen locked shields and marched down the slope in two lines to relieve their hard-pressed comrades.

Oystein Orri led his men into battle with speed and ferocity to which all his men responded. Despite marching five leagues, at the double, from Riccall in punishing heat the Norsemen did not let fatigue slow their progress. On the contrary, they burst upon their enemy like a breaking dam and the Saxons, so close to achieving victory, were pushed back to the bridge. The encircling army of ten thousand Saxons felt the biting steel of

Orri's storm, and the expected victory might well have been snatched away from them when they least expected it. His men broke the ring of steel that threatened their comrades inside it and hacked away until the attackers became defenders. The beleaguered Norsemen inside the circle took heart and rallied and the counter-thrust found the larger army pushed back. One of Oystein's men retrieved the battle standard of the 'Land Ravager' and hoisted it high, giving hope to all his countrymen who looked upon it. The ground was littered with the fallen of both sides as thousands of bodies lay dead or dying. The English King, realising that the tide of battle had turned against him, threw in his reserves and the sheer weight of several thousand fresh warriors finally overcame all Norwegian resistance. When Jarl Oystein fell to his knees, bloodied and exhausted, a Saxon dane-axe removed his head, and all hope was over.

The slaughter did not stop for the next hour and thousands of exhausted Norsemen were dispatched to the next life. The battle of Stamford Bridge was finally over and barely four hundred Norsemen staggered from the field, leaving almost eight thousand of their dead comrades behind them. Harald Fitzroy did not wait until the bitter end and departed the field when he saw the Land Ravager fall for the second time. He had seen enough, and too many good men had fallen for a lost cause.

2

The retreat back to the boats was a bitter experience for the men of Ambrières who had seldom tasted defeat. They were silent as they trudged off the field and away from the noise of the slaughter at their backs. As the cries of wounded men became evermore distant the only sound from the long column was the creak of saddle leather, the jangle of bits and the occasional whinnying from the horses. There was no conversation between any of the riders as they cantered away in twos, each man lost in his own thoughts. It was still uncomfortably hot despite the lateness of the day but as the big horses had seen no action since the morning they were rested and fit enough for the journey to the boats. They passed the bodies of Norsemen at the side of the rode, visibly uninjured, but dead from exhaustion, trying to run the five leagues to the battle.

Harald wanted to put as much distance as they could between his column and the Saxon army and when he was confident that they were not being pursued he gave orders for the pace of the march to slow. In his long career as a warrior, he had inured himself to the triumphs and occasional disasters of a campaign, but this one had been as ignominious as he could ever remember. He shook his head and cursed to himself. The King of Norway had been lulled into believing that England had been there for the taking, and for all his glorious reputation, forged across Europe and Asia Minor, had been defeated by his own complacency. Despite Harald's repeated warnings to Hardrada that the enemy would be retaliating for the defeat at Fulford, he had been politely but firmly rebuffed. The army of the dead now covered the field of battle, where their bleached bones would bear testament to the King of Norway's folly for years to come. The great age of the Norsemen was over, and with the flower of their warriors fallen and left for the crows and wolves to devour, few of their number would make it home to tell their desperate story. With their passing a part of Harald died too.

Dusk was falling as the column reached the fortifications of the vast inland lake at Riccall harbouring the great fleet of the defeated army. There were only two guards manning the entrance to the camp, old veterans carrying a variety of wounds who lolled listlessly against their spears. They stepped aside wordlessly to let them through, and Harald led his men along the dry mud banks surrounding the vast lake, to where their own ships lay. They passed hundreds of ships, either beached or anchored in the shallow water that lay silent and empty. The camp that had bustled with activity only days before with thousands of men preparing for war was now empty and barren. The enthusiastic vigour that had coursed so virulently through the expectant ranks was now but a memory. Nightingales and reed warblers trilled their evening songs unabashed and uncaring of the great disaster that had befallen the camp. Around the great bowl of the lake there were dotted a few cooking fires, where small handfuls of men gathered to cook their evenings rations. They rode on to the other side of the lake, passing the King's deserted pavilion and his great long ship which had sailed its last voyage. Next to it was the camp of the men of Bergen, bearing the obvious signs of a hurried departure earlier in the day, with unwanted arms and equipment tossed carelessly away in the panic to join battle. Beyond that lay Harald's camp where he prayed that Hedda and Richard would be found safe and well. His heart leapt with joy as he saw the two of them running toward him in the half-light, and he jumped down from his horse and swept them both up with unashamed relief. The Commander stood the exhausted column down, and while the men tended to their horses he gave the final orders for the day. They would be unable to leave the lake tonight and would have to defend themselves as best they could if the Saxons followed up their victory. Tomorrow they would take stock and get ready to leave as soon as was practical. A perimeter of Norman spearman was deployed for the night, while the remainder of the men went in search of food and rest. Hedda led Harald to a small bed she had made up where the three of them sat and she let him eat in silence. When he had finished, he realised that he was weary to his bones, and she cajoled him into lying down without a further word. She lay next to him, and with his arm around Richard they slept deeply beneath the northern sky.

3

Dawn broke bringing a misty drizzle, and they were woken by the sound of a commotion coming from the main entrance to the camp a thousand paces away. Harald, dragged from deep sleep by the noise jumped to his feet. He was joined by Jeanotte and Hedda, and called the rest of the men to arms, marching towards the camp's entrance. What they found was not an army of Saxon warriors but the bedraggled remnants of the once mighty host of Norsemen. No more than five hundred beaten warriors limped through the entrance to the camp, led by King Hardrada's son, Olaf.

Each man carried several wounds, and they were all bloodied and battered as they trudged back to their ships, oblivious of the watching Normans. One of their number, a man from Bergen leading a horse carrying the body of a mailed warrior, hailed Harald.

"Lord Fitzroy, it is me, Erland. I would speak with you," he shouted. "I have brought him back to you."

Harald recognised the young warrior immediately as Oystein Orri's companion and rushed toward him, putting a large arm around his shoulders to steady him.

"Come, Erland. You are wounded. Let us take you to our camp - it is not far," said Harald

"I have Brenier's body, Lord. They let me recover him from the bridge," said Erland through the pain of spear wounds to his leg and torso. "They have respected him in death - he is whole."

Harald mumbled his thanks, whilst Jeanotte appeared on the other side offering his support and together, they all walked slowly back to the Norman camp. It took a while, but eventually they carried the wounded Norseman back and laid him gingerly on the makeshift bed that Harald had only recently vacated. Erland was exhausted and in great pain but keen to explain the final actions of the battle. He was the last of Oystein's warriors to be left standing and with his liege lord dead and his friends and comrades lying at his feet he expected to join them - but the battle suddenly stopped. Olaf Haraldson had surrendered on behalf of his dead father and the Saxon king, in order to preserve his own men, ordered the fighting to cease immediately. He was allowed to leave the field with any Norsemen still alive, provided they returned to their ships and left the shores of England forever. None of Hardrada's companions survived the battle and all, including Halldor Snorrason, died beside their King.

"And how did you find the body of my cousin?" asked Harald.

"It was a curious thing. As the survivors gathered together to leave the field the Saxon King ordered that the body of the 'warrior on the bridge' be bought forward on a horse and returned to his people. He spoke of him with great reverence, almost as if he knew him. See - his armour and helm are still intact, and his body has not been abused," said Erland.

"You have done my family and comrades a great service and I thank you for returning him to us," said Harald, ordering two of his men to lay Brenier's body down on the ground.

"There is something else, Lord Fitzroy," replied Erland. "My Lord Oystein, insisted that you take the *Sea Viper* with you in the event of his death. He ordered that should he fall in battle you were to take his ship and everything onboard. He said you should treat it as a wedding present and that you would need a new ship to replace the one you lost to the Jarl of Rogoland."

Harald gave a bitter laugh.

"You have done well, my friend. Now rest - you will soon be going back across the water to Bergen and you will need all your strength for the journey home.

4

Hedda tried hard to conceal her tears for her dead father. She would grieve for him in due course but that would come later when she had time. She also needed to grieve for other lost comrades, and she was inconsolable at the loss of Brenier who had protected her like an older brother. Later that day he would be seen into the next life on the funeral pyre of the *Lady Alberada* but more immediately his body needed preparation for the ritual. With the help of Thomas and Gilbert her mentor's body was stripped and washed, his armour cleaned and mended, and his weapons polished until they shone.

Harald had decided that as Jarl Torbjorn had fallen and he was unable to hand his ship over as the bride price for Hedda, the vessel would be sacrificed to the dead. As Brenier was the only warrior to have been returned he would be laid out with his meagre possessions on the deck and the ship incinerated. The men hauled the *Lady Alberada* from her anchorage in the shallows, high up onto the dry mud bank, and filled her with dry brush and wood collected from the nearby forest.

The Normans stood around the ship and when all was ready Harald stepped out and recited the prayer to the fallen. In a loud, clear voice that could be heard from the other side of the lake he began to intone.

Lo there do I see my father;
Lo there do I see my mother and my sisters and my brothers;
Lo there do I see the line of my people, back to the beginning.

Lo, they do call to me, they bid me take my place among them, in the halls of Valhalla, where the brave may live forever.

When he was finished, he took a lighted torch and threw it into the ship, which had been doused with pitch, and the assembled warriors watched in silence as the flames licked around their friend's corpse. The conflagration grew and all the Norman warriors, both pagan and Christian, said goodbye to their comrades. Other groups were doing the same and soon ships all around the lake were set alight by little knots of survivors saying farewell to the fallen dead. Before long, hundreds of longships were burning, and the sky was black with acrid smoke. When the flames from the *Lady Alberada* finally consumed her and there was nothing left, some of the men dug a pit and scattered the cinders into it. They refilled it, leaving a carved wooden totem standing upright around which each warrior left a pebble in memory of their friend. When this final ceremony was over the men went back to the business of loading the remaining ships ready for departure and, tired as they were, they worked until the hours of darkness.

Harald stood alone with Hedda watching the first of the Norwegian longships depart the basin to go back down river and head across the North Sea.

"There are precious few going home," she said as another of the sparsely crewed ships left the sanctuary of the lake.

"At least most of us made it through the fighting," he replied, "we should count ourselves lucky. I cannot bring back the two hundred warriors we lost but they all died rich men, and their families will want for nothing. Richard has been returned to me and when all is said and done, that was our mission."

"And what now, Hari?" she asked.

"Now we shall head home," he said.

"And where might that be?" Hedda asked.

He turned to her and smiled.

"Wherever you are is my home," he replied opaquely "but first we must sail back to Maldon, for there is still unfinished business with these Saxons."

"Indeed, my love," she agreed touching the silver amulet at her neck.

It was well into the evening before the men and horses were loaded. Everything that had been removed from the *Lady Alberada* had to be stowed away on the *Sea Viper,* and it was dark before Harald and Hedda made their way aboard. The *Dreki* longship was a large, beautifully built craft, exemplifying the skills of the Bergen shipwrights. Unusually it had a small cabin in the stern of the ship and Hedda took Richard by the hand, making their way by the light of an oil lamp. Inside they found two wooden cots and with cloaks and blankets they made up the beds. In the corner of the cabin, they found the Jarl of Bergen's sea chest and, unable to contain his curiosity Richard lifted the lid. His eyes opened wide with delight as he saw the *Ulfberht* sword with its richly bejewelled hilt lying on top of an equally splendid mail coat. They lay next to several leather bags of gold coins and jewellery and the boy shook Hedda's arm to get her attention. She gave an ironic laugh as she saw what the chest contained.

"Well, at least it cannot be said that I will be a bride without a dowry," she said.

Although Richard did not understand the joke he laughed along with her with great gusto.

They were interrupted by the creaking of clinkered planks as the *Sea Viper* was rowed out to the centre of the lake, where she dropped anchor with the rest of the Norman flotilla.

Twenty-four ships carrying the tattered remnants of Hardrada's great army of ten thousand troops made their humble exit throughout the day. There were barely enough Norsemen to man the ships and they had nothing to look forward to except a shameful return to Norway. The epoch of the last great Norse Sea King was over, and his proud army lay rotting in their fallen ranks many leagues from their homes and families.

The next morning the *Sea Viper*, at the head of the Norman fleet, rowed into the deep channel of an ebbing River Ouse, toward the Humber Estuary and into the North Sea. The main sail was lifted, catching a favourable northerly wind that took her south and away from the despondency of Northumberland.

5

They spent four days reaching Maldon and, for most of that time, Harald stood at the tiller of the *Sea Viper* steering her south. Apart from taking time to eat and sleep, he stayed at the stern of the ship for most of the voyage, in contemplation. He was now forty-three years old and had spent most of his life fighting on battlefields far from home. He had loved and lost many women along the way and his two sons were complete strangers to him. Harald was a wealthy man of great reputation with lands in England, France and Sicily and had taken these riches by force and deed. For the first time in his life, he was tired of war and continual conflict. Much as he hated to admit it, but the thought of retiring his sword and destrier, spending his days sitting around the hearthfire with his old comrades was not without its appeal. The death of his cousin had been a bitter blow, and he felt it deeply. But he also knew that there was still a score to settle with the Saxons and in particular with Harald Godwinson. His family would be avenged, of that he had no doubt, but how he would be able to achieve it he had little idea. Their small army of a thousand men would need the luck of the gods to defeat a Saxon army perhaps twenty or thirty times their size.

"Long odds, long odds," he muttered to himself.

Hedda was sitting on the deck, with her arm around Richard, and she turned to see him looking down at them and beamed him a dazzling smile. He returned it and for the first time in a long while he felt fortunate and whispered a silent prayer to the Norns beseeching them not to cut the cords of fate which bound them together. As he finished his invocation, a large wave broke over the stern of the *Sea Viper* and the salty spray ended his moment of reverie, soaking them all.

The flotilla approached Maldon on the morning of the fourth day, and all appeared to be as it had when the army left two months before. The harbour was busy and there were four large Byzantine *dromons* flying the flags of Apulia tied up against the stone walls, with half a dozen smaller ships beached further away down the shoreline. The *Sea Viper* approached the jetty first and ropes were thrown to eager hands on the dockside. As soon as his new ship was secure, Harald jumped down without waiting for the gangplank. He nearly fell, cursing himself for his clumsiness and looked up to see his steward, Clifford striding towards him, arms outstretched in greeting and with a huge smile on his face.

"My Lord, it is good to see you. What news?" he shouted before looking up at the gunwales of the *Sea Viper to* see Richard's face smiling down at him. "Master Richard, you are a sight for sore eyes," he continued delightedly.

"Fate has dealt us an uneven hand," replied Harald, looking toward the gathering group of women and children anxiously searching for the faces of returning husbands and fathers as they started to spill down onto the jetty. "We have visitors, I see."

"Yes, the Duke of Apulia has sent his brother Roger with five hundred men," said Clifford, "I have billeted them in the garrison."

"Ah, when is a Hauteville ever on time? Well, better late than never, I suppose? Now let's get everything onshore and you can tell me news of your own. But first I have an urgent errand to make," replied Harald.

He took a deep breath and trudged off in the direction of Brenier's house to deliver the news to his wife that she was a widow.

With all the ships now docked, men arms and horses were unloaded with customary efficiency. The precious horses were taken off to the stables to be fed, watered and groomed. Married men were met by jubilant families while the single ones went in search of refreshment in the nearby ale houses. Hedda and Richard made their way up the hill to the longhall, and hearing the wails of despair from the newly made widows discovering the deaths of their men, only heightened her sense of loss for her father.

Chapter 26: The Duke's Great Gamble
Hastings, September 1066

1

Between the towns of Pevensey and Hastings the Normans had left a smoking wasteland. Like locusts in a biblical story, they had swept the land of everything of value. Saxon communities caught in the hellfire of destruction were given no quarter and with their lands destroyed, homes pillaged, and womenfolk violated, the lucky ones that lived joined a growing band of refugees on the road heading toward London. It was rumoured that King Harald would be returning from the North with a mighty army to cast the invaders into the sea.

Robert Fitzroy threw himself into the destruction of the Saxon homeland with zealous fervour, sending his men out with orders to create as much damage as possible. They had followed the missive to the letter, returning to the camp at night with wagons full of food and booty, ensuring that the army of eight thousand men were well supplied and motivated.

The matter that irked the Chancellor was that their camp in Hastings was situated on a peninsula - a good place for defending but less valuable to launch an attack on the English heartland. Their army was well supplied for the moment, but he knew they could not possibly spend too long there. Come what may they had to move or starve before the onset of winter. For a long week he waited for news of their adversary and Robert knew only too well that they were isolated within the smouldering Saxon ruins on the small triangle of land they had taken so easily.

When the news came, it was not what had been expected and emanated from an unusual source. Robert and the Duke had chosen quarters on the abandoned estate of the thegn of Hastings, a man of great wealth and property, who had occupied a palatial and heavily fortified house that reflected his station. The two men were taking dinner together in the great hall when an emissary from Harald Godwinson arrived from the north of England.

Roparzh Fitzwymark was a Saxon Lord of Norman descent and had kinship with Duke William. He was also well-known to the Fitzroy family and, whilst not a close friend to the brothers, he had a reputation as an honest man. Now, he stood outside the Duke's quarters with urgent news for him. He was admitted by the guards and stood before the Duke and his Chancellor, mud-spattered and covered in the dirt and grime of the road. He was at least ten years older than the men he before him and despite a florid complexion and a slight paunch that betrayed an over-fondness for wine and ale, he stood upright and tall.

"Lord Roparzh, welcome. It has been a while since we saw you last. Your visit to Mortain with my cousin King Edward, I think. The hunting was good that day, if I recall correctly?" said the Duke cordially. "Come take some food and refreshment with us. You have travelled far it would seem?"

"Indeed, my Lord. You are correct on both counts," said Fitzwymark with a bow, "but before I accept your hospitality, I feel I should explain the nature of my visit."

"Oh? Whatever your purpose is, cousin, we are still kin, and you are amongst friends. Please, sit with us," said the Duke, feigning surprise.

Fitzwymark shuffled anxiously before sitting down at the proffered seat, while a servant brought him wine.

"I am here at the behest of King Harold, who commanded me to deliver his message," he said without prevarication. "I am here to persuade you to give up this enterprise and return to the Duchy. You will find nothing but grief here, my Lord. The King has won a great victory over the Norsemen and Harald Hardrada and his army have been destroyed."

The Duke shot a look at his Chancellor.

"Interesting news, Roparzh, but it does not affect my position greatly. I am here to claim the English throne which has been promised to me. Why, we were all present when King Edward pledged his Kingship to me on the event of his death," said the Duke calmly.

"Indeed I was, but today I am only here as a messenger," continued Fitzwymark steadfastly. "As a friend of the Norman court and your kinsman I would be deeply sorry if any harm befell you. Do not stay in England, my Lord, where you will meet with certain destruction. I beg you to go home while you have a chance. King Harold will soon be in London with a countless host, and you will be defeated. Your army cannot stand against his, as justified as you believe your cause might be."

Duke William snorted derisively.

"You are a man of some integrity and know well what was promised to me. Desist with this folly and I will bear you no grudge. I thankyou for delivering this news and when I am King and the pretender has been cast down, by the will of God and my own strong hand, I will allow you to keep your lands," said the Duke pompously.

The man shifted nervously in his seat.

"You will be granted safe passage out of here." said Fitzwimark, ploughing on relentlessly, "Ten thousand Norsemen lie dead in Northumbria and their monarch lies with them. King Harold slew his own brother, Tostig Godwinson without mercy … and there is more."

Fitzwymark turned to look directly at Robert.

"I regret to inform you, Lord Robert, that your brother Harald lies among the fallen. He died a hero's death, alongside his kinsmen, fighting the Saxon army."

The blood drained out of Roberts face and he felt the earth shift beneath him. Completely lost for words, he shook his head in disbelief, unable to comprehend what he had just heard. He was shaken to his core at hearing the news that he had dreaded receiving all his life and struggled for words.

"You saw him fall?" he finally managed in a quiet voice.

"Not I, Lord, but there were many that did. He was killed holding up the Saxon advance to allow his comrades time to retreat," replied Fitzwymark.

"We will sit together in the great hall of Valhalla, brother," Robert mumbled to himself, staring into the hearthfire.

He tried to compose himself and lifted his cup of wine to his lips draining it completely. The room fell silent until the Duke spoke.

"That is unwelcome news, Roparzh, and the death of our friend and brother, the Lord of Ambrières, is a great loss to all of us. We shall all mourn his passing. Now, the hour is getting late and you will be in need of a bed. You are my guest for as long as you like. We shall meet again in the morning, if you will excuse us," said the Duke politely.

Fitzwymark thanked his host and was shown to his quarters. They waited for him to leave the room before William spoke again.

"I am sorry for your loss, Robert, but your brother chose to leave his duty behind him when he left the Duchy," said the Duke dispassionately. "The men of Ambrières failed to answer when they were called. A sore loss to our numbers but we have had to do without them all the same."

Robert did not seem to take in the words and looked blankly ahead before finally speaking.

"My brother is dead, and my son is lost. What will become of the boy?" he said with great anguish.

"We will look for young Richard when Harald Godwinson has been put to the sword. Do not fear, my friend, your family is my family, and we shall leave no stone unturned," replied the Duke.

He tried to engage in further conversation but saw his Chancellor's thoughts were far away, and after saying goodnight he left for his rooms. Robert did not notice the Duke leave and after a while he looked up to find himself alone. He could not remember how long he sat there, but by the time he got up to leave the fire had burned low and most of the candles had all but guttered out. He needed to pray and left to find the chapel. The thought of his son lost and alone in some forsaken part of this awful land was more than he could stand, but if God could hear him there might still be a chance.

2

The next morning there was another meeting with Roparzh Fitzwymark in the same room they had met previously. The Duke and his Chancellor had met beforehand and decided on the best course of action. Both of the veteran warriors had agreed that the Saxon army would be weakened by the battle with the Norwegians, a factor that needed to be exploited before they had time to regain strength. They had goaded Godwinson by burning his land but now they needed to force him into a decisive confrontation and strike while the iron was hot. If the English King stayed in London long enough his banner-men would join him, swelling the size of the army many times. Robert estimated that Godwinson had ten thousand men at his disposal, but that number could double within a week. Once the Northern earls rallied to the muster, the Saxon host might exceed thirty or forty thousand men - more than enough to sweep the invasion force into the sea. Beyond wasting the English countryside, a different tactic was needed to force Godwinson's hand.

Fitzwymark was admitted to the room when their meeting was finished and the Duke, adopting the same polite manner from the previous evening, spoke first.

"Lord Roparzh, I trust you are well-rested from yesterday's journey. You know Bishop Oddo, of course," he said gesturing to the heavily set man in a long hauberk sitting next to him.

"Of course, we are well acquainted," replied Fitzwymark, nodding courteously to the Duke's half-brother.

Bishop Odo, looking more like a knight than a holy man, fixed their guest with an unblinking stare but otherwise did not respond. He was a powerfully built man with Duke William's dark facial features, but an opulent lifestyle had taken its toll, and the shape of a large belly was obvious beneath his mail. Robert, looking tired and listless, with dark rings beneath his eyes, muttered a greeting.

"I have considered the King's offer and my answer is the same as yesterday. I am here at the invitation of King Edward who, before he died, asked me to inherit the crown of England. I am here to discharge my duty to him and you, Roparzh, were witness to that wish, were you not?" continued the Duke with a steely edge to his voice.

"Yes, my Lord, but the deathbed wish of King Edward was that Harold Godwinson should be his heir and that must take precedence," replied Fitzwymark as stridently as he was able.

Duke William reacted with well-rehearsed fury and banged the table with his fist.

"That is a lie!" shouted the Duke. "Not only is he an oath-breaker and guilty of fratricide but now he has also killed my own kith and kin in Northumbria - and for that I demand justice. I challenge your King to single combat so that God may decide the destiny of the English crown."

Fitzwymark's face coloured at the outburst and he held up his hands.

"That will not be necessary, my Lord but I shall take your offer back to London with me."

The Duke continued to express his effrontery and blew out his cheeks theatrically, but it was now the Bishop's chance to speak and Oddo drew his large frame upright in his seat.

"Never have I experienced such larcenous behaviour in all my days and neither has the Holy Father in Rome," said the Bishop menacingly.

The mention of this last statement caused Fitzwymark to cease his protestations, and he was struck silent. Odo reached beneath the table and produced a piece of sealed parchment and placed it in front of their guest.

"And if any more evidence of his sins were needed, this document is the Papal Bull of Harold Godwinson's excommunication," continued the Bishop.

Fitzwymark was dumbstruck and the Duke spoke again.

"I swear by the holy relic of St. Peter, around my neck that your King will be punished," he spat. "How will his people react when they discover that their monarch is a heretic? We view this enterprise as a pilgrimage and our holy duty to the Church. We are here to save the Saxon people not destroy them."

"But if God requires us to spill some blood in our endeavours then we will not shirk our duty," added the Bishop, placing an ugly looking mace on the table.

Roparzh continued to be harangued by the Duke and his half-brother for some time until there was nothing left unsaid. He excused himself and bid his hosts farewell before mournfully taking his leave and returning to London.

Robert quietly observed the theatre in relative silence. He had said little, nor did he need to do so for he had orchestrated the response perfectly, and it was abundantly clear that the Normans had God and the Pope on their side. King Harold needed the hearts and minds of his army in the coming campaign, and they might not be so keen to follow him were it known their leader was a heretic.

"You think that will be enough to lure the pretender into battle?" asked the Duke.

Robert considered the question and nodded thoughtfully.

"Bravery without forethought causes a man to fight blindly and desperately like a mad dog. Harald Godwinson will not be defeated by brute strength alone and our trap is now well-baited."

Chapter 27: Unfinished Business
Maldon, October 1066

1

Harald recognised the unmistakable long, languid form of Roger de Hauteville as soon as he caught sight of him, over five hundred paces away. He was stretched out on a bench outside the longhouse, patiently waiting for the arrival of his old brother-in-arms. Harald's face cracked into a broad smile as Roger saw him coming, shouted a greeting and got to his feet. The two friends embraced warmly.

"I bring greetings from the Kingdom in the Sun. Age has not withered the strength of your arm, I see. Just a little more snow on the mountain-top," said Roger, laughing and releasing himself from Harald's huge bear hug and standing back to observe his friend.

"It does the heart good to see you, my old friend," said Harald joyfully. "You have changed a little yourself from the skinny boy we took with us to Italy twenty years ago."

"Aye, Hari," said Roger casting his mind back to the time when they had both left the Duchy of Normandie as itinerant soldiers of fortune. "The gods smiled upon us then, I hope they have not forgotten us since."

"They have not forgotten you; it would seem. You look like a Byzantine prince in that rich attire," joked Harald. "Now let us take some wine together - I have had enough English ale to last a lifetime."

"Then it is a good job I do not come empty-handed," said Roger, pointing to several barrels of fine Apulian wine standing in a nearby wagon and handed the older man a wineskin. "Here try this. It will remove some of the dust from your journey."

Harald drank deeply and the rich, summery taste of the wine took him back to a different time and place.

When he had first fallen out with the young Duke of Normandie, Harald had left the Duchy as an outlaw in the company of Roger's brother, Robert Guiscard, and a small warrior band. They went to southern Italy seeking fame and reputation against the turbulent backdrop of their new home. They found both in great measure and became a driving force in the Kingdom in the Sun. After leading his army to victory at Civitate in 1057, Harald became not only an important military figure but also a friend to the church of Rome.

The wineskin was quickly drained and Roger produced another before both men retired to a bench out of the sun. After the briefest time catching up the younger man came straight to the point.

"My brother sent me to persuade you to come home. He knows you have business here that must be settled but says he cannot wait forever to conquer Sicily. Your lands and property in the south are all in good order and you have been sorely missed," said Roger earnestly. "We are here to help you fulfil your quest, in the hope that you will return with me when it has been accomplished."

"A return to the Kingdom in the Sun has been much on my mind of late, but, as you rightly say, I have duties here that need to be discharged before I can think of the future," answered Harald unequivocally.

"Then we shall talk of that again and until we do, we are at your service - that is if you are in need of your old comrades of St.Marks," asked the younger man.

"I think you know the answer to that question. Let us leave our reminisces a while longer for there is much to tell and we have little time," said Harald, and began to share the events that had occurred since the first return to Maldon. Before he could fully share all the details of the last year, they were interrupted by Jeanotte striding towards them, and after a brief reunion the veterans of St. Marks sat down to discuss what needed to be done.

2

Hedda and Richard had slipped quietly back to the longhouse. They were both exhausted from the journey but there was food and relative comfort waiting for them, and after they had eaten, the boy fell asleep over the table. She struggled to get him to his feet and noticing how big he was getting, ordered one of the servants to take him to her chambers and put him to bed. It was not long before she did the same and climbed in beside him. It was not quite dark, and she quickly fell into a deep sleep. When she woke up in the early hours the sound of the men talking outside had stopped, and she looked around in the half-light looking for Harald. He was not beside her and the sleeping boy continued to snore away gently. She tried to get back to sleep but the events of the past weeks came back to her and the grief returned.

Hedda had loved her father deeply and was still coming to terms with the fact that she would not, at least in this life, see him again. She was still tired and closed her eyes but knew that sleep would not come back and sitting upright, swinging her legs over the side of the bed, she walked over to the table on the far side of the room and washed her face from a bowl of water. Hedda promised herself she would bathe later in the day when she returned, but at the moment she had other things on her mind that took precedence. She pulled on the clothes discarded so hastily the previous evening and swept a long woollen cloak over her shoulders. With her boots in one hand, she crept past the sleeping men and dogs in the hall and went outside to greet the day. The sun had yet to rise over the sleeping town, which showed little sign of movement, although smoke from the cooking fires began to rise into the early morning air. There was another clear morning sky, and the crisp chill of early autumn was evident. She went to the stables and saddled up a palfrey that gently nickered a greeting to her as she led it out, mounted up and walked away toward Northey Island, just over a league away.

Hedda did not know why she needed to go to the place where the Voyage of Tears had begun, taking Harald's people away from their home to make a new one in Normandie. She only knew that she needed to visit it once more and as she traced their footsteps toward the causeway, the sea frets began to blow in from the distant ocean covering her path in a thickening mist. She was a little nervous as the fog descended, but knew her horse well and it walked confidently and sure-footedly onwards. It was then that she started to hear the voices.

It began as a whisper then grew in volume, and although she could not yet discern what they were saying she heard the fearfulness in their voices, mothers urging their young charges forward to the boats. She looked around and passed dim shapes in the gloom, but they did not feel malign in anyway; just ghostly forms with heavy loads, hurrying to reach their destination. The noises from the fog changed as she reached the causeway, and she smelled the salt water and mud. She heard the clash of steel on steel, of men shouting as they fought and of others dying in anguish and agony. Hedda recognised the noise all to well and imagined that these were the sounds that her father had heard just before he died. Great salty tears ran down her face and fell, unchecked, onto the horse's neck. She tried to wipe her face with a fold of her cloak, but it did no good, the tears could not be stopped, and she sobbed uncontrollably. The ghostly forms in the fog seemed to join her in her grief and she heard faint cries of the women's despair and loss as the dark forms rushed past her. A gust of wind blew and the air began to clear and lighten, enough for her to see the causeway up ahead of her. Horse and rider stopped at the point where the stony pathway made its way onto the island and Hedda jumped down to lead it over the slippery rocks. As they walked across, a man's voice rose above the cacophony of the others, emitting a bellow of wild laughter behind them. Hedda looked back and saw nothing except the briefest of thrashing in the water, before she turned again and led the horse forward. When she got to the other side of the causeway to Northey Island, they continued along a muddy bank. The murk had lifted and with it the spectral voices and dark shapes also disappeared. The day was dawning and although the struggling sun could not yet be seen, it was at least getting lighter. Hedda looked around her and had little difficulty imagining the plight of the people as the warriors fought to keep a vengeful army away from their women and children. When she looked up again, she saw a dark shape standing in front of her a hundred or so paces away. She stopped and peered intently at the small, hooded figure, clad in dark clothes. This was no apparition or ghostly form, and as Hedda stared, the person pulled back the hood to reveal a woman's face, her straight, yellow hair pulled back and plaited into a long ponytail. She called a greeting to the woman, who did not reply but levelled a hunting bow in her direction and loosed an arrow. Hedda watched the arrow sail into the air in a high arc above her head, landing behind her on a patch of dried mud. When she looked back the woman was nowhere to be seen and she went to the arrow which had landed deep in the ground, pulling at it hard to get it out. What she found was a hunting arrow, seemingly unextraordinary in any way, but when she looked down at the hole it had made, pulling it out, she saw a loose piece of leather. Hedda bent down and tugged but it was stuck fast and so she took her *seax* from her waist and began to dig. Before long the hole revealed a small bundle, wrapped in leather and she pulled it out to find it contained a pair of identical throwing axes. The wrought iron heads had keen steel edges, and the handles of oak were inlaid with runes of walrus ivory. She picked one up in each hand, admiring their weight and balance, until her attention was taken by the harsh 'caw-cawing' of two ravens flying overhead. She looked up at them, waving the axes in greeting and smiled at the palfrey who stood patiently waiting for her.

"I understand what I must do," she said, patting his neck before mounting the horse to go home.

3

The residents of the town of Maldon had taken the news of the Norman invasion better than many of the other coastal towns in southern England. They had a Norman lord and their citizens were of mixed Norman and Saxon origin who, despite their history, all managed to coexist in peace. Most of them reasoned that with such a benevolent Lord as Harald Fitzroy, whoever prevailed in the battle, that would surely take place before the year was out, there was little reason for alarm.

The day after Hedda's visit to Northey Island, one of the town's merchants, a salt trader by the name of Eadfrith, returned from London in some haste and went in search of his Lord. The man held an exclusive *fief* to produce and transport salt from a large area of land around Maldon and had grown rich in the lucrative trade under his patronage. Eadfrith traded his wares directly with the royal household in West Minster and had been delivering sackfuls of salt to the palace where the Godwinson brothers had all been present for a council of war. The Royal

Steward, a close confidante of Eadrith, had told his friend that he had heard the brothers arguing for the King to be prudent and wait on reinforcements before marching out to meet the Duke of Normandie's army in Kent. According to the steward, the King would brook no argument and had insisted on marching as soon as his army were able - whether reinforcements had arrived or not. Gyrth, Leofwine and all the noble names of southern England were ordered onto the road to Kent to gather at a place known as Senlac Hill. Eadrith had stationed one of his servants at an inn on London Bridge, with orders to send word the moment the first cadres of the Saxon army set foot on the road to Canterbury. Harald thanked the man, who refused to take payment for his services and called a meeting of his captains.

They met an hour later in the longhall and Jeanotte, Wolfgang, Rolf and Roger all joined the Commander around the table.

"Gentlemen, it may come as no surprise to you that I will ask you to take the field once more. You are all rich men now and if you do not care to join me, I shall miss your presence but will not think ill of you," said Harald looking around at his comrades who barely seemed to register the question. "Then I shall begin."

A large parchment map of England had been unrolled and they all looked at it intently as the Commander continued, pointing at Hastings.

"As you all know, our brothers from the Duchy have landed here on the south coast and are in danger of being trapped. Duke William is many things, but a fine navigator is not one of them. The Saxon army will be on the march to meet them before we know it and given time will crush them if given the opportunity. I do not intend to let that happen. Jeanotte, what is our intelligence regarding the Duke's army?"

"Eleven hundred ships carrying almost ten thousand men and three thousand horses, all told, left Dives and landed safely in Kent. There was a rumour that they lost a few ships to the great storm but other than that it was a success," answered Jeanotte. "They are stripping Kent of everything they can and an army that size will need to move constantly just to feed itself."

"Then the Duke is lucky to have my brother at his right hand," interjected Harald, secretly delighted at the news. "The Saxons will field at least fifteen thousand men, but we shall even up the odds. Godwinson will be leaving London as soon as he is able and will form up his host here, where the Duke will join battle."

He pointed to Senlac Hill on the map and shook his head.

"We cannot outpace the Saxons. The men might be fit enough but the horses need another two days and even then, they are not built for a long march," said Jeanotte.

"True, but we can out-sail them. A strong northerly wind will take us to Dover under sail and we can row from there. We will disembark here, at Winchelsea. We have a man of Kent in our town who knows the terrain and will act as our guide. Perhaps the horses can be ready in a day?" Harald asked rhetorically and Jeanotte nodded reluctantly. "Then if there are no questions, we shall meet at the ships at first light the day after tomorrow."

There were none and each man murmured his assent.

"Before you go, we should make a toast, let us drink to absent friends," he continued and raised his cup to the empty seat where Brenier should have been.

The others raised their cups in a similar fashion before going out into the cold night air.

Harald sat alone with only his dogs for company, listening to them snore contentedly in front of the hearth-fire. In under two days he would be taking to the sea again in search of his enemy to right a good many wrongs. For the first time in a while he felt his old confidence begin to grow within him, and wondered with some amusement how Robert would welcome him when he turned up to fight by his side. Hopefully they might be reconciled one more time and resume their brotherhood, which had always been so close. He would miss Richard, of course, but the thought of returning him safely to his parents would be a cause for celebration for all of them. He tried to imagine the look on Duke William's face if they met again, which they would undoubtedly do, and laughed out loud.

Hedda heard him laughing and came to join him at the table. She leaned over and kissed him, letting him breathe in her sweet, musky perfume of ambergris and he was filled with desire for her. She took his hand and led him past the sleeping dogs to their bed chamber. When finally, they were spent he wrapped her in a tender embrace and whispered his love for her. Taking her hand, he slipped a gold band onto one of the fingers.

"There, we are married, and you are now my wife. We shall celebrate the union when I return. Now I must go away to the war and this time you must obey your husband and stay here with Richard - out of harm's way. I will not let the Norns cut the strings binding our fate." he said, drawing her into him and falling asleep.

She said nothing, feigning sleep, knowing that if she answered him, she would have to lie.

4

The next day another messenger came from London and the salt trader's servant arrived around noon with important news. The first of Harold Godwinson's troops had been seen crossing London Bridge, heading down the pilgrim's road to Canterbury. It was now a race against time to ready the ships to meet the tide in dawn's early light. Some of the women came to bid their men farewell but Hedda was not one of them. Harald was disappointed not to see her on the dockside, but was soon caught up in the excitement of the departure as his new ship the *Sea Viper* led the thirty strong fleet of vessels out past Northey Island and into the River Blackwood. A strong neap tide helped them get into the Tamsye estuary by mid-morning and by noon they raised their sails in the open sea where a stiff northerly propelled them toward Winchelsea and their destiny.

From a vantage point on one of the Byzantine *dromons* a diminutive warrior watched Harald Fitzroy lean into the tiller and turn the *Sea Viper* across the wind. The billowing sails filled, and the elegant longship sped over the choppy surface of the sea as if it were about to take flight. The warrior, bedecked in a full-face helmet, knee length mail and two elegant throwing axes hanging from the waist, watched him as a wave broke over the stern and sprayed the resting oarsmen with salt water. Harald threw back his head and laughed as he gripped the tiller. Hedda mouthed a little prayer for both of them and asked the old gods that they should be together soon, in this world not the next.

Her task had become even more onerous when she awoke that day, realising beyond any doubt that she was carrying Harald's child.

Chapter 28: Battle of the Hoary Apple Tree
Kent, Autumn, 1066

Robert Fitzroy also received news of the Saxon army when they began their march from London. A veteran of a hundred battles, he willed the confrontation to hasten and looked forward to delivering vengeance. He had shared the news of their sibling's demise with Floki, who was distraught at the sad tidings and together they had made a solemn pact to avenge him.

When the Norman scouts reported sighting the enemy, Duke William, ordered his men to 'stand-to' in expectation of a night attack. The meeting of the two adversaries did not materialise and the Saxons camped for the night on Senlac Hill two leagues from Hastings. The Duke declared that in the morning they would meet their foe and by nightfall he would be the new King of England. The night before battle was an anxious one for both sides and every hardened warrior knew what the following day's ordeal would likely bring. Men drank, took whores, prayed and gambled or simply slept if their nerves allowed them, for tomorrow's terrors would soon be upon them.

The Saxons had taken a strong position on a hilltop, with their flanks and rear protected on each side by dense woodland and it would take a great effort to dislodge them. The Duke ordered his army forward at first light to engage with King Harold, before he could be bolstered with reinforcements, due to arrive from all over England. The Norman advance guard found an army of ten thousand assembling in the early dawn light and a brightening morning revealed rank after rank of spearmen emerging from the hilltop woods. Beneath the fluttering standards of the 'Fighting Man' and 'Dragon of Wessex', the Saxon lines took shape, and their ranks began to swell in a tightly packed crescent formation over eight hundred paces long.

Aside from the two armies stood a small hill and both commanders, realising its strategic importance, sent men to secure it. Norman archers hurried to meet Saxon mounted infantrymen, and in the salvo of arrows and crossbow quarrels released into English ranks the first casualties of battle fell. Despite the early loss of dozens of men, the King's troops rallied with the arrival of a force of spearmen and drove the Duke's bowmen back to their own lines in search of reinforcements. With the first skirmish of the conflict over, both armies dusted themselves down and prepared for the first major clash of arms. Once the Norman cavalrymen were ready, after hastily pulling on armour and preparing their horses, the assault would begin in earnest. The seasoned professionals of Duke William's force of heavy cavalry, archers and crossbowmen stood ready, waiting for their commander's word. From his vantage point on the top of his hill King Harold looked down on the invaders from within a solid phalanx of armoured *huscarls* clutching a variety of javelins and cudgels they would hurl down on the enemy as soon as they came in range.

When he judged his army ready, Duke William rode out in front of his men and faced them.

"My friends, my comrades, at last the moment is upon us. Today we shall need courage, and only outright victory will suffice. Retreat from this place cannot be contemplated and defeat will only consign us to a painful death. Do not tremble when you look upon the enemy for they have been defeated many times before. We have God on our side, and we fight beneath the papal banner against a usurper and heretic. I swear on the holy relics around my neck that I will build a church here on the place of our great victory. Our crusade is just and you must not doubt yourselves today," he cried out.

As if to add weight to his master's words, the Duke's magnificent Spanish warhorse reared up on his hind quarters and screamed its defiance. His men cheered and Duke William drew his sword and saluted them. Robert and Odo walked their horses out to stand next to him and they turned to look up the hill at their enemy. In the Norman centre stood the vanguard, archers and infantrymen to the fore. A *conroi* of three thousand horsemen men waiting in the rear watched their commander, Floki Fitzroy for his signal to attack. On the right wing stood the French troops and foreign mercenaries, while on the left the Breton, Angevins and Poitevins waited nervously for hostilities to begin, knowing they would be the first division to close with the enemy.

As eight thousand men waited for the war-trumpets to sound their advance, a Norman knight broke clear of the massed ranks and raced his horse up the hill toward the Saxon lines. When he got within fifty paces he stopped and threw down a challenge for any man of Harold Godwinson's host to fight him in single combat. A mounted Saxon warrior duly obliged and charged out toward his opponent with his spear levelled. The Norman warrior, a man named Taillefer, met the charge and killed the Saxon with a lance strike through the chest, silencing the cheering for their champion. Flushed with success, the victor turned on the enemy shield wall and charged again. At the moment of impact, a gap appeared, and the shield wall opened, swallowing horse and rider whole. Man and beast were slain before they advanced much further, and Taillefer's headless corpse soon reappeared when it was tossed out of the defensive line of shields.

Trumpets at the bottom of the hill sounded and the Norman advance began. Archers raced within range of their enemy and shot volley upon volley of arrows toward the Saxon lines. The air was thick with deadly projectiles which landed to little effect, for they were being shot uphill and easily caught on the great round shields at the top. Then it was the infantry's turn to engage, and they moved swiftly forward to meet their enemy. As soon as they were in range a fusillade of missiles erupted from both sides and hatchets, javelins and pieces of stone attached to wood were hurled, filling the air. But it was when the two sides came within stabbing distance that the real bloodletting began, and shield clashed with shield and every warrior looking for a gap through which he could stab a sword or a spear. Despite their valour and bravery, the Norman men-at-arms struggled and their march up the hill ended in failure accompanied by the clamour and reek of battle as guts were spilled and men voided their bowels in terror. In desperation the cries of *Dex Aie* could be heard all along the line as Norman infantrymen beseeched the heavens for help as they were skewered or scythed to the ground. The packed ranks and sheer physical strength of Harald Godwinson's army were more than a match for their adversaries and their exultant battle cries of 'out, out," celebrated the grisly deaths of scores of Normans, their bodies run through or spilt by a Dane-axe. The assault had lasted less than an hour and the defeated infantrymen retreated back down the hill signalling the entry of the heavy horses into the fray.

Floki Fitzroy slowly marched his cavalry men through lines of retreating archers and infantry. He looked to the left and right to see the Breton and French divisions in the same position at the foot of the hill. More trumpets sounded and he led the first *conrois* of a hundred warriors at the Saxon shield wall. As they moved off, another *conrois* followed close behind them until wave after wave of mounted men could be observed charging up the slope in close formation, lances couched and looking for enemy heads and chests. This time it was the men behind the shield wall who suffered more than their assailants but not in any great number. By the time Floki's *conrois* and the subsequent waves reached the top of the hill on their heavy horses, much of their impetus was lost, and the destructive force that had crushed so many armies in the past was diluted. They claimed a few lives but the power of the *huscarls* fighting from height and the sheer physical strength of their axe men turned back each charge.

If Floki and his commanders were disappointed by the results of their labours, it was nothing compared to the abject failure of the Breton left-wing, who foundered and broke on the Saxon right, where they encountered the men of the *fyrd*. Long before Floki had led his men from the field to regroup, the Bretons had lost their nerve after taking a fearful mauling. Streaming down the hill in complete disarray they rode back to the Norman lines pursued on foot by triumphant *fyrdsmen* who rushed after them thinking that the battle was won. In defiance of their King's orders they broke from the impregnable shield wall that had resisted everything thrown at it, creating a gap in the line. Many of the *fyrdsmen* ran ahead of their comrades and were quickly picked off by the Bretons who, realising the folly, turned on their isolated pursuers. This phyric victory was quickly overshadowed by further movement in the Saxon lines, as the King seized on the opportunity presented by the confusion of the Norman left and gave the order to advance. The Saxon shield wall began to advance *en masse* downhill in a long impenetrable line of steel.

Isolating and slaying handfuls of Saxons who had strayed out of line was one thing, but trying to find a gap in an impregnable and rapidly advancing shield wall was another. Duke William was in trouble and Harald Godwinson pressed home his advantage, intending to rout the Normans and drive them into the Sea.

Chapter 29: Unfinished Business
La Manche, October 1066

The thirty ships of Harald's fleet rounded the Isle of Thanet in good order. The crew reefed the sail to slow down the speed of *Sea Viper,* which had threatened to arrive far ahead of the rest of the fleet once the wind filled her sails. They were making good time and in less than a day he estimated they would be landing in Winchelsea for the long-anticipated reckoning with the Saxon King and his host. He did not doubt for one moment that he would be denied the opportunity to set right the wrongs that he and his family had endured at the hands of the Saxons for generations. He was resolute in his quest and once again felt the blood of his forbears coursing through his veins. Whatever had happened to him since his return from Northumbria he could not fathom, but he knew that the old warrior in him had reawakened, and it was time to take his place on the field once more to exact justice.

Their destination of Senlac Hill was four leagues from Winchelsea and if all was well and the gods favoured them, they would arrive by tomorrow afternoon. He prayed to *Njord* once again and promised the old god a sacrifice of a whole army if the sea and the wind took him and his warriors safely to their destination. *Njord* must have been listening for as they turned from the North Sea and into *la Manche,* preparing to drop sail and row, the wind changed from a northerly to easterly direction allowing them to sail on at speed. They passed Romney on the Kent headland at midday and sails were spotted in the distance. As his fleet drew closer, Harald called his guide to join him at the tiller.

"Where are we, Oswald?" he asked the man, an old fisherman from Dungeness.

"We are close to Dover, my Lord. We shall reach Winchelsea by nightfall, I believe," said Oswald.

"And what do you make of those sails?" asked Harald, pointing ahead.

Oswald squinted into the distance.

"The King's navy," said Oswald without hesitation, "they were rumoured to be on the Isle of Wight, but with the invasion they will want to make it difficult for any Norman ships to get past them."

"Let's see what they are made of then," said Harald with relish.

He ordered the standard of the 'two leopards of Normandie' to be run up the mast, the sails were hauled down and signals sent to the rest of the fleet to make ready. As they rowed ahead, he saw a long line of ships tethered together, bow to stern, creating a barrier for any other craft passing the port of Dover within half a league. Their sails had all been lowered and the ships were anchored fast to hold them in position. The Norman fleet was about a thousand paces from the enemy line, close enough to see the faces of the crews looking toward them. Harald saw that two of the larger vessels carried *trebuchets* and as they rowed forward, the Saxons began to hurl large rocks which fell woefully short of the target. At his signal a hail of arrows from two of the Byzantine *dromons* replied in kind, killing many enemy seamen and rendering the catapults useless. He ordered four men with axes to the bows of the *Sea Viper* and headed for the tethering ropes between two of the ships. The crew shipped oars and as they approached the gap between the two craft fifty men leapt off the *Sea Viper* and onto the Saxon vessels attacking their terrified crews with swords and axes. As they were dispatching the enemy their comrades set about the thick tethering ropes with axes until they cut through them. Meanwhile the boarding parties, having completed their lethal mission, leapt back aboard, took up their rowing stations and propelled the *Sea Viper* forward, leading the rest of the ships through the gap in the blockade line like a brood of ducklings following their mother. The Saxon vessels on each side were now burning fiercely and a strong wind fanned the flames carrying the burning embers to the other ships in the line. Harald ordered the sail raised once more and took off back down the Kentish coastline at speed,

"That will teach them to use chains in future," he roared to the men. "Now, look lively boys, let's see what this beautiful old girl can do. I want to be ashore by nightfall."

He got his wish and well before dusk, all the men and horses had disembarked. Weapons, armour and supplies were unloaded and taken past the high-water mark on the beach where they stood in neat piles.

The little town of Winchelsea was completely unprotected, for their *fyrdmen* had left to join the main Saxon army. A small group of cowed locals appeared with wagons full of food and waited patiently for the Normans to relieve them of their peace offering. The Commander refused their food with good grace, for they had plenty of supplies, and from the look of the local people and the burnt surrounding countryside, this community was likely to be starving. He kept the ale but ordered his hosts to build a fire on the beach. Harald wanted his men and horses fit and rested for the morning's march and sharing the modest amount of local ale among the warriors he toasted their health and wished them luck. He slept well under the Kentish sky and his last thoughts were reuniting with his new wife when he returned to Maldon. Hedda did not sleep quite so well, choosing to make her bivouac as far away from her husband as possible.

Chapter 30: The Shieldmaiden's Curse
Senlac Hill, 1066

1

Duke William was hard pressed and unpleasantly surprised by the scale and speed at which his forces had been pushed back. He was not a man to take a single step backwards and was certainly not used to facing defeat in the field. He simply refused to contemplate anything but outright victory, for everything else meant certain death for him and the eight and a half thousand men under his command. The Duke dispatched Robert to rally the Norman cavalry, still his most devastating weapon, and in which he had complete trust. He had been unhorsed twice already and mounted his third horse before pitching forward once again into the fight. Beside him, Odo of Bayeux waited for him resolutely, battle mace in hand and the Duke gave the order to advance once again, leading the two hundred men of his bodyguard directly toward the battle standards of Harold Godwinson that swirled aloft the solid Saxon shield wall.

Robert, a hundred paces to the rear of the Norman vanguard, looked at the hole in his brother's *hauberk* from which protruded the shaft of arrow.

"It is not too deep, just pull it out. I cannot ride like this," said Floki between clenched teeth to his squire.

The young man grasped it gingerly and tugged it free before packing a wad of wine-soaked rags into his master's tunic.

"There, I told you, now help me back into the saddle, I must lead my warriors back," he continued.

"Wait," shouted Robert above the din of battle. "Listen to me, brother, you have new orders. You will take two thousand horsemen and wait here in reserve. I will lead the rest back. Be ready for the call when it comes. Their line cannot hold too much longer and I will need you to strike it with everything you have."

"Then be careful, I could not bear losing another brother so quickly," said Floki nodding furiously. "As soon as I see your signal I will be at your side,"

It was difficult to hear anything above the noise of battle, and the two men had to shout to be heard in the chaos all around them, but somehow the word was passed amongst the men. With a thousand heavy horsemen at his back Robert looked for the banners of the Duke, before plunging forward to meet the resolute line of warriors before him. He attacked with a fury that he did not recognise but embraced it all the same. From his position in the first *conrois* he smashed into the shield wall which yielded a little, but did not buckle, and looked to the left and right to see his men doing the same. Their lances broken, thrown down or simply discarded, they hacked down on enemy heads with swords and axes. For their part, the Saxons fought back with venom, thrusting spears or lashing out with long handled axes and obstinately refusing to give up any of their hard-won ground. If the Norman horsemen needed a leader, they saw one in Robert of Mortain that day as he fought on relentlessly. But even the doughty Chancellor could not fathom what happened next, as the words which he had been dreading all day were heard up and down the Norman lines.

"The Duke has fallen. He is dead. Duke William is dead," shouted a mailed horseman on his shoulder.

Robert, failing to comprehend the full import of the words, continued to hack and slash away at the heads and shoulders in front of him. He heard the words but could not believe them and as he fought on the distant sound of trumpets blared out from the left of the battlefield. It was not a sound with which he was familiar, and he did not recognise the orders they were relaying. Fearing the worst and that a fresh attack was coming from that direction, he ordered his men to draw back and all eyes turned to where the new trumpets were blasting out from. An eerie silence descended over the battle-front and both sides parted, if only momentarily, as eighteen thousand men looked to the east to see what and who was coming from that direction.

2

Harald Fitzroy was in high spirits as he surveyed the battle below him and planned his grand entrance onto the field. The journey from Winchelsea had been uneventful and the hard, mud road, yet to suffer the depredations of winter, had been good enough to travel fast. Oswald had guided him to Colbec Hill where he and Damascus looked down on the drama below them. He sat with his commanders, and they watched in fascination as the scene unfolded. The solid line of the Saxon shield wall looked impregnable, and the Normans appeared powerless to prevent its forward progress. Their attention was drawn to the far side of the line where local *fyrdmen* milled around untidily pursuing an even untidier body of horsemen; their action was completely at odds with the discipline of the rest of the Saxon army.

Roger de Hauteville and Jeanotte sat astride their horses beside their leader.

"Breton mercenaries," spat Harald, "they never fail to disappoint."

"The Duke appears to be hard-pressed," said Roger. "What is our plan, Commander?"

"I want those Saracen archers of yours to give King Harald something to think about, while you, Jeanotte, will attack the Saxon right wing where it looks suspect. We need to put some gaps in their shield wall and the best way to do that is to start rolling up that weak flank."

"Very good, my Lord. And then?" asked Jeanotte.

"Then we shall put an end to the House of Godwin for good," said Harald unequivocally leading his horse off the summit where his men waited for him.

Harald's army had been together for over ten years. Not all of them had followed him to England, but those who did were the finest of his warriors. They had fought together in many different theatres of war and their respect and admiration was mutual. He had made rich men of them all and in return they would risk everything that he asked for. He faced them now and asked them to deliver victory one more time. The Commander sat straight and upright in the saddle, his long, fair hair, tinged with grey was pulled back from a care-worn face, and he swapped greetings with his brothers-in-arms. He smiled broadly at all the familiar faces as he met their eyes.

"My freinds, we are the victors of Civitate, of Varaville and Dol, and you have given me nothing but dedicated service. This may not be our fight, but we will not desert our brothers beyond," he said, unsheathing *Gunnlogi* and pointing her toward the clamour of battle. "We have always fought for honour, reputation and each other, and today will be no different. Look for my standard and you will find me there, where the fighting is thickest, and we shall prevail together," called Harald in a strong, resonant voice that carried on the wind to the furthest ranks.

Hedda sat, shrouded in steel from head to foot, in a line of her comrades several ranks back, and a tear ran down her cheek at his words. She had work to do and knew that she would have to block out all of her fears to play her part in the drama to come. Harald led them down the far side of the hill, his war trumpets sounded, and the horsemen galloped towards the enemy lines.

One hundred mounted archers were the first to arrive from the hilltop, propelled on small, fast-running horses. In their tasseled helmets and gaily coloured silk tunics beneath light mail shirts, they raced along the English shield wall, looking for targets for their arrows. With speed and precison they found them and all along the enemy line men began to drop. The Saxons, completely taken aback by the assault, were stunned and all progress forward came to an abrupt halt. When the archers found the end of the line they simply turned back and repeated the same exercise, felling those in the front ranks, too slow to raise their shields.

At the same time as the Saracens archers were meeting their marks, Jeanotte's *conroi* were making their presence felt. The English line, their flanks no longer protected by the dense woodland, was exposed. The *fyrdsmen* on the far right, still flushed by their initial success against the Breton cavalry, were slowly walking back into position when they were hit hard by the first wave of horsemen. They had no answer to the steel-tipped lances that pierced boiled, leather armour with ease and were slaughtered without mercy. Despite offering a spirited resistance the *fyrdsmen* were no match for the professional Norman warriors and fell back beneath the crushing waves of continuous charges. On Jeanotte's signal they changed the point of their head-on attack and began to press on the enemy ranks from a sideways direction, continuing to hit it hard enough for the shock waves to reverberate from one end of the defensive wall to the other. As soon as one *conrois* hit home and wheeled off another one would follow and Saxon warriors way down the line felt the impact along the wall of locked shields.

The gap between the armies of the Duke and the English king began to widen and a clear channel of almost a hundred paces appeared between them. The mounted archers raced away to rejoin their comrades on the nearby slopes and more trumpets sounded.

The air was filled with the sound of a thousand horses galloping down from Colbec Hill and across the face of the Saxon shieldwall. With the banners of the papal standard and the two leopards of Normandie streaming out behind him, Harald led his men charging across the field, screaming defiance at a surprised enemy. He led them close enough to the Saxon line to see the fear on the enemy faces and the huge column hurled a fusillade of javelins over the defending shields and beyond, causing havoc to the rear. Harald rode on, impervious to the Saxon spears and arrows aimed at him, all of which went well wide of their mark. He was now in his element, knowing that this was his destiny, and he had been put on earth for this role. As he approached the midway point of the charge, he noticed the Normans on his right busying themselves back into organised ranks, whilst on his left the enemy appeared to be growing quiet and unsure. He saw the billowing standards of Harold Godwinson, within densely packed ranks of *huscarls* and as he did so he gripped Damascus's powerful flanks with his knees and hurled his javelin. He did not follow its flight, which arched into the air and flew over the packed ranks of English warriors, piercing the chest of a Saxon knight close to the King. Unseen by his killer, Gyrth Godwinson sank to the ground dying, felled by an unknowing enemy, with a spear through his chest.

Harald Fitzroy knew that Duke William needed time to reorganise his forces before the next assault, and had made a promise to himself to give his liege-lord that time. He also knew that the fate of both his brothers depended on the outcome of this battle and if they failed there would be no tomorrow - at least not on this earth. When he had finished his gallop to the end of the battle lines, he turned the long column and headed directly toward Duke William and the Norman camp.

There was little time for polite conversation and the Duke and his entourage looked up in amazement as Harald approached the little knot of officers. Harald removed his magnificent Byzantine helm, which had last seen action on his cousin's head at Stamford Bridge and bowed low in the saddle. Robert and Floki Fitzroy stared at him in amazement, their mouths open, as if they were seeing a ghost.

The Duke of Normandie was also lost for words and not wishing to waste any more time than he had to, Harald spoke first.

"My Lord, we have little time to make the decisions that will determine whether we live or die so please accept my brusqueness. The news of your death precedes you and it is a pleasure to still see you here before me. The Saxons are weakening and with a united attack we might yet carry the day and crush them," announced Harald breathlessly above the hubbub.

"Be that as it may, Lord Fitzroy, you are a little late, and as you can see I am very much alive," said the Duke with annoyance, his face and armour covered in the detritus of the field.

"I rejoice in that fact but let us cast our differences aside for another time, my Lord. The hour is late and we must act decisively if we are to secure the throne of England for you. My men have shored up the left flank and we can break the enemy line with a concerted effort. I am at your command and await your orders," shouted Harald above the noise. "I believe this barrier of steel will buckle before we do but let us not prevaricate."

The Duke, clearly uncomfortable at Harald's appearance, did not argue and with a shrug of his shoulders he replied.

"Very well, Lord Fitzroy - I welcome your support. Tell me what we should do."

3

The lull in the fighting did not last long and the Saxons, once recovered from Harald's lightening attack, reignited their advance, albeit at a more considered pace. Duke William stood in front of his troops, bare-headed so they could all see him and exhorted them forward. Hostilities began once more with venom and purpose and the combined Norman forces hurled themselves back into the fray.

Harald's men lined up, but without Jeanotte, who continued to chisel away at the Saxon right wing, and together with the Duke's vanguard they threw themselves against the Saxon centre. Robert and Floki's divisions on either side of them did the same and together they battered away at the lines in front of them with no quarter given. Behind the lines of heavy horses which began to impact the Saxon shield wall marched the ranks of Norman infantry and their allies, and slowly and with great purpose, they began to assert themselves. It began with the withering of the Saxon flanks as both Floki and Jeanotte fractured the opposition in front of them. Then came the loss of the second of King Harald's siblings, Leofwine, delivering a grievous blow to English morale when he died at the end of a Norman lance.

It was late in the afternoon and the expected Saxon reinforcements had not appeared. The fighting had been long and unremitting and Duke William's trumpets, signalling his forces to disengage, came as a welcome relief to their hard-pressed adversaries. The Normans fell back and as they did so the iron discipline that had held the English line together for so long began to dissolve. The Saxons, thinking they had broken the Norman spirit, broke from their solid formation in pursuit of Duke William's army and with it the course of the battle changed inexorably.

4

Harald Fitzroy led the 'feigned flight' of the cavalry from the field. He left in a wide arc and doubled back on himself with the whole of the Norman cavalry behind him. As they reentered the fray, deploying all away along the splintering Saxon shield wall, they found their enemy in a broken formation and the formidable *huscarls* in smaller, isolated cohorts. The Duke's opportunity had finally presented itself and he and his bodyguard of knights set about the enemy once more with fury. Harald looked across the field to see Duke William and his brother Odo dispensing holy justice, bringing down heavy maces on the heads of a confused enemy. He looked further afield to his left and right, to see both of his own brothers in the thick of the action, engaging and felling enemy warriors. Satisfied that his comrades were in the ascendancy, Harald could focus on carving a path toward the banners of the Saxon King less than one hundred paces away. His column made for a gap in the shield wall and hacked its way forward like a gigantic centipede, snapping at everything in front and beside it. After the initial impact of the horses hitting the line, the column slowed as it met densely packed armoured axe-men. Harald's frenzied attack showed no let-up and the more resistance he encountered, the harder he fought. Jeanotte, fighting at his Lord's right shoulder fought with equal ferocity while on his left Leif and Rolf stood guard, their axes cleaving the heads of anyone in their way. None of Harald's comrades could have prevented what happened next and the blade of a Dane-axe, swung through the air towards his head on a downward path. The blade missed its target by a finger's width but caught Damascus square on the back of the neck, severing bone and muscle. The stallion screamed in pain as the axe bit deep and he dropped to his knees like a stone, throwing his rider into the blood and filth of the battleground.

Harald, still clutching his shield and his sword staggered to his feet to find the *destrier's* killer about to aim another blow at him. The huge Saxon warrior was despatched before he had a chance to strike again and as he fell Harald looked up to see Leif grinning down from atop his horse.

"Dismount," shouted the commander, "the horses are no good here. We will go forward on foot."

The whole column, moving as one, dismounted in an instant and formed up in a single line behind their leader. Kite shields held over the left shoulder, they continued the bloody march on foot. Harald surged forward, the loss of his faithful companion fuelling his ire to even darker passions. The rage of his advance was channeled by the rest of his men, and they drove forward like some dark beast of the underworld, devouring everything in their path. But beneath the savagery of his assault, Harald fell calm in the primal intensity of battle. He felt the presence of his grandfathers urging him forward and, with his blood-brothers at his shoulders there were few places he would rather be. In front of him stood a loose phalanx of a dozen axe men blocking his path to the Saxon King. They stood a spear-shaft's distance apart, enabling them to swing their fearsome weapons with whistling intent as they cut the air. A javelin hurled from the advancing column took down one *huscarl* whilst the fellow next to him lived a little longer after dispatching Rolf with a flailing axe, the old warrior's head removed from his body at a single stroke. Harald continued to lead his men forward, through the chaos of noise and foulness, and as he did so he stepped into a clear space where the banners of his enemies flew.

King Harald stood within a small knot of his loyal earls, swords drawn to protect him and ready to sacrifice themselves. He stood stock still as he took in the interloper who had just broken through the secure cordon of his household guards now lying dead at his feet. The King lifted his head and turned toward his masked adversary with a look of bewilderment.

"Who are you?" commanded the King in a strident voice that could be heard above the battle's roar that still raged all around them.

Harald, his moment of destiny arrived, was deaf and blind to the fighting that still boiled all around him. He looked upon his former friend who had betrayed him so readily and removed the bloody helm. He saw the King quail as he recognised him.

"You are dead, Hari," cried the King in astonishment. "What conjurer's trick is this? I saw you fall at Stamford Bridge."

"Alas, my Lord. I am alive and well and in search of justice," Harald shouted back and moved toward him, both hands clutching *Gunnlogi*. He moved with a single purpose stepping over the bodies of recently fallen friends and foemen, oblivious to anything other than his intended victim. Normally, so aware of any danger around him, Harald did not see the movement to his left of a wounded *huscarl* rising to his feet. With all the remaining strength in his dying body the man unsheathed his *seax* and plunged it into the Norman commander's side. Harald turned toward his assailant and thrust his sword through the man's chest, killing him in an instant. He turned back toward the King and took a few halting footsteps before tumbling to the floor himself. Godwinson looked at his would-be assassin dying on the muddy ground in front of him and his lips drew back into a triumphant sneer as his earls tightened the protective barrier in front of him.

The Saxon King did not see the small axe spinning toward him until it was too late. It tumbled relentlessly in a shallow arc and with deadly accuracy from the ranks of the Normans and struck him in the eye, lodging in his brain. He was dead before he hit the ground. Had Godwinson had time to inspect the ancient axe before it killed him he might have appreciated the beautiful, well-balanced weapon inlaid with ancient silver and gold runes. A small warrior broke from the stunned Norman ranks and raced toward the prone figure of Harald Fitzroy lying in the mud. Releasing the matching axe to the one that had just killed the Saxon King from her grasp, she dropped to her knees at the side of her stricken husband. She pulled back her mailed *coif* and lifted up his head to cradle it in her lap before an uncontrollable torrent of burning tears ran down her dirty face and onto his.

5

The news of the death of their sovereign reverberated around the decimated ranks of the Saxon army and the effect was immediate. They deserted the field in droves and in the fading light of the day the Normans chose not to pursue them. The victors had wounds of their own to lick and reports of the great warlord Harald Fitzroy's demise had been a bitter blow. His men formed an honour guard around their fallen leader and fifty grieving warriors stood in a ring of impenetrable steel around him while his wife kept vigil.

Hedda Halldorsdottir's grief was interrupted by the Fitzroy brothers, who galloped to the scene as soon as they heard the news. They found their brother barely conscious, but on hearing their voices he rallied briefly. They knelt down beside him and each grasped a hand.

"Brothers," he croaked, "we are victorious?"

"We are, Hari. The Godwinson's are all dead and the Saxons have fled the field," said Robert.

"And I have your forgiveness, Robert?" he asked.

"We are brothers, Hari, we argue and then all is forgotten," he answered.

Floki tried to speak but the words would not come.

"You will take good care of my wife," Harald ordered, looking up at Hedda who had not moved from her position since she had found him.

"She is a Fitzroy, is she not?" said Floki.

"Then nothing more needs to be said. I shall see you both in the great hall when your time comes. But see you both die with a weapon in your hand. That is my final command."

Harald coughed and a little blood trickled from his mouth before he passed into darkness. He closed his eyes and the last thing he heard were two ravens 'caw-cawing' as they passed overhead.

Epilogue:

The battle of Hastings marked the end of the line of the Godwins and the fall of the Saxon Kingdom, as its stewardship passed from one King to another. Harald Godwinson's body was discovered on the battlefield by his mistress, Edith Swanneck, and had been mutilated by vengeful Norman knights. The bodies of Gyrth and Leofwine were found near their brother's corpse and were left with the rest of the Saxon dead where they had fallen, on unconsecrated ground, for more than a year.

The Duke of Normandie was crowned William the First of England by Christmas, and during his reign the Saxon people suffered as he exerted his iron will over his new subjects. The might of the Saxon earldom was broken forever, never to recover, their lands and possessions were seized by voracious new rulers, and they were scattered to the four winds.

Turid Skjaldmær's curse, uttered after the Saxon betrayal in 1002, was made flesh and vengeance was delivered by her grandsons at the Battle of the Hoary Apple Tree near Hastings in the Autumn of 1066. It lasted for many years before it finally lifted.

"You are all cursed and will once again reap the wind from the North. My people will return here again and your homes, your wives and your children will be put to the axe and the flame. Your land will be burned, those of your families who live will be enslaved and your God will desert you. You will long for the time when we offered you peace instead of death and destruction. This curse you have brought on yourselves shall not be lifted for generations."

.... to be continued

Main Characters

Harald Fitzroy: aka The Papal Shield, Marquis of Ambrières, Lord of Maldon
Robert Fitzroy: Chancellor of Normandie, Count of Mortain
Richard Fitzroy: Son of Robert
Floki Fitzroy: younger sibling to Harald and Robert, Count of Regneville, Marshal of the 'Riders'
Torstein and Sigrid Fitzroy: Parents to the Fitzroy brothers
Lanfranc of Pavin: Archbishop of Caen, Advisor to the Duke
Edwin: Earl of Mercia
Eleanor of Mortain: Wife to Robert
Duke William of Normandie: aka 'the Bastard, 'the Conqueror'
Harald Sigurdson: aka Hardrada, the King of Norway
Mathilda of Flanders: Wife of William,
Baldwin of Flanders: Count of Flanders, Regent to the Dauphin of France
Thomas & Gilbert: Harald's squires
Grimnir: The travelling stranger
Henri: Robert's squire
Hedda Halldorsdottir: daughter of Halldor Snorrason, Icelandic *seiðun* (seer)
Halldor Snorrason: Advisor to the King of Norway
Brenier Fitzroy: Cousin to the Fitzroy siblings
Oystein of Bergen: aka Silvertongue, the Jarl of Bergen
Olaf Knarresmed: Master shipwright of Regneville
Stephen Fitzaird: Master mariner and captain of the Mora
Jeanotte of Ambrières: Captain of harald's cavalry
King Edward: aka 'The Confessor', King of the Saxons until his death in 1066
Harald Godwinson: King of England

Tostig Godwinson: Deposed earl of Nortumbria, brother to the King of England

Leofwine Godwinson: Brother to the King of England

Rolande of Countances: Marshall of Mortain

Leif: Veteran and comrade of Harald

Morcar: Earl of Northumbria

Rolf: Veteran and comrade of Harald

Wolfgang: Teutonic knight and comrade of Harald

Glossary

Fyrd: English militia

Thegn: Saxon nobleman and landowner

Huscarls: Highly trained, feared Norse warriors, loyal to the crown of England.

Asgard: Place where the Norse gods lived

Midgard: the realm of men n Norse mythology

Lymer: Scenthound, used on a leash to find large game before it was hunted down by the pack

Alaunt: Large hunting dog, bred to bring down large game

Milites: Trained regular soldiers

Dromon: Swift war galleys, powered by oars and sail.

Skeid (also Dreki/Dragon): Large longships

Palisade: Wooden perimeter fence

Gambesson: Heavily padded leather jacket

Knight's Fee: The stipend demanded by a knight to go to war

Gunnlogi: Harald's famous Ulfberht sword

Jotun: A giant (Norse mythology)

Norns (The): Deities of Norse mythology who controlled the fate of men

Margygr: Mermaid (Norse mythology)

Donjon: Fortified castle within a castle

Seiðun: Seer, witch

Baronie: A collection of barons

Holmgang: Duel to the death (Norse)

Londenvic: Medieval London

Londinium: Roman London

Haverfest: Saxon harvest festival

Spangelhelm: Conical helmet (Norman)

Conrois: Line of closely-formed Norman cavalry

Conroi: Multiple Conrois

Tamsye: Saxon name for the Thames

Talbots: White hunting dogs

Svinfylking: Battle formation (Boar's Snout)

Seax: Short stabbing sword

Dex Aie: Battle cry of the Norman troops "God be with us."

La Manche: the English Channel

About the author:

Peter Richards has a home in Normandy, France. He is a dedicated historian who after a visit to Hambye Abbey, close to his home, was inspired to investigate the possibility of studying medieval history at university as a mature student. The available syllabuses did not match his requirements and so he decided to create his own; one that focussed on medieval history in the region. After a great deal of research and library time, he discovered that despite being an interesting subject to study, not everything was 'going in and staying in' and so he decided to write a historical novel or rather a series of them. The more he researched, the more he discovered that Normandy was a treasure trove of historical fact and a perfect setting for his series of historical fiction, 'The Leopards of Normandie'. The series focusses on the turbulent years of medieval history in Normandy seen through the collective eyes of many generations of a local family. Starting with the colonisation of the region by Viking settlers and including the invasion of England in 1066 through the following centuries.

The author is also a keen cyclist and the region provides memorable cycle routes along which he takes groups of touring riders to and from the objects of his research.

The Fitzroy Blood-Line

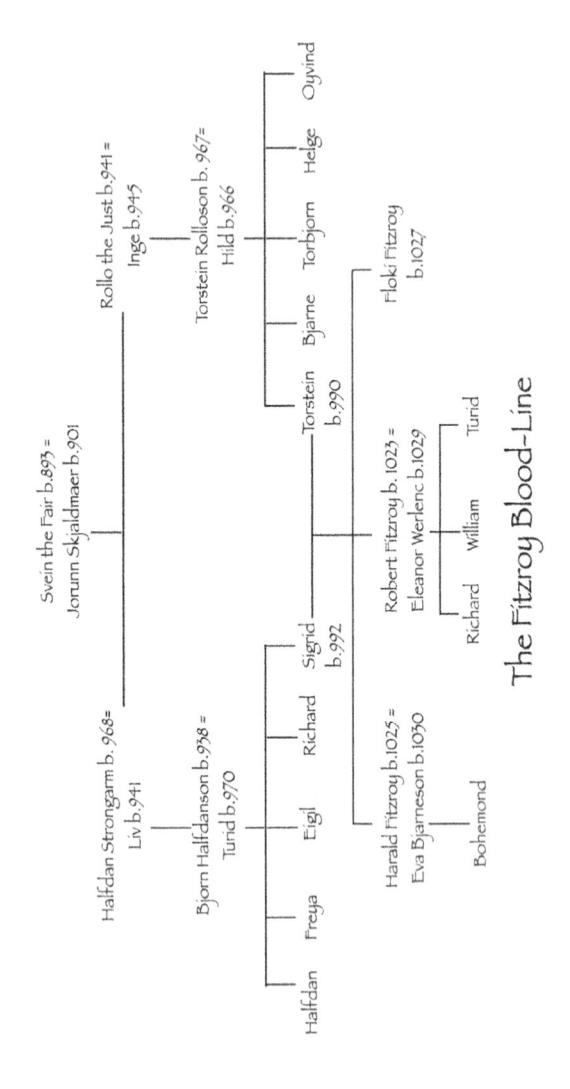

Svein the Fair b.893 = Jonunn Skjaldmaer b.901

├── Halfdan Strongarm b.968 = Liv b.941
│   └── Bjorn Halfdanson b.938 = Turid b.970
│   ├── Halfdan
│   ├── Freya
│   ├── Eigil
│   ├── Richard
│   └── Sigrid b.992
│   └── Harald Fitzroy b.1025 = Eva Bjarneson b.1030
│   └── Bohemond
│
└── Rollo the Just b.941 = Inge b.945
    └── Torstein Rolloson b.967 = Hild b.966
        ├── Bjarne
        ├── Torbjorn
        ├── Helge
        ├── Ojvind
        └── Torstein b.990
            └── Robert Fitzroy b.1025 = Eleanor Werlenc b.1029
                ├── Floki Fitzroy b.1027
                ├── Richard
                ├── William
                └── Turid

Printed in Great Britain
by Amazon